Seeds of Light

Lilies of the Underground Trilogy

Book 2

Steven Hamilton

Cover Design and Interior Formatting by BespokeBookCovers.com

Please visit our website:www.insidepassagebookroom.com

Other Novels by Steven Hamilton

Dragon Slayers

McSally and Company

From Where I Stood

Journey Home

Steeno Six

Twisted Truth

Lilies in the Dark (Book 1, *Lilies of the Underground*)

Coming 2025

Garden of Lilies (Book 3, *Lilies of the Underground*)

Acknowledgments

My deepest gratitude goes out to those who helped bring the second of three novels in this trilogy to completion. My Thursday Writer's Group—Gretchen Day, Richie Goldstein, and J. J. Waller: Thank you for the long hours, hard work, and, most important, the critical feedback on my work. To my editor, Diane Luehrs: Once again I am in your debt. I am forever grateful that you see things that I manage to overlook. As always, I am grateful to Peter and Caroline O'Connor of BespokeBookCovers.com for the remarkable work they do. Not only do they produce beautiful covers, but also all the internal formatting for this book. They make my life so much easier. Finally, once again, to my beautiful wife, Mary. She not only nudges (gently) but also edits and keeps me on track.

Special Thanks

Toward the end of this installment, we are introduced to a character—Boris Bunin. He is a Russian mob boss in New York. Boris appears courtesy of author Richie Goldstein. Bunin is a central character is Goldstein's Sasha Kulaeva trilogy, *Crime on the Alaska/Russian Border*. Richie was kind of enough to grant permission, for which I am grateful. His fictional work is engaging and paints vivid images of the complicated web of organized crime and law enforcement in Alaska. All of Richie's work is available on Amazon.

Visit his author's page on Amazon https://www.amazon.com/author/richiegoldstein.

Author's Note

This is a work of fiction. The characters are fictional and not inspired by true events. While some organizations in the story exist in the real world, characterizations are presented to move the story forward. They are in no way meant to be true representations of the actual organizations.

One element of this novel that does reflect our society is the blight of domestic violence. The horrifying events that I've portrayed in this novel are all too common. One has only to keep up with current events to understand this.

As of this writing, my home state of Alaska has the third highest rate of domestic violence in the United States. If you look at the data, it is striking. In the top tier states, more than 40% of women report experiencing domestic violence at some time in their lives. These numbers hold across multiple data sources. That our culture tolerates this evil is an indictment of who we are. It is not a pretty picture.

The Story So Far...

A violent husband guns his wife down in a law office parking lot. Reverend Janet Polasky, who is there to accompany the woman to an appointment with a divorce attorney, witnesses the murder in horror. That nightmare infuses the minister with a sense of purpose. Certain that it is her calling, she sets out to help abused women who fear for their lives—help them disappear. Her plan is to give them new lives in new cities and states.

In addition to inspiring Janet to action, this tragedy robs twelve-year old Abby Miller of her mother. The grandmother, Roberta Klein, assumes custody, but it quickly becomes evident that the woman is herself so grief-stricken that she struggles to care for the young girl. Janet feels a duty to help the young girl survive the traumatic event.

Meanwhile, working on her idea of rescuing women, she scores a quick initial success securing funds from a wealthy businessman to accomplish this mission. Then Janet suffers her first brutal defeat. As she moves to save Luellen Pickering and her children, the woman's husband manages to locate and murder the kids. Despite the resources and passion, Janet's efforts aren't enough. Once again, violence destroys a family.

Janet begins to understand that she will not be able to carry out the day-to-day work of rescuing women and their children. After all, she has responsibilities to her church. On the recommendation of a friend, Detective Dee Martin, Janet hires a woman who has gone through domestic violence trauma herself. Valentina Gomez had just spent ten years in prison for killing her abusive husband.

Things begin to take shape. Janet establishes organizations to comply with requirements—payroll, taxes, expenses, banking, and other elements that go with any enterprise. Spiriting women to safety requires a sophisticated infrastructure.

Along the way, she encounters Leah Bowman, the wife of a local gang leader. Leah comes to Janet for help through Detective Martin, who is attempting to get the woman to testify against her husband. Leah claims to be trying to escape him, although she is by no means the victim of his abuse. Despite her reluctance, Janet allows her to stay in a rented condo that they have access to. The world turns upside down when the husband comes looking for his wife at the condo. Conveniently, Leah isn't there. Janet is. As she stares down the barrel of the man's gun, her world once again flips. Anton Bowman, gang leader, and his two associates are themselves killed by an unseen shooter from just outside the condo.

Janet suspects, although she has no hard evidence, that this had been Leah's plan all along—to lure her husband into a trap and kill him without exposing herself. Janet sweeps the traumatic incident from her mind. She already has too many other irons in the fire.

Meanwhile, Janet's funding source—billionaire Greg Stottman—struggles with his own problems. His niece, Dani, for whom he is legal guardian, becomes involved with a controlling and abusive boyfriend, Billy Robinson. Compounding the problem is Dani's rejection of her uncle's help. In his desperation to keep her safe, Greg turns to an old college acquaintance who operates mostly on the wrong side of the law. Rico Enretti is known as the *go-to guy* for anything desired but not legally allowed. Rico recommends a security expert with unique talents.

Enter Dimitry Kazarian. Kaz accepts the task of keeping Dani safe while he and Greg together strategize a longer-term solution. Their plans are dashed when Greg discovers that Dani's boyfriend is regularly beating her. Greg and Kaz find where they are staying and physically remove her. This, however, didn't end the saga. Within weeks, Dani runs away, leaving a note telling Greg to leave her alone.

During this time, another woman comes to Janet for help. The circumstances, however, make this a seemingly impossible case. The woman, Lucy Young, is married to Janet's board president at the church, Rob Young. The minister begins the delicate balancing act of remaining professional while interacting with him and, at the same time, working to help his wife escape. Despite her efforts, though, Janet suspects that Rob knows of her involvement.

He enlists the help of his cop brother, Phillip Young, who attempts to strongarm Janet to find the runaway wife. When his first attempt fails, he accosts her on the street while she is on an early morning run. He comes for Janet and there seems to be no possible escape route. Suddenly, Leah Bowman shows up. She has taken over her husband's gang operation and, as luck would have it, Phillip Young is on her payroll.

The cop and his friends retreat, but Leah warns Janet that the road she is on will lead to increasingly dangerous situations. Because Janet helped her, Leah promises friendship; a resource that Janet is reluctant to accept.

During this time, Valentina Gomez—Val—escorts Lucy Young to safety in another state. Despite their efforts at secrecy, Val finds that she is being followed… two states away. The breach is traced back to a tapped telephone in the office of the attorney who helped set up Janet's organization.

Greg once again calls on his friend, Rico Enretti, to find a technical wizard who can unravel the mess. Eisen, a very expensive tech contractor, quickly finds the bug on the phone system and traces it back to its source—Seattle attorney Reba Stillings, who has made a name for herself advocating for men's rights, especially men accused of domestic violence. There are hints and signs that this powerful lawyer is providing the technical means for men to track down and sometimes kill their runaway wives. There is no hard evidence of her involvement, though, so she is free to continue her crusade.

A phone call brings Greg Stottman's life crashing down around him. His niece, Dani, has been brought to the emergency room. She's been beaten, shot, and left for dead. There is no doubt who was responsible, but Billy Robinson has long since disappeared. What he left behind, was a young woman whose world has been turned inside out. Dani struggles, alternately blaming Greg for the entire event, and defending Billy. With Janet by his side, Greg tries to talk to her but begins to understand that there is a very long road ahead for his niece.

During the investigation into Dani's shooting, we are introduced to Detective Charlotte Wharton of the King County Sheriff's Department. She butts heads with Greg as she investigates the case. He has a strong inclination to try and find Billy Robinson and dispose of the man himself. Greg's clumsiness in this endeavor, though, brings Wharton down on him as she warns him off.

Tired of tiptoeing around the issue, Janet finally confronts Rob Young. With his wife safely relocated, she has to deal with the reality that she has a violent, abusive husband as the president of her church's governing board. She takes a bold approach. Accompanied by Kaz, she meets with Young and gives him an ultimatum—resign from the board and leave the church or she will bring the entire issue into the public eye. The coup is successful, although Janet is under no assumption that it was the end of the issue.

Meanwhile, her involvement deepened with Abby Miller, the young girl whose mother's murder started all of this. The grandmother's mental health has deteriorated, leaving Janet to try and fill the empty spot in the girl's life.

With all of these issues and problems converging, Janet feels increasingly stretched. The magnitude and pace of events suggested that the entire mission was an impossible dream.

1

The Sniper eased the rear sliding window of his pick-up camper to the left. The sun peeked over the hills, its rays slicing the early morning haze and illuminating his target, seventy-five yards away. Birds chirped merrily in a nearby tree as though all was right with the world. The faint drone of traffic on a nearby highway provided comforting background noise. He put the binoculars to his eyes. "Right on time."

He considered the fifty-ish woman as she trudged from her front door to the car. The flowing dress, he imagined, was intended to cover the extra weight she carried. Her short blonde hair by all appearances had not been washed in at least a week. *Such a small life.*

He set the binoculars aside. Hefting his Remington 700 rifle, he slid the barrel out the window opening. His cheek against the composite stock, he peered through the scope. The woman struggled to retrieve her keys while shifting an oversized briefcase and to-go coffee cup from one hand to the other.

"Not just yet," he muttered.

She gave up. Dropping the briefcase and setting the coffee cup on the car roof, she took her keys from the purse slung over her shoulder.

The Sniper muttered, "Stupid. Why didn't you grab the keys before you picked up the other junk?" The soft laugh carried the full measure of his contempt for the woman he'd never met.

He'd watched her for two weeks, following her every move. The early autumn morning represented the culmination of his effort. Here she was, right on schedule… and every bit as frazzled as ever.

He swept those thoughts from his mind. He centered the crosshairs on her upper back and ever so slightly to the right—a clean lung shot. He pulled away from the scope and surveyed the trees around them. Lush green leaves rustled as a slight morning breeze blew from left to right, no more than ten miles per hour. Still, at this distance it would matter. He pulled the rifle inside and made the adjustment to the scope windage.

With the weapon back in place, he re-acquired his target. She picked up the briefcase as he clicked off the safety. The doomed woman reached up for the coffee cup just as he squeezed the trigger.

The noise suppressor dulled the sound. Even if someone happened to hear it, they would think nothing of it. The recoil rewarded him with the familiar assurance he had grown so fond of over the years. Through the scope he saw the coffee cup go flying. She stiffened straight up before crumbling into a heap on the pavement. He pulled the bolt back, ejecting the spent shell and rammed a fresh round into the chamber.

He studied the motionless body for a moment. No doubt—he had delivered a killing shot. Still, there was no point in taking chances. He placed the crosshairs on the

2

base of her skull and fired another round. The blood splatter on her late model white Chevy Malibu comforted him.

There was one final task. Taking a small camera from his satchel, he zoomed in all the way. Even with the target seventy-five yards away, the image was good enough for his purposes. The photo composition included the crumpled body as well as the blood splatters. After clicking twice, he removed the SD card and set it aside. Stuffing the camera back into the pack, he tossed it toward the front of the camper.

He gathered the two spent shells and placed them, along with the rifle and the SD card, into the hard-shelled plastic case. Skooching to the side, he rolled up the rubber matting and accessed a trap door in the bed of the pick-up. The case fit perfectly in the hidden compartment. Closing the door, he rolled the matting back into place.

He crawled through the front window of the camper cap and through the rear window of his truck. Once behind the wheel, he fired up the ignition and eased out onto the side street. Five minutes later he maneuvered to the on-ramp of I-90 East. Checking the rearview mirror, he saw golden sunlight of the new day falling like a spotlight on the skyline of Spokane.

After a couple of miles, he pulled off the freeway into a wooded area. Springing from the cab, screwdriver in hand, he quickly switched out the Washington plates and replaced them with his own Idaho ones. Later, he would toss the stolen plates into the Spokane River south of Huetter, Idaho.

First things first. Remaining on the access road, he turned off into a McDonald's for his usual celebratory meal. Pulling up to the drive-through speaker, he rolled the window down.

A scratchy voice greeted him. "Welcome to McDonald's. Can I take your order, please?"

"Yeah, gimme two Egg McMuffins, hashbrowns and a cup of coffee, black." He pulled a twenty out of his wallet.

A warm feeling of well-being, of accomplishment, washed over him.

* * *

Sitting in a dimly lit study, he booted up his notebook computer. He opened the Tor browser and navigated into the dark web. As the application did its work, his comfort level increased. The familiarity, security, and anonymity wrapped around him like a warm blanket on a cold winter's night.

A few clicks took him to his destination. The list was a short one—four names. Tammy Newsom was the second down. He clicked on the check box. The font color for her name changed from red to black and a small skull icon appeared.

The SD card slid effortlessly into the reader, which he connected to the computer. Seconds later, he hit the upload icon on the dark website. A thumbnail image appeared next to Tammy Newsom's name, immortalizing the day's efforts.

2

The calendar app on the notebook computer showed a red dot on the current day. Before Senator Thomas Corel could click on it, the door opened, and a striking young woman entered. Her lustrous blonde hair fell onto her slight shoulders. Her azure blue eyes sparkled. "Senator, I had a call earlier from Sue Hartman, director of the King Country Domestic Violence Network. She wanted to confirm the fundraiser this evening." Alicia Wilkins closed the door behind her.

"Yes, please confirm that for me." Senator William Corel offered a warm smile and added, "Please check with staff and line up someone to attend with me. This will be a pivotal meeting if we want to galvanize the women's vote in the election."

The young aide cleared her throat. "I'd be happy go. I know several of the players in that field and I'm up-to-date on their issues."

"Perfect. Thank you. Oh, and could you get me a rundown on the Violence Against Women Act. I'm particularly interested in any changes we might want to suggest in the legislation."

"I'll get right on it."

"Good, excellent. I'll pick up you up at quarter to seven, if that works for you." While he and his wife maintained a Seattle home, his Washington, D.C. staff secured hotel rooms for campaign trips back to the home state.

"That would be perfect, Senator. Thank you," she smiled as she left the office.

Taking note of the time—4:30—he phoned the local florist and ordered a bouquet. For ordinary people, such an order might take a full day to get ready. Senator Corel, though, knew the value of subtle name-dropping. He would pick them up on the way home to change. Another evening lost to campaign business would disappoint Bonnie, his wife. Hopefully, the roses would help.

* * *

He checked his watch when he stepped through the automatic door into the hotel lobby—6:30. Taking the elevator to the 12th floor, he got off and automatically turned left. When he reached her room, he knocked. The door opened and Alicia stepped aside, allowing him in. She wore nothing but a towel around her upper body and hips.

"It'll just be another ten minutes or so. I got out of the office late." She retreated into the bathroom.

He forced his frustration aside. He was, after all, early. He called out to her, "Did you get that information I asked for?"

She stuck her head out of the bathroom and nodded toward a small worktable in the corner. "It's all there."

He wandered over and picked up the packet. Thumbing through the material, it all came back—the reauthorization of the Violence Against Women Act and closing the boyfriend loophole. *No problem. I can handle this.*

Alicia took less than five minutes. She appeared in a stunning pale blue dress that accentuated her curvy figure.

Senator Corel nodded his approval. "You look very nice this evening."

She blushed and smiled warmly.

Still, she could have let him know she wouldn't be ready on time. Arriving late would make him look like he didn't care about women's issues.

3

The call came as Janet Polasky, sole minister at St. Luke's Methodist Church in Bellevue, opened the parsonage door. She glanced at the display—Sue Hartman, the director of the King County Domestic Violence Network. She connected and, after listening to the pitch, she sighed and dropped onto the couch.

Politics. Janet wanted none of it. "I'm really tied up right now. This isn't a good time." Her only employee was still on the road with Lucy Young, their first client. Things remained unsettled with Lucy's violent husband, Rob Young, former of the church governing board. He'd been officially removed from office, but Janet was under no illusion that it was over. She knew that Rob was unlikely to let this go.

On top of that, it seemed like only yesterday that she'd nearly been killed by three gang members in one of their leased condos. Greg Stottman's niece had been shot right after that and was still hospitalized. On top of working through this, Reverend Polasky worried that she was short-changing her congregation. "Sue, if I could squeeze it in, I would."

Sue shot back, "I'm not asking you to join his campaign. It's a one-night fund-raiser. Senator Corel represents a big hope for us. We've talked about this before. The federal Violence Against Women Act comes up for reauthorization next year and there are some improvements we'd like to see. He's behind us on this one. He needs to see that women can present a formidable political constituency. Come on, it's just one night."

Janet closed her eyes and tried unsuccessfully to find an escape route. "What kind of event is it? I mean, what's the appropriate attire?"

"It's business casual, maybe. Your minister's garb would be perfect. That would send a powerful message that the faith community is also behind the effort."

"I've told you this before and I'll tell you again. I'm not a token representative of the faith community, as you call us. People of faith are diverse. They hold different values and believe different things. Under the best of circumstances, I'm a Methodist minister. You know as well as I do, even the Methodists don't always see eye-to-eye."

Sue's voice remained upbeat and positive. "For our purposes, it's the perception that matters. Your clerical collar seen at this event will speak volumes."

Janet shook her head in resignation. "Where and what time?"

* * *

Janet was used to crowds. She conducted church services each Sunday in front of several hundred people. It wasn't as though she needed to make a speech at this event. It was a political fundraiser. Still, she felt out of her element. People held their glasses, sipping wine, martinis, and bourbon as they carried on conversations that, from what she could discern, came across as more than a little pretentious.

Just listen to the spiel, shake a few hands, and you're done. She tried to make herself feel good about it, but it was a losing battle. She felt a wave of ambivalence. Nothing she could say or do was likely to make the least difference here. Janet couldn't help feeling that she was here as window dressing.

"I'm glad you made it." Sue gave her an obligatory hug, which Janet returned with a measure of indifference —a brief embrace with and quick disengagement. She didn't fit in at these kinds of events.

Sue, on the other hand, seemed born to this life. "Come on, I'll introduce you to the senator." The sparkle in the woman's eyes and the giddy excitement in her voice said it all. Sue was definitely in this guy's camp. The logical extension was that they were all on the same team... maybe.

They wove through the crowd and approached a small cluster of individuals. Janet recognized Senator William Corel from his campaign photos. Sue Hartman stepped close to him. "Senator, I'd like you to meet Reverend Janet Polasky. She's the minister at Saint Luke's Methodist Church in Bellevue."

The man smiled warmly and offered his hand. "Reverend Polasky. I'm so glad to finally meet you."

His handshake was firm but brief. His demeanor grew more somber as the smile faded. "Sue told me about your experience with the woman who was killed last spring. I can't even begin to imagine the horror." He kept eye contact, shaking his head... just the right amount, as he spoke The words flowed like honey on a warm summer day.

Chapter 3

Janet searched for a response. Nothing seemed appropriate. The smooth but sincere voice and the sparkle in his eye—all horribly out of step for a discussion about a woman being gunned down. "It was... yes...." She lowered her head and let her voice tail off.

"That can't be allowed to become the new norm. I'm honored that you could make it tonight. We're going to need all the help we can get to end the violence."

An attractive young woman touched the senator on the shoulder and whispered something in his ear. He nodded and turned to Janet. "Please excuse me. I think they're wanting me to say a few words. It was a pleasure to meet you."

As he turned away, Janet thought that she saw the warmth on his face fade. In that instant, he seemed to be without emotion—a machine going through the motions. Alarms went off in her head. This was not about violence and women. It was about a senator running for re-election.

She immediately cast the thought from her mind. She knew that she was tired. It had been a long day and her list of things to do continued to grow. *I'm imagining things.*

Still, his words were too spot-on. The smile, the eye contact, and the confidence came across as too perfect. *He's a politician. It's what he does.*

The evening stretched on forever. Janet wanted nothing more than to get home and fall into bed. She convinced herself, though, that she should at least remain to hear his comments.

Sue Hartman's voice blared from the speakers in the front of the large banquet room. "Thank you all for coming tonight." She went on to introduce herself and plug the network and its work. After a few minutes of self-serving promotion, she continued, "I'm honored to present Senator Thomas Corel." She stepped back from the microphone and nodded to the Senator, who stepped onto the raised platform.

"Thank you, Sue, and thanks to all of you for coming out tonight. I'll respect your time and keep my comments brief. I'm sure that you all have things you'd rather be doing than listening to a crusty politician." He smiled and waited for the polite laughter to subside.

"We stand at a crossroads, faced with difficult choices. I won't bore you with numbers, but we all know that it's long past time for our great nation to move out of the dark ages. It's been far too easy for our government to give lip service to women's rights. It's time to act."

He lifted his right arm, his index finger extended upward.

"It's no longer enough to say that women have rights and opportunities. They must take their place alongside men in leading this nation. Even more urgent is the need to, once and for all, end the violence against women."

His balled fist came down on the podium with measured force—fierce enough to make his point but light enough to be civilized—just the right amount of force.

"My opponent has thwarted all attempts to secure full rights and opportunities for women in our great state of Washington. His record in the State House speaks for itself. He opposes the right to reproductive choice. He smirks at and dismisses the evidence of unequal pay. He openly mocks the need for childcare assistance and parental leave. Finally," he pointed a finger up as though to signal that an important point was coming, "he has repeatedly advocated for the repeal of the Violence Against Women Act, which is currently up for reauthorization. At this time and place in history, we simply cannot afford to have him sitting in a position of power." The crowd responded with applause, cheers, and whistles.

He fell silent for a moment, as though allowing the words to be absorbed. The accusation about his opponent's position on VAWA struck Janet as odd. She'd never heard that. Surely Sue Hartman would have said something about it if that were indeed the case. She glanced around. Everyone in the audience leaned forward slightly, hanging on his every word.

"My record is clear. My position is clear. I stand solidly with the women of our great nation. I ask that you stand with me. Together we can do this."

He finished to rousing applause and cheers. He descended the platform, shaking hands with people along the way. Throngs of supporters gathered around him.

Janet found herself smiling. She wanted to like him. His words made sense, and God knows, there was plenty of work to do on domestic violence. There was just something about him. In her heart, though, she knew what it was. He was a politician, a smooth talker.

"What did I tell you? Pretty impressive, huh?"

Janet turned to face Sue. "Uh, yeah." She felt that she should gush a little more, given that Sue was so excited, but she couldn't summon the words. "Thanks for inviting me." She turned toward the door. "I'm going to take off. It's been a long day and I need to get an early start tomorrow."

What she wanted, though, was to be at the hospital with Greg Stottman.

4

Greg Stottman didn't expect miracles. Thus far, there had been none. He sat in the hospital room with his niece, Dani, as she stared out the window in silence. His questions—did she want something to drink, did she need anything, did she want to talk—were all met with one-word answers... mostly *no.*

She had been beaten, shot, and left for dead by her boyfriend, Billy Robinson. By all appearances, the emotional damage was every bit as bad as the physical injuries.

"The doctor says that you should be able to go home within a couple of days." He thought that the notion of her leaving the hospital and getting back to some semblance of a normal life might cheer her up. He was wrong.

"Hmmm." Her responses were barely audible. Her gaze never shifted. She stared into the gathering darkness outside as though it alone contained the answer to all her problems.

Greg thought about bringing up the subject of

school… getting back to classes again. The look on her face warned him off. She was clearly someplace else.

The door opened. Greg turned to see Detective Charlotte Wharton of the King County Sheriff's Department. Even though their last encounter had left him angry and bitter, she seemed a welcome respite. He stood and eased his chair to the side, giving her access to a second chair. He nodded and offered the only greeting he could summon. "Detective."

For her part, she seemed not to notice him. Instead, she pulled the chair up close to Dani's bed. "We need to talk."

Dani turned and blankly stared at the woman.

"Billy Robinson, the man who shot you, killed two police officers in Spokane this afternoon." The words came out matter-of-factly. The detective's face offered no clue as to what she was thinking.

Dani's eyes grew wide as she shook her head. "No. He wouldn't do anything like that."

"It wasn't a question. It was a statement. I don't need your opinion. I'm here as a courtesy. Every cop in the state is looking for him right now. Odds are, when they run across him, it won't end well for him." She paused for a moment, as though to let her words sink in.

She continued, her voice taking on a more casual tone, "This is where you come in. If you care anything about him… and frankly I'm lost as to why you would… you might want to consider helping us find him. If we can locate him and plan around that, we have a good chance of bringing him in alive."

Wharton smirked. "If he's innocent, as you suggest, that would give him a chance to clear himself. Problem is, of course, if we keep flying blind, whoever finds the boy is likely going to shoot first, simply to be on the safe side."

Tears gathered in Dani's eyes. Her voice trembled as

she spoke. "You… you're lying. Billy wouldn't kill anyone. He's not like that."

Greg, watching the exchange, fully expected Detective Wharton to unload on Dani. Instead, the detective cleared her voice and touched Dani's arm. "I know you think that, and on the off-chance that you're right, being able to bring him in alive will allow him the opportunity to make his case. If it ends up in a gun battle on the street, he'll die. End of story."

Wharton leaned back and clasped her hands in her lap. "It's up to you, Dani. You can help us and maybe give him a chance to live." She shrugged and cocked her head. "Or you can remain silent and let things take their own course." She fell silent.

For the first time in the conversation, Dani turned her head to look at Greg. Her eyes pleaded. She licked her lips as she appeared to grapple with the dilemma.

Greg wanted to say something to help. He wanted it to all make sense for Dani. He came up empty. He didn't, for one instant, buy the *help us help Billy* line of bullshit that the detective was spouting. The cops wanted this guy, and it probably didn't make much difference to Wharton or any of the others whether he was alive or dead. In all honesty, it didn't make much difference to Greg either, although a part of him favored *dead*.

Dani let her gaze drop. "What do you want to know?"

Wharton leaned forward, her eyes intense. "Good. Now, we know that his parents split up a long time ago and that he was never close to either of them. His father's in prison right now. He had one brother who was killed in a car wreck about five years ago. Do you have any idea where his mother might be?"

Dani shook her head, her eyes seeming to lose focus.

"He didn't talk much about her, except to say that he hated her. I don't know where she is."

"Fair enough. What about other relatives?"

"I don't know. He said something about a cousin over in Idaho once but he didn't mention a name."

"Where in Idaho?"

"He didn't say." Dani paused, her gaze focused on the detective. "He didn't talk much about any of that. He didn't have much use for family. He used to say that I would be his family."

The words cut Greg. The idea that Dani would turn away from him to be family with Billy Robinson hurt.

The detective responded, "Okay, thanks, Dani. That's helpful. I promise you that, if we can get to him, we'll try to bring him in alive." The words sounded sincere. "One other thing. I doubt that he'll try to contact you, what with everything that's happened. On the chance that he does, please get in touch with me. Right now he's running scared and there's no telling what he'll do. No matter what you think of him, he could well pose a serious danger to both you and your uncle. Just call me. I'll take care of things, okay?"

5

J anet already felt stressed to the breaking point, and yet she had barely gotten her feet wet in this new undertaking of hers. She had gotten Lucy out the door when the onslaught from her husband, Rob, had started. Even at this point, Janet wasn't certain how the issue with her former boss would ultimately play out.

Then came the phone call. She checked the display before connecting. "Hi Sue."

"I was wondering if we might chat. I could meet you for coffee about two if you can get away."

Taking the afternoon—a time at which she was supposed to be working for the church—to spend on something that her new board president had specifically warned her against… this seemed fraught with problems. "Can it wait until this evening. I'm booked up solid here at the church this afternoon."

"I'm sorry. I've got a board meeting tonight and you need to know about this. I promise, I wouldn't ask if I didn't think it was important."

Thirty minutes later, against her better judgment, Janet

took a table near the window at Common Grounds to wait for Sue. Less than five minutes later, her friend slipped through the doorway and made her way to the table. "Thanks, and I promise this won't take long." She hung her coat on the back of the chair. "I'm going to grab a coffee. Do you want one?"

"Sure, black. And make it a to-go cup, please."

Once Sue returned with their drinks, she went straight to business. "Something happened about a week ago that could pose some problems for us. So far, it's remained under the media radar. It might, though, have some long-term implications. Are you familiar with the name Tryp Gamble, you know, the whiz kid financial investment guy?"

"Can't say that I've heard of him? Should I have?"

"I think he fancies himself more of a heavy hitter than he actually is. Anyway, early last week the police were called to his home. His wife had made a call to nine-one-one alleging he was beating up on her. The cops got there and the two were arguing but neither appeared hurt. I guess the kids were in bed. Anyway, the protocol at Seattle PD is to separate the couple when this kind of call comes in. Usually they end up arresting one of the parties, which accomplishes that. In this case, though, they apparently didn't feel they had probable cause. The wife downplayed the whole thing. Still, they had this policy to separate the two. They ordered Tryp to leave—told him to get a hotel room or some such thing."

"Okay, so, what's the problem? Why all the urgency? Sounds like a reasonable solution. Nobody got hurt. Nobody got arrested. All good, right?" Janet wasn't sure where this was going.

"Well, yes and no. That was the end of the issue for that night. The guy shows up at the mayor's office a few days later and, by all accounts, tears into him for this policy. Says that, because of the cops' actions, he was separated from his family and now his kids are all upset and, well, you get the picture."

"Except that, in the long run, everybody won, right? No violence, no charges, and I assume that this Tryp guy is free to return to his family. If he can just keep from beating up on her, everything should be fine."

"Janet, there's something that you may not have seen before. There is a school of thought that keeping families together and focusing on reconciliation is a more effective and morally just approach than just assuming that bickering couples need to be separated."

"Whoa, wait a minute." Janet stiffened, feeling the urge to lash out. "You're use of the term *bickering couples* paints this in an inaccurate light. The women you serve as well as the ones I'll be working with could hardly be termed as part of a *bickering couple*. Just ask Hanna Miller. Oh, sorry, you can't ask her. She's dead. Her bickering husband shot her three times." Janet felt her face turning red and her voice rising. She stopped and looked around to see if she had an audience.

Sue held her hands up, as though in defense. Her eyes pleaded for Janet to listen. "You're preaching to the choir, you know. I agree with you, but the truth is, yes, there are times when husbands and wives argue, and it doesn't rise to the level of danger. Yes, in those cases it may well be a good approach to try and get them talking so they can solve their problems. What makes this a problem, though, is that the police are required to make a call on the spot. They often operate with incomplete information and the knowledge that a mistake could cost a life. That's why they operate from policy and procedure rather than just going with gut reaction."

Janet shook her head, not sure where the conversation

was going. "So, again, isn't it better to err on the side of safety. I mean, if reconciliation turns out to be the best approach, then they can always do that later. If we go the other way and we're wrong, the woman may end up dead, maybe the kids too."

"Good, you see the dilemma. Unfortunately, I think this is going to grow legs. It's not going to end at the Mayor's office."

Janet narrowed her eyes. "Why not?"

"Because there are some powerful people in town who would like to push this agenda. Some of it is religious, some political, and some social. It's possible that this will erupt on several fronts at the same time, especially if these people and groups are able to coordinate."

"Okay, but if this hasn't even materialized yet, what am I supposed to do about it?"

"Right now, there's nothing you can do, but if it hits full force, it may affect what you're able to do with those women you serve."

"How so? Is it against the law for me to help women get out of town?"

"It's not that simple. There are no laws that dictate the details of how domestic violence services are provided. There are standards of care, which in Washington, are integrated as grant conditions. Most police departments have protocols on how to handle DV calls. The most common is to separate the two parties—get them apart so no one gets hurt."

"And? Sounds about right to me."

Sue leaned into the table, her eyes ablaze. "That could easily change. Seattle PD, for example, could change their protocol so that keeping the couple together is the default and separating them would require some level of probable cause. Or, the state legislature could pass a law that dictated this condition. It's not far-fetched to think that some guy like Tryp Gamble will take this straight to the governor. When it comes to politics, money and influence trump principles. This is where it could impact you and the services you're providing. If the policy changes and the default becomes to leave the couple together, more women could die before they even have a chance to ask for your help. In fact, these kinds of changes could affect your ability to even help these women."

Janet sat dumbfounded. "How so?"

Sue scooted up closer to the table and leaned in, her voice low. "I could only speculate right now, but it's worth keeping this on your radar. If it starts to grow legs, we may want to mount a serious advocacy campaign."

"Are you serious? They could do something like that?" The last thing Janet needed at the moment was to take something like a PR campaign on.

Sue put her hands up as though holding off some unpleasant invader. "I don't know yet. It's a possibility. There are other ways they can approach it as well. I just wanted to alert you that this has reared its ugly head and it's not likely to go away."

6

The door shut behind Detective Wharton as she left. Greg slid his chair closer to his niece, hoping to comfort her. Tears streamed down her cheek. It was only then that the final few words the detective had said struck home.

He bolted from his chair and raced out of the room. Detective Wharton had crossed the waiting area and paused in front of the elevator. "Detective, wait up." He raced to her side.

"What can I do for you, Mister Stottman?" Her face looked stern, her mouth drawn into a tight line.

"What you said, about Billy Robinson making contact with Dani or maybe even coming back here…." He struggled to frame the question he wanted to ask.

"I said that it's possible. I have no idea what the guy will do."

He grew frantic. "He beat her and shot her. Now he's killed two police officers. What if he just shows up here?"

She considered him for a moment, then motioned him toward the waiting area. She took a seat opposite him and leaned in close. "Like I said, I don't know, but odds are that he's on the run. If that's true, the last thing he'll do is come back here." She took a deep breath, looked away for a moment, and then turned towards him again.

"He crossed a line. Shooting your niece was a crime of passion. He likely lost control. Although it may not seem this way to you, it was sloppy. He beat her, shot her, and left her alive with large amounts of evidence in the room. It doesn't get much stupider than that. Killing the two officers, though, that was different. They knew he was dangerous. They would have been ready, and yet he managed to get both of them. That tells me that he's become far more deliberate and cunning in his behavior. He has to know that things are closing in. I suspect he'll try to get as far away as possible."

Greg asked, "If you can tell me, how did he manage to get the jump on the two officers?"

"I don't know and, even if I did, I wouldn't share that information with you. What I can tell you, though, is that he's evolved from a hot-tempered, emotionally stunted asshole into a predator. That's a problem for us, but it works in your favor. He's not likely to care much about coming back for Dani or to get even with you."

Greg felt guilty for his earlier behavior with regard to the detective. He tried for redemption. "Is there anything I can do to help?"

"You're doing it. Keep your niece safe. Stay close. Talk to her and listen when she talks. If you want an extra measure of safety, given your resources, you might want to relocate her. Rent a place that can't be easily connected to you. Keep her away from places she used to frequent—school, restaurants, coffee shops, and the like. Beyond that, call me the instant you hear something, no matter how trivial you think it is." She handed him a business card.

As he made his way back to Dani's room, he noticed himself holding the card with both hands, as though it was some priceless artifact. He wanted to trust Detective Wharton. He wanted to believe the things she said. Surely Dani would be safe. There would be no way Billy would return for her.

Back in her room, he pulled the chair up. "Thanks for talking to her. I know it's hard, but she really does want to help."

Dani appeared to have not heard. "Did you know that Reverend Polasky used to be married?"

The statement came out of nowhere and took Greg by surprise. "Uh, yeah, I did know that."

"He died. That was… like… ten years ago, but she's still alone. She loved him and they planned a life together, and then he was gone, just like that. Now there's nobody… nothing… in her life. Empty." The words seemed bathed in pain.

"She told me, yes. But I wouldn't say her life is empty. She's the minister of a church. People depend on her. She touches the lives of others. She's there when people need her. That's not empty."

Dani shook her head. "She does all that for *other* people. What does it do for *her*?"

The question made Greg uneasy. "I guess you'd have to ask her that question. From what I see, though, she does have meaning… purpose in her life. She has friends. I'm sure she has both sadness and joy." He was guessing. In truth, Janet's private life was still a mystery to him.

"I can tell you this, Dani. I don't have anyone in my life romantically, but I don't feel empty. I have you. I have friends like Melissa and Janet. I have things that interest me, that make me feel good about getting up in the morning."

A laugh escaped from his niece. "Like that stupid video game?"

A wave of relief swept over him. He could deal with the banter. "My video games are not stupid. I'll have you know that it takes a great deal of skill and knowledge to be successful. If you'd spend more time on video games and less time studying, you'd know that." He forced a laugh, hoping she'd engage.

Dani closed her eyes and smiled softly. "Being in love was incredible—once in a lifetime incredible."

Greg took her hand. "You're going on nineteen years old. I wouldn't write off the possibility of love just yet. I promise you, Dani, there is someone out there... someone special... someone that deserves you."

She smirked. "Are you going to welcome him with open arms?"

"Like I said—someone who deserves you."

7

It had been one week to the day since Janet's last contact with Rob Young. He'd not submitted his resignation letter, although it didn't matter much at this point. The board had chosen an interim president and, sometime down the road, they would take the necessary steps to formally remove Rob from the board. The personal clash between him and Janet was another matter. Rob's wife had come to Janet for help getting away from him. Rob would not forget that any time soon. Although he hadn't contacted her since the last phone call, she lived with a sense of foreboding, afraid that at any moment, he would turn up.

Janet shuffled through the door, office supply bags in both hands. "Any calls?"

"Aylin Freyberg from the Church Association called. She left a voice mail." Margaret Shemanski, the church secretary, responded without looking up.

"Thanks." Once settled at her desk, Janet played the message.

"Hi Janet. It's Aylin from the Association. Sorry I

missed you. Please give me a call when you get a chance." Her voice sounded pleasant enough, but a hint of concern made its way out.

Janet stared at the phone. The last thing she needed was more trouble. Aylin was paid staff for the King County Church Association. Her portfolio, as they referred to issues, was family violence. Given that Janet was no longer on the Association Board of Directors, it was rare for the staff to contact her.

On the other hand, it could be nothing. Maybe Aylin just wanted some background information or to ask a question or two about the Hanna Miller murder. That was probably it. The killing made front page news, along with the fact that Janet had been there. Aylin was probably just putting together some material for the annual report.

That certainly wasn't urgent. It could wait until the next day. Almost immediately, though, the issue resolved itself. Her cellphone chimed, and she connected. "Hello,"

"Hey Janet, this is Aylin."

"Hi. I just got back in the office. What's up?"

"Just a head's up. Pastor Millard Conyers has asked to be placed on the agenda for our board meeting next week."

The last person Janet wanted to talk about was Millard Conyers. "Okay, so, why is that important?"

There was a short pause before Aylin responded softly, "The word is that he's going to push for us to advocate for a family preservation priority in Seattle family violence services."

This was the very issue that Sue had warned about. "I can't imagine the Association will go down that path. We generally don't get that involved in specific policy. We've always advocated for services but have avoided the details."

"Maybe you're right. All the same, you might want to

show up for the meeting. You have a lot of credibility with the board. You could be the voice of reason."

"I don't know, Aylin. I have a full plate. I'll call Tam and Carl and try to convey my concerns. On the other hand, you might not want to give this any more airtime than it deserves. If you instigate a full-blown argument at the board meeting, it works in Conyers' favor."

Still, she had promised to phone Carl Broward, the Association board president and Tam Wiggins, the Executive Director. That would, however, have to wait until the following day. With that settled in her mind, Janet moved on to her next task.

The lined yellow pad sat in front of her, as though inviting the words that would ultimately become her sermon on Sunday. The service was still three days distant, but focus eluded her.

She tried to force her mind into *the zone*, as she called it —that state of mind in which the scripture inspired visions of real-world lessons. Nothing came. When she managed to wipe her mind clear of all the distractions that had plagued her through the day, she saw only a blank page. There were no inspirations, no flow of thoughts, and no sense of God's great plan.

Finally, she gave up. Switching gears, she reluctantly punched in the phone number for Tam Wiggins and connected. "Good afternoon, Tam. How are things going?"

"Oh, about the same. How are you doing?" The sincerity rang true. The Association, and specifically Tam, had been solid in their support and comfort during the days following Hanna's murder.

"I'm doing okay, all things considered. The reason I called is that I understand that Pastor Conyers is on the board agenda for next week... something about family preservation and restoration in domestic violence services."

"Yes, that's true."

"I don't want to make more of this than is there, but that concept is a very controversial one and, in my opinion, a bad approach in general. Before you say it, yes, I realize that sometimes families can get back together and work through their problems. It's dangerous to use that as a default, though."

"You're getting ahead of yourself, Janet. He just wants to chat with the board about his concerns. You and I both know that we've always been reluctant to delve into the minutia of services, regardless of the field."

"Yeah, I know, and I trust you on this. I just wanted to touch base and air my opinion. Tell me, in your view, would it be worth my time to attend the meeting?"

"Our meetings are open. Attend if you want to. We intend to listen to what he has to say. I will promise you this, though. The board will almost certainly not act on anything based on a single night's testimony. The worst case is that they would take it under advisement and schedule further discussions. In that case, you could participate later, if you choose."

"Yeah, that sounds good, Tam. I've got plenty to do right now. Besides, getting into an argument with the guy in front of the board would just give him more attention."

After disconnecting, Janet decided on one more call. She punched in the numbers.

"Good afternoon, this is Reverend Broward. How can I help you?" Carl was the minister at the Bellevue Baptist Temple.

"Hi Carl. This is Janet Polasky. Have you got a minute?"

"Sure, what can I do for you?"

Chapter 7

"I understand that Pastor Conyers is on the agenda for your board meeting next week to talk about family preservation and restoration in violence cases. I don't intend to be there, but I'm hoping that if the board decides to take up the issue for consideration, you'll give me a call."

"I know that you're involved in that field. I have to confess that I'm not sure about the details of what he has to say, but certainly… if we decide to move on it, I'll make sure that you're notified."

After they disconnected, Janet replayed the conversation. Something hadn't sounded right—not the words so much as the tone. It was as though he was expecting her call and wanted mostly to put her off. They'd always gotten along well when she was on the board. While they were never best friends, they had always managed a collegial relationship. Just then, though, he had sounded different.

8

The living room lights were still on when Senator Corel pulled into the driveway at 3:30 a.m. *Shit.* He had told her not to wait up. She didn't listen. She never listened. He could feel the pressure building. He slammed the car door and stomped to the front door. He looked around at the stately homes in the immediate area. Interior lights all appeared to be off with only porch lights illuminated. *Good. No prying eyes.* Punching in the security code, he opened the door.

Bonnie sat on the couch in her robe. Her eyes were red and swollen, which only made the black eye look worse than it really was. The look on her face was hopeful. "I was so worried about you." She stood.

"I told you not to wait up."

"I wanted to spend some time with you tonight. We don't get much time to talk."

"You need to learn to listen when I tell you something. You don't pay attention."

"I'm sorry. I just wanted to be with you."

"I had this meeting tonight. You've known about it for

weeks—how important it is to the campaign. You never think about what I need or what the campaign needs. Everything has to be about you."

Tears rolled down her cheeks and her lips quivered.

God he hated those quivering lips. Why did she have to play the helpless victim?

She sniffled and used a tissue to wipe the tears.

"Knock it off, for Christ's sake. Why do you have to pull this shit over and over?"

She shrank into the couch, fear in her eyes.

The dam broke. His righteous anger won out. Suddenly he was across the room. He grabbed her up by her horrid pink robe and shoved her back toward the center of the room. Her legs buckled and she crumbled. He kicked her in the ribs. It was as though his legs had taken control of his body, while he stood on the outside looking in. He understood clearly that she deserved this. His foot connected again with her midsection. This was her fault and hers alone.

She screamed and curled into a ball.

He grabbed both her arms and pulled. The force brought her off the floor, but her legs folded. She melted to the floor. His legs kicked her again—more screams.

She fell away and rolled over with her face toward the wall.

Why had she done this? Why had she brought this on herself? It seemed he was the only adult in the room.

Gradually he felt the rage subside. He once again took control of his body. Seeing her rolled over on the floor, he took in the full measure of what had happened. She had driven him to the point where he lost control.

"I'm sorry, Bonnie, really I am." He knelt beside her, his hand stroking her hair. Let's get you cleaned up and we can talk. We'll spend some time together."

She whimpered. Her body relaxed.

He rolled her over. Standing, he reached out his hand. "Let me help you up."

* * *

He didn't mean to hurt her. Senator William Corel never meant to hurt anyone. He was just not wired that way, and it pained him to see her bruised body. She never seemed to pay attention, though. She knew that this was an important time for him. She should support him. His re-election campaign was a central fixture in his life—*their life*, but she insisted on making everything about herself. It was always about Bonnie Corel.

He brooded as his coffee cooled on his desk. He tried to focus on the list of items he needed to accomplish. His wife's tear-streaked face kept intruding. *Damn her!*

The door opened and Alicia stepped in. "I wanted to remind you, Senator. I'm leaving early today. I'm driving over to Spokane for my grandparents' fiftieth wedding anniversary." Her smile and easy demeanor gave the impression that she expected no objection.

If that was indeed what she thought, then she was in for a shock. He glared at her. "This is not a good time, you know that. We have several fundraisers over the next few days and the governor's hosting a benefit dinner for me tonight."

She looked as though a wall of bricks had come crashing down. "But I told you a month ago and reminded you last week. This is their golden anniversary. I have to be there." Her eyes moistened, a sure prelude to tears.

He held his anger in check. He was, after all, the adult in the room. "What time does all this happen?"

Chapter 8

"They're going to renew their vows in the church at six. The party starts at seven."

"You should be able to do the church thing, make a showing at the party, and still make it back tonight. I need you with me tomorrow. We have a full day."

"It's a four-hour drive. That would put me back at midnight or later."

"And?"

Her lips tightened and she nodded. "Yes sir." She closed the door behind her as she left.

His anger smoldered beneath the surface. Neither his bore of a wife nor Alicia seemed to grasp the gravity of his situation. If he was to win re-election, it would be on him completely. Everyone around him seemed eager to desert him at the first opportunity. He gritted his teeth as he tried to force his attention back to the to-do list.

* * *

"I told you about this weeks ago, Bonnie. The governor and his wife are hosting a dinner for me at the Space Needle. You know perfectly well that the election is only a little over a month away. This trip is a campaign trip."

"I can go with you, then. I'm feeling a lot better." Bonnie gestured meekly to her face as her words trailed off.

"That's absurd and you know it. No, you need to stay here until you're well enough to get out." He knew that the bruising to her ribs and stomach would make moving about nearly impossible.

She started to say something but stopped, her mouth open. The glare that he shot her had done the trick. "We're headed back to D.C. at the end of next week. We'll go out to dinner when we get back there. After that, I have to come back here for the last two weeks in October. I'll do

35

that alone so that you don't have to suffer through all this tension."

"But I don't mind, really. I want to help you. Remember in the last election, I was with you and even gave two speeches myself. I can do this."

He shuddered at the thought. The last thing he wanted was for her to speak to anyone. She knew next to nothing about politics and, the worst part was that she didn't realize just how stupid she was. He closed his eyes and willed away the frustration. "Thank you, Bonnie. I appreciate it. You know that I love having you with me. This is something I need to do alone, though. I need you to keep the home fires burning." It was a stupid excuse, he realized, but he hoped she wouldn't notice.

Her voice came out meek, barely more than a whisper. "Will you be late tonight?"

His mind wandered to Alicia. He was pissed... well more like disappointed in her. Still, she would be back by midnight. That meant that they could spend at least a couple of hours in her hotel room. "I'm afraid it will be rather late. The dinner itself shouldn't go past ten, but the governor is going to have some deep pocket friends there. I suspect we'll discuss the state of affairs over a few drinks." He forced a laugh. "Anything to grease the skids."

She nodded and lowered her head.

* * *

The guests started leaving the venue around ten-fifteen. By ten-forty-five, he was shaking the governor's hand and thanking him. As Corel made his way to the elevator, he retrieved his cellphone and checked his messages. He listened to the last one, and he felt a surge of anger.

"Hello Senator. This is Alicia. Things got kind of

turned around here and the party started late. I'm going to stay overnight here and hit the road early. I should be in the office by mid-morning. I'm so sorry. Will talk to you then. Bye."

He felt like hurling the phone against the wall. Goddamned women—none of them were worth a shit. All around him—betrayal at every turn. There was no one that he could count on. He checked his watch—eleven o'clock. He shuddered at the thought of what awaited him at home.

9

Greg committed to spending the day in his office. Dani was home and settled in. He was in the process of searching for a short-term rental for her as Detective Wharton had suggested. To keep it anonymous, though, he had asked Melissa, his business partner, to help. This process was eating most of his time and, thus far, had produced no results.

He was determined that today would be different. He pulled up financial reports for the past two years on one monitor and loaded up the past two years of macro-economic data on the other. How had the company performed compared to other tech firms?

Greg heard the click from his desk phone before the voice burst forth. "I have a Mister Trowbridge for you on line one." This was exactly the kind of interruptions he hated. Pouring through financial reports was hard enough without this kind of crap.

"What does he want?"

"He wants to talk to you."

"About what?"

"He just said that it was important."

He exhaled and slumped in his chair, frustration building. It wasn't Tanya's fault. She generally did an excellent job of screening his calls. Every once in a while, though, it came to this. "Okay, thanks."

He put the phone on speaker and pressed the button to connect. "Good morning, this is Greg Stottman."

"Thank you for taking my call, Mister Stottman. My name is Nicholas Trowbridge. I'm with the Council for Safe and Healthy Families. I wonder if I might have just a few minutes of your time?"

"What is this Council—a non-profit or what?"

"We are tax exempt, but not really a 501(c)(3). We're a political action committee."

"I'm sorry Mister Trowbridge. I don't do politics."

The caller laughed. "No, no. It's not really about politics."

"I don't contribute to political campaigns, either." Greg struggled to keep his tone civil. He hated these kinds of pitches.

Another laugh. "I hear you." Trowbridge paused and then continued with a soft and obviously contrived sincerity. "I'm not after your money, Mister Stottman, although I wouldn't be averse to having that conversation at some point in the future. No, I just wanted to have a discussion with you about family violence. I know that you've contributed to organizations that provide DV services."

"And?"

"Could we meet for drinks? I promise I won't take much of your time."

Greg closed his eyes and took a deep breath. "I don't mean to be rude but where is this going? I'm not much of a drinker and I certainly don't discuss business over drinks."

"How about lunch then, I'm buying."

Greg wondered where this clown had come up with all of these cliché lines. "I can meet you for coffee if that works. Common Grounds in Bellevue. Two-thirty today." He knew he was going to regret this. In fact, why had he even agreed to it? Normally, he would have just refused. It occurred to him that he had crossed a fair number of lines these past months. Maybe his partner, Melissa, was right. Perhaps he had become far too agreeable in helping others. On the other hand, domestic violence had become an important issue for him.

After the call ended, he dialed Melissa's number. "Hey, Mel, you ever hear of a guy named Nicholas Trowbridge. He's with some outfit… let's see… oh yes, the Council for Safe and Healthy Families. It's a PAC."

"Never heard of him or the organization. Why?"

"He just called and badgered me—wanting to meet to discuss something. Says it's not political or a pitch for money."

"So what?"

"I don't know, it's just a pain in the ass. I'm up to my eyeballs in financial reports right now."

"Did you shut him down?"

"Naw, I agreed to meet for coffee this afternoon… against my better judgment." He understood how absolutely stupid that sounded the minute he spoke the words.

Melissa apparently agreed with his assessment. "You know, of course, that they just added a new word to the English vocabulary—*No*. You're free to use that word when appropriate."

"Spare me. I'm just trying to keep a good PR front."

"Good luck with that."

Chapter 9

* * *

He had no trouble spotting Trowbridge. He was the only one in the place in a suit and tie. He sat at a corner table tapping furiously on his cellphone.

"Mister Trowbridge?"

The man looked up, a grin spreading across his face. He stood and offered his hand. "Great to meet you. Please, have a seat. Can I get you something—a latte or cappuccino or something?"

Rather than sitting, Greg said, "I'll grab a coffee and be right back."

Everything about the man grated on him—the polished look, the plastic grin, and a rather obvious sense of self-importance. Greg stood in line regretting his capitulation in even agreeing to the meeting. As he made his way back, weaving through the tables with his cup of steaming coffee, he resolved to get through the ordeal with as much grace as he could muster.

Sliding into the seat, he placed his cup on the table. "So, what can I do for you?"

"As I said, this isn't a pitch for money or any kind of political endorsement. I'd just like to discuss domestic violence services. I know that you've contributed to the King County DV Network in the past."

"I contribute to a lot of different things."

"Yes, yes, I'm sure you do. We at the Council are just starting to come up to speed on the violence issue and I thought we might offer you some of our thoughts."

Greg took a sip of coffee and shrugged.

Trowbridge, not appearing the least bit put off, continued without missing a beat. "As you likely know, the Network's current approach to dealing with bickering couples is to separate them, according to their staff, for safety purposes."

Greg cut in, "Before you go on, just a point of clarification—I doubt that the Network is providing services to *bickering couples*, as you call them. My understanding is that they serve victims of violence and abuse. Big difference."

"Yes, well, rather than get into a long discussion about semantics, I'll cut to the bottom line. When the husbands and wives are separated, it pretty much destroys the family."

"I'd say right off-hand, that when a man batters his wife, that... as you say... *pretty much destroys the family*."

"We agree that sometimes the violence has progressed to a point where the separation is needed. We question, though, whether that should be the norm. What we're after is just a slight shift in the way that these cases are viewed. We think that the default should be that every effort should be made to keep the family together. If that can't be safely accomplished, then certainly the victim's safety must be assured. It is heartbreaking, though, that we might see families destroyed when it's possible that safety is only an issue in about twenty-five percent of the cases."

"Where did you come up with this twenty-five percent figure?"

"Our own independent research indicates that this is the approximate percentage in which there is a real danger. It's not my intention to quibble over numbers or details. I'm just suggesting that, rather than assume that the couples must be separated, simply assume that they will stay together. If the situation at hand dictates differently, so be it."

Greg stuffed his growing rage. "I find it odd that you're concerned about the issue but don't seem care about data or even definitions. That aside, what is it that you want from me? I don't set or recommend policy. In fact, I don't even have policy discussions with these agencies. If you don't like the way they operate, why not talk to them?"

Trowbridge put his hands up as though to calm the troubled waters. "Please, Mister Stottman, I'm sure you know that these are feminist organizations. Surely you understand that they're not going to listen to us."

Greg's rage built. He felt the heat rise in his face as he clenched his jaw. The urge to lash back at the man nearly overwhelmed him. Instead, he took a deep breath, determined not to rise to the bait. "That still doesn't say what you need from me?"

"I'll be blunt. You contribute a lot of money to them. If you weigh in on this, making clear that you have concerns in this area, they might pay attention, even if begrudgingly."

"Well, that is blunt. So, I will be equally precise with you. My answer is *no I will not*. My role in these kinds of affairs is to donate to worthy causes. If I have to attach strings, then I don't contribute. Otherwise, I leave the program design to people who know about such things." He paused and sipped his coffee. "Now, is there anything else?"

Trowbridge's smile slipped and his gaze became a glare. "We're putting together a campaign to help shape public opinion on this. We intend to roll it out in the near future. If you're not willing to step up and do the right thing, this could come back to haunt you."

Greg burst out laughing. "I assure you, Mister Trowbridge, this wouldn't be the first time that someone in politics or the media vilified a business owner. Additionally, if you have any inclination of seeking financial support for your organization from me in the future, you're shooting yourself in the foot right now."

Trowbridge lifted his napkin to his mouth and dabbed it gently, his smile returning. He stood and put his cell-phone in his vest pocket. "You're going to find that this issue is bigger than you think. When it takes off, you aren't going to want to be on the wrong side."

10

The phone call caught her off-guard. Janet had already put the finishing touches on her sermon for Sunday. The packets for the next board meeting were ready to go out. She finally felt as though she had the luxury of time to engage in some planning for her project. No such luck.

"Good morning, Aylin. What's up?"

The Church Association staff member sounded stressed. "Janet, I was wondering if maybe you'd reconsider about the meeting tonight. Something's up and I'm feeling a little alone right now."

"What do you mean?"

"I can't put my finger on it. Tam is avoiding me and there seems to be kind of a chill in the air."

"I'm sure Tam's busy preparing for the meeting. There's a lot that goes into that, you know."

Aylin's voice sounded frantic. "It's not just today. Several times this past week I've tried to schedule some time to brief her on the background for this issue that Pastor Conyers is intending to bring up. She shut me down every time. It wasn't blatant, or anything. She would just make excuses about having to do other things or not having time to talk. I tell you, Janet, it's not like her. Something's going on."

Janet didn't feel like debating the issue over the phone. Besides, in all likelihood, there was nothing to it. Conyers would come and rant, as he did on most issues. The board would thank him for his input and move on. This would not be the first time something like this played out. "Okay, I'll show up. Keep in mind, Aylin, getting into a debate with him will work against you. Just let him rant."

* * *

The proceedings started promptly at seven. By seven-fifteen, Janet remembered why she hated these meetings so much and had refused to sit on the board again. They went through the minutes of the last meeting, with several requests for changes or clarifications. Proposed changes were detailed and voted on. On and on and on it went.

The financial report was presented with its usual flurry of questions and concerns, which dragged on for half an hour. As the president, Carl Broward, called for approval, Janet felt the tension building. She knew in her heart that it had nothing to do with the budget. She turned her attention to those present and it hit her. The board members that had historically been the strongest supporters of DV advocacy were not there. The board had a quorum, to be sure, but it was comprised of members that were less enthusiastic about social issues. She suddenly understood Aylin's apprehension.

Broward put the financial report aside and studied the agenda for a moment. "Okay then, moving on. The next piece on the agenda is... Pastor Conyers has requested the opportunity to address the board regarding advocacy for family violence services." He nodded toward the portly man who appeared to be in his early fifties. "The floor is yours, Pastor."

Conyers stood and made his way around to the head of the table, standing behind Tam Wiggins, the Executive Director. She scooted her chair to the side and turned it so that she could see him.

Janet immediately spotted the pastor's blatant power play. He apparently came ready for battle.

"Thank you, Carl, and thanks to the board for agreeing to hear me this evening. I appreciate your consideration and promise to keep this concise." He cleared his throat and studied the piece of paper in his hand. Janet was fairly certain that was for effect. Millard Conyers was never at a loss for words and always confident in his presentation.

"As all of you are well aware, family conflict has been around for… well… as best we can know, since the beginning of recorded time. We find it addressed again and again in the Bible. Although the Lord abhors violence, we are reminded to consider all sides. In his letter to Ephesians in the fifth chapter verses twenty-two and twenty-three, Paul urges women to submit to their husbands. First Timothy, Chapter Two, in verses eleven and twelve, women are directed to learn in silence with all submissiveness. I could go on and on. But of course, you all know this."

He took his glasses off and wiped them with a piece of cloth before replacing them and smiling at the group. "I know what some of you are thinking—that I am trying to cast blame on the victim. Nothing could be further from the truth. Violence is wrong, period. We have in the past decade begun to make progress on this front. We have shelters to protect vulnerable women. We have counseling and assistance programs to help them restart their lives. All I am saying is that maybe now it is time to take a closer look at how we respond in general." He paused for a moment.

Janet watched him make eye contact with each board member. Conyers was good at this.

Tam Wiggins took that opportunity to interject, "Before you continue, Pastor Conyers, I wanted to clarify something. We don't promote any specific service delivery approach. We advocate for services for those in need, but we leave it to the professionals to determine how best to accomplish that."

"Of course. I realize that and I'm not suggesting that we take on the task of designing programs. All I'm saying is that we must speak up on behalf of the family. Not every incident is worthy of destroying an intact relationship. Many of these situations are nothing more than bickering couples. Sometimes they drink too much—both of them. They say and do things that they regret the next day. Just because the police may be called doesn't justify destroying God's holy union—the marriage."

The words—*bickering couples*—struck Janet hard. This was the second time in as many days that she'd heard that phrase. She fought the urge to lash out at the proselytizing pastor.

Aylin Freyberg, who had been simmering in the seat next to Janet, blew up. "What does it take, a dead wife? Is that the bar that we have to reach in order to keep a violent man away from his wife? Maybe men who can't control their temper should shoulder the blame for destroying the family."

Janet put her hand on Aylin's arm and applied pressure. When the woman glanced over, Janet signaled with her eyes—*don't do this, not here.*

It was too late. What was done… was done. Tam spoke

in a crisp and authoritative tone. "Enough, Aylin." She blushed, nodded to Carl Broward, and then spoke to Conyers. "My apologies, Pastor. Please continue."

Aylin bolted from the room, which fell silent as the door slammed shut. After a moment, Janet spoke quietly. "Excuse me. I'll check on her." She left the room and found Aylin sitting on the stairs at the end of the hall.

"Ouch." Janet sat beside her.

"I knew it. I knew something was at work here."

"What was at work? All that happened was this guy made a speech that you knew ahead of time he was going to make." Janet knew, though, that Aylin had a point. Her explosion in the meeting, though, had not helped.

Aylin turned and glared at her. "You don't get it, do you. Do you think the absent board members were just accidently not here? You think this was random? This entire thing was orchestrated. That sanctimonious jerk is playing them like a fiddle, and you know it."

"So, do you think your performance in there helped?" Janet put her arm around the young woman's shoulders. "The DV community has a lot of friends in this organization. You may not like the guy's message, but he has the right to voice it. Frankly, we're better off getting it out in the open where we can deal with it than having it fester in the dark."

"Fester in the dark? Really? Did you see Broward and Tam in there? This guy has them cowed."

"If you get yourself fired, how's that going to help?"

11

He took a deep breath before punching in the security code and opening the door. With any amount of luck, she would be asleep. Senator Corel had resigned himself to a scotch on the rocks in his easy chair with his feet up.

"Is that you, Thom?" The shrill voice made its way from down the hall as a shape appeared in the half-light of the corridor. "I wasn't expecting you home so early."

"The dinner wound up a little early. I'm going to sit up and go over some things for tomorrow. Go back to bed, Bonnie."

"Do you want me to fix you a drink?"

"I said, go back to bed." He closed his eyes and clenched his jaw, hoping against hope that she would just this once, follow direction.

No such luck. "You need a drink, and I'll fix you a sandwich."

"I can get my drink... *thank you.*" He forced the last two words out more to calm himself than anything else. "Go back to bed."

"But I'd like to stay up and talk to you. I'll fix us both a drink."

He had tried, truly he had. He had been determined to keep the peace. One of them had to play grown-up and it certainly wasn't going to be his wife. He could see it in her face; hear it in her voice. She knew the buttons to push and delighted in pushing them. He felt the last vestiges of control disappear. He shot across the room and back-handed her. "Listen, for the love of God. I said no. That means no. When are you going to learn to listen?"

Bonnie stumbled backwards, slamming into the wall. Blood trickled from her mouth as she wiped her face with her hand. Her eyes widened. "I'm sorry, Thom." The words filtered through her sobs.

"You never listen," he shouted. "You never pay attention. You only live in your own world, and you screw everything up," He grabbed both her forearms and pulled her towards him.

She tried to put her hands over her face, but he held her arms out with one hand and punched her in the face with the other. Her head snapped to the side. He let go of her and she crumbled to the floor. He kicked her midsection twice, then stepped back and took a deep breath.

The darkness washed over him. She'd done it to him again—made him lose control. Only this time he'd really *lost control*. Her bloody face displayed the results. This would never do. How could he hide this? Now he'd have to deal with the mess she'd made.

It wasn't his fault, though. She'd provoked him again. He didn't want to hurt her. She forced him to do it. Kneeling beside her, he spoke softly. "Here, let me get a wet towel." His mind raced. He needed to fix this?

She buried her face deeper in her hands as she sobbed deeply.

He rushed into the bathroom and wet a wash cloth with cold water. Coming back to her, he placed it on the side of her head. "This will help."

He tried to caress her hair, but she recoiled.

"Please, Bonnie. Let me hold you. I'll get us a drink. Here, let me help you up." He took her hand as he stood. "Come on, let's go into the living room."

Her crying had subsided to a whimper. With only minimal resistance to his pull, he lifted her to her feet, continuing to cover her face with her free hand. He took her in his arms and held her, caressing her hair and assuring her that everything would be all right. He knew that he needed to be stronger. He couldn't continue letting her provoke him like this.

* * *

Senator Corel sat in his office as the morning dragged by. He had gotten only a couple hours of troubled sleep. He had a full afternoon and evening ahead of him. But what he needed most was to straighten out this mess with Bonnie. He somehow had to make her see that he wasn't trying to be cruel. He just needed her to pay attention and do what he said. It didn't seem that hard, but the more he thought about it, the angrier he grew.

To make matters worse, ten o'clock had come and gone and Alicia had not arrived yet. As infuriating as his wife could be, at least she was reliable. When Bonnie said she would do something, she did it. Alicia had failed him now twice in two days, well, three times if he counted the fact that she went to the stupid anniversary party ignoring the fact that he needed her.

No sooner had the thought swept through his mind, when his door opened, and his aide stepped in. "I'm so sorry, Senator. There was a traffic accident on I-90 and it tied things up for an hour."

He forced a smile. "No problem. I was just trying to catch up on a few things and get ready for our two o'clock at the university. Why don't we get some lunch and take it back to your room."

"Sounds perfect. You want me to call in an order to go?"

"Yeah, that would be fine. I need to make a quick phone call and then I'll be ready to go." In truth, it would be more than fine. It had been nearly a week since he had spent any quality alone time with Alicia.

She shut the door on the way out. He steeled himself for the conversation and then dialed his home phone—no answer. He left a message. "Hey hon. I wanted to touch base with you before I headed out for the afternoon. I've got a full schedule and then a dinner meeting. I'll try to connect with you later. Love you. Bye."

He started to grab his coat, but something gnawed at him. He dialed Bonnie's cellphone number—no answer. He didn't bother with a message. Standing in the middle of the room, he felt conflicted. She always answered the phone.

The senator swung by Alicia's office as she was putting her coat on.

"I need to run home and pick something up. I'll meet you at your room."

She looked disappointed but nodded and said nothing.

He tried both the main landline number and Bonnie's cellphone again while driving—still no answer. His sense of worry deepened. This was not like her.

When he arrived and let himself in, the house was deserted. There was no note and no sign of his wife. This was definitely not like her. Then he found it—her cellphone. It was lying on the bed. Her suitcase was gone along with most of her clothes.

He powered up his computer. Fortunately, he knew how to check her airline account. Maybe she'd decided to go back to Washington, D.C.

No, she hadn't purchased a ticket. There was no activity on her account since they'd flown in from D.C. She did have a reservation to go back with him as they'd planned. Nothing else.

He opened the display on her phone using her ID Code. Pulling up the telephone call record, he could see that she'd made no calls. He checked the landline handset controls—again, no calls out.

She had no car. She'd not made any calls, so she hadn't gotten a taxi or car service. Bonnie was simply gone. She'd disappeared. She'd done it again, just to hurt him when he needed her most.

He plopped down in the overstuffed chair in the living room, cellphone in hand. He dreaded making this call. He pulled out a card from his wallet and set it in front of him. He dialed the number. "Dylan?"

"Yes."

"We're in Seattle. She's gone again. Find her. Bring her back."

12

J anet's first instincts were right, it seemed. There had
been no good reason for her to be at the Association
board meeting the previous night. Nothing Conyers
said had been unexpected. The responses from Tam and
Carl had been more docile than she would have predicted.
On the other hand, they had both made clear that they
didn't intend to debate the issue. The only unexpected
development was Aylin's outburst.

As she put her breakfast dishes in the dishwasher, she
made a mental note to give Aylin a call and maybe set up a
lunch date. The young woman was a member of the
Duwamish Indian Tribe and had worked on domestic
violence issues her entire adult life—she was passionate
about it. She'd seen it first-hand growing up and lived
through it herself. She was still struggling, though, to navigate the political minefields that existed within the faith
community. The previous evening was proof of that.

Settling into what she hoped would be a quiet morning,
the first inkling that something was amiss came when she

received a phone call from Greg Stottman. "Good morning, Greg."

"Hey, Janet. I was wondering... have you ever heard of a guy named Nicholas Trowbridge or the Council for Safe and Healthy Families?"

"Uh, no to both. Why?" She swiveled her chair around so that she could take in the sunny day.

"Well, I met with him yesterday afternoon, at his request. The organization turned out to be a political action committee. The gist of what he wanted was for me to put some pressure on the DV organizations I contribute to—try to get them to focus more on keeping couples together."

"Seriously? That's odd." It seemed a strange coincidence. Maybe there was more to Aylin's concern than Janet thought. She related the events of the previous evening.

His voice sounded concerned. "It seems curious, you know, that both of these situations related to the same topic happening at the same time?"

"Yeah, it seems that way to me too."

"I told him that I don't get involved in detail or in pushing any kind of service approach. He didn't take it very well... hurled a thinly veiled threat."

Her day was already starting to turn sour. "What are you going to do?"

"Same as I told him—nothing. Even if I wanted to get into that level of detail, I don't know enough to have an intelligent conversation. I contribute because the issue is important. How services get delivered isn't my focus."

"I take your point, although I think maybe you're selling yourself short. You know more about the issue than most people. More importantly, you're willing to listen."

"What about your Church Association, what are they going to do?"

Janet thought about the question for a moment. "Probably nothing. We're not financial contributors. Our role is advocacy—we keep the issue in the public eye. How the women are helped is something we leave to the professionals. My guess is that the board will thank him for his interest and let it go at that."

After a brief pause, she continued, "I was hoping to drop by and see how Dani's doing. Would tonight be okay?"

His voice changed. The seriousness and concern she'd heard only a moment before changed into a tone of... *excitement*? "Tonight would be perfect." He added quickly, "Dani will be thrilled."

After they ended the call, Janet felt increasingly uneasy. Greg's question about coincidence was a good one. The topic of family preservation came up from time-to-time, but there was virtually no support among the professionals for making that the default goal. Every program that she was familiar with placed the safety of the victim above all else. Historically, the best way to tackle that was to initially separate the couples for a cooling-off period. In some cases, they reconciled later. Many times it worked, but most often the assault resumed within a relatively short time.

Something else bothered her. She'd now heard the term *bickering couples* from several different independent sources. It was as though this whole issue was being coordinated by some overarching entity.

She dialed Aylin Freyberg's direct line at the Church Association office. The call went straight to voice mail. Something felt off. While it wasn't unusual for a call to go to voice mail, it was strange that it went straight there with no delay. She phoned the main reception desk and asked to be connected to Aylin.

The voice that finally answered was not Aylin's. "This is Tam Wiggins. How can I help you?"

"Tam, this Janet. I was trying to reach Aylin."

"I'm afraid she's no longer with the Association." The tone was crisp.

"She quit?"

"We had to let her go. I'm sure you understand"

"Oh come on, Tam. That's crap. She was passionate about it and, yes, she might have toned down her reaction a little. She's a superb advocate, though. You don't just toss people out on the streets for a minor incident like what happened at the meeting."

"It was a board decision. You know as well as I do that I don't get a vote in those matters."

"You're telling me they fired her last night, after she left?" Janet suddenly regretted not going back into the meeting.

"It was unanimous."

"Let me guess. It was *unanimous* among those who attended. What about the members that were not there last night? What would they say about it?"

"You'll have to talk to Carl about that. It was not an administrative decision. That came straight from the board."

Janet closed her eyes and tried to calm down. "Has anyone told her yet?"

"I spoke to her when she came in this morning. We agreed to pay her the two weeks consistent with notice requirements, but the board didn't want her in the building anymore. We had her leave first thing this morning."

"Tam, you're better than that."

"It isn't about me, Janet. You can phone Carl if you

want, but I can tell you now what the response will be. Look, if it'll make you feel any better, I'll contact Aylin and make sure that I get her a good recommendation."

"Oh, so you're going to fire her but give her a *good recommendation*. I'm curious about how that works. What happens if a prospective employer calls you to talk about her. How will you explain firing her and then recommending her at the same time? That seems a little hypocritical."

"It's the best I can do."

Janet sighed. "Can you at least give me her personal phone number?"

13

Janet sat in silence. Yet it wasn't an uncomfortable silence. Dani lay curled up on the couch, an afghan wrapped around her. Greg had migrated back to his study. A softness settled over the room—a sense of shared humanity.

Janet avoided the trite *how are you feeling* kind of questions. She knew that the emotional pain that haunted Dani would take time to heal. "It gets better. I know it doesn't seem that way now, but it does."

The young woman focused on the minister for a moment, her head cocked and her eyes questioning. "What was your husband like?"

The memories washed over Janet.

"Hey, Hon. What's got you down today. You haven't smiled all morning." Mark's eyes sparkled as he slid onto the couch next to Janet, putting his arm around her.

"This sermon's not going to write itself." She half-heartedly

laughed and continued, "And I'm not giving it much help. I just can't seem to come up with anything today."

He sat silently and pulled her closer to him. Resting his head on hers, he spoke softly, "Speak from your heart. You have the warmest, most incredible heart of anyone on earth. Remember, you were called to this for a reason. Just share what's inside."

Why this memory? There was nothing earthshaking or unusual there. It wasn't a pivotal moment in their lives. It wasn't even out-of-the-ordinary, but it was Mark. He was always there for her, no matter what. Even when he was sick and getting worse by the day, he always managed to look at things from her perspective. He made her the center of his world. Janet's eyes teared up. He had a way of making even the worst situations better.

"I'm not sure where I would start. If you're looking for the short version, Mark always managed to make me feel like I was the most important thing in the world to him. Whether I was having a good day, a bad day, or a completely non-descript day, he wanted to make it special for me."

Dani seemed to drink the description in. After a moment, she responded, "You said he died ten years ago. That's a long time. Do you think you'll ever find someone else?"

The question jolted Janet's emotions. It was something she didn't want to consider. "I don't know. None of us can know what the future holds."

"But living alone, that has to be… I don't know. I'm not sure I could do that."

"I'm not alone, Dani. I have friends. I have a congregation that depends on me. I have God with me every single day. My life is full. What's down the road… I can't say. For today, this is what I have. I love my life. I consider every day a gift. I know from hard experience that if I squander the gift of the moment, I can never get it back."

Janet could tell that Dani wanted to push back. The young woman's jaw clenched, and her eyes became intense. She wrung her hands in her lap. But she remained silent.

The minister smiled softly. "I think I know what your question is. How do you get through the day without the one person you want to be with? I could sit here and rant about how Billy is wrong for you, but I think you know that already. As for getting through the day alone, you're only as alone as you choose to be. Your uncle is here with you and, whether you realize it or not, he needs you as much as you need him. There's so much that you can do to help him through the day—little things—a hug, a kind word, sitting together in the quiet. Those things will mean the world to him. You'll be surprised at how much they'll mean to you."

Dani stood and turned toward the window, pulling the afghan tighter around her shoulders. "I know it seems that way to you, but after everything I've done to him—the lies, the betrayal, the words—things will never be the same."

"Change is inevitable. What used to be between the two of you was always going to change. The last few months have been unsettling, I know. Here's the bottom line, though. It's up to you now. Greg has done everything he can. Heaven knows he's not perfect. None of us are. It falls to you to let him know how you feel about him. You can start to rebuild the bridge, or you can watch the relationship completely crumble."

Tears filled Dani's eyes. "I'm sick of everything always being up to me."

14

The call came around mid-morning. Janet checked the display before connecting. "Hi Sue. How're you doing?" She offered a soft laugh. "Have you recovered from that political fundraiser yet?"

Sue Hartman spoke in a soft, urgent voice. "We need to talk."

"What's up?"

"Not on the phone. We need to meet in person." The words were barely more than a whisper.

"Where?"

A scant half-hour later, Janet rolled to a stop at the north entrance to Bellevue Square. Sue emerged from the shopping complex just as Janet arrived. Opening the passenger door, she slid in and buckled up. "Thanks. Get on Five-Twenty and head over to the city. Take I Five north from there."

Janet stared for a moment. "What's this about?"

Sue turned to look behind them as though to checking to make sure they weren't being followed. "Just drive. I'll fill you in on the way."

Janet eased her Subaru out into the street and turned left at the next light. "On the way *where?*"

Sue continued to scan the surroundings, her eyes darting from side street to alleyway. After a moment of silence, she spoke in a voice that sounded like forced calmness. "You remember Senator Corel, right?"

"Of course. I was at the fundraiser the other night, remember?" Janet turned onto the onramp and merged with traffic headed across Lake Washington to Seattle.

"I've got his wife, Bonnie, stashed at a hotel north of the city."

Silence enveloped them. Senator Thomas Corel, who only a few days prior had given his stirring speech about ending violence against women, was apparently a batterer himself. Looking back, though, she wondered if maybe she had suspected it when she met him.

After a moment, Janet responded softly. "I'll assume that you want to talk to me because you're not going to help her." She knew from Sue's words and tone what was taking shape.

"I'm sorry, Janet, but this is going to take some time to sort out with my board. Senator Corel has been a consistent supporter of our program. He's done a fantastic job getting federal funds into the state. Not to mention that he's good friends with several of my board members." Sue watched the cars around them, occasionally turning to check out what was behind them.

Janet retorted, "Unless I miss the mark, he assaulted his wife and probably more than just this one time. If that's true, there's no way that you can just pretend it's not happening." Janet's grasp on the steering wheel tightened until her knuckles ached.

Sue hurled the response back with no small amount of bitterness. "Spare me the lecture. I'll take care of my business. You signed on for this, remember? You took a billion dollars of Greg Stottman's money to help abused women. This is what you're supposed to be doing."

Janet swallowed the retort that she so wanted to spit back. Sue was right. "Other than the name of the hotel and room number, is there anything else I need to know?"

"I booked the room using my own credit card. The only connection to the network is that she initially called in from a neighbor's phone to our central reception and asked for me. I've handled everything else without agency involvement. It would be nice if you can get her moved quickly." She turned and looked at the road behind them and then over to the side. "One other thing, although I'm not sure how relevant it is. Bonnie Corel is the wealth behind the senator. She comes from old money."

Janet wondered about the relevance. "So?"

"I'm not sure if it'll make a difference, but given that she has at least some control over their collective fortune, he'll likely be anxious to get her back... very anxious. I'm not sure how well she can hold herself together right now. She seems rattled and desperate to get away."

"Was the... whatever happened... was it a one-off kind of thing or has it been going on for a long time?"

"She didn't say, and I didn't ask. I don't know her that well. The few times I've met her, she didn't give any indication of problems. On the other hand, some women can keep it bottled up for years, even decades."

"Do you have any idea exactly what she has in mind, I mean, for help?"

"The only thing she said is that she needs to find a safe place. Beyond that, you'll have to see how it goes once she's out of immediate danger."

"What kind of immediate danger are you talking about?"

Sue hesitated a moment, as though searching for words. "According to Bonnie, the senator uses a team of what she refers to as 'mercenaries' to do his dirty work. She implied that this isn't the first time that she's run away. You can talk to her in greater detail, but I figure the best bet is to get her out quick."

"My employee is on her way back to town. She should be here day after tomorrow. I can move Bonnie then."

"How about you move her to another hotel? Since she called into our network, it's only a matter of time before questions start to come up. Once it's out that Bonnie talked to me, it won't take long before they figure out where she is."

Janet walked through a process in her mind. "I'll get her out this evening."

Her cell ringtone interrupted the conversation. "Hello."

Margaret Shemanski's voice sounded full of urgency. "I just got a call from Lena Severtsen. Her husband, Richard, just had a heart attack. He's in ICU at Overlook. She wanted to know if you could come over."

15

J anet slid into the seat next to Lena Severtsen, who stared anxiously at the nurse's station as she wrung her hands in her lap. Janet put her arm around the woman and asked quietly, "How's he doing?"

Lena glanced over at Janet and then back at the nurses, who appeared to be lost in their paperwork. "I don't know. They're not telling me anything." Tears streamed down her face, which was lined with the evidence of her age.

Janet pulled her close. "They have best doctors in Seattle here. Between them and the grace of God, Richard will be just fine."

"Why won't they tell me anything?"

"I'd say that they're probably spending their time working on him. I'm sure when they get a few minutes, they'll come out and talk to you. For now, though, they're focusing every bit of their attention on getting him through this."

Lena sobbed, putting her hands over her face, her muffled voice full of pain. "What if he's already dead?"

"He's not, Lena. Richard's too ornery to die that easily.

You know that. You two have been married more than fifty years. He'd never die without talking to you about it." Janet wondered in passing if the lame attempt at levity was the right approach.

The old woman didn't respond. She wiped her eyes with a handkerchief and sniffled, continuing to look with despondency toward the oblivious nurses.

Late morning became early afternoon. A doctor came out shortly before 1:00 pm to say that Richard was out of danger for the moment. The hitch was that they needed to install a stint in a collapsed artery. They could get it done that evening.

Lena turned ashen as she sucked in breath. "But he's going to be alright? That's what you said."

"He's stable for the moment, but we need to get that stint in, if you grant permission." The doctor handed her a clipboard with a piece of paper.

Janet felt like a voyeur peeking into the woman's most painful moment, remaining silent as she watched the exchange.

The papers signed, Janet and Lena settled back into the waiting. They walked down to the chapel and offered prayer. The low lighting and intimate setting brought back horrible memories for Janet—Mark in his final hours while she prayed intensely for the miracle that never came. Perhaps Lena's prayers would be different.

As the afternoon aged, Janet became increasingly aware of the commitment she'd made to Sue Hartman—to get Bonnie Corel moved to a safe location that evening. The tension ramped up substantially when the doctor informed Lena that the surgery was scheduled for six that evening.

"You can stay here with me during the operation, can't you?" Hope sparkled from Lena's eyes as she made the request, which Janet was certain was more of a formality to the woman.

"I'd love to, Lena, but I have something I have to attend to early this evening. I'll be back as soon as I can, I promise." Janet felt nauseous as she watched the Lena's face reflect the anguish. "It'll only take a few hours." She had absolutely no idea how long it would take to get Bonnie Corel settled. Without splitting herself into two pieces, though, Janet had no idea how she could fulfill her obligation to Bonnie Corel as well as her duty to her congregation.

Janet left the hospital just after 4:00 pm. She carried with her the nagging worry that the conflict would not end well. The worst part, though, was that this incident would likely play out again and again. Her job demanded that she be available during these kinds of situations and yet the women she served depended on her for their very lives.

16

J anet dreaded the conversation, but she needed to take care of it before she started getting Bonnie Corel settled. If there were some magic thoughts that would make everything okay, they eluded her. Finally, she dialed the number printed on the paper in front of her.

"Hello." The voice sounded empty and hopeless.

"Hello Aylin. This is Janet. Tam told me about…."

"Yeah."

"Hey, look, would you like to meet for coffee sometime this week?"

"I'm busy."

"Please don't give up hope. I'm going over to talk to Carl Broward. I'm sure we can find a way to work this out." Janet tried to force some confidence into her words. It felt like a failure, though.

"Don't bother."

"You can't just give up. The work you do is too important."

"I don't do work. I just write and talk. It's not that big a deal."

"Okay, I understand where you're coming from. At least don't close the door. Give me a chance to see what I can do."

Anger seeped into Aylin's voice. "What part of *no* don't you understand, Janet. Just *no.* I couldn't go back there. I couldn't walk down the halls without a sense of anger and betrayal. I thought I was part of something important. As it turns out, I was just an expense line on the budget and a voice they didn't want to hear."

"Whether you reconsider or not, I do intend to speak with Carl. What they did isn't right and, I can't let it pass. If they call and offer your position back, you can take it or not. That's up to you."

Janet decided to close the loop on this and make the call to Carl Broward at the moment rather than waiting." Thanks for taking the time to speak with me, Carl."

"Certainly, Janet. It's always a pleasure."

"I wanted to discuss what went on last night at the board meeting."

"How so?"

"Let's not be coy. You know exactly what I'm talking about. You ambushed Aylin. You goaded her into a very predictable reaction and then fired her with no due process whatsoever."

"Not at all. We went through the process with precision. Her behavior was inappropriate and at odds with our core values. It's not as if she hasn't been warned before. After her outburst, a motion was advanced to terminate her employment. We entertained discussion, and then voted. That's the way it works."

"The association personnel policies stipulate that she has the right to appeal that decision."

"Yes, she can. Her appeal needs to be in writing,

submitted to the board within thirty days. When we receive it, we will consider it and render a decision."

"I see. I'd be willing to bet that decision has already been foreseen and finalized."

The line remained silent.

"It's not right, Carl. You don't treat people like that."

His voice came across hard and precise. "Janet, you know as well as the rest of us that we work in an organization. There are rules. There are standards of behavior. Our board meetings are managed in a way that allows us to get our work done. Miz Freyberg has been counseled in the past on acceptable participation in these meetings. She was a staff member and, as such, her job was to serve the organization and policies set forth by the board. The board is the governing body. Aside from being rude and unprofessional, she somehow felt that she alone was allowed to set policy and that anyone who disagreed needed to be shut down."

"You're oversimplifying it. The issue at hand was not some minor administrative detail. How women and men in violent situations are handled is a matter of life and death. We were fortunate to have someone as knowledgeable and passionate as Aylin, especially given the slave wages we pay."

"Our council is in a position to make a difference in the lives of women and their families. It's important that we are able to enter into dialogue with all sides and hear different points of view. Your voice is a strong and important one. You need to be at the table. I'm asking you not to get wrapped up in this personnel matter. It's a distraction. There will be lots to discuss in the coming weeks. There is a new and welcome attention that has come to this issue, and we need to harness it. In order to do that, our council has to focus. We have to have influential voices present."

Chapter 16

"What you did was wrong, Carl. I will advise Aylin as to her right of appeal. Whether she takes advantage of it will be up to her. You may want to carefully consider the message that you send to our other employees—that they are infinitely expendable, and their livelihood is always at risk. The problem with that situation is that the truly exceptional staff will find other work quickly and the ones who remain will likely not be the ones you want."

"Or maybe the employees we really need are the ones who know how to work with boards and take direction."

17

Senator Corel heard the ringtone on his cellphone and checked the display—Unknown name. This would be his hired help. "What do you have for me?"

Dylan Strauss sounded tense but reserved. "She hasn't used her credit card. As you know, she left her cellphone at the house, which means, in all likelihood, that she's got a burner. She's not registered at any hotel in the area, at least under her own name." The voice paused and, in a softer tone, continued, "I don't yet know where she is. I'll keep looking."

The senator fumed. "Could she be at the local DV place? Do you think that Hartman, their director, is a part of this?"

"It's possible, but we don't have anything yet. Whatever the case, there's no buzz about it—the police haven't been called and, as far as I can tell, the press isn't on it."

Corel's tone turned to ice. "Get her back here, now."

Strauss' words came back equally cold and assertive. "I'll hack into the video surveillance feeds around. Some are businesses. Others are residential. I'll target the more sophisticated ones that have internet connectivity. I'll check hotel data and see if we can isolate potential hits based on check-in times. I need eyes inside the shelter." He sounded as though he was the one giving the orders.

Fucking insolent asshole. Despite his desire to put Strauss in his place, Corel decided to put it off and focus on the problem at hand. Dylan Strauss could be dealt with later. "Get on the video feeds. I'll find out about the shelter."

"I'm on it."

The senator disconnected and tossed his phone onto the office sofa. Of all the goddamn times for her to pull this shit… right in the middle of the fucking campaign. He muttered under his breath, "I swear to God, when that bitch gets back, I'm going to—"

A knock on the door interrupted. "Come in," he barked.

Alicia stuck her head in. "Is this a good time?"

He started to send her away, not trusting himself to keep his mouth shut when he was this angry. He couldn't go into isolation because of this, though. He softened his voice. "Yeah, sure. Come on in."

"We just got the AP polling numbers." She sat on the couch, a sheet of paper in her hand.

"And?"

"They have you up by seven. With males over fifty, you're in a dead heat. With males under fifty, you're ahead by just over three. Keep in mind that the margin of error is plus or minus two point eight."

Corel processed the numbers. "So, what you're telling me is that my strength is with women."

"Yes. Most definitely. You're ahead by a solid twelve points with women under fifty. Over fifty, they favor you by about eight."

This worried him. If this crap about Bonnie saw the

light of day before the election, that comfortable seven-point advantage would evaporate. "And?"

"I can do breakouts by race, economic status, and education, if you like." She looked hopeful, her eyes wide, seeming to hang on his every word.

"Write them up and shoot them to me by e-mail."

She spoke quietly, with uncertainty laced through her words. "If you'd like, I can arrange for some dinner to be delivered here this evening." She paused for a moment, searching his eyes. "Or, if you prefer, we could order up some room service over at my hotel and work from there."

So, this was his problem. Yes, he definitely wanted to work at her hotel room, but he also needed to be on his game right now. Things were in play, and he couldn't afford to miss a beat. *Damn her! Bonnie picked the perfect fucking time to pull this shit. I don't know why I married that stupid bitch.* Of course, he did know why. She came from money—real money. Without that, he'd still be struggling to get elected dog catcher. Too bad there wasn't a way to get her money without getting *her* in the package.

"Thanks, but I'm going to need to stay close to the office tonight. You go ahead and take off, though. You've put in a few tough days, and the schedule ahead is going to get worse." Turning her down took every ounce of discipline he could muster. It couldn't be avoided, though. He was the adult in the room, after all.

She looked hurt but she nodded her understanding. "Very good, sir. If there's nothing else, then, I'm going to take off. I'll see you in the morning."

Alicia left, along with most of the rest of his campaign staff. He sat in his office as darkness fell over Puget Sound. A light rain had set in, common for early September. It felt as though nothing was going right. Yet he knew that he was overreacting. He was up in the polls. He had a solid war chest with more contributions coming in by the day. The Democratic National Committee was prepared to feed him money, while outside PACs were pummeling his opponent with attack ads. Senator Thomas Corel was indeed the bright spot in the progressive line-up for the Pacific Northwest. The only thing standing between him and a perfect victory was his stupid wife.

He took a deep breath and reassured himself. "Yes. We can manage this." He switched on the lights in his office and turned his attention to some tasks that he'd neglected. First thing up, he needed to work on a speech that he was supposed to give to the Seattle Women's Coalition. *Women. Why is it that women are such a pain in the ass?* Then again, they had their uses. His mind wandered to Alicia. She definitely had strong assets.

He reminded himself that he'd committed to checking out the situation at the shelter. He closed his eyes and took a deep breath and held it. This was a phone call he wasn't anxious to make. He released the breath, and opened his personal hard copy address book—the place where he kept his most sensitive information. He moved his index finger down the list until he came to the entry he sought—R.S.

Shit, shit shit! He really dreaded this call—Attorney Reba Stillings.

18

The Sniper clicked on a checkbox and the font color next to the woman's name changed from red to black. A skull icon appeared beside her name. A deep sense of accomplishment and satisfaction settled over him. He inserted the SD card into the reader, connected the reader to his notebook computer and uploaded the image of a blood-spattered woman lying on the ground. Another successful mission.

He stared intently at the list. One of these women would be his next target. He had narrowed it down to four names. He needed to decide. Which would it be? The woman in Spokane would be the easiest. It would be only a few hours' drive. He could go there and back in one day. A couple of weeks visiting every other day would be enough surveillance. Easy enough. Out in the morning. Back in the afternoon. The problem was that he had already struck twice in Spokane. No need to tempt fate.

He had already ruled out Bellingham, Washington. His last mission had been there. He had always made it a point never to do back-to-back hits in one location.

Chapter 18

Portland, Oregon was farther than he wanted to travel. He could do it one way in a day, but it would be a long day. With another day to scope out the target and a day back—a three-day commitment. Too much, at least for the present. Maybe later.

That left only Seattle. "Hmmm." He focused on the second name on the list. "Aylin Freyberg." The name sounded like one of those lesbian feminists—always sticking their nose in other people's business. Always trying to tear families apart.

He sighed, a smile stealing across his face. He muttered, "Well, Aylin Freyberg, looks like you drew the short straw."

After a series of mouse clicks, he emerged from the dark web and began his more mundane tasks. Where did she work? What was her home address? What kind of car did she drive? All of this information is readily available, if one knows where to look. All told, it took less than an hour.

He reclined back in his rickety computer chair, his hands laced behind his head. Mentally, the Sniper stepped through his to-do list—check ammunition stock and replenish cash supplies. Added to this, he needed to sweep his car and house for any electronic surveillance—tasks that he compulsively accomplished weekly.

The organization to which he belonged—*Truth is Strength*—remained obscure, even to members such as himself. He had been carefully screened before being brought aboard. He assumed that the same applied to others, although he didn't personally know any other members. They all operated in near complete secrecy, resembling the cell structure of many terrorist organizations.

Having fought against these elusive cells while serving in Afghanistan, he felt a degree of security and safety.

Cracking them had been nearly impossible. Now, the very things that frustrated him all those years back gave him comfort in his current life.

He swept the clutter from his mind. *Back to work.* Throwing on a light jacket, he left the house and started down a narrow path into the woods. Fifteen minutes later, he emerged into a small clearing. He made a careful scan of the area, and then moved a pile of brush aside. Reaching down, he grabbed a piece of rope, pulling upward. A heavy wooden door pulled open, exposing a ladder disappearing downward into the darkness.

After a quick glance around, he pulled out his flashlight and descended the ten steps to the bottom. The light revealed a tight compartment, barely large enough for him to stand among the boxes. One box held his weapons—a sniper rifle, a semi-automatic assault weapon, and two Smith and Wesson handguns, one 9 mm and one .45 caliber. He moved past that one to a smaller container.

Opening the lid, he focused only on the sniper rifle ammunition. He hadn't used any of the AR-15 nor the handgun ammo in the last year. He counted the Winchester .300 bullets—thirteen loose and another two boxes of twenty. This would be plenty for the time being. He closed the lid and moved on to the final box.

This was the part he hated most. He counted out the bills—thirty 100-dollar bills and seven 50s. With the trip to Seattle coming up, not to mention his living expenses, he'd need an infusion. Replenishing cash was an annoying but necessary process.

Back at the house, he decided not to put it off. *Might as well get it done today.* Grabbing a spare, scrubbed notebook computer, he donned a sporty looking fleece vest and a pair of worn but fashionable jeans. He added a pair of wire-rimmed glasses for effect.

Five minutes later, he turned off the back road onto Idaho Highway 55 headed south. Lost in thought, he ignored the trees that gave orange and yellow hints of the coming autumn. The trip took only an hour and a half. He zipped past the Boise city limits sign and began scouring environs.

Within a mile, he pulled into his favorite McDonald's. The Sniper slung his pack, which contained the notebook computer, over his shoulder and sauntered across the parking lot, noticing the pleasant warmth of the early September sunshine.

After picking up his order—two cheeseburgers, large fries, and a coke, he grabbed a seat by the window and broke out the computer. He smiled, silently thanking the restaurant management for providing free wi-fi access.

To avoid leaving any consistent trails, The Sniper chose to access the financial element of the organization from sites other than his cabin. His fingers flew across the keyboard as he navigated to the website—*scenicnorthwestphotos.com*. He perused the beautiful photographs of mountains, meadows, streams, and wildlife until he found what he needed. The grizzly bear stood on its hind legs, its front paws stretched high as though curious about the photographer.

He clicked the icon labeled *free download*. A scant few seconds later, he opened the photo and verified what he was after. *Got it.* Minimizing the browser, he accessed the file with his graphics program and pulled up the meta data for the photo—date, time, and location where it was taken along with some camera information. To the casual user, it would be completely innocuous.

To the Sniper, though, it held vital information. Buried within the meta data he found the statement of funds—starting balance for the year, amount drawn, and balance remaining. It was early September, and he still had a hundred and fifty thousand available. He had no idea where the funds came from. He just knew that when he asked for money, it magically appeared.

He pulled up the browser again and put his cursor in the comments section below the photo. The words appeared as his fingers clicked the keys—"Fantastic photograph. Impressive that you were able to freeze the action with an exposure of 15. My compliments." This was the pre-determined format. He needed fifteen thousand. He knew that the person who handled the money would see the message and arrange for delivery to the drop site within a day. It would mean another trip to Boise, but, what the hell. McDonald's two days in a row would be a treat.

He powered down the computer and savored his cheeseburgers as he watched the coming and going outside the window. It was an incredible day.

The Sniper luxuriated in the drive home. The road wound its way northward into the forests. Several times, he caught sight of sun rays breaking through the canopy of trees, illuminating clouds of tiny bugs. He never ceased to be impressed with the beauty of his state.

His joyous mood came to an abrupt halt as he pulled up to his house off the side road. A gray Ford Focus SUV with Washington plates was parked in his driveway. A stranger sat on the porch, waiting for… who knows what. The Sniper discreetly reached over into the glove box and pulled out a thirty-eight handgun. As he exited the truck, he reached around and stuck it into his waist band beneath his vest. "Can I help you?"

The man stood, brushed his pants as though sweeping away some dust, and smiled. "Hey, it's me. Don't you remember? You know… your cousin—Billy Robinson."

19

G reg gestured toward a wing-backed chair. "Thanks for getting here so quickly, Kaz. Have a seat and I'll grab us some coffee."

Dimitry Kazarian slid into the chair, nodding in silence. He displayed his typical neutral expression, giving away nothing regarding his thoughts.

Greg popped a pod into the coffee maker and grabbed a couple of cups from the mug tree. He turned his head toward the living room, speaking in a loud voice, "I apologize for being out of touch for so long. Nothing ever seems to go like I want it to these days."

Silence.

A couple of minutes later, Greg placed the mug in front of Kaz and took a seat at one end of the couch. "How are things going for you?"

Kaz cocked his head, his eyes questioning. "I suppose we need to discuss the status of our arrangement." He took a sip of coffee and set the cup back down, leaning back in the chair.

Greg sighed. "Yeah, probably. Dani's staying here for now, but I'm not sure that's a great idea."

"How so?"

"Billy Robinson's still out there. Like I told you on the phone, he's killed a couple of cops out in Eastern Washington. Now he's dropped out of sight. Maybe he's on the run and will try to stay underground, but it's just as likely that he'll come back and...." Greg couldn't bring himself to finish the sentence.

Kaz picked at a piece of lint on his trousers as he seemed to consider the words. "Maybe. It could go either way." He leaned forward, clasping his hands together in his lap. "What do you want to do?"

Given the size of Kaz's fee, Greg was in no mood for the casual back-and-forth. "I'm asking for your ideas."

"You're playing the odds no matter what you do, Greg. You can play it safe, but that will mean putting more restrictions on Dani and, to a large extent, controlling her life. That's not going to do wonders for your relationship. On the other hand, if you assume that her ex-boyfriend is done with her and you're wrong, well...." He paused as though waiting for a response.

Greg wanted a suggestion, recommendation, or, at the very least, encouragement. "What would you do in my place?" He knew that, with his resources, he could send Dani off on an extended vacation in Europe. The problem was that she would be alone and he wouldn't be able to help her if she needed it.

Kaz's face hardened and his eyes lost focus for a moment. When he came back, he spoke in a matter-of-fact tone. "I want to be clear that I'm not trying to feather my nest. That said, given what's gone down so far, I'd come down on the side of safety. To put it bluntly, better that Dani be pissed off and alive than the alternative. Keeping her safe gives you the opportunity to repair the relationship down the road. If you let your guard down and you're wrong, there won't be a *later*."

This mirrored Greg's own assessment. "Okay, let's say that I agree with you. Where do we go from here?"

Kaz picked up his cup and sipped, this time holding it with both hands rather than setting the cup down. "Mix it up. The only thing that Robinson knows for sure about you is that you're very protective of Dani. Which, in his mind, would likely mean that you'll try to keep her here and protect her. I suggest taking a different approach. Go through some obscure channel and lease an apartment, condo, or whatever. Have her move in there. Get her a new vehicle, but lease it in a different name, like your corporation. Make it difficult to find her electronically. You'll need to stay away, since he could be watching you. I can keep an eye on her, though. Scrub her online presence and get a new one—new e-mail, new streaming accounts, and the like. Just to be sure, set up flags on her credit card accounts so that you'll see if she jumps the rail again."

"I don't know." Greg tried to visualize what it would be like for Dani, all alone in an apartment. She had few friends, and the ones she had wouldn't know where she was. Going to class was out of the question. "I'm not sure how well she'd take that." He knew, though, that it was question that would be answered in time.

He pulled himself back into the moment. "What about a leased unit? If you can locate something, I can have my attorney and accountant make the arrangements."

Kaz answered. "Let's do it."

20

Senator Corel tapped his foot nervously. He hated this place... and yet it felt so perfect. Reba Stillings and her business occupied an entire floor of what was undoubtedly the most opulent building in Seattle. It made his office at the Capitol in Washington seem like the slums.

"Miz Stillings will be with you shortly, Mister Corel. Would you like something to drink? We have coffee, tea, water, or I could make you a latte or espresso." The woman, who looked to be in her early thirties, was dressed in black wool slacks with a burgundy blazer over a silky white blouse. Her auburn hair rested gently on her slight shoulders. She offered the softest of smiles.

Corel fought to keep his temper in check. He was not *Mister Corel*. He was *Senator Corel—Senator Thomas Corel*. Was it too much to ask that the hired help observe the simplest of courtesies? "How long will she be?" He checked his watch.

"She's on a conference call with the appellate court judge. I'm sure it won't be long." She paused and repeated her question, "Can I get you something?"

Chapter 20

"No." He turned his head toward the expansive picture window with the panoramic view of Seattle and the Space Needle. He hoped she got the message. He had no desire to engage in small talk.

Fifteen long minutes later, the receptionist's phone buzzed. She picked up, listened for a moment, and then spoke briefly, nodding at the same time. After she hung up, she turned to the senator. "You can go in now."

He fumed. He didn't need permission to enter a room from anyone, least of all this twat of a file clerk. He nodded curtly and opened the door.

"Come in Thom, please, have a seat." Reba Stillings, sitting on the other side of her grandiose desk, stood and moved around to greet him. "It's been a while. Would you like something to drink?" She nodded toward the door, apparently in reference to the availability of coffee and tea. Smiling, she added, "I have something with a little more substance if you prefer." She arched an eyebrow.

"Scotch, rocks." He fought to keep his anger inside. This bitch really knew how to punch his buttons, starting with her insistence on addressing him by his first name.

She turned to a side table where a small bar was set up. Dropping a couple of ice cubes in a whiskey glass, she poured a generous serving of deep amber liquid from a bottle of Johnny Walker Black.

Handing it to him, she gestured toward a chair and took her own seat behind the desk. "How is Missus Corel?" The look in her eyes told him that she knew the entire story. Why shouldn't she? It wasn't a new one. They'd been down this road before.

He cut to the chase. "What can you tell me?"

Her smile disappeared. She studied her computer monitor as though looking for something specific. Finally, she turned back towards him and leaned back in her chair. "I'm not sure how much you know already, but your wife is not at the shelter. She did, though, work through them. She called Sue Hartman, who then left the building for several hours. I can only assume that Hartman put her up somewhere, although, at the moment, I'm not sure where. I just know it's not at the shelter. Besides, Sue's too smart for that. She wouldn't want to risk losing your support."

Corel narrowed his eyes. "How is it that you came by this information?"

Stillings burst out laughing, although he could tell it was more for effect than genuine. "If Sue wanted to destroy you, this would already on the news. Relax, Thom."

"Cut the shit, Reba. I'm not asking for state secrets here. I just want to be sure."

She grew serious, her eyes piercing his. "Senator Corel, when I tell you something, you can take it to the bank. Period. We've been over this before. I won't share my methods or sources with you. Now, you can take me at my word or you can go."

He forced himself to stifle the rage as he tried to digest what she'd told him. "If I'm understanding you correctly, you know for certain that she's not at the shelter and that she did call Hartman. That tells me, and correct me if I'm wrong, that you have eyes and ears inside the shelter."

"We need to talk about what you're going to give me in return."

This was why he hated Stillings. Everything was a transaction to her. She might try to frame things as doing favors but, in the end, it was always quid pro quo. "What is it that I can do for you?" He spit the words out, dreading the answer.

"Let's keep it simple, shall we? VAWA is coming up for

reauthorization this coming session. Since I'm confident in your re-election, you'll be a part of that."

"That's a fucking joke and you know it. There's no way I could stop that reauthorization, even if I wanted to."

There came that laugh again. "Oh, Thom, you have so little faith in me. I just don't understand it. I would never ask you to stop the reauthorization. I only ask that you tweak it a little." She grew serious. "Let's keep the boyfriend loophole in place. Also, I want to place a limit on the amount of time that convicted men are prohibited from owning firearms. A couple of years maybe, but it can't be indefinite."

His mind raced as he calculated the costs and benefits. "I can work on the time limits, but the boyfriend loophole has to go. I've got too much exposure on that already."

She countered, "One-year time limit."

Back and forth. "Review at two years and, if not removed, at each year after that."

"Review at one year and…." She waved her hand as though idly shooing a fly away. "You drive a hard bargain."

"Where did Hartman stash my wife?"

Stillings shook her head. "I have no idea."

"What's Hartman's next move?"

"Why would you expect me to know that?"

Corel seethed. He was a goddamned U. S. Senator. Nobody treated him like this. "I'm just asking. You want a huge favor from me. I don't think it's too much to ask that you pony up what information you have."

She stared at him for a moment, as though running a complex analysis of the situation. "Okay, here's what you have. Hartman obviously intervened personally, but there's no shelter involvement. Your wife is not a client there. That means that Sue is likely going to pass her off to someone else, either an individual or another agency."

"Would you have any ideas on who or what organization?"

"There's this new invention called the Internet, Thom. You can search for DV agencies in the area as well as I can. I assume that you have some hired help that will get information for you."

That sealed it. Senator Thomas Corel made a mental note to find a way to exact revenge. Out of necessity, he'd tolerate her for the moment. As soon as the situation was resolved, however, he'd deal with Miz Reba Stillings.

Her tone changed to a less contentious and more collaborative one. "Oh, there is one possibility. There is a minister lady in Bellevue. Her name is... let's see..." she checked the papers on her desk again. "Yes. A Reverend Janet Polasky. She's over at Saint Luke's Methodist. I think you may have even met her once or twice. Word is that she's building a network to help women. You might check her out."

21

Janet took a scrap of paper from her coat pocket — Bonnie's burner cellphone number. The sense of conflict deepened. Beyond the current situation with the Severtsens, she had not made any calls on congregation members. Her last sermon had been *on the fly* and fell flat. She needed to go over the budget in preparation for a meeting with the Finance Committee chair later in the week. All of these things nipped at her ankles while she confronted the challenges of the project.

One bright spot was that, instead of putting Bonnie up in a hotel, Janet had gotten the okay from Greg to use the condo where they'd stashed Leah Bowman all those months ago. That would give them a safe haven while Val and Bonnie came up with a plan of action.

She swept the concerns from her mind as she dialed the number. She stared out the window at the gathering darkness as she waited.

A quiet, meek voice answered. "Hello."

"Hi Bonnie. This is Reverend Janet Polasky. I think that Sue over at the DV Network told you I'd be calling."

"Yes." She sounded frightened and alone.

"What I suggest is that we get you moved out of that hotel room this evening. You'll move into a condo that we use while we come up with a more permanent solution."

"Okay. What time are you coming over?"

"I'm on my way now and should be there by six at the latest. Does your room have a view of the parking lot?"

"Yes."

"Okay, watch for me. I'll be driving a forest green Subaru Outback wagon. I'll park in a lighted area near the building." Janet thought about it for a moment before adding. "When you see me, keep an eye on the lot for a few minutes. Look for anyone who seems to be following me. When you're sure it's okay, give me a call at this number and let me know you're on your way. I'll meet you right in the unloading zone, so you won't have to walk far."

* * *

As she pulled out of the church parking lot, she saw something out of the corner of her eye. She turned her head in that direction in time to see a silver Ford SUV leave a parking spot across the road. It entered traffic slowly then whipped around other cars and sped off. Something about it bothered Janet, although she couldn't put her finger on it. She shrugged it off as she headed out in the opposite direction. She muttered, "Getting a little jumpy, aren't we?"

Still, it bothered her... and the stakes were high. She phoned Bonnie to let her know she'd be running a little late, maybe as much as a half-hour. It could have been nothing... probably *was nothing*. There were probably thousands of Ford SUVs in the Seattle area. Rob Young certainly wasn't the only person who owned one.

Chapter 21

The reassurance didn't take. There was just something about the car that stuck out. She replayed the entire few minutes in her head—nothing. She decided to err on the side of safety.

Janet pulled out headed north on Elm Street. She put her blinker on, slowed, and turned right on 34th. After pausing at a stop sign. She eased her speed back up, proceeding leisurely along hoping to appear oblivious.

She turned on to the access road for I-5 south and came up to speed. Maneuvering over the far-right lane, she set the cruise control to 65. The miles zipped by, and she saw the signs for Sea-Tac International Airport. Easing toward an exit on the right, she swerved at the last minute, back into the center lane and accelerated.

In the rearview mirror, she saw no sign of the silver SUV. She moved back to the right lane and exited onto the access road. From there, she cut off on a side street, circled around, and picked up I-5 heading north. She checked her mirror and breathed a sigh of relief. She couldn't see anything resembling his car. Just to be sure, she moved on and off the interstate into residential areas from time to time.

Janet finally parked her Subaru wagon in the Rainier Budget Lodge just off I-5 north of Seattle at 7:45 p.m. It had been a jarring experience. As she sat waiting on Bonnie's call, a stark realization hit. She was picking up was the wife of a U. S. Senator.

It suddenly occurred to Janet that she'd set her regular cellphone to silent mode. Worrying that she might have missed a call from Lena Severtsen, she pulled the phone from her purse. There it was—a voice mail. It was not, however from Lena. Instead, she listened to the voice of Gayle Roundtree, her board president.

"Hi, Janet. This is Gayle. I'm here at the hospital with

Lena Severtsen. I understand that you have another commitment this evening. I'd like to get together with you sometime over the next few days. Give me a call and we can set up a date and time."

22

Valentina Gomez passed through Issaquah on Interstate 90 headed west toward Seattle. Exhausted from her job working for Janet Polasky—relocating Lucy Young—she longed to see the skyline of the Emerald City. *It'll be good to get home*.

She wanted… no, *needed* to talk to Detective Dee Martin. Something had changed for Val. The bitterness from spending ten years in prison for killing her abusive husband still gnawed at her. Blaming Dee, though, had been wrong. This epiphany had come after being hired by Reverend Polasky based on Dee's recommendation. Helping Lucy Young escape her violent life had shown her that there were good people—people who cared. Contrary to what she had believed, it was not the entire world against Val.

She felt a burning need to apologize to Dee, and to tell her how much her support meant. Val had offloaded ten years of hate and anger on the detective. It was time to make things right.

Her phone, mounted in a holder on the dash, rang. She

glanced at the display seeing nothing only a number. It was Janet's burner number. She pressed the connect button on the steering wheel. "Hello."

"Hi Val. How's it going?" Despite the casual words, the tone was all business."

"I should be in town by lunch."

Janet paused for a moment. "We've got a new client. Pick her up at the same place you picked up your last one."

The cryptic instructions were not lost on Val. They had been compromised by a landline phone system once already. Cell phones, while being a little more secure, were still vulnerable. "When?"

"As soon as you can get there."

"Is she safe right now?"

"For today. But we have to move as quickly as possible."

"I need to do some laundry and take care of a few things. Will tomorrow morning work?"

"It'll have to do."

After disconnecting, Val considered her options. She decided to go straight to her apartment, get laundry started, and then make a phone call.

Getting home was surreal. It was the same cramped apartment with the same dingy furniture, tacky art prints on the wall, and worn carpet. The inevitable musty odor hit her full on. The place had been shut up tight for the past ten days. The thought crossed her mind that, with the new, well-paying job, she could afford better.

She brushed the notion aside for the moment—there were more important things to deal with. With the first load of clothes in the wash, she dropped onto the couch and punched in Dee's number.

"You're back?" Dee's voice was laced with enthusiasm.

Val smiled. "About an hour ago. I thought that maybe,

if you're free, we could grab a pizza later." She paused and added, "Unfortunately, I'm back to work tomorrow."

An uncomfortable silence came from the other end. When the words came, they were bathed in uncertainty. "Okay. What's up?"

"Work. Other than that, I don't know. I guess I'll find out when I get there."

"Get where?"

"How about that pizza?" She hoped that Dee wouldn't push.

A sigh floated over the connection. "Okay, then. I get off at five."

"How about I pick you up at your place... six o'clock?"

* * *

A medium pizza sat on the table between them. The aroma of oregano, basil, garlic, and melted mozzarella cheese wafted up, stimulating Val's appetite. She had forgotten how hungry she was. Sliding a slice from the pan onto her plate, she set it to the side to cool and took a sip of the draft beer.

"I'm glad you made it back safe," Dee said, "Although I have to say, you had us worried there for a bit. The bug on Paulette's phone caused quite the stir."

Val laughed. "It didn't exactly make my day, either." She held the pizza slice in her hand as she put her thoughts together and grew more serious. "We're going to have to come up with better ways of doing this. I have to be able to communicate with Janet... and you. I can't keep having to worry about the wrong guys hearing the conversation."

"For sure. Talk to Janet about it. She's got some people helping her who might be able to figure this thing out."

Dee took a long draught of beer. "So, any idea who your client is?"

"I'll meet her tomorrow morning."

Dee nodded and took a bite of pizza. Silence descended over the table. They ate without speaking for a few minutes. Finally, Val put down her slice, took a drink, and cleared her throat. "Dee, I need to apologize. I'm so sorry for the way I treated you."

Dee shook her head as though to dismiss the idea.

Val continued, "The truth is, you're the only one that stood up for me. It's hard to see when you're in the middle of the shit, but it would have been so much worse if not for you. I know that now. I hope that one day you can forgive me."

Tears flooded Dee's eyes. She nodded as she attempted to recover. "Of course, yes. How could I not forgive you? You're...." She bowed her head without finishing the sentence.

The reaction stunned Val. She'd never seen Dee this emotional. "Yeah, well, if I ever get that way again, just kick the shit out of me... please." Val forced a laugh.

Words came and went with little notice or effect. It was as though conversation didn't matter. Peace had been made.

They left the restaurant all smiles, although Val sensed that something had changed. It wasn't what had been said but rather what had gone unsaid. She felt it deep in her gut. The air had grown heavy, and she could feel the weight of expectation.

They drove in near silence. The words that passed seemed forced. She pulled into Dee's driveway just after eight o'clock. The sun had just set and the air had begun to cool.

Dee unbuckled and opened the door. Pausing, she turned to Val. "Would you like to come in?"

At that moment, Val knew. She responded quietly, as though she was afraid that the entire world might hear her answer. "Yes. I'd like that."

Inside, Dee asked, "Can I take your coat?"

Val shed the jacket and handed it to her. She stood in silence as the detective hung up both coats and then turned around. They stood facing each other in silence. Finally, Dee took a step forward, reached up, and touched Val's cheek.

It was Val's turn to experience the tears. She took Dee's hand and held it tightly. The two each took another step toward each other. Val's arms slid around Dee's neck. Their lips met, tentatively at first. Their lips parted gently. Val tasted the warmth of love that she'd unknowingly longed for.

*   *   *

Val rolled over and checked the clock on Dee's night table. "I have to go—I have to pick up my new client first thing in the morning." She stroked Dee's hair and kissed her gently.

Dee pulled her tight. "You have to know that I don't want you to go. I don't ever want you to go."

Val smiled and then offered a soft laugh. "As lovely as it would be to stay right here forever, your boss and mine would likely have some minor objections."

"Screw 'em if they can't take a joke." Dee snuggled closer.

"Very catchy phrase. Did you just make that up?" Val gently touched Dee's arm. "I promise, I'll be back before you know it."

Dee sat up, pulling the covers up to her chin. "Before you go, Val, there's something I need to tell you. This isn't just a casual thing for me. I've thought about you for... I don't know... it seems like forever. I love you. If it's a little too sudden and fast for you, I understand. For me, though, this is what I want—a life with you."

Val turned to her, gazing into her eyes, and trying to imagine what it all meant. She'd been married before, and it hadn't worked out. Dee was different, though. Being together forever, though, was a lot of work. "I wouldn't say it's sudden. I mean, I felt it too. I don't know how fast is too fast. I'd just say that we should work on building what we want together. Where it takes us, I can't say right now, but I love you, too."

With that, she eased out from beneath the covers and got dressed. A feeling of warmth and belonging cloaked her.

Dee, still lying in bed, said, "I understand that you can't tell me who the client is."

"I don't know myself. Janet didn't give me a name. She just gave me a pick-up location. She's worried about security, even with the burner cellphones. I have to say that I agree with her on that. Back in Sacramento when we found that guy following us, I felt like I was on my own. I didn't care for that one bit."

Dee reached over and touched Val's arm. "You be careful, girl. None of this hero stuff, okay?"

"Promise."

23

Senator Corel's irritation increased to anger, which evolved quickly into rage. Incompetence and disloyalty surrounded him. Everyone he depended on failed him at every turn. He fought to regain his composure. Sitting in his office, he stared out the window, his jaw clenched so hard it hurt.

His cellphone brought him back to the moment. "What do you have?"

Dylan Strauss got straight to the point. "Your attorney friend was right. We accessed Sue Hartman's credit card records, and she did rent a room. Unfortunately, by the time we got there, your wife had checked out. Whoever picked her up managed to avoid the cameras in the area. We're back at the beginning. I'll keep checking surveillance in the area and along the I-Five and I-Ninety corridors. Of course, we'll keep tabs on Hartman's credit card, and I'll try to get a fix on her cellphone."

Corel fumed. "No, we're not back at the beginning. Sue Hartman knows something. She's our only lead."

Strauss laughed. "Yes, of course. If only she'd sit down and talk with us, you know, tell us everything she knows."

"Don't be a dick. You know exactly what I'm talking about."

The connection went silent for a moment before Strauss answered softly. "You need to be sure about this, Senator. There's no coming back. If we grab her, we can't let her go. You know that. We can get the information out of her, but after that...."

"I pay you a goddamned ton of money to solve problems. This is a problem I need solved. If you're not up to it, maybe we should re-think our arrangement. Besides, don't act as though you've never done this kind of thing before."

"Since you know my reputation so well, you also know that I discuss consequences before these kinds of decisions are made. The time to consider risks and rewards is now; not after we act." Strauss paused for a moment and continued, "I'm going to assume, then, that you've thought it through."

Corel was rapidly losing patience. "Don't fuck it up, then. Remember, if this goes wrong, you're up to your ass in it just as much as I am."

Strauss let out a hearty laugh. "In your fucking dreams, Senator. You can labor under that illusion if you choose, but I promise you, I can disappear and be out of this country before you have time to clean the shit out of your pants. Before you get on your high horse, I'm going to tell you this. I'm not your whipping boy. You don't get to fuck with me like you do those starry-eyed twits of yours. You want to talk shit to me, you're going to get it right back in your face. Is that clear enough for you? If this doesn't work for you, I suggest you go shopping for someone else."

The rage built to the boiling point. Corel closed his

eyes tightly, forcing down the string of epithets on the tip of his tongue. "Find out what Hartman knows—now."

He disconnected and threw his phone at the settee on the other side of the room. There were still nearly two months to go before the election. What if people began to notice that his wife was not around and starting asking questions? He simply could not afford to have this shit hanging over his head. He tried to focus. *Where could she go? She doesn't have much cash on her.* And then it an uncomfortable truth washed over him. She was co-owner of all their financial assets as well as having a comfortable stash of her own. With that kind of money and some help, she could go pretty much anywhere she wanted. This needed a remedy.

Things just went from bad to worse. Not only did he have to take incompetence and insolence from Dylan Strauss, who was nothing more than a common thug. Now he needed to call that twat of a lawyer again—Reba Stillings.

He stood, shuffled across the room and retrieved his phone. Connecting, he tried to put on his best demeanor, at least for the moment.

"Good morning, Thom. What can I do for you?" Her voice sounded as though she had not a care in the world.

"I have a small legal problem I need solved. I'm hoping that you might help me with it."

"Your retainer account is in fantastic shape, so I'd be happy to do what I can. What seems to be the problem?"

"Nothing major. I just got to thinking. Bonnie, in her current state of mind, isn't in the best position to make decisions. It occurs to me that she has access to all our financial accounts. I'm just afraid that, in her condition, she might, well, you know, make some very unwise money decisions. Is there a way we can get her taken off the accounts, or at least freeze them so that she can't access anything?"

He could hear the smirk.

"In my world, that's the epitome of something *major*. She's co-owner, as you said. In order to terminate that status, you'd need her approval. Absent that, you could try legal action to force it, but she would be entitled to a hearing. You and I both know how that would go. If memory serves, she has funds outside of those jointly held by the two of you. That would be nearly impossible to close down without her approval."

Is there nobody that can accomplish a simple fucking task? "I thought someone with your connections and skills would be able to work a little magic."

"Yeah, that would be quite the magic trick. Look, there are a few simple things we could do. I'm not sure how much it'll help in the long run, but it might ease things a little. First set up a private account—your name only—and transfer funds into it. Then notify the institutions with joint accounts that you think you've have been hacked. Freeze them. You can set up some new joint accounts later."

She paused and then continued, "You could also liquidate real property assets and move those funds as well. The problem with this course of action is that it would likely draw all kinds of attention."

Corel clenched his jaw in anger for a moment. Forcing himself into a calmer space, he considered the options. "Forget the real property assets. Is this something you can take care of for me?"

Stillings sounded mildly amused. "Of course, Thom. I'll have one of my assistants take care of it. You'll need to give me your account numbers and any security PINs or phone passwords. We can get it done today. How much of your joint funds do want to move? Before you answer, keep in mind, this may be all the funds you can access for weeks to come."

"Make it a fifty million. You'll have to access our investments as well regular checking and savings accounts."

She hesitantly said, "That's a lot of money. They may want to talk to you personally. Also, there's something else you need to keep in mind. You still have two months before the election. You have a lot of balls in the air right now. If any of this leaks out, it's going to come home to roost. You have to know that your strength is with women. If you lose them, you lose the election. It's that simple."

24

Rattled, that was the word. Val supposed it was a good kind of rattled. The night with Dee had left her with a warm sense of belonging, accompanied by a lot of really hard questions. First among them—*am I really a lesbian?* She'd never thought of herself that way. She'd been married to a man, and, before the beatings, she'd loved him. When they made love, he touched her in the most incredible, sensual way.

What changed? She gripped the steering wheel so tightly that her knuckles turned white. Was it so different with Dee? Was it the ten years in prison. Val didn't think so. While on the inside, staying alive and out of trouble was her main concern. Unlike many of the women she was incarcerated with, Val knew she would be free at some point. No, prison had not shaped her feelings toward Dee.

The entrance to the gated community loomed ahead, pulling Val out of her thoughts. "Here we go." She pulled up in front and parked in the assigned visitor's space. Out of the car, she strolled casually up to the front door, trying to keep watch on her surroundings.

A moment after she rang the bell, the door cracked open, and a face appeared. The eyes spoke of uncertainty and fear. "Yes?"

Val showed the woman her driver's license. "I'm Val. Reverend Polasky told you to expect me."

The door opened and the woman stood aside. "Come in, please." She turned her back and retreated into the living room.

"Are you ready to go?"

"Where?"

"I don't know. We can talk about it and decide on the way. The first step, though, is to get you out of here."

The woman plopped onto the couch. "Why?"

The question took Val by surprise. "Why what?"

"Why leave until we know where we're going? Do you think I'm in danger here?"

Val dropped into an easy chair. "I don't know anything about you or your situation. All I know is that I'm supposed to get you to safety and then work with you for longer term arrangements."

"You don't know who I am?" The woman, who appeared to be in her early fifties, arched an eyebrow. She had lush brunette hair, hazel eyes, and a trim figure. Her clothing appeared to be expensive. There was only faint bruising on her face. Her husband had obviously learned how to inflict pain without leaving marks.

"No. Reverend Polasky didn't give me anything except this location."

"I'm Bonnie Corel."

Val nodded but remained seated. "I'm pleased to meet you, Bonnie Corel, but that doesn't help us figure out where to go."

The woman looked confused. "Then you don't know who my husband is?"

Val stared at the woman for a moment, not quite sure where it was going. "Afraid not, but if he's violent, which I assume he is, then we just need to get you away from him."

"My husband is Senator Thomas Corel." She narrowed her eyes and fell silent, as though expecting some sign of recognition.

"Okay, well, he's a politician, then."

"He's a U. S. Senator, and a very powerful one at that." Bonnie paused for a moment. "Also I guess you should know, he has a bunch of thugs that he uses to chase me when I run."

"I take it this isn't the first time you've tried to get away."

"Twice before. They always found me. There's this one man—Dylan Strauss. He's the leader of that little band. He comes across as soft and understanding but, make no mistake, he has ice water running in his veins. I have no doubt that he'd kill me if I didn't go back with him."

Val shook her head. This didn't sound good. "Did you ever think of going to the police?"

Bonnie's laugh came out with no small amount of bitterness. "Yeah, right. You clearly don't understand how power works. He has it and I don't. The system is owned and operated by those in power. My father had it, and he used it brutally on me and my mother. Now my husband has it and he uses it when and how he chooses. There's no fighting it, at least there hasn't been... until now."

"Oh, so you're going to fight him?" That really didn't sound good.

Bonnie stood and eased over toward the window, staring out into the morning sunshine. "Everything is a step at a time. The first step is getting to safety. After that, I'll go to the next step."

Val smirked. "And what might that next step be?"

"Financial resources. After that, I'll decide what's next."

Val felt more than a little put out. "It sounds like you don't need me. You have this all figured out."

"On the contrary. You and Reverend Polasky, you are the only lifeline I have right now. I have nowhere to go where I'm safe. If you can give me that, I can find a way to claw my life back."

And that made sense to Val. "Which brings me back to my first question—where to?"

"Seattle."

The response dumbfounded Val. "What? Are you really that dense?"

"It's the last place he'd expect to find me. When I ran before, I tried to get out of the state. They'll be watching the interstates and major roads in and out of the city. No doubt he's put a freeze on my credit cards. I'm certain his hired criminals can hack into phone systems, video surveillance, and even banks."

"If I'm hearing you right, then, what you want is a place to regroup here in the Seattle area. You say that you'll try to access financial resources. Won't that tip him off? If you're in the area, well, it will make you an easy target."

"That won't be a problem. None of my new accounts are located in Seattle, and I have no need to visit any of the banks in person. I need time in a safe place. If you can give me that, then I should be fine on my own after that."

Val sighed. "We'll find you a safe place. After that, I have some pre-paid debit cards that you can use for expenses. One thing, though, and this is not something that I'll compromise on. You cannot have any contact with anyone in your prior life. From here forward, at least for the time being, it's you and me. Is that okay with you?"

Bonnie nodded. "Reverend Polasky explained that. As for the money, don't bother. I have some of my own." A slight smile stole over her face. "I actually did a better job of planning this time."

25

Greg dreaded the conversation he needed to have with Dani. She'd been home from the hospital for not quite two weeks. The best he could say about her state of mind was that she seemed lost. She suffered wild mood swings and had little appetite. If there was a positive side, it was that she seemed to comprehend that her life with Billy was a thing of the past. It was clear she didn't like it, but she did seem to accept it.

Saturday morning he decided—*today is the day*. He prepared a cup of coffee as he brooded over how to go about it. She wandered into the kitchen as though she was trying to find her way back to someplace familiar.

"Good morning. How are you feeling today?" He put his cheeriest tone into the question.

She mumbled a response, "I'm okay." She stood at the kitchen counter staring at the coffee maker as though contemplating some great life decision. Mostly, though, she seemed frozen in uncertainty.

"Would you like coffee? We have French Roast, Italian Blend, and French Vanilla."

She remained silent for a moment before shrugging. "I don't know. Maybe. Uh, not right now."

She turned toward the living room.

"Dani, wait up. Can we talk for just a minute?"

His niece slid into a breakfast room chair without answering.

"I know this conversation's not going to be easy for either of us. Unfortunately, we have to have it."

He waited in silence for a moment. When no response came, he continued, "What the detective told you about Billy—I know it's not something you wanted to hear. I know it's going to take some time to put this all together so it makes sense. Believe me, Dani, I don't want to rush that, but there is something that's urgent. He's still out there. They haven't found him yet. Hopefully, he's running and will try to get as far away as he can. I'm worried, though, that he might double back this way and…." He unsuccessfully tried to find the right words to complete his thought.

She looked blankly at him. "What do you want me to do?"

"I need to make sure you're safe. That's the only thing that matters to me right now. I worry that this may not be the best choice of locations. He knows where we live. We have surveillance and alarm systems, but all of that can be beaten. No matter how many precautions we take, there's a chance that he can get around them."

"Why would he come back?" Her tone sounded slightly more engaged.

"I don't know. I have no idea what's in his head. What happened to you was most likely his temper getting the better of him. Killing those two police officers, though, was not a temper tantrum. They should have been prepared for him and he got them both. He's become something else. If he can get the jump on two cops who knew about him, he can certainly find a way past me."

"He wouldn't hurt me." The look of worry on her face didn't fit the words.

Greg felt the exasperation rise. "He's already done that... and left you to die. No, Dani, hurting you came natural to him. I suspect that's doubly so now."

She turned her head away, looking toward the kitchen window.

"We're going to find you another place to stay, at least for the time being."

She whipped her head around. "What? Where?"

"I don't know. A guy that works for me, Dimitry Kazarian, is going to help find a place. He and I spoke about it. He thought it would be best if you were part of the discussion. Once the two of you locate a good place, we'll make the arrangements through some third party so it's not traceable back to me or you."

"When's all this going to happen?" She suddenly seemed interested.

The increased engagement took Greg by surprise. "I don't know for sure. I wanted to see how you reacted first. I suppose you can start looking right away."

Dani picked at the corner of the table with her fingernail. "What's going to happen to him, I mean, when they catch him? Will they execute him?"

"I have no idea what the courts will do. If I'm not mistaken, though, there's a moratorium on capital punishment in Washington. So, I'd say the death penalty is out. Hopefully, though, they'll send him to prison for the rest of his life."

Tears came to her eyes. "How does this kind of thing happen? How do I go from being in love and happy to almost being killed, and the man that I love turning out to be some kind of monster?"

Greg shook his head. "I wish I had some profound answer for you. The truth is, I don't know. What I *do* know is that it's not that unusual. Women find themselves in relationships with men they love and dream of building a life with, only to live in constant fear. A lot of them are killed every year. Their children are killed."

He choked up and his heart pounded. "It could have been you." What he wanted to say, though, was *It almost was you.* "Anyway, I'll ask Kaz to come over. You and he can talk about it."

26

The Sniper was no stranger to on-the-fly life-or-death decisions. His time in Afghanistan had taught him to assess situations, act without delay, and move on. Regret and second-guessing served no real purpose other than to help him be more prepared for the next crisis.

Now he was under no illusions. Cousin Billy showing up at his door constituted a life-or-death decision. He studied the young kid… that's all his cousin really looked like—a snot-nosed kid. The whelp stood there on the porch like he was expecting a royal reception.

The Sniper glanced over at the SUV—Washington plates. It figured. He hadn't heard from the boy in ages. They'd played together when they were kids, although the Sniper had a good ten years on his cousin. *A long time ago. That life's over.*

Feeling the reassuring pressure of the handgun tucked in his back waistband, he offered a smile. "So, Cuz. It's been what, ten years?"

Billy's face lit up. "Yeah, I believe you're right. Back when we were kids, I guess."

The Sniper gestured around the clearing. "What brings you here?"

Billy stuffed his hands, which he had been rubbing together nervously, into the front pockets of his jeans. "Nothing, really. I just got to thinking about reconnecting, you know, family stuff."

The Sniper glanced around, while he worked the pieces through his mind. This kid, who he hadn't seen in years had unexpectedly shown up at his cabin. Why he came was, at the moment, less important than how he found the place. "How'd you think to find me here?"

"This is where we used to play, don't you remember? We even tried to build a treehouse over there." He pointed across the clearing. He laughed and continued, "That didn't turn out so well. I just figured you might have ended up building a cabin here. You used to talk about it."

It all came back. The Sniper felt the sense of danger recede even more. He organized his thoughts. The explanation made sense, but why was his cousin here? "Are you working in Idaho?"

"Not yet. I was doing some construction over in Seattle and decided to take a break. I though I'd check things out over here."

The decision to be made hung heavy in the air between them. Either he would invite Billy into the cabin for supper, or kill him straight up. It didn't feel right. The kid was leaving a lot unsaid. The Sniper decided to delay the decision. After all, a few hours one way or the other wasn't going to make a big difference. "Let's go inside. It's more comfortable there."

A few hours later, the two sat down with bowls of chicken rice soup and a loaf of homemade bread. The Sniper pulled out two bottles of Miller beer from the refrigerator. Twisting the top off of his, he held it up toward Billy. "To family." He took a deep drink and set the bottle on the table.

Billy grinned and turned his bottle up, guzzling down a third of it. Wiping his mouth with his sleeve, he echoed, "To family."

Tearing off a piece of bread, the Sniper popped it into his mouth and chewed slowly. He chased it down with another draught of beer. "Are you thinking about another line of work or are you looking for something in construction over here?" He gestured toward the front door, as though it were the gateway to Idaho. "Not much going on in this part of Idaho right now. The economy in this area is nothing like Seattle."

Billy took a spoonful of soup as he nodded his head. "I'm looking for a change of pace. I figure I'll just see what's floating around and figure it out as I go."

Alarms went off in the Sniper's head. Billy was hiding something. The decision options narrowed. Could there be some use for Billy—a purpose he might serve in the grand scheme of things? The Sniper started to click through some ideas but stopped abruptly. He knew nothing about Billy.

Well, he knew one thing. Either he would find a use for his long-lost cousin, or he would have to kill him. There was a chance that the kid was just what he seemed— distant family who was trying to reconnect. The Sniper dismissed that notion immediately. It made no sense. Since his cousin was dancing around whatever had brought him here, it would take a more nuanced approach. They finished the meal with meaningless small talk that eased into an uneasy silence.

After the dishes were washed, dried, and put away, the Sniper set Billy up in the spare room. "It's not the most comfortable bed in the world, but it'll have to do." He was not interested in any more conversation.

Down the hallway to his combination bedroom and study, he booted up his notebook computer. He activated the camera system within the cabin and set motion alarms. If Billy tried to leave his room, for whatever reason, it would be readily apparent.

With his computer powered up, the Sniper navigated onto the dark web. He knew he could probably get most of what he needed on the regular internet. The dark web, though, assured him of anonymity. The first order of business would be to gather more information about Billy. It didn't take long. The Sniper smiled as he shook his head. "Well, Cuz, you've certainly been a busy boy." The newfound information made his decision much easier. He might well have a use for this kid. Life was complicated. The work he did targeting feminists was his passion. Unfortunately, that arrangement barely paid enough to keep him afloat. He supplemented this with independent income, contracting out his unique services. If he could make things work with his cousin, he could easily double his productive output, taking on more contracts. If it didn't work out, then he'd feel no qualms about offing the boy.

He powered down the computer, leaned back in his chair, and laced his hands behind his head. It had been a long day and he was exhausted. As he pulled back the covers on the bed, he put his thoughts together. He and Cousin Billy would have a heart-to-heart discussion in the morning. Hopefully, things would go well. If not, Billy Boy would not live to see lunch.

27

There was no great mystery about the meeting. Janet knew that her duty to the church demanded that she be at the hospital with Lena Severtsen during her husband's operation. The fact that she had an important commitment to Bonnie Corel, one that could well have spelled the difference between life and death, did nothing to change her church obligations. She fidgeted as she waited, moving papers from one stack to another and tidying her up cluttered desk.

A knock at the door announced Gayle's arrival. Her board president came in and offered a curt nod that foretold an unpleasant conversation ahead. "Thanks for making the time, Janet. I know that you've got a lot on your plate, so I'll try to make this quick."

"Would you like coffee or tea?"

"I'm fine, thanks." Gayle cleared her throat and took a deep breath. "As I said, I know you've got a lot going on, and I know that you put in far more hours in the job than we pay for. The truth is, Janet, that Lena Severtsen needed you the other night and you had other commitments. I'm not going to ask you about them, but I need to say that there are times when your duties here need to take precedence. The other night was one of them." She fell silent, her lips drawn into a tight line.

The board president hadn't said anything that Janet didn't already know—nothing that she hadn't expected... or deserved. Still, it stung. It had been a no-win situation. No matter what she'd chosen—Bonnie Corel or Lena Severtsen—there would be one person left out. "I know, Gayle. I understand and take full responsibility for the lapse." She had no problem taking the responsibility but bristled at the notion that it had been a lapse in duty. Janet had done the best she could under impossible conditions.

Gayle exhaled as though relieved. "Good, that's good. Look, I know it's tough. I appreciate... the whole board appreciates your effort." She fell silent for a moment and then stood. "I need to be going. Please let us know if there's anything we need to do to make thing work smoother."

Janet stifled the urge to smirk. *Can't think of a thing unless you can clone me.*

28

The summer's end triggered a guilt attack in Janet. She had ignored young Abby Miller and her grand-mother, Roberta Klein, for weeks. The school year had already started. It was time to reconnect.

Janet thought of calling ahead but decided against it. Talking with Roberta on the phone in the past had proved an exercise in futility. The woman's depression had hampered discussions since her daughter's murder. The last few times that Janet had spoken to her, it seemed to have gotten much worse.

Parking in the driveway, Janet was struck by the dark, ominous appearance of the house. She rang the doorbell and waited. After a moment, the door cracked open, and Roberta's sallow face appeared. The blank eyes and flat affect were enough to confirm that things hadn't gotten any better.

"Good afternoon, Miz Klein. May I come in?" Janet struggled with how to broach her request.

"What do you want?" The words came out not as a challenge but rather as a pointless question.

Janet shuffled in place and responded, "With school just starting. I thought it might be nice to take Abby out shopping for a few things."

"We don't need your charity."

"It's not charity, Miz Klein. It's simply me wanting to do something for Abby." As an afterthought, Janet added, "And it would be nice to spend some time with her."

The woman seemed to consider Janet's words for a moment.

Before she could respond, another idea occurred to Janet. "Maybe you could come along. I'm sure she'd love that. We could get some lunch while we're out. I'd really like it if you could come along."

An hour later, the three of them navigated the aisles of a local discount department store. Their first stop was at the school packs. Janet began looking at brightly colored backpacks with flowers and birds. Abby seemed drawn to a blue pack with a rainbow arced across the back. Roberta was transfixed on a plain gray one. She stared at it as though it might offer some answers to life's problems.

Janet set down the one she was looking at and focused on the pack that Abby held in her hands. The young girl ran her fingers over the rainbow arc. "This is pretty." Tears welled up in her eyes. "Mom loved rainbows."

"I'm sure that she'd be thrilled for you to have one, and this one seems perfect." The deep sky-blue color provided the perfect backdrop for the rainbow. "What do you think?"

Abby glanced over at her grandmother, as though for approval or confirmation. Neither came. Roberta continued to stare at the gray backpack on the shelf in front of her.

Janet touched Roberta's arm.

Chapter 28

"This one's cheaper. It would work okay." The words lacked any emotion.

Janet said softly, "The other one gives something of her mother."

"Her mother's dead."

Janet wanted to scream *I know she's fucking dead. I was there, remember?* Instead, she offered the only alternative she could come up with. "Her memory's not dead. For now, that's what matters." She tried to keep the tone as non-confrontational as possible.

If Roberta heard, she chose not to respond. She turned away from the backpacks. Her jaw clenched and she closed her eyes.

Abby set the backpack down and shuffled over next to her grandmother, wrapping her small arms around the woman's waist. "It's okay, Grandma. I can get whatever pack you want me to have."

Tears welled up in Roberta's eyes.

Janet watched the scene unfold with disbelief. The young girl became the caregiver, comforting her grand-mother. Roberta hesitated for a moment and then put her arms around Abby. They stood in the aisle by the back-packs, the two of them, in tears.

29

The early morning hours were the best. The Sniper washed the dishes and poured himself a second cup of coffee. Out on the porch, he dropped into a straight wooden chair and leaned back against the wall. It was going to be a beautiful early September day.

It was nearly eleven when a disheveled Cousin Billy stumbled out onto the porch, stretched, and yawned. He looked as though he'd slept in his jeans and sweatshirt.

The Sniper squinted into the morning sun before considering his cousin. "The day's half over." With the tone and words carefully calculated, the accusation hung in the air without being overpowering.

"I ain't slept that good in I don't know how long." He plopped down on the front steps, staring out into the woods.

I can only imagine. The Sniper found this amusing. He sat in silence, waiting for Billy's inevitable discomfort to kick in.

"Things have been a little crazy."

The exchange was turning out to be quite entertaining.

"I got some home fries, elk sausage, and buttermilk biscuits in the kitchen." The Sniper sat, waiting for the response.

"That sounds good. Some coffee'd be good." Billy sat still.

Oh… and would you like to be served out here in the open air or would you prefer the formal dining room? The Sniper kept his snark in check. He nodded toward the door. "Help yourself."

Five minutes later, Cousin Billy chowed down like he hadn't eaten in a week. The Sniper watched in quiet disgust. *Not an awful lot of promise here.* "How long will you be here?"

Billy apparently didn't catch the sarcasm. "Hard to say, I guess. I figure it's going to take me a few days just to get adjusted to the slower pace of life here." He stopped eating and rubbed his chin. "I'm guessing probably a few weeks," he remarked slowly, turning toward the Sniper and adding quickly, "I mean, if that's okay with you."

The Sniper gestured in a generally southern direction. "There might be some things going on down in Boise. Not a lot in this area."

Billy's face darkened. "I was hoping to maybe stay away from the big cities—too much hustle and bustle. I think I might like the country life." The after-the-fact smile seemed forced.

Repulsion set in. How could this miserable excuse for a human being believe that he could skirt around the truth, and no one would ever question him. "Seems a big change —Seattle to central Idaho. Anything in particular lead you to this?" The Sniper, of course, knew exactly what the kid was running from.

His cousin's apparent discomfort heightened. "Not really. I mean, I'd just kind of like to lay low and take it easy for a while."

"I thought you wanted to look for work." Extracting information from this imbecile was more tedious than the Sniper had patience for at the moment.

Billy rubbed his hands together and appeared to gather what few thoughts could possibly fit inside his head. "Look, if you don't want me here, I'll leave. I just thought that maybe since we're family, you might be able to help me out."

"What kind of help do you need?"

Billy's uncertainty morphed into agitation. "I need a place to hang out. You know, someplace to stay while I sort things out."

"What do you need to sort out?"

It came down to this moment. Billy would either have to come clean or start out-and-out lying. He squirmed in his chair for a moment and looked away. "I got into kind of a scrape with the law. I need to lay low until it blows over—that's all."

The Sniper laughed internally—*kind of a scrape?* "So, you're in trouble with the law?"

His cousin's demeanor immediately turned defensive. "I know what you're thinking, but it wasn't my fault. I was minding my own business. There were a couple of cops that decided to hassle me for no reason at all."

The Sniper pulled at the threads. "And?"

Billy's voice increased in pitch and volume. "I tried to stay away but they pushed me into it."

"Into what?"

The dam broke. "I shot 'em. I swear, I wasn't trying to cause no problems or anything. I was just minding my own business." Billy had begun to repeat himself.

Okay, I guess that's enough. Time to come clean, Billy. "You shot a couple of cops and somehow it was their fault. I find that hard to believe. Just out of nowhere, they picked you out and decided to hassle you… for no good reason at all."

"I don't need no lecture from you."

The Sniper smiled gently. "Yet you do need me to give you a place to live, food, and safety."

"If it's that big of a deal, then fuck you. I'll find something else."

The Sniper leaned forward, his hard gaze focused on his cousin. "And just what else would you find, Billy. You killed two cops. Unless I'm wrong, I'd say that vehicle you got there is boosted. You just seem to dig yourself deeper and deeper into shit."

"Yeah, like you ain't never been in trouble." Billy returned the glare.

The Sniper understood the reference. He'd broken into a gas station and got caught. It was what teenagers did. That, like his entire relationship with Cousin Billy, was in another life a long time ago. "This isn't about me. I'm not the one who's running from the cops."

Billy sat in stony silence.

"If you want my help, you need to come clean. Those cops didn't come after you for no reason. What was that about?"

"It was no big deal. I just had a run-in with my girlfriend and her uncle. He's a rich asshole who didn't like his pretty little niece screwing me."

"And?"

"And what? I told you. I had a little run-in, that's all."

The Sniper struggled to contain the sarcastic laugh. "Define *run-in*."

"We got into a shouting match. It was nothing. I left her in a hotel room. I was done with her. I guess her uncle came along later and they must have got into it. He killed her."

The Sniper probed. "Let me guess. They tried to pin it on you."

A look of relief washed over the boy. "Yeah, exactly. They tried to say that I did it. Her uncle is rich and I'm sure he bought his way out of it. Just like all them rich assholes—blame it on the poor guy."

"Yes, well, I see what you mean by *a scrape with the law.*" The Sniper smirked. "I'm guessing that all that stuff about looking for employment opportunities and starting over was pretty much just a smoke screen."

Billy grew sullen, quiet.

The fun was over. It was time to get to work. The first piece of business would be to pull this asshole's ground out from beneath him. "Well Cousin Billy, I'm going to share some things with you. Please take these comments in the spirit with which I offer them. In other words, I don't want to hear any defensive arguments from you. You fucked up… not once, but again and again and again. Now, if you want, you can walk away right now—no harm, no foul." The Sniper smiled inside. There is no way he'd let Billy Robinson just walk away at this point.

"Okay. Go ahead." Resignation bathed his voice.

"First, what the fuck is that car doing in my yard. You drove all the way over, presumably on Interstate Ninety, and then into Idaho with a stolen vehicle. On top of that, you drove down through Idaho with a set of Washington plates. Whatever else you might think of the bozos in Idaho, they're not completely stupid or unaware. At the very least, someone was bound to notice your license plates. Assuming the vehicle is stolen, the description is probably being circulated."

Billy stared at the vehicle as though he were seeing it for the first time. He shook his head slowly but kept his mouth shut.

"We might as well get this out of the way, too. That line about the cops picking you, that's bullshit. If I'm understanding you right, there was likely a warrant out for your arrest. It was their job to execute that warrant. They were, in fact, minding their business."

Cousin Billy started to speak but the Sniper held up his hand as though to warn him off. "Here's what we have. You lose your temper and shoot your girlfriend. You go on the run. Two cops approach you and you kill them. You steal a car with Washington plates and drive half the length of Idaho to my place, where you say you want to get a new start. Do I have that right?"

"I told you, I didn't shoot her. Her uncle must have done it."

"Uh, no, you're lying again. Not only did you shoot her. You left a witness alive."

For the first time, Billy looked genuinely perplexed. "No. There was nobody else there. There weren't any cameras and no witnesses."

"Now, you see, this is another example of your stupidity. You didn't follow through on your girlfriend. As it turns out, she's alive. Oh yes, you shot her, but they managed to save her life. Now she's a star witness against you. That means that you killed a couple of cops for no reason."

"Dani's alive?"

For the Sniper, the crucial issue was that his cousin's presence posed a risk. "Cuz, you fucked up really bad. You're gonna have to fix that one."

30

The plate of Russian tea biscuits sat untouched on the coffee table. Janet sat and waited while Maddie prepared tea. The minister felt a tinge of guilt. After all, her friend and mentor was finding it harder and harder to get around. Yet she was the one shuffling about in the kitchen making tea. On the other hand, Maddie prized her independence. It was her home. She could make the tea.

Janet gathered her thoughts. As she waited, she absorbed the old photographs on the wall and the precious artifacts of a life well-lived on the shelves of the small house. Maddie's life had indeed been a rich one. That the old woman was willing to share all of this with Janet was truly a blessing.

With the teacups on the coffee table and the two women in their seats, Janet asked, "How are your children doing?"

Maddie laughed softly. "Still trying to get me into one of those assisted living homes. Like I need assistance just to live. Hmph." She reached for a tea biscuit. "As long as you keep bringing me these sinful things, I can do just fine right where I'm at."

"I know, but they're just trying to help. They're good kids." *Kids* wasn't really the right term. Maddie's children were both older than Janet.

"Yes." Maddie's eyes misted over, and she fell silent.

Janet asked quietly, "How are you doing?"

Her friend quickly came back into the moment. "Me? I'm good. Every day is a gift from God. I will not disappoint him by squandering these days on self-pity."

"I can't argue with that. The days truly are blessings."

Maddie blew across the surface of her tea and took a sip. "Enough about me. What's new with Reverend Polasky?"

Where to begin? "Things are as crazy as always. Do you remember me telling you about that young girl, Abby—the one who lost her mother?"

Maddie nodded. "How's she doing? I can't imagine the pain that young thing is going through."

Janet related the story of the shopping trip and that moment with the backpacks. "I'm hoping that it's a turning point for her grandmother. Roberta seemed genuinely moved. I tell you, Maddie, Abby needs her."

"It's hard, I'll warrant you that, but...." Maddie fell silent, seeming to reconsider what she had intended to say.

"But?" Janet probed.

"I understand that the child desperately needs her grandmother, but these things don't resolve themselves quickly. Whatever is haunting Roberta has been there for years. Losing her daughter like she did obviously hurt her. There's a lot more to it than that, though. Maybe the moment there in the store was something... maybe a first step, but I'd be stingy with my optimism."

Janet felt as though she was being criticized. She

wanted to argue about the virtues of hope. Instead, she asked, "What would you do, you know, if you were in my place?"

Maddie bit into a tea biscuit, chewing slowly. After she swallowed, she cleared her throat. "Maybe I misspoke. Optimism is good, I guess. Maybe look at what happened and where she is now as an opening—an opportunity. This may be the right time for you to visit with Roberta. I would talk about things less hurtful. Try to engage her in conversation about things which are perhaps more mundane."

Janet had never had a close relationship with Roberta Klein. Speaking with her had always been centered around Abby. Before the shooting, she hadn't spoken to the woman in years. Finding common ground to have social conversation would be a challenge.

Before she could respond, Maddie switched gears again. "What's going on with that project of yours?"

Janet sighed. "It's going. I mean, we got our first client relocated safely. I managed to get Rob Young off the board and presumably out of the church, although I'm not sure it's completely resolved. I haven't heard from him recently, but I don't know. I guess the next move is his."

She stood and wandered over to the curio shelf that contained old photos. Examining a few, she turned and continued, "We're working on our second client." In that moment, Janet wondered whether it would be ethical to share the details with Maddie. The pause, though, lasted only a moment. After all, she'd shared everything about the Lucy Young case.

"Do you remember me talking about Bonnie Corel?"

"Poor little rich girl. Yes, I remember." Maddie narrowed her eyes and shook her head. "I suppose I'm being judgmental. I don't know her at all."

"As it turns out, she's my new client." Janet poured out

the story. As she finished she remarked, "It's a little scary, what with her husband being a senator and all. Still, she does need our help."

Maddie sat for a moment, staring at the teacup on the table. Finally she spoke with what seemed some degree of hesitation. "I think I told you before—Bonnie's never been the helpless type. Her family married her off to that senator, but I get the sense that she was not the reluctant bride, nor was she starstruck with the man. I could be wrong, but from what little I know about her, she seems to be quite capable of spotting and taking advantage of opportunities. It's hard to imagine her groveling around her house waiting to be beaten up by her brute of a husband."

She looked up at Janet. "Don't get me wrong. I'm not suggesting that she wasn't beaten. Maybe, in her home, she was more dependent on him. There may be more to it than that, though. All I'm saying is not to take too much for granted."

Odd. Although Maddie had not said as much, the implication seemed clear. Her mentor seemed to suggest that Bonnie Corel was far more capable than Janet had imagined.

31

The situation had dragged on for far too long. Senator Corel's patience dwindled by the hour. Dylan Strauss had thus far produced nothing of value. Hopefully, Reba Stillings would be more productive. The senator sat in his chair, staring out across the Seattle cityscape, the gray, drizzly day reflecting his dark state of mind.

The ringtone on his phone buzzed. "Yes?"

"This is Reba. How are you doing today, Thom?" The voice was sugary—coated with insincerity.

He forced a cheerful response. "I'm doing well, Reba, and how are things there with you?"

"I made the financial arrangements you asked for. You will, of course, need to log into your accounts and verify with your electronic signature. The funds you wanted moved to a different account are in place. I used the same bank, so you should be able to activate that account at the same time. Your joint credit cards are all cancelled. I placed the order for new ones. They agreed to get them ready today and have them available at the downtown branch. You'll need to go in and pick them up."

Chapter 31

I don't have time for this kind of shit. What was the alternative? If he did nothing, Bonnie could get access to funds. That would complicate things and delay her return. "Thanks, Reba. Anything else?"

A short hesitation. "Well, as a matter of fact, yes. It seems that this little adventure your wife is on was not a spur-of-the-moment thing. She planned it. She moved a half-million out of your joint account about a week ago."

Corel exploded. "What the fuck? How does that happen?"

Stillings laughed. "Exactly the same way it's happening right now with you. She made the arrangements, verified with an electronic signature and boom, she's off to the races. There's more. You are aware, are you not, that she has a personal account—funds left to her from her father?"

The senator's head spun. This was not happening.

"She closed that account and moved the money to another one at a different institution."

"Which institution?"

"Doesn't matter. She closed that one too, moving the money again."

"No. That's not possible. Bonnie's not that smart, and she certainly doesn't have the wherewithal to make these kinds of moves. Somebody's helping her." A completely new and unthinkable idea crossed his mind. *Did she have a lover? Was she having an affair? He's likely some gigolo after my money.*

Stillings seemed to read his thoughts and responded. "We didn't find anything to suggest that there was anyone else. If you want a deeper dive into it, I'm sure you have the resources for that. It looks like she pulled it off herself, though."

Corel forced himself to calm down. *Think it through.*

There has to be a solution. "How do we get access to her accounts. I need to shut this down right away."

"In the near term, you don't get access. Over the longer term—months or years, you might get some traction trying to get her declared mentally incompetent. I'm sure you don't want to go that route. The only other option is to find her quickly and get her home so you can talk some sense into her."

"If I can find out which bank she's using, I can cut through some red tape and go straight to the top. There has to be an answer."

"Thom, I don't mean to sound disrespectful. You and I have a good working relationship, but you need to understand that your wife's family name and wealth carry as much power as your position, if not more. At the very best, it would end up a messy battle that would leak into the media. It's only a couple of months until the election. Your top priority right now should be to keep this off the radar. To do that, get her home."

After disconnecting, Corel fumed. He paced the office back and forth. He began to feel as though his mind had stepped out of his body. His fists wanted to crack his wife's thick skull. His legs wanted to kick her until her screams turned to muted moans. His eyes wanted to watch the blood flow from her nose and mouth.

He struggled to push these thoughts away. He didn't want to hurt anyone, least of all his wife. She just needed to understand that he was under a lot of pressure. *She should be supporting me. We're in this together. How can we change the world if I have to constantly babysit her?*

32

Kaz rang the bell and waited. Greg had arranged for him to connect with Dani and work on details for relocation. Presumably, that was what this meeting was about, but there had been something else in Greg's voice. Most people found it impossible to keep their feelings completely under wraps. Greg Stottman was no exception.

The door opened and Greg gestured him in. "We just finished dinner." He motioned Kaz toward the sofa and took a seat in an overstuffed chair. "Before you and Dani get started, though, there's something else I need from you."

Kaz waited without comment.

"I spoke with Enrico—told him I needed someone to do some rather sensitive investigations for me. I was a little surprised when he suggested you."

Kaz arched his eyebrows. "And?"

Greg reached over and brushed what looked like a spot of dust off the coffee table. "This is the second time he's recommended you. As I understand it, he gets nothing from the arrangement. What's up with that?"

Kaz eyed him for a moment, not sure where the conversation was going. Finally, he shrugged and responded, "I'm not a part of his asset inventory. You engage others, like Eisen, who do work through him. I figure he's pulling in some serious cash from that arrangement." He could see in Greg's eyes that the CEO understood that point quite well. "Anyway, what's the job?"

"There's an attorney in Seattle, Reba Stillings." Greg handed him a photo of a seriously beautiful blonde woman with a slight smile on her face. "Do you remember the bug that was placed in my attorney's office?"

Greg continued, "She's the one that ordered it. The thing is, the guy involved in the case she was working on… Rob Young… there's no way he could afford that kind of operation. He's a car salesman barely making ends meet. There's got to be something else going on."

Kaz leaned back in his chair. "I assume that you want me to find out what?"

"How much?"

"You purchased my time for six months. There's still two months left on the contract. If I can do it within that time, you're in luck."

Greg shook his head. "This has nothing to do with your original contract. Dani's not a part of this."

"Doesn't matter. You bought my time. Within reason, I'll do whatever needs to be done. If things run longer than the six-month term, we can talk about it."

Kaz watched the CEO process the information. Surely he understood about adding value to a contract. It's how high-end companies differentiated their products.

Greg exhaled and shrugged. "I'll get Dani."

* * *

He extended his hand. "Dimitry Kazarian—Kaz." He offered the warmest smile he could muster. Being warm and fuzzy had never been a part of his identity. He had, for all of his adult life, dealt with the darker side of things. He cared little about who liked him or didn't. He knew about contracts—protecting people, solving problems, and finding out things that others would prefer remain hidden.

Dani took his hand briefly and then let hers drop away as she turned toward the living room window. "Uncle Greg told me why you're here."

"I would hope so. I'd hate to come into this like a bucket of cold water."

"What am I supposed to do?" Her words seemed bathed in pain.

"Have a seat, Dani." He gestured toward the over-stuffed chair in which he'd just been sitting as he slid onto the sofa. "A lot's happened. I'm sure it's hard to make sense of it all. The upside is that you don't have to, at least not right now. As crazy as it may seem, you'll figure things out as we go on. No need to rush it."

She shook her head, tears in her eyes. "Just tell me what I have to do." The young woman—actually, she was still a teenager—seemed to have given up.

He leaned forward, his hands grasped together resting on his knees. "First, you don't have to do anything by yourself. I'm going to be with you."

Without waiting for a response, he continued, "Second, you need to know that I've done this kind of thing before. Helping people stay safe is what I do. Frankly, most of my jobs are much harder than this. We'll get through it fine. All I ask is that you trust me. If you have questions, ask. If you have concerns, express them. Don't stuff things—they just fester."

"Billy was never like that before." Her headshake was barely perceptible. "What happened?"

Kaz let a sarcastic chuckle escape. "Oh contraire. Billy has *always* been like that. You may not have seen it, but it was there. Men don't go from sensitive, loving beings to violent animals overnight. If you think back, he always wanted to control you... to possess you. In his mind, you belonged to him. Is that what you want, to be some man's property?"

"Uncle Greg didn't tell me you were a shrink."

"I'm sure there's a lot he didn't tell you."

"You sound like a know-it-all to me." She offered a half-hearted laugh.

"I wish. If I knew it all, this would be so much simpler. Sadly, you're going to have to be content with someone who only knows some of it. The rest we'll have to figure out together."

He let the silence work for him.

After a few minutes of fidgeting with her hands, she asked, "What now?"

"We start talking about what we need in a safe location and how to put it in place without leaving a trail to either you or your uncle."

Her voice softened. "Am I going to have to live alone?"

Kaz knew that the answer was going to hurt. "Not permanently, but you are going to have to spend some time alone until the thing with Billy is resolved. Maybe that's not a bad thing. A little solitude can help you reflect, to decide where you want your life to go. Besides, I'll stop by every day."

"Do I have to move out of state?"

"No, nothing like that. We can find a place locally. Most likely, we'll access it through the vacation rental network. They have a great website with lots of photos.

Once we narrow it down to several of them, we'll go have a look."

"What if he finds me?"

"He won't. Believe me, Dani. I've done this kind of thing for international business executives, government officials, and even some less savory types. Once we get started, you'll see. The arrangements will be so convoluted and obscure, a spy agency would have a tough time finding you. I can guarantee that Billy doesn't have those kinds of resources. You'll be safe."

"What's going to happen to him?"

"I don't know. Here's something to consider, though. His legal problems are tied to the two cops he killed. His attempt to kill you will pale by comparison. Every law enforcement official in the state is looking for him by now. If there's any chance he crossed a state line, the FBI will be on it as well as the police in the other state. He screwed up when he shot you. But he really iced the cake when he pulled the trigger on those two guys." Kaz shook his head.

She lowered her head and wiped a tear from her eye. "I just want all this to go away."

33

G reg had just come out of a production schedule meeting when he felt his cellphone vibrate. Checking the display, he connected. "Good morning, Detective Wharton." His first thought was that they had Billy Robinson in custody. A suitable alternative would be that the kid had been killed while resisting arrest.

"I've been trying to reach your niece, Dani. It seems her phone service has been turned off."

Greg spoke as he made his way back to his office. "We closed her old account and set up a new one. We didn't leave Billy Robinson with a path back to her."

"I need to talk to her."

"Meet me at my condo in an hour." He gave her the address.

Forty-five minutes later, he pulled into the garage. Inside, he found Dani slouched on the sofa watching TV. She looked up with boredom in her eyes. "You're off early."

"Detective Wharton from the King County Sheriff's office wants to talk to you. She'll be here in about fifteen minutes." He shed his coat and hung it up. "Have you had lunch yet?"

"Not hungry."

He sat in the overstuffed chair facing the couch. "Tell you what. After she leaves, why don't we go out and grab some lunch?"

Her attention shifted back to the reality show on TV. "Whatever."

Greg felt the need to engage with her. He knew that sitting in the house twenty-four hours a day was taking a toll on her. He hoped that she'd get settled in a safer place within a few days.

The doorbell interrupted his thoughts. "I guess that would be the detective." He answered the door and invited her in. "Can I get you some coffee or tea?"

"I'm fine." Wharton took off her raincoat and handed it to him. "I'd like to get on with the interview." The detective turned toward Dani. "How are you holding up?"

Dani remained immobile on the couch and shrugged. "Okay."

Greg pulled the wingback chair over closer to the couch. "Have a seat, please. If you don't mind, I'd like to sit in on this."

Wharton studied him for a moment and then responded, "If you want." She pulled a notepad from her briefcase and powered it on.

"Dani, I have some information for you, and I also need to ask you a few questions. First, Billy Robinson is still at large. We have BOLOs out across the state. We're also working with the Idaho State Police on the off chance that he's there. The FBI has been notified and will likely join the case. There's no evidence that he's back in this area, so I don't think you're in any immediate danger."

Greg interjected, "So, Dani's safe here?"

"We're not ruling anything out right now, but we have no reason to believe, based on what we know, that he's in the area at the moment." She paused and seemed to relax into the chair, crossing right leg over her left.

"What I'd like for you to do, Dani, is to think back to your conversations with him, especially anything he might have said about extended family. I think you told me once before that he mentioned Idaho."

Dani shifted her gaze toward the window as if trying to recall some bit of information that remained just out of her grasp. Finally, she said, "I don't remember much about it. He said something about a cousin in Idaho. Like I told you, he didn't say much about his family; mostly that he didn't have any use for them."

The detective swiped her pad and studied the screen for a moment. "We did some research and found that he had a cousin named Trey Costas who lived over in south-central Idaho. He was in the army, deployed to Afghanistan in twenty-fifteen. Military records show that he got into some serious trouble over there and was facing a courts martial. He went missing before he could be tried and hasn't been heard of since."

Dani stared at her as though not understanding what the conversation was about. "I don't know the name. Billy never mentioned it."

"The reason I bring it up is that the army lists him as missing in action. The people that I spoke with in D.C. seem to feel he's most likely dead. Still, if he found his way back somehow with a new ID, it could lead us to Billy."

Dani shrugged.

Wharton uncrossed her legs and leaned forward, her gaze fixed solidly on Dani. "I know this may not sound relevant to you. If that were the case and Billy managed to connect with him, it could provide the boy with some cover for the immediate future. I just wanted you to know so that, if you have any unexpected or strange communications with anyone, you can be aware of it."

Greg spoke again. "What kind of trouble did his cousin get into?"

"He went berserk one night and killed some Afghani villagers in cold blood. It created a small international *situation*. The local Afghan government wanted to take him into custody and try him for murder. The U. S. insisted that he face military justice. In the end, the military would have won that particular battle. In the interim, though, he just disappeared one night. They didn't say how he escaped confinement."

Greg's blood froze. "Great, a family of psychopaths." Kaz needed to know about this connection.

Detective Wharton put her pad away and stood. "I'll be going." She handed both Greg and Dani a business card. "Call me if you remember anything, no matter how unimportant it may seem. Let me know if he or anyone else out of the ordinary contacts you."

Greg appreciated that the police were obviously taking this seriously. He was relatively certain, though, that it was only because of the two cops that Robinson had killed. If it were just a matter of Dani being shot, this would probably have been a cold case by now. He let his cynicism slip out. "I guess it makes a big difference if the ones being shot are cops." He regretted the statement the moment the words escaped.

Wharton turned and considered him for a moment, as though studying a perplexing problem. "I know what you're thinking, Mister Stottman, and you're wrong. I'm in this because of what happened to Dani. Those two dead cops were in it because of what happened to her as well. I don't speak for anyone but myself, but I don't let these kinds of cases go."

"I'm sorry, I didn't mean any offense." He bowed his head.

Putting on her coat, she turned toward the door, speaking over her shoulder. "Call if you hear anything."

34

J anet turned her attention to the incoming call on her cellphone. The screen displayed only the telephone number of the caller, not their identification. Still, she knew who was on the other end. "Hi, how's it going?"

Val's voice sounded far too casual as it came through the speaker. "Do you have some time to talk?"

Janet swiveled around to look out the window into the gorgeous late summer afternoon. "Sure, what's up?"

"Maybe we could get together for a cup of coffee." There seemed to be an elusive edge to her words.

The minister focused—*get together?* Val was supposed to be on the road with Bonnie Corel, getting the woman to safety. "Uh, I didn't know you were in town."

"I thought maybe at Common Grounds in, say, thirty minutes. I'm buying." Far too casual.

"Yeah, that's good. See you then." As Janet disconnected, her stomach churned. Fear seeped in. What had gone wrong?

She powered down her computer and grabbed her coat. On the way out the door, she stopped at the church secretary's desk. "I've got to head out to a meeting. I'm going to swing by the office supply store on the way home. Do you need anything?"

Margaret Shemanski rubbed her chin as she pondered the question. "No, I think we're in pretty good shape."

"Good, then. I'll see you in the morning."

Twenty minutes later Janet slid into the chair opposite Val, who seemed to be desperately trying to hide the worried look on her face. Janet glanced around the room, wary of having any kind of substantive conversation in the public setting.

As though reading her mind, Val spoke in a soft voice. "Don't worry. There's plenty of background noise. We'll be fine."

Although not totally convinced, Janet relaxed. "Okay, so, what's up?" She listened intently as Val described the situation with Bonnie.

When the woman finished, Janet shook her head. "I don't understand. She wanted to get away to safety. Why stay in Seattle?"

Val shrugged. "You can talk to her about it. Like I said, though, she's set up resources and believes her husband is unlikely to look for her locally. I don't share that confidence." She paused and queried, "What do you want me to do?"

Janet felt a tinge of panic. Their model thus far had been that she wasn't supposed to know where the women were located. This hiccup blew that idea completely away. "Whether you or I agree or disagree with her, it's still her life. We do what we can, but I think we have to leave this kind of decision to her. If you feel it puts you in too much danger, we might have to revisit it."

"What do you think about the money thing? She says she doesn't need our money—she has her own. To my way of thinking, though, if she tries to access any of that money, it'll alert her husband."

Janet struggled to organize things in her head. "First things first. She's safe for the moment. There's food in the house. All the other usual expenses are taken care of for now. So, let's focus on where to locate her. Too many people know about the condo. We need to work on getting her moved out. That means finding a short-term arrangement, like a vacation rental. We could have either Jocelyn, the accountant, or Paulette, the attorney take care of that. After that, I don't know. We'll have to see how things play out, I suppose."

Val nodded. "That leads me to my next question. I have some things to take care of around my place. Is it okay to leave her alone in the condo? I don't mean all the time, but, you know, for stretches of time during the day. Do I need to stay there with her at night?"

Janet toyed with the question. She could sense that something was left unsaid. Val was not telling her everything. "I guess it depends on what's going on with Bonnie at any given time. Is there anything happening with you that I should know about—any problems that have come up?" It was an awkward question.

Val gestured with her hand as though brushing away the question. "Just some personal stuff. Nothing that impacts the job."

"Then I'd say to use your own judgment." Janet suddenly found it odd to give that advice to a woman whose judgment, or lack of it, had resulted in her killing her husband. *That was a long time ago. Things have changed.*

35

Compartmentalization. *What a fucked up word.* Still, Senator Corel struggled to keep each problem in its proper place. Whatever else was going on, he still had a campaign to run. When his cellphone rang, a shot of optimism ran through his mind. He checked the display for connecting. *It's about goddamned time.*

"What do have for me?" He barked the question.

"Not good. The Hartman lady didn't make it."

Corel laughed. "Of course she didn't. I thought we discussed that."

"No. I mean, she died before we got a chance to talk to her."

The senator exploded. "What the fuck? What does that mean?"

The voice came over quietly and with no hint of apology or regret. "It means exactly what I said. We didn't get a chance to question her."

"I'm sorry. Help me with this. I thought you knew what you were doing. How does this shit happen?"

"Easy there, Senator. We've had this discussion before.

You pay me to work for you. I don't have to take your shit. Now if you want the explanation, I can give it to you, but I'm not going to sit here and listen to you rant."

Corel fumed, the pressure building. He wanted to crawl through the cell network and strangle that arrogant motherfucker.

Before he could speak, though, Strauss continued. "To answer your question, I wasn't there. My crew grabbed her and took her to the site. One of my men administered the drug—the same one we use for all of these kinds of things. She seized and her heart failed within seconds."

The senator simply couldn't help himself. "Which one of your incompetent assholes managed that?"

"I'm not going to warn you again. We can work the problem like professionals, or you can head off to Google and find yourself someone else. Not that it matters, but the guy who gave the shot was Karl Unger. He's new. I just hired him a couple of months ago. He's not the issue, though. Some people have reactions to the drug. It sucks but that's just the way it is. Hartman's luck just ran out, that's all."

It occurred to Corel that her luck had run out anyway. Even if she had talked, she would not have survived. What pissed him off was that it turned out to be not only a wasted opportunity, but he incurred liability with nothing in return. He clenched his jaw and shut his eyes tight for a moment. As the calmness crept back in, he asked, "Were you able to get anything on the mole?"

"I was able to access phone records for the shelter and isolated a call from one of your neighbors' home phone. It matches the approximate time that your wife left. The extension that picked up the call belonged to an admin assistant. I was able to identify her and access her personal cellphone records. A call was made from that phone to your attorney friend, Stillings. There's your mole."

"Did you find out anything from her?"

"She just took the call and transferred it to Hartman. The only problem is that the young lady unfortunately knew more than she should have. Turns out she committed suicide. Probably all distraught about the way things happened... who knows?"

Finally, at least something goes right. "Okay, good. What's next?"

"With no information from Hartman, we're back to flying blind. We know that your wife was in a hotel, but she's gone now. We have no idea who's helping her or where she's gone."

The senator's mind shifted into overdrive. If the DV Network wasn't helping Bonnie, then it had to be someone else. The bitch didn't have it in her to do it alone. *But who?*

Stillings had indicated that it might be any of the other DV organizations in the area. He had no intention of doing the kind of research necessary to tease that out. She did, though, give him a specific name—Janet Polasky. He'd met the minister once or twice, although he didn't recall much about her.

He brought his attention back to Strauss. "Have you set up some system of checking video surveillance in and out of Seattle?"

"We've identified key locations that have cameras. We should have taps on them by the end the day. There are some things you need to know. The sites are only on the main corridors. There are side roads and complicated routes that could get her out without passing by these sites. There's no way, at least in the near term, of covering every single possibility. We're playing the odds."

"Yeah, I get that. It should be okay. Bonnie's not that

bright and the do-gooder bitches are likely no better. What else?"

There was a short silence before Strauss spoke again. "I just want to remind you that this entire effort is premised on her trying to leave town. If she has, for whatever reason, decided to remain local, we're not going to see her unless she emerges into the light."

"I've already told you once—forget local. She always runs."

There was no immediate response. Before Corel could add anything else, his phone beeped indicating an incoming call. "I have to go. Let me know when you have her."

He disconnected and answered the call without looking at the display. "This is Senator Corel."

"I need you in my office—now." The voice belonged to Reba Stillings.

He clicked through some possible responses in his head. Before he could speak though, the attorney beat him to it.

"In case you didn't understand that, Senator Corel, you will get your goddamned ass down here right now. I don't mean later today, and I don't need any of your flimsy excuses. Fifteen minutes." She disconnected.

He squeezed the phone so tight his hand hurt. He felt the pressure in his head building. His heart pounded. He fought back the urge to hurl his phone against the wall. *Nobody… NOBODY talks to me like that.*

His mind raced. He briefly considered ignoring the phone call. But the situation was… *complicated*, what with Hartman abducted and dead and Stillings' mole deceased as well.

He grabbed his coat and left his office, curtly speaking to the receptionist as he strode by "I've got a meeting in town. I'll be back later this afternoon." He didn't wait for a response.

Twenty minutes later, he poured himself into the chair opposite Stillings, applying every ounce of control he could muster. He forced himself to speak calmly. "So, Miz Stillings, what's so urgent that I have to drop everything for this little visit?" He offered the best smile he could come up with.

She glared at him for a moment before responding in a soft but menacing voice. "I said fifteen minutes—not twenty." She leaned back in her chair. "I'm going to take the gloves off for a moment. Excuse me if I injure your fragile ego. Let's be clear who's calling the shots here. When I tell you to do something, you do it. Now that the formalities are out of the way, I need some information from you."

Corel could feel his temper building and he knew he had to control it, at least for the present. "What is it you need from me?"

"Sue Hartman's disappeared. Do you know anything about that?"

He smirked. "Why would I know anything about the Hartman bitch?"

"Oh, just a wild guess. Your wife has disappeared, and Sue Hartman helped her. Unless I miss the mark, you've got some high-powered talent turning over every rock. One other thing. When I ask you a question, I want an answer... not a question."

"Sorry, can't help you on that one. I don't keep tabs on her and couldn't possibly care less."

"You're lying, but let's leave that for now. My contact inside the DV Network is dead."

No shit. Corel almost laughed. "And?"

She glared at him.

Chapter 35

Uncomfortable with the silence, he added, "What? Do you think I had something to do with it?"

Her words came out cold and shrouded in pure hatred. "I don't think anything. Here's what I know. You knew I had a source inside the network and now she's dead. Just for the record, I'm not a big believer in coincidence. So, here's what's going to happen. I'm going to have my best people investigate it. If I find that you or your thugs had anything at all to do with it, it will present us with a rather unpleasant situation. Either you will compensate me for the loss of an asset, which, I might add, has been a very, very expensive asset or...." Her voice trailed off.

"Or what?"

She relaxed and smiled. "Or your life as you know it will be over."

She's right in front of me. I could jump across the fucking desk and strangle the cunt. He summoned every bit of control he could find. "Okay, I let you make your points." He paused and tapped his index finger on the desk for effect. "First, don't ever speak to me like that again. I'm happy to have discussions and solve problems, but I don't take that shit from anyone."

Before she could respond, he continued, "Second, as for your mole, I have no idea who she is... or was. For all you know, maybe she killed herself. I'm trying to be as respectful as I can, so let's not escalate this. If someone died, the police will investigate—it's what they do. Let them figure it out."

Daggers of ice shot from her eyes. "I don't need the police, and your assurances mean nothing to me. I'll get the answers and you'd better be ready."

Oh, you can bet I'll be ready, bitch. "We're done here." He stormed out of her office, slamming the door behind him.

As he exited the building, he dialed Dylan Strauss' number. Perhaps it was time to widen the search.

"Hello."

Corel spoke as he walked. "I got a name for you. Janet Polasky. She's a minister of some sort... Methodist, I think... over in Bellevue. Give me everything you can find on her."

36

Summer faded quickly, and Janet felt increased urgency to spend time with Abby. The last time she'd seen the girl was on the outing to buy school supplies. It had been a hard day, but ended well, with at least some connection between Roberta Klein and young Abby. It would be nice to do something else before school started back.

"Good afternoon, Miz Klein. This is Janet Polasky. How are you doing?"

"Okay." The voice sounded empty.

"I was wondering if it would be okay if I took Abby out for dinner."

"I suppose that would be okay."

Janet waited for more… for some sign that the grand-mother approved or something. Nothing came. "Okay, then. If it's okay with you, I'll be by around five. I won't keep her out late, promise."

Three hours later Janet and Abby sat across from each other in the upscale burger bistro in Bellevue Center. "These are really good fries. I love the spices they put on them." Janet took a bit of the potato and closed her eyes as she chewed slowly.

Abby stared at the minister as though expecting some profound meaning to come. After a moment, she took a bite of her burger.

What bothered Janet most was that Abby had been thrown back into the school setting with virtually no support. She'd been excused from school for the last couple of months in the previous school year because of her mother's death. Now she'd be forced to face, not only with being behind other students, but also questions from her friends. She'd been isolated, for the most part, all summer. Now she'd have to deal with social overload for the first time since her mother died.

"How does it feel to be in middle school?"

Abby held her burger halfway between the table and her mouth, seemingly transfixed by the question. It was as though she hadn't understood what Janet had asked. After a moment, she responded quietly, "I dunno."

I dunno. It had become the go-to answer to every question Janet asked the young girl. Abby shrugged and set her burger down, her gaze wandering around the restaurant. She had taken only a couple of bites of the sandwich and her fries were untouched.

Janet acted on impulse. She scooted her chair around and embraced Abby. She hugged the girl tightly and kissed her gently on the head. "Abby, I'm your friend. I will always be here for you."

At first Abby felt rigid, but soon Janet felt her relax and lean into the hug. That was when she heard the sobs and felt the girl heaving.

"It will get better, I promise you. God will be with you. He watches over you and comforts you. You don't even have to ask."

Chapter 36

Through the sobs, Abby's voice broke through and chilled Janet to her soul. "It was my fault." Her small arms reached up around Janet's neck.

Janet held the young girl without speaking for a moment as she gathered her thoughts. Then she pulled back a little and spoke with a delicate balance of gentleness and force. "Abby, you need to listen to me. Listen carefully. It was not your fault."

"I didn't do my chores. I didn't do what Dad told me. When he yelled at me, Mom tried to protect me. That's what caused it all. If I had just been good. If I had done what he said, Mom would be alive. It was my fault."

The words tore into Janet's heart. "No, Abby. You have that wrong. What happened was something that neither of us may ever understand, but what he did was not your fault. It was not your mother's fault. He did what he did and nothing you or your mother could have done would've changed that. Please believe me, Abby. I would never lie to you... ever."

"He told me I was bad. He said I was no good... he said that all the time. I'm useless. I'm not good for anything." The sobs came again.

"Abby, you are one of the best friends I have. You are like a light shining in my life. I look forward to being with you. You have the purest, best heart I've ever found. Don't let anyone tell you any different."

Her sobs quietened but still she shuddered.

Janet made a quick decision. "Tell you what, let's get these burgers and fries wrapped up. I'll get us a couple of chocolate chip cookies, and we can take these back to my house. How would you like that?"

Abby didn't respond but, in their embrace, Janet could feel the girl nodding her head.

As they made their way back to the car, Janet's phone

rang. Initially, she thought to just ignore it. Surely whatever it was could wait until the next day. Checking the display, she saw that it was Greg Stottman. "I need to take this call. Is that okay?"

Abby nodded.

"Hey Greg, what's up?"

"I need to talk to you. Can you swing by my place this evening?" The voice sounded tense.

"I'm tied up right now, but maybe we can connect tomorrow."

"It won't take but a minute, I promise."

The insistence bothered Janet. It was not like him to be pushy. "What's this about?"

"I'd rather not talk about it on the phone. If you could drop by, I'd really appreciate it."

Her mind raced. She would have Abby home by eight and could be at Greg's by eight-thirty or nine. On the other hand, his condo was more or less on the way to the parsonage. She wasn't sure, though, how taking Abby with her would work out. "I'm out with Abby Miller, a young girl from my congregation. We can swing by there briefly, if you're okay with that."

A brief pause preceded his response. "Uh… sure, you can bring her. No problem."

37

His appearance struck Janet hard. Weary but determined—that was the look. Greg Stottman had been through a lot to be sure. He had responded enthusiastically at her initial request for funding. He jumped in without hesitation every time she needed him… which was far more than she'd anticipated. On top of all that, he'd been through hell with his niece, Dani. Yet, here he stood, apparently tired but undeterred. Janet's irritation at his insistence on seeing her this night faded.

"Hi Greg. How are you doing?" It was more than a perfunctory question.

"Okay, I guess, pretty good." He sheepishly shuffled his feet as he seemed to grapple for words. "Look, I'm sorry about pushing you to come over." He glanced at Abby, who stood to the side and behind Janet. "I'm trying to refocus on my business. Lately I've been an absent partner," he forced a chuckle, "and I get the sense that Mel isn't going to sit still for it much longer."

Janet nodded and smiled. "I completely understand. So, what's up tonight?"

Greg continued as though he hadn't heard her question. "I've committed to keeping my head in the company during the day and working on all the other stuff at night. Sorry."

She stood in silence, waiting.

At that moment, a realization seemed to overtake him. "I'm sorry. Janet, you know Dani." He gestured toward his niece, who sat silently on the couch, seemingly in a daze.

Janet turned toward the young woman. "It's good to see you, Dani. How are you doing?" The minister turned and put her hand on Abby's shoulder. "This young lady is Abby Miller. She's a member of our congregation. We were just out for burgers and fries." She guided the young girl forward.

Abby looked lost. She shifted her gaze from Janet to Greg to Dani and back again. She seemed at a loss for words.

Greg went down on one knee and offered a hand. "I'm pleased to meet you, Abby."

Abby took his hand, a bewildered look on her face.

He stood and turned to Janet. "Maybe we can talk in the kitchen. Dani can keep Abby company."

A minute later, they stood by the kitchen counter. Greg said, "I haven't talked to you recently, but I'm trying to work some things out with Dani. The big thing, though, is that Billy Robinson is still on the loose. I don't think he'll come back this way, but I'm trying to play it safe. I've got Kaz working on finding a rental unit for her but it's going to take some time. In the meantime, I'd like to move her into the condo that you've been using. It'll only be for a few days... a week at the most."

Her stomach did somersaults. "Uh, I've got a woman placed there now. Remember... I told you about it. We're looking for a place to relocate her, but it could take up to a week."

Greg seemed to consider her words before responding. "Well, okay. It is, you know, a three-bedroom place. Maybe the two of them could share it. I mean, we're trying to keep both of them safe."

"I don't know, Greg. The woman is going through a tough time. I'm not sure that having someone else living there with her would be such a great idea."

"It would only be for a few days. The place is big enough that they could stay out of each other's way. Besides, maybe some company would be nice." Desperation crept into his voice.

Janet fought back the urge to argue. Greg had gone above and beyond anything she'd expected of him. And one thing was certain—the danger to Dani was real. "Tell you what, let me check with the woman and just get her reaction. You may be right. Maybe it'll be fine. Can you give me until tomorrow afternoon?"

* * *

Dani sat slumped on the sofa. The last thing she wanted was company. Everything about her life sucked. The worst part of it was that she was beginning to wonder if maybe some of her problems were of her own making. She wanted to be angry with her uncle. She wanted to lash out at him and all of the people around him, but something the cop had told her stuck. When she was in the hospital, Uncle Greg and all his friends stayed there and stood by her. The man whom she planned to marry and spend her life with shot her and left her for dead. As far as she knew, he hadn't even phoned to check on her. It wasn't supposed to be this way.

The young girl—Abby, they said her name was—stood in the middle of the room. She looked even less happy than Dani felt. "Hi. I'm Dani."

Abby mumbled something unintelligible in response. She didn't move from where she stood.

"You want to sit down?" Dani forced a laugh. "My uncle talks a lot. They might be in there a while."

"Okay." Abby shuffled over to a chair and sat stiffly, the expression on her face never changing. Her eyes looked puffy and red.

"Are you okay? You look like you're upset or something." Even as the words came out, Dani wondered if she was wandering into forbidden territory.

The young girl suddenly seemed as though she noticed Dani… really noticed her. She appeared to think about the question. After a long moment, she responded quietly, her voice bathed in pain. "My dad killed my mom, and it was my fault." Tears gathered in her eyes.

Dani felt as though she was about to pass out. The simple statement took the wind out of her. *What the hell am I supposed to say to that?* The truth was, though, she'd asked the question. She beckoned to Abby. "Come over here, please. Sit with me."

Abby moved mechanically, sliding off the chair and shuffling over to the sofa. She sat, remaining just as stiff as he had been before. Dani put her arms around the young girl. "I'm so sorry." The words were wholly inadequate, but they were the only ones that came.

The young girl shrugged. No doubt, she'd heard those words countless times. From experience, Dani knew that they meant next to nothing in the face of so much pain. "I'm sure it wasn't your fault. People can do really bad things. I know. It's not you, though. Trust me. It's not you."

The irony struck Dani. She had repeatedly defended

Billy and his violence, lashing out at everyone around her. Now here she was trying to convince this young girl that her father was the bad guy.

"How do you know?" Abby's face had taken on a look of curiosity. She stared up into Dani's eyes, her head slightly cocked.

In that instant, Dani made a decision—one that she'd never imagined she could make. She decided to share her pain. "I had a boyfriend. We were going to get married, but he beat me and shot me. He tried to kill me. Then he ran off to let me die. Abby, I know that beyond any doubt at all. It was not my fault. Your father did what he did for reasons only he can tell. Whatever the reason, though, he owns it."

Abby seemed to consider the words. "I'm in middle school now. I don't know what to say to people."

Dani wasn't sure what that meant. "Well, I guess I'd ask what you want to say to people. What do you want them to know?"

"Nothing. I want everybody to leave me alone."

Dani heard herself in those painful words. In her heart she knew that the last thing young Abby needed was to be left alone. For the first time in months, someone or something else seemed more important than her own self-pity. "I understand, I really do. I know exactly how that feels. There's something you need to know. You may not want other people around you, but sometimes they need *you* to be around *them*. That lady in there, Janet, she's a good person, but she's alone too."

"I know. She lives alone."

"I'll bet you that when you're with her and you talk to her, it makes her feel good. I've seen her smile when she's happy. Have you ever seen that?"

Abby nodded. "I did a sleepover. We ate dinner and

watched a movie. It was a good time. Then at church, she smiled at me when she was preaching."

Dani felt a grin break out on her face. "That's what I'm talking about. You have the power to make her happy. You know what? Talking to you tonight has made me kind of happy, too."

The look of curiosity deepened. Abby's head cocked even more. She furrowed her brow as though trying to solve some complex problem.

In that moment, Dani understood that there was a way out of the grief.

38

Janet steeled herself. This was not going to go well. She had agreed to ask Bonnie Corel about sharing the condo with Dani, at least for a few days. It was, however, against her better judgment. She agreed to ask only because Greg Stottman, the sole funding source for her project, had been the one asking.

She rang the bell and then tried the door, which was locked. A few seconds later, the door cracked, and a face appeared out of the darkened room. "Yes?"

"May I come in?"

The woman looked her up and down briefly and then opened the door. She gestured toward the sofa. "Sure, have a seat."

Janet's eyes were drawn to the center of the living room floor. Just a couple of months prior, she'd watched three men die on that spot. She had witnessed the blood spread from their bodies onto the ivory carpet as the pungent coppery odor wafted through the room. The memory took her breath. Her heart raced. Then she forced herself back to the present. "So, is everything going okay?"

"I guess."

"Where's Val today?"

Bonnie eased into the wing-back chair, her hands folded in her lap. Whatever pain or fear she harbored, she hid it well. Her expression remained neutral. "She went to pick up some things at the grocery store. She said she'd be back in about an hour."

Janet shifted her weight on the couch, nervous about the request she was about to make. "She said that you've decided to remain in the area, at least for the time being."

"Yes."

Bonnie Corel's demeanor was unnerving. She displayed no clue as to her state of mind. Janet found it impossible to tell whether the woman was so terrified that she was unable to speak, or whether she was simply being cold and manipulative.

Janet paused before she asked the question that had brought her here. "I have a request. There's a young woman who is in hiding from an abusive boyfriend. This is currently the only location we have in Seattle. Would you mind sharing the condo with her for a few days."

Janet watched disapproval wash over Bonnie's face. Her jaw clenched. Her eyes narrowed. Before she could respond, however, Janet continued, "It's strictly short-term. We're working on other arrangements. It's only until we finalize those."

"Why can't she just stay where she is right now? Why move her twice?" The question came as a cold, callous challenge.

Janet gritted her teeth as she tried to thread the needle. "We have reason to believe she may be in imminent danger. Her partner has already shot her once. After that, he killed two police officers. This isn't something we're taking lightly."

Chapter 38

"Who is she?"

Janet stopped herself. Did she have the right to disclose that information? Did Bonnie Corel who had requested help to remain safe, even have the right to ask the question? In the end, Janet decided it didn't matter. If she refused to disclose the name, Bonnie could just say no. Then the ball would be back in Janet's court. She could override the woman's objection and put Dani there anyway. There were no good solutions.

"Danielle Stottman. She goes by Dani."

Recognition replaced the anger and reticence. Bonnie glanced to the side as though processing the information. "Stottman? Any relation to the tech guy... Greg Stottman?"

The change in the woman took Janet aback. Why would it make any difference who the girl was?

"She's his niece. Greg's her legal guardian."

The look of curiosity and interest morphed into a smile. "This place is large enough to accommodate both of us." She gestured toward the hallway.

Janet felt her stomach roil. She didn't like the sudden change in Bonnie's demeanor, and she didn't like the fact that she might be dragging Greg into yet another complicated web.

39

The Sniper navigated out of his usual dark website. There was one more thing to check. Most of his work—the missions he accomplished—were done out of devotion to duty. That he was supported financially in this effort seemed normal and appropriate. Out of necessity, though, he often relied on more transactional jobs, which provided him with resources that allowed a comfortable life. The nature of these assignments mattered little. It was about the money. Today he sought that kind of work.

His fingers moved deftly across the keyboard as he worked through layers of security, using codes, PINs, and passwords. Finally, he struck paydirt—The Bounty Board.

A list of names and photos appeared on his screen. Beside each, a reference code provided the link to a potential contract. In the final column, he noted a number— either one, two, or three digits. This number was the contract price, in thousands of dollars.

The three-digit targets were high profile, usually political figures such as the President of the United States, a high-profile state governor, or a Hollywood celebrity. The two-digit targets were mid-level government officials or corporate officers… CEOs and the like. Both groups were more than he wanted to take on.

The final category, the single-digit targets, were little more than annoyances to the payer. The targets were nobodies. The contract prices reflected this lack of importance—amounts ranging from a couple of thousand to just over nine thousand. He scanned the list and picked a name. Clicking on the validation icon, he entered his credentials and checked a box agreeing to the terms.

Powering down the computer, he prepared to talk to his cousin, who remained in bed. *This will change soon enough.* He brewed a fresh pot of coffee and put some elk sausage on to fry. These tasks accomplished he wandered out to the porch with his coffee to soak in the fresh air.

Within the hour, Cousin Billy shuffled out the door with a steaming cup of coffee in his hand. "Geez, I slept good. This country air does wonders for a man." He plopped down into a wooden rocker and closed his eyes as he took a sip.

The boy had arrived three days ago. *Time's up, Cuz. Today's the day.* "Anything new on your plan?" The Sniper kept his words to a minimum. He patiently waited for his cousin to respond.

"I can't say's I know, right now." He took another sip, not bothering to even look over. As though uncomfortable with the silence, he continued on, just as the Sniper expected. "I need to get my feet on the ground, you know, get situated." The words, of course, meant nothing.

The Sniper smiled. A warm feeling rushed through his body. This bumbling sack of shit was the most entertaining thing that he'd encountered in years. "There's sausage and biscuits in the kitchen."

Billy turned and grinned. "I'd love some, thanks."

The Sniper sat still, watching the sad excuse for a person.

After a minute or so a light seemed to go on in the kid's head. Apparently he'd expected to be served breakfast. With the realization that no one was going to wait on him, Cousin Billy stood and ambled into the house, returning a few minutes later with a full plate of food and a refill on his coffee.

After another five minutes of watching his cousin shovel the food in, the Sniper finally made his first move. "I did a little research about new identities. I think you may be on to something."

His cousin stuffed half a biscuit in his mouth and swigged some coffee. "That's great." The words escaped through the soggy glob in his mouth. He swallowed the food and swilled some more coffee. "What do I got to do?"

The Sniper leaned back in his chair, cupping his coffee with both hands. "There are several approaches. For a relatively small sum, you can get some false IDs—driver's license, Social Security card, and such. The problem with that is that, while they'll get you by a liquor store employee or a hotel clerk, you wouldn't make it past a traffic stop. If you want to immunity to that kind of thing, you have to go big."

"How big?"

"I know where to get you a new identity—a new Social Security account, a legitimate driver's license, and a birth certificate that checks out. It'll get you by any routine traffic cop and probably see you through a minor run-in with the law. I have to say, though, if you get hauled in by the feds on a major charge—you know, like murdering a cop—they'll make you. The trick is to keep your head down." He watched his cousin wince at the words *murdering a cop.*

Billy nodded. "That's the ticket. That's what I'm after. What'll it set me back?"

"A hundred grand."

Timing was everything. Billy had just taken a large gulp of coffee. When the Sniper's words landed, he sprayed the dark liquid across the porch. "Are you fucking shitting me? A hundred grand? Where the fuck am I supposed to get that kind of cash? That's bullshit, man."

The Sniper did little to conceal the intended sarcasm. "You can always file a formal complaint with the authorities if you think you getting gouged."

Billy looked confused for a moment and then shook his head, apparently missing the sarcasm. "Seriously, I can't go that route unless I take up bank robbery."

"Not gonna work. It'll just increase your already high profile. The minute you hit a bank, the feds are on it. Nope, Cuz, you're going to have to come at this differently."

"Okay, I give up. What do you suggest?"

That was it. He had Billy's complete attention. "You can earn the money. There's work out there if you're willing to do it. It's usually low to moderate risk. Most important, it doesn't involve walking into some bank loaded with security and trying to convince them to give you money."

Billy just stared.

"First things first." The Sniper reached down beside his chair and picked up two Idaho license plates, tossing them to his cousin. "Ditch the Washington plates and put these on. Don't get over-confident. These won't even get you past a traffic stop. If you keep out of trouble and obey the traffic laws, though, they'll be enough to keep you from getting noticed."

His cousin picked up the plates and tapped them together. "Okay. I can do that. Next?"

On a roll, the Sniper moved to the next step. "I got a job for you. I need you to go down to Boise tomorrow morning and pick up something for me. I'll give you the information you need. Easy-breezy. Drive down, pick it up, drive back, and deliver it to me."

"What am I picking up?"

"Cash, Cuz, cash. Fifteen grand. Your commission is a third—five."

Billy looked crestfallen. "Five thousand? At that rate, it'll take me forever."

"Not forever. Just a little while. At five a pop, it'll take twenty jobs. Once you prove yourself, we might find something that pays a little more."

The boy seemed to struggle getting his mind around the concept. Finally, he nodded. "Okay, then. What's after that?"

"One step at a time, Cuz. Let's stay focused on this first one for now. You bring me back the package and you'll get paid. After that, we can talk about the next job."

Billy took another bite of sausage and drink of coffee.

The Sniper continued, "I have to drive north to Coeur d'Alene in the morning. I'll leave at first light. Still, you'll probably be back before I return. Just bring back the satchel. Don't break the seal. We'll settle up when I get back."

He watched as the wheels in Billy's head appeared to turn. The Sniper knew exactly what his cousin was thinking. *Fifteen Grand—I could take that and run.* "Thing is, Cuz, you need to know that doing this kind of work is all about loyalty. I need to be able to trust you and you need to trust me. Otherwise, you know, things can go sideways. People get hurt. He stared into Billy's eyes and drew his mouth into a tight line. It was the Sniper's way of saying *don't even think about it.*

In any event, he had no intention of turning Billy loose on this mission without supervision. It would just be *hidden supervision.* If his beloved cousin so much as blinked in the wrong direction, he would be quickly on his way to hell.

40

Greg peered into the living room from the kitchen. He'd finished putting the dinner leftovers away and stacking the dishwasher. Janet had phoned him earlier in the day to let him know that it was okay for Dani to stay at the condo for a few days.

This left him with but two tasks. First, he had to break the news to his niece. Up until this point, she knew that looking for another place was her path. This arrangement, though, made it all real.

The second task would come around soon enough. He needed to connect with Kaz to make it happen. There shouldn't be a reason for problems with this one. Still, something teased at the edges of his mind telling him that his security expert might push back. He brushed that thought away. *I'll deal with it when the time comes.*

He eased quietly into the living room where his niece stared blankly out the window. "Hey, Dani. You seem quiet tonight. Is everything okay?"

Sitting in the overstuffed chair, she turned to face him with a totally flat affect. "I'm okay."

He slid onto the couch, facing her. "I know that you and Kaz are working on finding a place for you. I managed to get a temporary place, you know, to make sure you're completely safe while you look for something longer-term." He avoided using the term *more permanent*. This was not permanent. As soon as the thing with Billy Robinson was settled, she could move back in with him, and things would be back to normal.

The question came out of the blue. "That little girl that was here last night with Janet, what do you know about her?'

He sanitized the description. "Not much. Her mother died and she's living with her grandmother."

Dani slouched down in the chair, wringing her hands in her lap. "She said that her dad killed her mom. Did you know that?"

Greg felt a tinge of guilt at not being more forthcoming. He was trying to build up trust with her. Keeping things from her wasn't going to help. "Janet was there when it happened."

At this point, the conversation went in an unexpected direction. "The girl, Abby, she told me it was her fault." Suddenly, Dani's eyes, though teary, exuded understanding. "How does a kid that age deal with that kind of thought?"

Greg hadn't heard about this part. "What do you mean *her fault?*"

"She didn't say, and I didn't know how to ask. That can't be true. There's no way that a kid can be responsible for what some adult does."

"I'm not sure how a child that age even begins to deal with what happened. Of course it wasn't her fault. That's not the issue, though. The issue is that she *thinks* it is. How that gets changed... I don't have a clue."

"Janet will help her, won't she?" Dani's eyes were wide with hope.

"If there's anyone who can do it, Janet's the one. I honestly don't know how that works though. As I understand it, Abby lives with her grandmother. I have no idea what that relationship is like. Whatever it is that needs to happen, it won't happen overnight."

"Was it my fault about Billy?"

Greg steeled himself. He hadn't expected that question, but it demanded an answer, and he understood that his answer would matter. "The truth, as best I can figure, is that Billy has a temper that he can't control. After what happened with you, he killed two cops. It wasn't their fault either. For whatever reason, he is simply driven by the need to dominate and can't control that compulsion. I'm sorry, Dani, but you just happened to get in his way."

"It seemed like he loved me. I loved him back. I did what he asked. I did everything." Her tears flowed.

Greg slid off the couch, eased over, and sat beside her. He embraced his niece and hugged tightly. With her face buried on his chest, he stroked her head and spoke quietly. "You did everything you could to make it work. You loved him, and that's what makes this so hard. I can't get inside his head, so I'm not able to say whether he did or didn't love you. Whatever the case, people don't show their love with violence."

"Abby's dad did the same thing."

"Yes, he did. There are other men who do it as well. Good people—people like Janet—are fighting back... trying to stop it. Please remember, Dani. Not all men are like that. You'll meet someone, a man who will love you and know how to treat you. You'll see."

He offered a shallow laugh. "Please don't say that I've

never been in love, so I don't know. I'm painfully aware of that fact."

Dani pulled gently away, a soft smile on her face. "Thank you, Uncle Greg. Thank you for everything. I acted like a spoiled brat, but you always believed in me."

He lowered his gaze, unsure where to go with the conversation.

Dani leaned back in the chair. "Now, tell me about this temporary place."

41

The sidewalk stretched out in front of Janet. Her stride lengthened as she sought the rhythm that would allow the journey into her thoughts. The day held promise. The September morning had dawned clear and seasonably cool. It was still more than two weeks until the autumnal equinox. There was more summer to come. For the moment, though, the air was deliciously cool.

She found that magic spot. Her breathing settled into a comfortable pattern. She was ready. *What was Bonnie Corel's reaction all about?* At first, the woman had seemed adamantly opposed to anyone else staying at the condo, even for a few days. All of that appeared to change when she heard the name Stottman. Bonnie didn't know Dani. There was no doubt, though, that she was familiar with Greg. Her question was spot on. *"Stottman? Any relation to the tech guy… Greg Stottman?"* Why would Dani being Greg's niece change her mind?

Something Maddie had told Janet early in the summer came back. Bonnie Corel was not a weak woman. *If that's true, why did she live with a guy who beat her?* How does a woman transform from a helpless victim into a strong, assertive person overnight?

The sidewalk beside Bel-Road slipped by. The green street sign that she knew signaled her turning spot onto 132nd came into view just ahead. Janet approached the halfway point in her morning run.

She forced herself back to the original question. Why had Greg Stottman's involvement moved her? *It's not the money. She's no stranger to wealth. She inherited her own from family.* Could it be power? He was, after all, the CEO and co-owner of one of the largest corporations in the country. While he never displayed it for Janet, she was certain that he could wield influence with the best of them. Could that be it—Bonnie wanted to associate with power?

It seemed a monumental leap from helpless victim to power player. Maddie had said it, though. Bonnie Corel came from money and power. She was used to running in the most exclusive circles. Cultivating a relationship with Greg certainly couldn't hurt her prospects. *No, that's not it. At the moment, she's just trying to stay safe.* It seemed unlikely that, in her current situation, the woman was plotting power moves.

Could it be a romantic interest? No. Absolutely not. Bonnie Corel was close to fifty and Greg was not yet out of his thirties. He was almost young enough to be her son. *He's too young for her.*

Janet reminded herself that the woman was still married. She might even harbor plans to reconcile with her senator husband if they could straighten things out. There's no way that she'd get involved with another man this quickly.

She turned the corner onto 132nd. A light breeze came

from behind and helped move her along. Even if Bonnie wanted to pursue Greg, it was none of Janet's business. *He's a big boy. He can do whatever he wants.* Besides, if he got entangled with Bonnie, it would mean that Janet wouldn't have to worry about his intentions regarding her.

I'm not worrying. No. This is business. He's funding my project. I'm giving him status reports.

It was more than that and she knew it. He talked to her about personal things, like Dani. He worried about Janet's safety.

She picked up the pace. She needed to pound the thoughts of Greg from her mind. The soles of her running shoes slapped the concrete sidewalk. She pushed faster. Her breath came harder. More speed. *I've got a job to do. I can't get caught up in this kind of thing. Enough of this.*

She forced her mind onto a different subject. The board had approved the operating budget back in June. She needed to check with Margaret to make sure that the accounting software was set up to generate the current year's financials. This year she was going to do a better job of comparing budgeted revenue to actuals in real time.

That meant she needed to visit congregation members. Maybe they could plan some more celebratory activities. *Yes. We need to add a harvest celebration for late September.* As far as she knew, there weren't any hardcore farmers in the congregation. Still, it was a cultural thing.

The parking lot needs to be re-striped. I need to arrange to have the roof inspected. I don't want to get into winter and have to deal with a bunch of moss on the shingles.

She could see the Russian Jewish Cultural Center ahead. She would make the turn towards home. *Besides, Greg would never be interested in her.*

Thirty minutes later she stood on the stoop of the

parsonage, catching her breath and stretching. As she punched the numbers into the security lock, her cellphone buzzed. She checked the display and connected. "Hi, Dee. You're at it early this morning."

"Have you heard from Sue lately?"

42

Janet struggled to get her mind around everything. She'd tried Sue's cellphone—not in service. She phoned the network—Sue had not been to work in the past few days. "No," they had said, "she is not on leave." She apparently hadn't said anything to anyone.

Janet stared at Dee, waiting for something… anything.

"For now, it's a new missing person case. They'll check the usual—family members, financial accounts, phone records, and such." Dee sat in the straight-backed chair in Janet's office. Her voice remained calm but the look on her face screamed worry.

"What next?"

"The police will do what they can. If they don't find her, there's not much else to be done. They'll interview people out at the shelter. They're the ones who reported her missing. Maybe one of the employees or clients saw or heard something. Other than that, I honestly don't know."

"It's not like Sue to cut off contact. Her phone's out of service. I tell you, Dee, this isn't good."

Dee grimaced. "Tell me about it."

Another thought slammed Janet. "She knows about my project, including who my clients are so far. This could…." She couldn't bring herself to even think about consequences.

"Well, yeah. The problem is, there's more."

Janet stared.

"An admin assistant at the network turned up dead in her apartment yesterday. The guys down in the bullpen are talking suicide but we'll have to wait and see what the ME says."

"That's an awfully big coincidence." The knot in Janet's stomach tightened.

"It could be nothing, but, yeah, it does seem odd." Dee shifted in her seat and leaned forward toward Janet. My gut tells me the two cases are related. The problem is that, at least for the moment, they're being treated as separate incidents."

Janet searched her memory. Had she told Sue about the condo? No, in fact, she hadn't spoken to her since they'd moved Bonnie. "What are you going to do?"

Dee's laugh was half-hearted. "Me? Do? What would you like me to do? Both are Seattle cases and I'm not privy to what goes on there. I can ask around my shop and maybe talk to some friends over in Seattle. At best, though, I'm only going to learn as much as they know. If I try to freelance on this, the captain will have my ass. I suppose I'll do the same thing that you're going to do—keep trying Sue's number and wait."

A thought, not totally welcome, popped into Janet's head. "Do you think Leah Bowman might know something? She seems to have contacts just about everywhere." Leah was the woman that Janet had reluctantly helped some months prior… and the one who had killed her husband in the very same condo where Bonnie was staying and had taken over his criminal enterprise in the area.

Dee rubbed her chin as she considered the question. "I'm not sure how she would. As far as I know, there's no connection."

"Is it possible that Leah could be behind Sue's disappearance? I mean, Sue refused to help when Leah's friend needed it. Maybe it was revenge."

"Doubtful. Things don't work that way in her world. Revenge is reserved for competitors and traitors. Sue and the network were both distractions... nothing more."

Janet closed her eyes and tried to reorder everything she knew. Nothing made sense. Even worse, there seemed be to nothing she could do.

Dee switched gears and continued, "There're some other things you need to know. Several DV workers have been killed over the last two months—one out in Spokane and the other up in Bellingham."

Will it never end? Janet fought through the anger and grief. "Do they know who did it—husband or partner? Have they caught them yet?"

"No idea who did it. Partner would normally be a good guess, but it doesn't fit. Both women were killed with a high-powered rifle from a distance. According to some contacts in both departments, they've determined that it was the same rifle. Someone is hunting DV workers."

Terror washed over Janet. "Why? I mean, I get that a husband might go out and get revenge." She had watched Todd Miller make sure that Hanna would not have a life without him. Janet understood that some men were capable of cold-blooded murder. But hunting?

Dee continued, "There're a lot of bat-shit crazy guys out there. It could be revenge on a grander scale, like a man whose wife left him some time ago and he wants to get even with the world. On the other hand, it could be some kind of warrior who's fighting what to him is a holy war."

The idea was revolting to Janet. "A holy war? How is hunting down defenseless women and killing them holy?"

"Like I said, bat-shit crazy. Look, Janet, I'm telling you because you're in that group now. You're a DV worker."

Janet took a deep breath and tried to put things in perspective. She was, after all, a very small player. In fact, few people even knew anything about what she was doing. "Don't worry, I'll be careful."

Dee shot back, "There is no *careful* in this. Whoever is behind this is a hunter, a stalker. He strikes from a distance. The women he killed, they likely never saw him. They never heard the gunshot that killed them. One minute they were going about their lives and the next they were dead."

"You said 'he.' What makes you think it's a man?"

Dee slapped her knee and laughed heartily. "Really, Janet? You think there's some batshit crazy woman out there killing other women?" Her face turned serious. "No. The reality is that in the vast, overwhelming majority of these kinds of killings, it's a man. That's just the way it is."

Janet asked, "Okay, well, do you have any suggestions?"

Dee lowered her head. "Nothing you don't already know. Keep the information about your project close. Stay at arm's length from things. Don't leave any trails that someone could follow back."

"Do you think this is connected to Sue's disappearance or that admin assistant?"

Dee shook her head. "Doubtful. We don't know for sure what happened to Sue, but whatever it was most likely happened up close and personal. As for the admin assistant. If it was murder, it also had to be done from close range. Those don't fit what the hunter is doing. From what little I know, he's meticulous. Very little to go on other than the rifle and the fact that his victims are DV workers."

Janet asked, "Any idea why these two? How does he decide who to stalk?"

"Nobody knows how he's selecting his victims. It seems random. Since the two women were from different cities, the state is handling it. The thing is, though, that there may be other victims in other states. Right now, we only know what's happening in Washington. It wouldn't surprise me if the State investigators go back through some cold cases and find more."

Dee paused for a moment. When she spoke again, her voice had changed. Rather than being bathed in worry or anger, she sounded more pre-occupied. "One other thing. Do you remember that woman who was killed along with her kids up in Bellingham this past summer—Helen Cook?"

"Sure. Last I heard they were looking at the husband. If I recall, though, he had a strong alibi. I'm not sure where it went from there."

The detective continued, "Yeah, Peter Cook was his name and he was never charged. They found him dead in his driveway this morning. Had a single bullet to the back of his head. The word I got is that it looked like some kind of assassination."

Janet uttered a single word, immediately regretting it. "Karma."

Dee shrugged. "I guess." Then her voice changed again, this time to sound like someone who was asking a hard question but trying to sound casual. "I understand that Val's going to be staying local for a little while."

"I'm not sure how it's going to play out. It depends a lot on how things with our current client work. Why?"

The detective casually waved a hand, as though

washing away the question. "No reason, really. I don't know, it just seems unusual, you know, with what you're trying to do for clients."

Janet tried to navigate the tricky ground. "I'm trying to make sure that we keep the client at the center of our attention. That includes considering their preferences. I suppose that they'll figure things out soon. After that, who knows?" One thing was certain. Dee was far more interested than she was trying to let on.

Janet probed, "Have you talked to Val in the last few days?"

"I try not to contact her when I know she's working on something." It was a non-answer.

"And?" Janet arched an eyebrow.

"I might have checked in with her over the last few days." For whatever reason, it seemed like a struggle for Dee to say that.

There was something that Dee wasn't saying—something that she was holding back. "Dee, is there a problem with Val? Are you having second thoughts about recommending her?"

"No, nothing like that at all. If I were in the position these women are in, there's no one I'd rather have than Val. She's working out for you, right? You're happy with her performance?"

"No complaints." Janet almost poked further but decided against it. Dee was holding onto something but was unwilling to share it. *Faith. She'll tell me when she's ready.* That little nugget of wisdom felt particularly unsatisfying.

"You know, Janet, while your project might come into the public eye at some point, Val is more likely to be a target than you. She's hands on. You need to think about protecting her."

"I asked you about that a few minutes ago. You said

there wasn't much I could do. How am I supposed to protect Val?"

Suddenly, Dee gave the appearance of someone bathed in pain and fear. "I don't know, Janet. But I'm afraid for her."

43

The Sniper checked his watch. *Sunrise in an hour.* In the low light of dawn, he wound his way on the path back to his storage cache. Five minutes later, he emerged carrying his Remington 700 sniper rifle. He hoped he wouldn't need it this particular day but, one never knew.

He had made sure that Cousin Billy had all he needed —the address, the access code to the storage facility, the combination to the unit, and the codes needed to get into the specific safe. All the kid had to do was follow directions. Yet the Sniper didn't have much confidence.

Billy wouldn't likely greet the morning until after 9:00. *Lazy fuck.* The Sniper loaded up his truck and pulled out of the long dirt driveway onto Idaho Highway 55. Instead of turning north toward Coeur d'Alene as he had told Billy he would, he headed south toward Boise. If his long-lost cousin so much as looked like he wanted to bolt with the cash, it would not end well for the kid.

An hour and a half later he pulled into McDonald's and ordered his standard breakfast—two Egg McMuffins, hashbrowns, and a large coffee. He'd have plenty of time to find a discreet location to watch, and he could take his time eating breakfast while he waited.

It took only fifteen minutes to find the right spot. He parked on a low hill overlooking the storage facility with a clear view of the specific unit's door. Billy would have to park right there. If his cousin deviated from the instructions, the Sniper would have to make a decision—take him out right on the spot or follow him and take a shot of opportunity outside the city. *I'll deal with it when the time comes.*

No surprise. Cousin Billy didn't show up until just after eleven. *Probably pissed that I didn't leave him a full breakfast.* The kid pulled up in the SUV. At least he'd remembered to replace the Washington plates with the Idaho ones.

With the storage unit open, The Sniper had a clear view as Billy went about the tasks. He'd seen lots of inept people in his life, but watching the kid try to access units and open locks seemed to put him into a class of his own. Finally, he managed to get into the right safe. *How the hell did this idiot the drop on two cops?*

Through his binoculars, the Sniper watched as Billy removed the satchel and stood, staring at it as though hypnotized by what he knew was inside. Would he break the rules and open the satchel. *Lot of money there, Cuz. What's it gonna be?*

After what seemed like an eternity, Billy closed and reset the safe as directed, grabbed the unopened leather satchel, and left the unit. By all appearances, he was going to actually do what he'd been told. He secured the unit and drove carefully through the storage facility, exiting onto the main road as though nothing were amiss.

Color me surprised, Cuz. I guess you might have some promise after all. The Sniper laughed as he stuffed his binoculars in the case, made sure his rifle was stored in the secret compartment, and cranked up the engine.

Billy navigated to Highway 55 and turned north, remaining well under the speed limit. He used his turn signals and allowed plenty of space between his SUV and the car in front of him. *You're a very careful driver. You get a gold star.* The Sniper followed several cars behind until he was confident that Billy was headed for home, then he dropped back a couple of miles.

After crossing the North Fork Payette River outside of Cascade, the Sniper detoured over to the lake. He grabbed a coffee and muffin from one of the lakeside vendors and killed an hour before getting back on the road. During that time, he confronted the reality that he'd bet fifteen thousand dollars on this miserable excuse for a criminal. If it went south, it would be a bitter pill to swallow. On the other hand, he'd made the decision freely. If it worked out with his cousin, it would allow him to keep up with his missions while taking on some additional freelance work. The extra money would make a difference.

Thirty minutes after leaving the picnic area by the lake, he pulled off the main road onto his dirt drive. Despite his efforts to remain dispassionate and detached, his heart pounded as he rounded the final twist in the drive. He pulled to a stop and stared for a moment at the old SUV. Only then did he realize that he'd been holding his breath. He exhaled, shook his head, and laughed at himself.

Inside, the satchel sat unopened on the kitchen table. Billy was at the counter making a peanut butter and jelly sandwich. The Sniper quipped, "I see you made it back in one piece. Any problems?"

His cousin took a huge bite of the sandwich and shook his head. With a full mouth, he uttered, "Nope."

The Sniper smiled and nodded as he sat down at the

table. "Okay then. Let's see what Santa brought us." He pulled out his folding knife and broke the wire seal on the satchel. Opening the top, he poured out the bundles of bills—twelve bundles of fifty-dollar bills, twenty-five bills per bundle. "Fifteen grand, as promised."

He took four bundles and tossed them across the table to his cousin. "Your share—five thousand. You're on your way." The Sniper internally cringed at the idea of giving the kid a third of everything he'd gotten in this payment. Still, in the long run, it could pay handsome dividends.

Billy picked up one of the packets and turned it around in front of his face, examining it from all angles as though he'd never seen money before. "Shit. It's gonna take me forever at this rate."

The Sniper retorted, "Success comes with patience. There will be other jobs. Once you prove that you can take care of yourself, the amount could increase. Patience, Cousin, patience. You'll get there."

"I thought that's what today was supposed to show— that I can take care of myself." Billy whined.

"No. Today proved that you can follow instructions. It also was a good step in convincing me that I can trust you." The Sniper set the money aside and leaned into the table. "Here's the problem, Cuz. You got this demon in you. It's called temper. From what little I know, you don't control it. It controls you. That's gotta change. You shot your girlfriend because that fucking temper told you to. If you didn't like her, why not just dump her? Instead, you gave control to your temper and you shot her."

Billy snarled back, "You don't know anything. You weren't there, and unless I'm wrong, you're on the wrong side of the law just like I am." He gestured toward the pile of money.

"You may not be wrong about that, but I'm not the

issue. You are. Look, I don't give a rat's ass about the girl. I don't care about dead cops, but here's some hard truth about killing. If you want to live a long life, you need to learn that killing is something you do with deliberation and thought. If you can avoid killing and accomplish what you need to, all the better. If you have to do somebody, you need to be in control. Don't let your temper take over." The Sniper stabbed the tabletop with his index finger.

"That, Cuz, is what you have to fix. Until I'm satisfied that you have that monster under control, you're stuck with simple, low-risk jobs that pay shit."

Billy fumed. The Sniper could see it in his eyes. He could see the color rising in the kid's face. He turned up the heat. "Now that we have that out of the way, let's move along, shall we? We have work to do. That means that you're not gonna lay around in bed until mid-morning. You're gonna be up at six and doing chores. We fix meals, clean the cabin, and take care of any other details that come up."

The Sniper twisted harder. "This starts today. So, in the spirit of our new arrangement, you're making dinner —stew. There's venison in the fridge along with celery and carrots. There's some onions and potatoes in the cabinet over there." He gestured across the kitchen. "You need to get it started right away. That meat's tough—has to simmer for about three hours."

The Sniper scooped up the remaining ten thousand dollars and stuffed it into the satchel. "Everything you'll need's in the kitchen."

"I got no idea how to make no stew." Billy glared.

The Sniper broke out in laughter. "Well, then, today's your lucky day. You get to learn something new. They got this thing called the Internet."

44

Val didn't like the situation. "I find it hard to believe you agreed to this." Bonnie Corel had not seemed the type that would welcome a housemate.

"Why? Your boss asked me. Do you disagree with her?" Bonnie strolled across the living room and slid into an easy chair with her cup of tea.

Val shot back, "She's my boss, but I speak my mind. So far, she doesn't seem to mind. Does it bother you?"

Bonnie gestured with her hand as though discarding the argument. "Not at all. I couldn't care less about your relationship with Reverend Polasky. Based on what she told me, it doesn't seem like it would compromise my safety. So why not be accommodating?" She offered a smile that came off as insincere.

"Okay. You're happy; I'm happy." Val's phone pinged indicating a text message. *They're leaving now. Should be there in fifteen minutes.*

The doorbell chimed right on schedule fifteen minutes later. "That would be our guests." Val checked through the side window—a young woman and a man who looked to be in his late thirties. She opened the door. "Yes? Can I help you?"

The man spoke. "I'm Kazarian. This is Dani."

Val stepped back and opened the door wider, gesturing them inside. "Come in." She nodded toward the senator's wife. "This is Bonnie." Turning back toward the two visitors, she said "Dani and Kazarian."

Bonnie was all smiles. Up from the chair, she glided across the room and took Dani's hand in both of hers. "I'm pleased to meet you."

The greeting was so sweet and sappy that Val almost expected the woman to hug Dani.

Instead, Bonnie turned to Kazarian and nodded curtly. "Mister Kazarian."

Val moved closer to the man and spoke quietly. "Why don't you and I speak in the other room… let these two get acquainted?"

They migrated to the kitchen where Val sat in one of the barstools at a center island. "Have a seat. I can get us some coffee if you like."

Kazarian remained standing. "I'm fine."

"Okay, then. I'm not sure how you figure in all this, but I assume that I can trust you. Tell me, does this seem like a good idea to you, I mean, having these two here together?"

"It doesn't strike me as a particularly bad idea. I don't know anything about your client, but Dani is avoiding a guy who doesn't seem that bright. I doubt that he has the wherewithal to find her here. Besides, it's only for a few days, as I understand. Either your client or Dani will probably move on within the week."

"I have no idea when Bonnie will leave. As for Dani, I understand that she's the niece of the guy who's footing the bill for all this. I guess that makes her special, but my obligation is to my client. I guess what I'm trying to get at is the extent to which you expect me to take responsibility for her safety."

"Like I said, the guy that's a danger to her is not that well connected. On top of that, he killed a couple of cops, so law enforcement all over the state is looking for him. It's unlikely he would come for her and, if he did, I doubt that he could find her. That means that the biggest danger to her would come from whoever is chasing your client. Since you're charged with that particular problem, I don't see how having Dani here presents a problem.

Val smirked. "You're one arrogant son-of-a-bitch, I'll give you that." He came across as flippant and condescending.

"I assure you, Miz Gomez, any arrogance you perceive is not intended. I'm just trying to make sure all the bases are covered. This arrangement was not my idea, but I have no objections to it. One other thing—once the guy who's chasing Dani is caught... and he will be... this entire situation will resolve itself."

Other than a vague sense of discomfort, Val could think of no other objections. "Fair enough, then. This guy who's after her, does he have a name?"

"The guy *who might be after her* is Billy Robinson. He's been all over the news for the last few weeks. So far, no one's seen a trace of him. My guess is that he's on the run and finding Dani is the last thing he's interested in. This arrangement, though, should provide even more insurance."

* * *

Bonnie Corel gestured toward the couch. "Have a seat. You'll have plenty of time to put your things away and get settled later on." She poured herself back into the chair.

Dani shuffled over and sat on the edge of the couch, looking horribly out of place.

"I'm Bonnie Corel, by the way. Val doesn't like to deal in last names, but I figure if we're going to be roommates, we might as well get to know each other."

Dani spoke in a quiet and halting voice. "Dani Stottman."

Bonnie considered the answer for a moment. There would be time later to talk about her uncle later. "Are you in school or…?" She let the question drift off.

"I was. I may go back."

"Oh? Where were you going?"

"UW."

"Great school." Bonnie beamed. Her family had donated handsomely to the University of Washington, mostly to the Foster School of Business. "What were you studying?"

"Liberal Arts major." Dani's voice was empty, devoid of interest or emotion.

The time wasn't right. The girl needed her space. Besides, it would be easier to converse once Val and the Kazarian guy had gone.

"I get it. Tough times right now. Don't worry, Dani. We're here for each other."

45

The familiar comforted her. Janet stood at the curio in Maddie's small home and immersed herself in the black and white and sepia photos. Mostly stern faces stared back at her. She liked the occasional picture of Maddie as a child, all smiles—a ray of sunshine piercing through dark storm clouds.

"I can't get over how happy you looked, Maddie… at least compared to everyone around you."

The old woman shuffled over and stood beside Janet. "Don't let these old artifacts fool you, Dearie. My family was always happy." She picked up one of the smaller framed pieces. "I think that there was something about photographs that carried over from the old country. One never smiled. The best representation was always the dourest. No need to tempt fate." She laughed as she set the framed picture back on the shelf.

As she watched Maddie, Janet was struck by the fact that the shelves were all dusted and polished. The faint smell of lemon oil drifted up from the surface. "Why were you different? Why did you smile so much?"

Chapter 45

The old woman burst out laughing. "Why, because God told me to laugh. I couldn't help but smile. I felt safe and happy with my family. Also, I had only a small taste of Russia and the journey across Europe. What little I remembered stuck with me. I was grateful to be alive in America."

The two women took their customary seats—Janet in the Jacobean patterned wing-back chair and Maddie on the sofa. The old woman reached for a tea biscuit. "And how is my favorite minister this morning?"

"Pretty good." Janet paused, knowing full well what was bothering her. "Well, there is something I wanted to ask you about."

"Ask away." Maddie took a bite of the sugary treat and closed her eyes. "Mmmm."

"Do you remember the young girl I told you about, Abby Miller?"

"Yes, of course. She's the one who lost her mother. You took her school shopping and bought that backpack."

"We were talking the other day and she said something. I responded but I can't help feeling that I didn't get it right. Out of the blue, she told me that it was her fault that her father killed her mother. I tried to explain that it wasn't the case. She seemed to let it go, but I'm sure that my answer didn't take."

Maddie set the biscuit down on a napkin. "What else could you have said that would have made a difference?"

"I don't know. That's why I'm asking you. Have you ever had to deal with that kind of thing?"

The old woman cocked her head and arched her eyebrows. "Yes, I have, and I said pretty much what you did. Perhaps I spent more time on it, but it was the same sentiment. What else could one say?"

The response left Janet unconvinced. "There has to be more."

Maddie cleared her throat and took a sip of tea. "Tell me, Dearie, what is a young girl that age supposed to think? The only thing she really knows about the world she understands through her own perceptions. At her age, all those perceptions include her. In fact, she is the center of her own world. If things go horribly wrong, how could she not be the cause?"

Janet grew more frustrated. "That's wrong. It wasn't her fault. Abby just happened to have the bad luck of having a father who went down that path. She didn't push him down it."

"No, she didn't, at least not from any objective point of view. It'll take some time and no small amount of love and care for her to understand this."

Janet picked at the fabric on the arms of the chair as she turned the issue over in her mind. "What does she do until that happens?"

"She gets up, eats breakfast, goes to school, and, maybe with some love and gentle prodding, prays. You, on the other hand, will need to take a more active role. First, never miss an opportunity to tell her how much she is loved. Tell her about God's love. Keep her in the moment. Sometimes that comes with conversation and tenderness. Other times it will happen over an ice cream sundae. Either way, from what you tell me, much of it will fall to you, at least until her grandmother gets better."

Maddie had told Janet nothing that she didn't already know. "Thanks. I'll try. Now, tell me, how are things with you and your children? You haven't said anything about them the last few times I've been here."

"Nothing much changes," the woman chuckled, "except that I keep getting older. We need to find a way to stop that, you know." She grew more serious. "They're still talking about assisted living and I'm still telling them no. Not sure what else there is to say."

Janet thought back to the curio shelves, which were dusted and polished. "Things here seem good. Are you getting some help in cleaning and such?"

"Help? Sure. My vacuum cleaner helps me. The furniture polish does a wonderful job on the wood. Yes, Dearie, I have all the help I need."

Janet switched gears. "Maddie, you said you know Bonnie Corel."

"I know *of* her. Was never acquainted with the woman, though. She and her family were high society. Everyone knew about them. Nobody in our little circle actually knew them, though."

"You said that you thought she was strong, if I recall correctly. It's funny, because she asked me for help in getting away from her husband. Once she was out, though, she seemed to take on a very confident, strong persona— not at all what I would have expected."

Maddie took another bite of biscuit and chewed thoughtfully for a moment. "I'm afraid that I am no expert on family violence. On those few occasions I was called to counsel women who suffered such trauma, they ultimately received services from professionals in the field. So, please, Dearie, take what I say with a grain of salt."

She paused, shifted her body subtly on the sofa, and continued, "From what I understand, women in these situations often pour everything they have into trying to salvage the relationship. They go day-to-day thinking that if they can just keep from doing something that sets their husband off, everything will be fine. At the same time, the husband grows increasingly violent, regardless of what the wife does. It seems a repeating, escalating` loop. My guess is that, during that process, the woman comes to feel increasingly helpless. Some break free, many don't."

Janet considered the assessment. "That sounds about right to me."

"Now we have Bonnie. She comes into what I would call a *power marriage*. The rich, privileged girl marries a strong, ambitious man destined for great things. Together they move forward, he ultimately becoming a powerful United States senator. She, of course, is by his side as a strong, supportive partner. It appears a charmed life."

Maddie paused for a moment, as though reflecting on the situation. "Suppose the man, Senator Corel, is not anxious to share power. He wants no part of a partnership. Rather, he wants people to bend to his will. He craves power and attention. The more he isolates Bonnie from that power, the more she tries to placate him. So it goes."

Janet wondered aloud, "I wonder when the beatings started?"

The old woman shook her head. "I doubt that the dark road started with beatings. It started with words. I would bet that he berated her, belittled her both in private and occasionally around others. He sought to beat her down. Ultimately, though, it wasn't enough. He obviously wanted the physical domination. Perhaps he wanted even to completely destroy her."

"All that rings true, but why would she suddenly become strong and assertive in such a short time after she left?"

"Who among us knows? Perhaps when she walked out the door, she broke free of the spell that she'd been under. Do you know, right off hand, whether she was able to access any of her own money before she left?" Maddie narrowed her eyes.

Janet replied, "I can't say for sure, but she reportedly

said she had access to plenty of money. I assume that she arranged that before she left."

Maddie laughed. "Then maybe our Bonnie wasn't quite as helpless as her husband imagined. Maybe she had laid out some possibilities. It would take quite an effort to keep up the effort with the senator, all the while plotting to leave. As I stated, she never struck me as a weak woman."

Something else bothered Janet, something she was reluctant to even admit to herself. That was the very reason she needed to confide in Maddie. "There is one other thing that bothers me." She described the scene in which Bonnie Corel seemed steadfastly opposed to sharing the condo... until she found out that the other woman was Greg Stottman's niece.

Maddie nodded. "Yes. Well, Bonnie would be drawn to power, and to hear you tell it, this Greg fellow has plenty of that. As to what that might look like, I don't know. It could be romantic or maybe nothing more than just wanting to associate with power. Either way, it doesn't hurt anything."

For some reason, it *did* hurt Janet, although she couldn't really understand why.

46

Senator Corel barricaded himself in his office and fumed. He teetered on the edge, wanting desperately to beat the living shit out of anything that moved. He wanted to start with his bitch of a wife, then the cunt lawyer Stillings, and finally that weasel, Dylan Strauss, who had become far too full of himself. The only thing holding the senator's temper in check was the certainty that he would be the instrument that would usher these worthless individuals into whatever afterlife existed.

He paced back and forth. Callers were being told that he was in a meeting. He had informed the staff that he needed to review some material and didn't want to be interrupted. Now he waited. So far, Strauss had produced the grand total of nothing. In addition, his incompetent help had eliminated the one person who might have held the key to ending this bullshit.

Even more outrageous than the lack of control was the episode with Stillings. He muttered under his breath, "I should have just broken the bitch's neck right there in her office." He could imagine strangling her and watching with glee as the light of life faded from her eyes. It was almost enough to give him a hard-on.

He picked up his cellphone. Surely Strauss had found out something—if not about his wife, then some information on that preacher woman. Janet Polasky, that was her name. *What church was she with?* He searched his memory. The only thing he could recall was that she was Methodist. He changed his mind about calling Strauss, and tossed the phone onto the small sofa. Pulling up to his desk, he turned his attention to his notebook computer.

At his desk, his fingers danced on the keyboard. He searched for Methodist Churches in Seattle and stared at the search results. "Motherfucker. What's with all the goddamned Methodists in this town. There must have been thirty of the churches in the area.

Bellevue. That's what Hartman had said at the fundraiser. He narrowed the search and came up with what he wanted— St. Luke's United Methodist Church. He navigated to the church's website—underwhelming, to say the least. The home page had a photo of the church. They had a page for staff and board and another for the schedule of services.

He stared at the photo of minister. Was she helping women run away from their husbands? Is that why Reba Stillings had mentioned her? Looking like that, she'd never get a husband of her own. The only thing that would make her happy would be to break up marriages. Figures. If she had anything to do with helping Bonnie, he'd add the minister to the list as well. He smirked. *No one would miss her.*

The afternoon wore on. He covered the same mental ground over and over. He played out the revenge fantasy until it grew wearisome. Three o'clock rolled around. The sense of urgency grew—the need to do something. Unfortunately, there was only one avenue open to him at the moment.

He phoned Alicia, whom he assumed was working in another part of the office complex.

"Yes, Senator?"

He smiled. At least she knew how to show respect. "I thought we might get together this evening—order some dinner and a bottle of wine from room service." He felt the familiar, pleasant stirring in his groin. It had been over a week—far too long.

The pause on the other end of the connection caught him off-guard. "Well?"

Her voice exuded uncertainty. "Uh, yes, sure, that would be wonderful." The tone absolutely did not match the words.

If she expected him to ask if it was a bad time or whether she had other plans, she was delusional. What she wanted didn't matter. He needed her. She owed him that much. He'd brought her into the campaign. She was nothing without him. The fact that she was able to spend time alone with him was something she could never have imagined.

"I'll be there at seven."

The uncertainty in her voice eased slightly. "Would you like me to order dinner—the usual?"

"Yes, that would be good. And I prefer a red wine, maybe Merlot." In his current mood, he wondered briefly if one bottle would be enough.

* * *

The lights filtering through the sheer drapes in the hotel room reflected off Alicia's blonde hair. She snuggled next to him, her head on his chest. He was spent. The effects of the wine lingered but the combination of the heavy meal and the alcohol on top of everything else going on pushed his stomach into turmoil. He was restless.

In his initial passion and desire not to be interrupted, he'd silenced his phone. Now he found himself wondering whether Strauss might have tried to phone him. He eased out from under Alicia's head and swung his legs over to the floor.

She whined, "Ooooh. You're not leaving now, are you?" She propped up on one elbow. "Can't you stay the night?"

"I need to check something on my phone." He didn't feel the need for any further explanation.

Indifferent to his nudity, he shuffled into the adjoining area. He'd left his phone on the table in the midst of the dinner remains. Unlocking the screen, he checked the record of incoming calls—nothing.

Shit! What the fuck was the man doing? How hard could it be? For what his contractor was being paid, the senator should have been swimming in information. Instead, this is what he got—silence.

A voice filtered in from the other room. "Are you coming back to bed?" There was a hint of an erotic invitation.

He ignored her. He started to phone Strauss but thought better of it. Once he connected, he couldn't have the conversation with Alicia in the next room. He set his phone down with more force than he'd intended. The sound shattered the soft quiet of the room.

"Are you okay in there?" She sounded concerned.

He called to her, "It's nothing." Corel needed to get back to his office and talk to Strauss. If he couldn't get anything useful out of him, then the next step would be to get the goddamned information himself.

Shaking his head, he returned the bedroom and turned on the beside lamp. The sensual look on Alicia's face turned to one of distress as he began to get dressed. "You're going now? It's early."

Enough was enough. Was there nobody who could just do what they were supposed to and keep their goddamned opinions to themselves? He whirled to face her, feeling the heat rise in this face. "I can tell time. I have things I need to take care of." He struggled to keep the anger from his voice.

A hint of fear crossed her face. "I'm sorry. I didn't mean anything. It's just that…." She let the sentence hang.

Fury built within him. God he hated that fucking scared look. It was the same one that Bonnie put on every time she goaded him into violence. He wouldn't give in this night, though. He turned his attention to his socks and then his shoes.

"Can you come back later tonight?'

He hated being handled and that's exactly what she was trying to do. He was gracious enough to spend time with her, but she was never satisfied. No matter how much he did for her, it was never enough. He closed his eyes and clenched his jaw. He would not be distracted.

Her tone changed. A touch of defiance came with her next words. "I cancelled all my plans for tonight."

That was all it took. "I don't give a fuck about your plans. We're in the middle of a campaign. We have a lot riding on this. You're either with me or you're not. It's nine o'clock. I spent the evening with you. That's more than most people get."

He pulled on his coat and stuffed his tie in his pocket.

Chapter 46

"If there's nothing else, I'm going. You need to spend some time tonight thinking about your priorities."

Senator Thomas Corel slammed the door as he left the room. Everyone had turned against him. He stood alone against the world.

47

Janet took the call from Tam Wiggins, the director of the King County Church Association, at mid-morning. The purpose seemed innocuous—the invoices for annual dues would be late going out due to an admin staff shortage. The Association still hoped for payment on or before the due date—November 1. Apologies and such.

There was something else in Tam's voice, though. With her obligatory notification out of the way, the director seemed to linger nervously. "Everything else is going okay. I just wanted to give you a head's up so you didn't get blindsided."

St. Luke's budget included the payment. While the invoice served as a reminder, it certainly wasn't a crucial thing. Margaret would have caught it. "It's not a problem, Tam."

"Good to hear. How's everything going with your church?"

Janet's interest piqued. It wasn't like Tam to make small talk. "We're good here. Anything interesting there?"

Chapter 47

A brief silence preceded an uncertain answer. "I don't know, more of the same, I suppose."

Janet's concern deepened. "You sound worried. Is something wrong?"

Tam deftly avoided the question. "Have you spoken with Aylin lately? How's she doing?"

Janet lashed out without thinking. "How should she be doing. You ambushed her and orchestrated her firing. She has a teenage child to support and no job. Off-hand, I'd say things suck for her, but that's just a guess."

Tam shot back. "I didn't ambush her, and I didn't fire her. We've been over this ground. I work for a board just like you do."

Janet had given it some thought over the past few weeks. Something had gnawed at her when it happened. Now as Tam tried to defend herself, the issue came into clear focus. "Let's be real here, Tam. You know as well as I do that the board can't fire employees. Only you can do that. It's right in the policy manual. The only employee that the board can terminate is you. They can recommend. They can suggest. They can coerce. They can't fire. Whatever happened, you own this one."

Stone silence. After a moment, a timid voice responded. "Whatever the manual says, the board fired her. You spoke with Carl. I'm sure he made that clear. I didn't terminate her. The board did."

Janet shook her head. Tam kept repeating the party line—the board had fired Aylin. The tone of her voice, though, revealed the truth. She was running scared. The director was doing everything she could to retain her own job. Browbeating the woman wasn't going to change anything. "So, what else is on your mind?"

"I know you disapprove. I get that, but this isn't the hill I want to die on. I love this job. Between the two of us, I don't agree with what the board did. I told them so. You know how it works, though. Whether the manual says I terminate, or they do, the end result is the same."

"Give it a rest, Tam. We simply don't agree on this."

"It isn't just that we disagree. You don't seem to understand that, whatever I would've done, they were going to get rid of her. If I had stepped in and stood my ground, they would have fired me and immediately appointed someone else who would have gone along with them."

Janet retorted, "I know how it works. I work for a board too. I sometimes have to do things I don't agree with. There are other times when I push back and force them to do the right thing. It's not easy. Every time I go that route, I risk losing my job, but it goes with the territory. When you take the leadership role, you sign up for that reality."

Tam pivoted. "There's a special board meeting being set up for this coming Thursday."

"And?"

"Conyers pressured Carl into calling it. They picked Thursday rather than our usual Wednesday night because…." Tam left the sentence unfinished.

Suddenly it made sense, all of it. The phone call was not about annual dues or Aylin. "Thursday night has conflicts for some members, if I recall."

Tam answered hesitantly, "Yes, I suppose so."

"And those conflicts are mostly with members who are passionate about domestic violence and are not on the same page as Conyers."

"That's probably true."

"Let me guess. The agenda includes a revision of the Council's position on delivery of domestic violence services. We're going to emphasize family preservation over safety."

Tam's voice sounded tired. "It's not worded exactly that way."

"I hope you're not allowing this as a closed meeting."

"You know better than that, Janet. Our only closed meetings are executive session. No, this is an open meeting, but…." Her voice trailed off.

"You're not providing notice, though. No PSAs. No e-mails to member churches. No advance agenda with arrangement for proxy votes. You're counting on a bare quorum with hopes that the complaints will fade."

"I need to go. I have a ton of things on my plate this afternoon. It was good talking to you."

48

J anet moved fast. The Thursday Church Association meeting was only two days away. She knew that if they proceeded on their present course, the association would end up taking a position that would endorse keeping partners together after a DV call rather than separating for safety. This had been Aylin's fear.

Opening the Council roster, she selected two names, and dialed the first number.

"Good morning, this is Reverend Wallace."

"Devon, this is Janet Polasky over at Saint Luke's. I need a really big favor."

"Shoot."

"Carl Broward has called a special meeting of the Association board for Thursday night. The agenda is consideration of a position on domestic violence services that would prioritize keeping husband and wife together over safety."

The response was steeped with incredulity. "That's madness. Whose idea was that? Wait... don't tell me. Conyers."

Janet responded. "Normally, he wouldn't have enough votes to carry it, but there are three board members with a conflict on Thursday night. As it happens, those board members are ones who would oppose the move."

"What a weasel." Reverend Devon Wallace of the Pine Creek Lutheran Church. He rarely minced words.

Janet continued, "If I could get a proxy for you from one of the conflicted board members, would you be willing to attend Thursday's meeting."

The response sounded full of fight. "I'd love to."

A second call went to Reverend Susan Ashton of the Greater Redmond United Presbyterian Church. The discussion went very much as the one with Reverend Wallace. The final piece was to obtain the proxies, which proved easier than Janet thought. This brought to bear a touchy problem. Should she warn Tam about the proxies or simply show up and ambush the other board members?

As much as Janet despised under-the-table tactics, playing her hand ahead of time was too risky. It would allow Broward and his crowd to react. No, better to show up ready to fight and surprise them.

* * *

Carl Broward called the meeting to order at 7:00 p.m. sharp. Surveying the meeting room, his face betrayed confusion. "I see we have some Association members here for the meeting this evening. Welcome." His demeanor, though, was in no way welcoming. He scowled for a moment, as though trying to figure out what was about to happen.

He nodded at a man sitting to his right. "We also have another guest this evening. I'd like to introduce Nicholas Trowbridge, with the Council on Safe and Healthy Families." Broward smiled warmly. "In speaking with Mister Trowbridge, I've found that our interests overlap with theirs on many issues." He smiled warmly at the man. "Welcome.

The name struck a chord with Janet. He was the man who attempted to strong-arm Greg Stottman about domestic violence services and separating couples.

Trowbridge seemed to survey the attendees, stopping ever so briefly on Janet, as though he somehow knew her. "Thank you, Carl. I appreciate the invitation." He appeared ready to continue, but fell silent instead.

Broward said, "Board members all have a copy of the agenda." He turned to Tam. "Do we have extra copies for the others?"

Tam shook her head. "No. Since the board didn't want this publicized, we didn't expect anyone else to show up." The look on her face mirrored the confusion on Carl's.

Janet raised her hand and Tam recognized her.

"If I may, Reverend Broward. We all have copies of the agenda and supporting documents, thank you."

Broward's look of consternation turned to one of alarm. This was clearly not going as he expected. "Very well. If you want to be heard on the issue, we can start a sign-up sheet."

Janet shrugged. "Thank you, but I don't believe that will be necessary. I don't need to offer testimony. I'm not sure about Reverends Wallace and Ashton." She turned to each of them, eyebrows arched. Each shook their head. She turned and smiled at Broward. "No, I guess there's no need of a sign-up sheet on our account." She paused and gathered her words.

Janet continued, "With the board's permission, I'd like to submit a vote proxy for Reverend Gonzales, who could not be here tonight. I have the completed and witnessed form here." She handed the proxy form to Tam.

Before anyone could respond, Reverend's Ashton and Wallace both provided copies of board vote proxies from two other absent members.

Tam collected and examined all three before handing them to Carl Broward. "They seem to be in order."

Reverend Broward was shaking with rage. He glanced over at Millard Conyers, who sat with a look of total bewilderment pasted on his face. Broward stole a glance at Nicholas Trowbridge, who maintained a flat affect, appearing not the least bit moved by the turn of events.

Without waiting for any further reaction, Janet spoke again. "Additionally, I would like to add one item to the agenda before we all vote to accept it." She handed a piece of paper to Tam with a single line typed on it—*Proposed Agenda Addition: Reconsideration of Aylin Freyberg Termination.*

Tam froze as she stared at the paper. After a moment, she handed it to Carl without speaking.

Broward glanced at it and then shoved it aside. "Has Miz Freyberg filed a formal notice of appeal? If not, then there is nothing to consider."

Janet cleared her throat. "This has nothing to do with an appeal. If you re-read the bylaws, you will see that her termination was not processed in accordance with our own rules. The board is not authorized to terminate employees. The only staff member that you can fire is the director. Termination of any other employee must be done by the director."

She removed a copy of the bylaws from her purse, opened them to a marked page, and handed the booklet to Carl. "Chapter three, section B, paragraph one A." She pointed to a highlighted section. "You can see… right there."

Reverend Broward turned bright red. "You're splitting hairs, Reverend Polasky. It is simply a matter of looking at it in the correct light. We, of course, directed Miz Wiggins to do the actual firing."

Janet narrowed her eyes and cocked her head. "I'm not sure that's accurate, Carl. I distinctly remember you telling me that the board fired her. Tam confirmed that when I spoke to her. Now, as you know, you can certainly remedy the situation. In order to make it work, you'll need to bring Miz Freyberg back, make good on the back pay she's owed, and then you can order Tam to fire her. That would work." Janet offered a broad smile.

No one spoke for a moment. Finally, Janet glanced around and said, "I didn't mean to have this discussion at this moment. I only wanted to add the item to the agenda."

Broward countered, "This is a special meeting called for a specific purpose. This would more appropriately be put on the agenda for our next regular meeting."

Janet almost laughed. "The next meeting is three weeks away. That would add three more weeks of back pay. Is that really what you want?"

Her adversary made little attempt to conceal his rage. He glared across at Janet as though he wanted to strangle her. Finally, he cleared his throat. "The item is placed on the proposed agenda. Are there any other changes before we move to approve?"

Millard Conyers rose, slid over, and whispered in Broward's ear. Carl nodded as he listened. When the interchange was over, he said, "We'll pull the main item from the agenda and reschedule it for a future meeting. The proposed agenda is amended to have only the reconsideration of Miz Freyberg's termination. Anything else?"

A voice from the other side of the table responded, "I move that the amended agenda be approved."

A second person added, "Seconded."

Broward nodded. "Moved and seconded. All in favor, please raise your hands."

All hands went up.

"The agenda is approved. Reverend Polasky, you have the floor."

Janet drummed her fingers on the tabletop. "I'm not sure there's anything left to discuss. I move that we rescind the termination of Aylin Freyberg and strike it from her personnel record."

Broward shot back, "That sounds lovely, but it doesn't work that way. We can vote on the rescinding and the modification of personnel record if you like. We'll also vote on a motion to recommend her termination."

Janet smiled broadly. "Of course, but since they are two separate actions, I think it only appropriate to treat them as two separate motions. My motion stands. Rescind the termination and change her personnel record. If someone wants to advance a motion to recommend her firing, then we can vote on that separately."

A low round of grumbling filled the room for a moment. Broward called for order and then said, "We have a motion to rescind the termination and make personnel record changes. All in favor indicate by raising your hand."

All hands went up.

"The measure passes. Miz Wiggins, will you please take the necessary action. Are there any other motions with regard to this issue?"

A hand went up on the other side of the table. Broward nodded in that direction. "Yes?"

One of Carl's cronies spoke for the first time that

evening. "I move that the board recommend to Director Wiggins that Miz Freyberg be fired for insubordination."

Broward responded, "So moved. Do I hear a second?"

"Seconded." Janet didn't see who it came from, not that it mattered.

"Moved and seconded. All in favor please raise your hands."

This is where the surprise hit. The hands that went up appeared to be about half the board. When Tam counted, they came up two votes short. She turned to Broward. "The motion failed."

The voice that had seconded the motion called out again. "I call for reconsideration."

Broward sounded tired. "So moved. Is there a second?" He appeared beaten; his actions mechanical.

"Seconded."

"Moved and seconded. All in favor please raise your hands."

Tam counted again. "The motion fails to carry."

Broward glanced around the room. "That completes our agenda for the night. Is there any other business to come before the board."

Silence.

He continued, "Anything for the good of the order?"

Conyers stood. "This fight isn't over. This institution is a place of faith and devotion to God's word. I will not stand by idly and see it corrupted by the false promises of secularism. There are those here who would turn this into the domain of Satan. You may think yourself clever, but God will smite you all."

Broward looked embarrassed. That he was angry at Janet was obvious. The battle was not over. The outburst by Conyers, though, didn't play well with any of the board members. Janet could sense that all saw it as weakening their moral position. The difference, though, was that they most likely viewed him as a loose cannon. Janet, on the other hand, saw him as a dangerous predator.

As the meeting participants filed out, Carl pulled Janet aside. "Do have a minute?" He motioned her over to a corner of the room out of earshot of the others. "You could have gone about this differently, you know."

Janet stared at him for a moment, deciding which tack to pursue. Finally, she opted for a genuine, honest exchange. "I understand Conyers. He is what he is, and we all know it. I expected this kind of show from him. Despite our differences, though, I've always thought you above this kind of thing."

Broward pushed back. "You ambushed the board. That's never been your style."

Janet stood, taken aback. "*Ambushed*? Who did the ambushing here, Carl? You called a special meeting for a night when you knew that those who held differing opinions from you couldn't make it. You held the meeting without providing notice to the membership. Those actions are the very definition of *ambush*."

"I'm the president for the entire Council. I try to consider the views of all. My goal is to move forward on common ground. I know that you're passionate about domestic violence. Your views, though, are not shared by everyone. That means that we have to find a way through this while respecting everyone's values. That's what I'm trying to do."

"Sorry, Carl. I'm not buying it. If you were pursuing a middle ground, you might generalize that the Council supports DV services without making any distinction regarding separating couples or keeping them together. I think we all agree that we want to eliminate the violence. If you were looking to honor everyone, you'd stick to that.

You're pursuing a path that flies in the face of every bit of research available in the field. You may well buy into this myth that keeping a violent husband and his wife together preserves the family. The data says that all you're doing is putting the woman at risk. The consequences of failure in this case are death. I promise you that I've seen my fair share of that recently."

Broward held his hands out as though to defend himself from the argument. "You're reading this wrong. Nobody is saying that the couple has to be kept together. All we are asking is that, if they are to be separated, there be some clear evidence that it's necessary. If the separation is what's indicated, so be it. If not, then leave the family intact."

Janet gave up on trying to reason with him. "I'll leave it at this. If you push that kind of position through, you're going to lose membership. I promise you that."

The wild card in all of this, though, was Nicholas Trowbridge. She'd heard the name before. This was not good.

Sitting in her car in the Association parking lot, Janet decided to make a quick phone call. There was something she didn't want to get lost in the shuffle. She brought up her contact list, selected, and punched the connect icon.

"Hi, Janet." Greg's voice sounded tired but cheerful.

"Do you remember back a ways, you mentioned that a guy named Trowbridge tried to strong-arm you?"

"Yeah, what about it?"

"He showed up at the Church Association meeting tonight. Predictably, the only topic on the agenda was the idea of family preservation or reunification on DV calls. He was apparently invited to the meeting by some of the association members."

Greg's voice sounded concerned. "What did he say?"

"Nothing. Just introduced himself and then watched the proceedings. Honestly, it appeared to me as though he wanted to address the group but, at the last minute, remained quiet."

"How did the meeting play out? Anything significant?" he asked.

Janet responded, "Well, it didn't go the way several of the members hoped. I get the sense, though, that the topic isn't going away. We beat them tonight, but they'll be back."

"I guess we take it as it comes."

49

Senator Corel scanned his calendar—a full day. Then something caught his eye. At 1:15 pm, he had a thirty-minute slot allocated to a Nicholas Trowbridge from the Council on Safe and Healthy Families. Neither the name nor the organization meant anything to the senator. Normally such a meeting wouldn't be an issue, but as the election approached and every minute became valuable, his staff was usually more protective of his time.

Complicating things was the fact that his wife was still out there. Dylan Strauss had not found her. The senator was finding it increasingly difficult to focus on mundane matters such as these kinds of meetings. He picked up the handset and punched in Alicia's extension number.

She answered on the first ring, her voice sounding enthusiastic. "Yes, Senator?"

"What's the deal with my one-fifteen? Who is this guy?"

"He's with the Council on Safe and Healthy Families. They're a political action committee focused on family issues. I did some research on them. They come mostly from the faith community." She sounded as though she was reading from a set of notes.

"Any idea what he wants?"

"I didn't talk to him personally, but the staffer who calendared it said that he wanted to speak with you about the Violence Against Women Act renewal."

Fuck! Just what I need right now. "Thanks. I'd like for you to sit in on the meeting with us. I may need to step out. If that happens, you should be able to wrap things up with him."

* * *

Corel stared out the window into the early October drizzle. Although he was used to the incessant rain in the Pacific Northwest, on this particular day it irritated the shit out of him. *Would a little sunshine be too much to ask?*

The officer intercom sounded and he punched the speaker button. "Yes."

"Senator, Mister Trowbridge is here. I have him set up in the conference room whenever you're ready, sir."

"On my way."

He stood, putting on his suit coat and straightening his tie. He considered waiting a few minutes, if for no other reason than he was in charge. Shaking his head, he reluctantly opened the office door and started down the hall. Putting on his best smile, he opened the door.

"Mister Trowbridge, welcome. I'm Senator Thom Corel." He nodded toward Alicia, who sat across the table. "I see you've met my aide. Can we get you anything—coffee, tea, water?"

Trowbridge stood and offered his hand. He stood

about six feet tall with a trim build. His dark hair was carefully coifed and sported a touch of silver at the temples. He was dressed in a dark navy suit, white shirt, and a maroon tie. His smile, indeed everything about him, seemed deliberate, planned. "It's an honor to meet you, Senator. Thank you for making time in your busy schedule. I'm sure things are crazy with the election right around the corner."

Corel's laugh was precisely measured—enough to convey a good mood but not so much that Trowbridge might feel too comfortable. It was interesting that the man had not answered the question about a drink. Perhaps he was sophisticated enough to realize that it wasn't a genuine offer. "Yes, things are hectic right now, but it's always good to be back in Seattle... home." He took his usual seat at the head of the table with Trowbridge on one side of him and Alicia on the other.

"Now, what can I do for you?" Corel avoided asking about the Council on Safe and Healthy Families. Alicia's brief summary had told him all he needed to know.

"I won't take much of your time, Senator. We at the Council have only recently begun to work on the issue of family violence. Fortuitously, the federal Violence Against Women Act is up for reauthorization this coming session. I know that you've been active in that arena in the past, so we hope that you'll be able to take some of our concerns to the table."

This was not a subject Corel wanted to wade into right now. He had campaigned hard on the issue of domestic violence, but his unfortunate circumstances with his wife made this an uncomfortable spot to be in. "What might those concerns be?"

Trowbridge shifted in his seat and offered a shallow laugh—the first sign of discomfort the senator had seen. "I

guess I'd start out by saying we think the title of the legislation is far too limiting. This is an important topic and it's
crucial to understand that violence happens not just to
women but to their husbands and boyfriends as well."

Corel shook his head. "Be that as it may, Mister Trowbridge, these things are really all about the art of the possible. This piece of legislation, regardless of what you may
think or even what other reality might exist in the world, is
known by that name. Trying to rename it would be an
exercise in futility, given our current political environment.
I'm sure you understand that."

"Yes, of course, Senator. I just wanted to lay some
groundwork to let you know that we take this seriously.
What we would like to see, though, is some language
inserted that empowered and even encouraged local and
state authorities to prioritize family preservation when it
can be safely accomplished. As I'm sure you're aware,
there are many instances in which tempers flare, words are
spoken in haste, and maybe even things turn physical. That
doesn't, however, always mean that someone is in danger. I
want to stress, if there is danger, absolutely separate the
two bickering parties. If there's no clear indication of that,
though, we'd like to see the default action to be keeping the
family together."

A part of Corel agreed. Couples could indeed work out
their differences. He and Bonnie could fix the problems if
only.... "I understand your concerns. As you indicated,
though, these types of protocols are developed at the state
and local level. As I'm sure you're aware, there's a strong
movement, especially among the conservatives, toward
more local and state autonomy. Getting this act reautho-
rized will necessarily require us to honor that to the
greatest extent possible. That means that, regardless of

how I or anyone else feels about this, prescriptive requirements likely won't make into the final reauthorization."

Trowbridge's smile faded. "Yes, we do understand the current situation. We also know that you're nearly certain to win re-election, if the polls are to be believed. That makes you less vulnerable and allows you to take bolder, more decisive action. All we're asking is that you bring our concerns to the table. Whether our preferences make into the final version will only be revealed in time."

Corel wondered about the statement. It seemed as though this request was part of a larger strategy. "Tell me more about this organization of yours, the Council on Safe and Healthy Families, I think it is."

"As you likely know, we're a faith-based political action committee. We focus on the issues that we believe will put families back at the center of our society. While we realize that conservatives and progressives disagree on many things, I think all of us can agree that safe and healthy families are a good outcome."

Corel almost allowed a laugh to escape. He couldn't count the number of times he'd heard the different versions of this position. *We all want the same thing. Horseshit.* He smiled, slid his chair back, and stood. "I'm sure that your position will come forward at some point in the negotiations. You said it yourself, though. The extent to which your views carry the day will be revealed in time." *When hell freezes over.*

While the senator understood the opposition to the act, he also knew beyond any doubt that his constituency would not tolerate any backpedaling on it. This was, at least for him, one of those inevitable "third rails."

"I'm afraid I have to go. I have another meeting in a few minutes. Thanks for bringing your concerns to me and

I assure you that they will be brought forward." He offered his hand along with his standard PR smile.

Turning to leave, he caught just a hint of what seemed a flash of anger on Trowbridge's face. Just as quickly as it came, though, it was replaced by the same plastic smile that the man had worn at the start.

50

The Sniper decided on Cousin Billy's next mission—making a pick-up of fentanyl and heroin in Boise.

"Tomorrow morning." The Sniper sat at the kitchen table with Billy. "This is the big leagues, Cuz. You fuck this up, and it won't end well." *For either of us.*

Billy laughed it off... just as he did just about everything. "Have some faith, Trey."

The Sniper shuddered. The thought of his inept and temper-driven cousin using his name sent waves of nausea through him. He rarely interacted with anyone on a personal basis. He used cash for purchases. His relationship with his network, including his drug transport business, were all based on a username. There was simply no reason for his real name—*Trey Costas*—to ever be uttered. Besides, he'd spend a small fortune constructing his new identity and leaving that old name... and life... behind. He was no longer Trey Costas.

Yet he had no doubt at all that if Cousin Billy got in the slightest jam, he would squeal like an infant. One of the first things out of his mouth would be the Sniper's old identity and business. *I should have just killed the motherfucker and been done with it.* It still wasn't too late. He could easily put a round into his cousin's head and the idiot would never see it coming. *It might still come to that.*

On the other hand, the idea of expanding his service capacity offset the risk. The Sniper could easily double his revenue. Even if he paid Billy a substantial fee, it would still be a hefty increase in his own income. *No risk... no reward.*

Back to the matter at hand. "Here are the rules. They are not subject to debate or negotiation. You follow them to the letter. I need to know that you understand that," He waited for his cousin to process the idea.

"Yeah, sure, okay."

"First. You're going to pick up a sealed package. Don't open it. Make sure the seal is intact. Your contact will be in an office space. They have a scale available. He will likely weigh the bundle in front of you as a matter of routine. If he doesn't do that, ask him to. Copy down the weight— exactly as it reads out on the scale. Make sure that the two of you agree. Make sure you have a copy of that weight. Got it?"

Billy rolled his eyes, as though impatient with the simplistic orders.

The Sniper repeated the question, with greater volume and emphasis. "Do you have it?"

"Fuck yeah, man. Lighten up."

"Second, you leave at eight in the morning. Eat breakfast before you go. It's an hour and a half down there. Pick-up shouldn't take more than fifteen minutes, thirty at the most. With an hour and a half for return, that puts you back around eleven-thirty. You can eat lunch when you return. We'll gas up the car today. What this all means is that you make no stops other than the pick-up. No stops at convenience stores, bathrooms, liquor stores, or gas stations. Nothing. Understand?"

Billy glared, apparently pissed that he had to listen to the lecture. *Good. The more pissed, the better.* The Sniper needed to see how the kid controlled his temper. The only way to do that was to stress the fuck out of him. "Okay, now, here's the important one. You need to know that if you have a run-in with the law, you're toast. You're wanted for killing two cops and you're driving a stolen car. You won't be able to talk your way out of it."

His cousin picked up his Smith and Wesson 9 mm handgun and waved it, barrel up. "That's what this is for," ending the flourish with a laugh.

The Sniper sighed. "If it gets that far, you're finished. You might fight your way out of one traffic stop. But if you kill another cop, especially one here in Idaho, your days are numbered, Cuz. They'll hunt you down. There won't be any place you can hide." *And if you come back here, I'll finish you myself.*

Before Cousin Billy could make another statement, the Sniper continued on with his final instructions. "So, it's just like last time. Observe the speed limits but don't go so slow that it draws attention. Staying with traffic will work in your favor. Go with the flow."

"I bring it back here. What are you going to do with it?" It was the first time Billy had asked an intelligent question.

"I'm not going to do anything with it. You, on the other hand, are going to take it to Spokane and drop it off the day after tomorrow. Just so you know, we're going to have another conversation tomorrow night about how to conduct yourself over there, given that you killed two of their cops."

"What's my cut of this?" Cousin Billy looked at the Sniper expectantly.

"Your payment for this service will be five thousand, just like last time."

"I thought you said that I'd be getting more money as the jobs got more complicated." A note of anger crept into Billy's voice.

The Sniper broke out laughing. "You call this complicated? There's nothing to this. You go pick up a package and bring it back here. After that, you drive to Spokane and drop the package off there. Your only concern is not getting caught. If you can pull this off, we'll talk about something with a little more substance."

51

No one talked about it. The world plodded forward without so much as a pause, but Sue Hartman's disappearance overwhelmed Janet. As the days went by, her anxiety increased. No news. Nothing. The minister grew increasingly pessimistic. Still, she'd been reluctant to press Detective Martin for information. Dee was, after all, not involved in the case. Sue's disappearance was being handled, to the extent that it *was* being handled at all, by the Seattle Police Department.

Finally, the combination of anger, frustration, and fear drove Janet to call. "Hi Dee. I hate to bother you, but I was wondering if you've heard anything about Sue yet?"

"Nothing. I've asked around here and even called some of my contacts over at SPD. Either they know nothing or they're being very tight-lipped. With the Admin Assistant death, the best that I can learn... and it seems nothing more than rumor... is that the ME is likely going to rule it suicide. That will close the door on that angle, at least for now."

Janet's agitation ramped up. "You can't tell me that

they don't know anything. Someone doesn't just up and disappear, leaving absolutely no signs. That's ludicrous."

"I only know what people are willing to tell me at this point. Whatever happened with Sue, either they're finding nothing, or the captain over there has a gag on it."

"What do you figure is next?"

Dee's voice sounded edgy. "How am I supposed to know? I can't even find out where the investigation is, much less where they intend to go next."

Janet tried to digest all she was hearing. "This whole thing has me rattled."

"I do have one thing that might interest you. Do you remember I told you about those DV workers who were killed?"

Janet vaguely remembered, but the details had been overshadowed by the situation with Sue Hartman. "The ones shot by a rifle?"

"The same ones, yeah. The task force came up with a lead. It's a thin one, to be sure, but it's something. There's a website, or at least there was one—righteousfire dot com. Supposedly, it was all about vilifying undesirable segments of society. Talked a lot about gays and immigrants. Interestingly, it also came down hard on the entire domestic violence movement. This isn't really that unusual, but accounts I've heard said that it went so far as to advocate violence against these groups."

Janet's interest piqued. "Did you visit the site yourself?"

"That's the thing. It was taken down about six months ago. The task force found a dead link in one of the online forums. The description I gave you came from that forum. As it turns out, the website was hosted on an offshore server, and we haven't had any luck prying information out of them."

"Do you think the site might be part of the killings?"

"Could be. The state cops are still working on it but they're mostly keeping a lid on things."

"Is it possible that it could be related to Sue's disappearance? I know her case is different from the others, since she's missing, and the others were killed outright. Still, maybe they're linked through that website."

"Except that the website doesn't exist anymore. I don't see how it could have played a role, at least in Sue's case."

Janet responded, "Maybe they just moved it to another server."

"That wouldn't matter if they used the same or a similar name. The site itself has been shut down." After a brief pause, Dee spoke again, this time softer and with greater uncertainty. "Janet, I was wondering if maybe we could get together sometime over the next few days. We could do coffee, or I could come by your house in the evening, whichever would work best."

Janet mentally went over her schedule before answering. "I'm free this evening if you'd like to come by."

"Not tonight. There's something I need to check on first. How about tomorrow evening?" Her voice sounded ominous, like something weighed on her soul.

"Sure, tomorrow's fine."

After disconnecting, Janet stared at the scribbling on the paper in front of her.

www.righteousfire.com

52

Silenced cloaked the room. Val focused for a moment on her own steady breathing; the gentle rise and fall of her chest. She felt a sense of peace, of rightness. The nightlight plugged into the far wall provided a faint golden light.

Snuggling closer, Dee spoke softly. "This is wonderful, you being in town like this." She rested her head on Val's chest.

"We shouldn't get used to it. This particular client prefers to stay in town. My guess is that there won't be many like this."

"I know." Dee propped up on an elbow and kissed Val lightly on the lips. "That's why I want to savor every second of this."

Val smiled to herself. She had never known anything like this. Even when she and her husband were first married, it was never this way. "Well, Love, we have all night to *savor*." She wrapped her arms tight around Dee and kissed her. Deep inside, the passion began to build again.

Suddenly, Dee pulled back. "Val, I need to ask you something—a favor."

"And that would be?"

"I was talking to Janet today. It felt strange. We somehow got to talking about you. I had to shut down. I wanted to tell her about us, but I wouldn't ever do that without your knowledge and okay. I guess it came off kind of weird because she pressed, asking what was bothering me."

Val thought about it for a moment. Having been alone for so many years, she'd never thought about what it would be like to have someone special and how to share the information. "What would you tell her?"

"That I love you. That you're the person that I always knew I would find. That I want to be with you for the rest of my life." She paused. Her next words came much softer and with greater uncertainty. "That I want to marry you."

Electricity shot through Val. She imagined coming home to Dee at night. The two of them cooking meals together seemed an intriguing but disconcerting vision. What would it be like to live with Dee, to laugh over little things that came up, and to disagree over other things? The idea of crawling into bed next to this woman every night, sometimes making love and sometimes just kissing her goodnight sent a wave of passion coursing through her body.

She also thought about her last marriage—the one that had ultimately led to her incarceration. This would be different, though. Dee was not like her husband. On the other hand, her husband and been loving and tender when they first met. *It's not the same.*

"So, this favor you want to ask—is it permission to tell Janet or do you want me to marry you? Which is it?"

Chapter 52

Dee eased over on top of Val, kissing long and deep. As she eased her face away, she whispered, "Yes."

Val reached up and caressed Dee's hair. "Yes." The passion took over. Her hands sought out Dee's soft shoulders. They kissed, longer and more sensually.

* * *

The next morning, Dee poured a cup of coffee for each of them and popped some bread in the toaster. "So, yes?"

Val's laugh came out soft. "I assume that you're going to talk to Janet today. Let me know how that goes. Yes, to the proposal. We can talk more about it tonight."

Dee shot her an inquisitive look. "Oh, you mean we're not going to meet at the court today and fly off on a honeymoon tonight?" It was clear, though, that she was trying to keep the laughter inside.

Val's deadpan reply came without hesitation. "I was thinking a romantic getaway to downtown Tacoma. We could leave late this afternoon and be back by breakfast. Or we could save money by getting a cheap hotel across from SeaTac."

"Tempting. Maybe we could just stay here tonight and do a repeat of last night."

Val smiled, eased over, and kissed Dee lightly. "Your toast is burning."

Dee spoke while she spread the butter. "Are you going to be tied up all day?"

"The client is adamant about remaining local. Since she's all set up with the housing, there's not a lot for me to do. I'm mainly providing some company and acting as a sounding board."

"I don't know, Val. She doesn't sound like a typical

woman who's afraid for her life. Whoever she is, she's taking a huge risk by remaining in town, close to her husband."

Val thought about it for a moment before answering. "Yeah. I can't get a good read on her. She doesn't come across as helpless or even afraid. In fact, she almost seems defiant. Maybe that's a good thing. Who knows?"

"Be careful. This thing could be a huge explosion waiting to happen. Don't get caught in the middle of it."

Val pivoted away from the topic. "I'm going to talk to Janet today. Why don't I break the news to her. After all, I'm the employee. Better to hear it from me than you, I think."

Dee turned toward her, concern on her face. "How do you think she's going to take it?"

Val shrugged. "How should I know? You know her a lot better than I do. What do you think?"

"No idea. I mean, Janet's been a close friend for a lot of years. My first thought is that she'll be happy for us. On the other hand, she's a minister. I'm not sure how her church feels about these things."

Val laughed. "Do you mean about lesbians?"

Dee rolled her eyes. "No, about a honeymoon in downtown Tacoma."

"So, how will she react if we go to Tacoma for a honeymoon?"

Dee grew serious, nodding her head. "She's my friend."

"That's good enough for me."

* * *

242

Val sat in her car outside the condo. It was as good a place as any to make the phone call. Composing her thoughts, she pressed Janet's icon in her contact list.

"Good morning, Val."

"Hi Janet. Do you have a minute? There's a couple of things I need to run by you."

"What's up?"

"First, I guess I'm wondering how long you envision me keeping the client company." Val was careful not to mention Bonnie's name.

"It's not really an issue unless we get another client. If you get the sense that she would rather you not be hovering, we can talk about our next steps. I don't think this arrangement with current housing shouldn't last any more than a month at the longest, especially given the extra person there."

"Sounds good." Val paused and moved on to the real reason for the call. "Second thing—I was talking to Dee last night." She closed her eyes and continued, "I spent the night with her. We both agreed that you should know about our relationship."

Silence for a moment. Val stifled a laugh. Clearly Janet had not seen this coming. Finally, the minister said, "Uh, what kind of relationship?"

The question stunned Val. What kind of relationship did Janet think it was, a golfing partnership. She blurted out, "We're sleeping together."

Janet's words came out soft and tender. "I understand that. What I'm asking, and please tell me if it's none of my business, but are you talking about a long-term relationship or something else?"

"To answer your conditional point, I'm telling you because I think it *is* your business. I work for you and what we do is… well… a little sensitive, to say the least. As for the relationship, it's serious and long-term, at least we both hope so."

Janet smiled, her words coming out as sincere and heartfelt. "Then let me be the first to offer congratulations. Dee is an incredible person and one of my best friends."

53

The Sniper slid the bundle of bills across the table. "Here you go—five thousand." Billy had done exactly as instructed, albeit not without considerable grumbling. This mouthiness would have to change. That would be for another day, though.

Cousin Billy's face oozed disapproval. His mouth drew into a tight line and his jaw clenched. He stared at the stack of bills, bound together with a rubber band. "Oh good. I need a hundred grand and I have ten. In another twenty years or so, maybe I'll save enough."

"Maybe, if you live that long." The Sniper folded his hands on the table and gazed into his cousin's eyes with as neutral a look as he could summon. "I've been up front with you from the git-go. Your first few jobs would be for five each. Just so we're clear, your next one is coming in at that price as well. Keep up the success, though, and we'll get you moved up to the ten grand level. At that rate, you'll be there in six to nine months."

Billy shot back, "In the meantime, I risk getting caught

every time I leave the house. I got nothing to fall back on except my gun."

"That same gun got you into this shit to begin with. Discipline yourself. Go out only when you have to. Keep to the plan. Have patience. Nine months to get a completely new life isn't so bad."

Billy breathed deeply and snatched up the bills. "What's next?"

"What's next, Cuz, is that we're going to work on your weapon skills. After that, we'll talk about your next job."

"I know how to handle my gun. I got the jump on those two cops, didn't I?"

The Sniper laughed, shaking his head. "Yet somehow, at close range, you couldn't finish off that girlfriend of yours. Yep, Cuz, we need to improve your skills." He stood and started for the door. "I'm going to grab some things. I'll meet you out back in five minutes."

He wound his way down the path, through the thick stand of fir trees until he arrived at the small clearing. Inside his cache, he grabbed the Remington 700 sniper rifle and a Smith and Wesson 9 mm handgun, along with ammunition for both. Reaching up to a shelf on the far wall, he selected a noise suppressor for each and a couple of paper targets.

Back at the house, he found Billy sitting on a stump in the back yard, still apparently brooding over his situation and the verbal dressing down he'd gotten just a few minutes earlier.

The Sniper stapled up a paper target on a large tree at the edge of the woods. The target consisted of a full-length silhouette of a man with a three-ring bull's eye in the chest.

As he approached Billy, he said, "This is twenty-five yards. It's a good starting point. Before it's over, you need to reliably hit at fifty and hundred yards."

His cousin eyed the target as though trying to assess how best to approach it.

The Sniper handed him the rifle. "This is your preferred weapon. Theoretically, it's accurate to about eight hundred and fifty yards. For your purposes, this rifle will be dead on at the ranges you'll be working at."

Billy reached around to his back and pulled out a handgun. "This here's all I need. I like to get up close and personal. I want to see the look in their eyes as I pull the trigger."

The Sniper shook his head. "Cuz, that's one of the stupidest thing I've ever heard. Why the fuck would you want to see the look in their eyes? This is a goddamn job, not a social outing. You have to get them and then get away without anyone seeing you. In addition, you don't ever want anyone to have seen you with, or near the target."

"Then why do guys use pistols all the time?" Billy's eyes screamed defiance.

"What, you mean gang bangers? Maybe you're talking spies like James Bond. Is that it? You see that shit in the movies?" The Sniper paused for a moment and lowered his voice. "This is what I'm talking about, Cuz. You have all these crazy ideas about how things are supposed to be. I do this for a living. The fact that I've been doing it for nearly fifteen years without getting caught means that I have a pretty good idea how to do it right."

Billy glared but kept quiet.

"Here's the way it works. We have a target. We scope them out first, from a distance. We watch and we map out a strategy. We pick our time and place. When it's time, we position a good fifty to a hundred yards away."

He picked up the suppressor and handed to his cousin. "This will dull the noise so that anyone nearby won't even notice it. By the time someone realizes the target's down, you'll be long gone."

A peaceful stillness descended over the backyard. Birds chirped and a squirrel chattered in a nearby tree. A light breeze cooled off the otherwise warm early autumn day. The Sniper added, "In my work, I don't know the targets personally. I have no relationship with them. That makes it nearly impossible for the cops to track it back to me, unless I fuck something up."

Billy shrugged, apparently ready to give up the argument for the moment.

The Sniper, though, needed to make sure his cousin was completely convinced. "Before we start with the rifle, I want to show you something. Let me see that handgun."

Billy handed him the 9 mm. The Sniper checked—a round in the chamber and the safety set. He gave it back to his cousin.

"I take it you keep it in your waistband, in back, right?"

A shrug. "Yeah, I guess."

"Okay, Cuz. You can either set the safety or not, your choice. If you don't set it, you risk pulling the trigger accidently when you pull it out. You could shoot your ass off." The Sniper laughed.

"On the other hand, you could set the safety, which means that when you draw it, you have to take it off before you fire, which costs you time." The Sniper paused before continuing.

"So, here's what I want you to do. Put your weapon in your waistband. Walk toward the target. When I say 'NOW' draw your weapon and fire. Keep in mind that, at that range, your target will see you and likely take some kind of action. He may pull his own gun. He may lunge at you and try to take yours. He may simply dodge away, roll on the ground, or take some other evasive action. Your job is to nail him within a couple of seconds. That's all the time you'll have. Got it?"

Billy didn't speak. Instead, he set the safety on his handgun and tucked it into his waistband. When he was set, he nodded.

"Okay, then do it. Start walking."

His cousin strode toward the target, his hands loose at his side.

At about the ten-yard mark, the Sniper yelled, "NOW!"

Billy reached and around and fumbled to get the gun out.

The Sniper shouted even louder. "Shoot the mother-fucker, now!"

His cousin brought the gun to bear and began firing. After five shots, he stopped, set the safety, and lowered the gun.

As the two of them approached the target, the Sniper smirked. "If this had been the real thing, you'd either be dead or in some kind of weird chase with everybody around looking at you." He pointed to the target. "See? Not a single hit. This is why we don't do it your way."

"This was just practice. I'll get better."

"Not at this, you won't. At least not with my help. If you're going to work for me, you're going to do it my way. Now, Cuz, go pick up the rifle and we'll get to work."

54

G reg stared at the website name—*righteousfire.com*. With no capitalization and all run together, it appeared like nothing more than a jumble of letters. When spoken, though, it carried an ominous sound. Janet had talked it to him about it, wondering if there might be some way he could track it down.

He had, of course, attempted to access the site. The message that came up confirmed what Janet had told him. The website had been shut down. She'd told him that it had been hosted on an offshore server, although she had no other information. He'd jumped at the opportunity to help; to show that he was more than just a source of money. This was an area where he had some expertise.

Unfortunately, he'd promised Melissa… and himself… that he'd devote his days to the business. He also committed that he would step back from the operational aspect of Janet's project. He was a funding source and nothing more. So far, at least for the past week, things had gone well.

He retrieved his phone, opened up his contact list, and selected a name. Eisen answered right away.

"Yeah?" The response is pretty much what Greg had expected.

"Could you swing by my place this evening? I have a job for you." Eisen had finished up with Paulette's phone system and had agreed to remain in town for another week or so… on his own dime. Greg figured it wasn't that generous of an offer, given the money he'd spent employing the kid so far.

"Eight okay?"

"See you then." Greg went back to the R and D report on artificial intelligence and switching devices.

Eisen showed up at 7:55 that evening.

"Thanks for coming. I appreciate it. You want something to drink?"

"I'll take one of those Sam Adams if you have any."

Greg headed off to the kitchen, calling over his shoulder, "Grab a seat." On his return from the kitchen, he slid onto the couch opposite Eisen, who had staked out the overstuffed chair. "Here you go."

Eisen took a deep draught and closed his eyes as he swallowed. "Yep. Good stuff." He set the bottle on a coaster. "What can I do for you, Mister Stottman?"

Greg handed him the scrap of paper. "I need everything you can get me relating to this website."

The tech genius considered it for a second. "Okay, simple enough. Is there anything special I should know before I get started?"

"Well, as you could probably guess, it's no longer up. My best information is that it was on an offshore server, but no idea where. In fact, I don't know anything else about it."

"I assume you're wanting information on the owner and probably any kind of successor that he might have put up in place of this one."

Greg responded, "Like I said, anything you can tell me."

"Fair enough. Same financial arrangements apply. Hopefully this won't take me more than a few days."

"Sounds good." Greg appreciated the confidence in the guy's voice.

With business completed, Eisen leaned back in his chair, took another swill, and asked, "How's your niece? Is she still recovering?"

"She's doing as well as can be expected, I suppose. Getting shot in the chest and having her head bashed in did a number on her, not to mention that the guy who did it was supposed to be in love with her."

"That's some crazy shit, for sure." He scratched at the corner of the label on the bottle. The look on his face was solemn but not intense. It seemed more a look of resignation and realization that bad things happened all the time.

Greg said, "You must see a lot of crazy stuff in your line of work."

Eisen eyed his employer for a moment, as though sizing him up. "Yeah, I guess. I try to stick to the tech side of things. I don't mix well with the guys who carry the artillery." He paused and his voice changed back into that *matter-of-fact* tone. "I take it they didn't catch the guy yet."

Greg suddenly remembered that Eisen had been one of those who urged him against seeking revenge. "Not yet. I'm not sure whether you heard, but he ended up killing a couple of cops over in Spokane. I guess I'm lucky I took your advice." He left unsaid what he was really thinking—*I could have ended up like those cops.*

Eisen killed the rest of the bottle, stood, and handed the empty to Greg. "I'll try to get you something in the next day or so." He started to leave but turned back toward Greg. "Hey, tell your niece I hope she's getting better."

Odd. The guy sounded like he actually cared.

55

The call came at mid-morning. Corel paced his office trying to force his mind back on track. His relationship with Dylan Strauss had soured. They had never been friends, but of late, things had deteriorated even more. Strauss, it seemed, couldn't even manage the simplest of tasks and produce anything resembling a positive outcome.

The odd part was that the contractor had the perfect disposition and lack of emotional connection. His utilitarian approach to morals was refreshing—anything that benefitted the man was okay.

Corel, for his part, had the money to pay for the services that Strauss had always been able to deliver. Always, that is, until this moment. Now he was producing nothing of value and charging a fortune. It had been several days since the senator's last contact with him. The senator's patience wore thin.

Barely a month and a half remained until the election. He needed Bonnie back under wraps so he could finish with a power burst. So long as she remained at large, though, he felt the need to remain low key. The more attention he drew to himself, the more likely it was that someone would ask questions about his absent wife.

He checked the display and connected. "Yeah, what do you have for me?"

Strauss said, "Still nothing on your wife. We haven't spotted her on video surveillance for corridors in and out of the city." He paused for a moment. When he spoke again, his voice came soft and slower. "I think we need to look more closely in town. We've completely ignored that."

"I don't agree. If she remained in town, she'd be in contact with friends. She's incapable of surviving on her own."

The contractor's voice grew harder. "Okay, your call. If that's your position, though, you're screwed. It's been a couple of weeks. If she was going to leave, as you suggest, she's long gone. Scouring local corridor videos makes zero sense."

Corel seethed. He didn't appreciate being contradicted by the hired help. For the moment, he'd let it slide. "What about the financial arrangements she made?"

"We verified that accounts were created, and money moved around. Just like you told me, she's shifted the funds enough times that we haven't been able to find them yet. Keep in mind that we know she did it while at home. So, unless she's actively managing the money now, finding it wouldn't help us understand where she's at physically."

Before the senator could retort, he continued in a placating voice, "We'll keep looking, and let you know the minute we find something."

Corel pushed his rising temper down. He needed to stay focused. "What about that minister, Polasky? What did you find out?"

"Not much to say. She's a minister at Saint Luke's in Bellevue. It's a medium-sized church. According to their website, she's the only minister. They have one other steady employee. I found their last year's budget posted on the site. It's pretty basic—salaries, utilities, supplies, and such."

"Do they have any kind of program or anything." Corel couldn't bring himself to say the words *domestic violence.*

"Nothing. The closest thing they have to any kind of community services is a free, used clothing closet. People apparently donate old clothes. Whoever needs that kind of thing can get the items free. Nothing else."

"What about her personally. I seem to remember being told that she witnessed a murder last spring."

Dylan replied, "Yes. That was in March. She does seem interested in the issue, but she's not a member of any organizational board related to domestic violence. As far as we can determine, she doesn't do anything other than counsel her own congregation members. She lives in church-provided housing, a parsonage. We watched it for a couple of days. She goes for a run in the morning around six and then to work at eight. We didn't see any lights on or movements during the day when she's not there. There doesn't seem to be any unusual comings or goings."

Fuck! "Why would my attorney tell me to check her out if there's nothing there?" Reba Stillings was not known for dolling out useless information.

"You'd have to ask her, but I can tell you this. Your wife is not staying at the parsonage, and Polasky doesn't go out at night. So, it seems unlikely that she's involved in any of this."

Corel closed his eyes and fought to hold in the contempt that he felt for this incompetent piece of shit. "Okay. Have you found anything at all in looking at the other organizations in the area?" Of course, he knew the answer to that already. If Strauss had found anything, he would have offered it earlier.

"Nothing. But, as you directed, we've put most of our effort into watching the corridors and checking agencies in other towns. How do you want me to proceed from here?"

Just fucking die, how about that? Dylan had produced nothing. At the moment, he seemed incapable of doing better. Still, the notion of Janet Polasky teased at the edges of the senator's mind. "How about we grab that minister like we did the Hartman bitch? If we can get her talking, that may unlock the entire thing."

The response came after an awkward moment of silence. "Bad idea. We've got a missing agency director and a death that, for the moment, is being looked at as an unrelated suicide. If we take the minister, then we're going to have to dispose of her when we're done, no matter what she tells us. If the bodies start to pile up, it's only a matter of time before someone's going to notice your wife is gone and begin to connect the dots."

Corel smirked. "I've never known you to be squeamish."

Strauss shot back, "I'm not squeamish, but neither am I stupid. Part of my job, at least as I see it, is to advise you against doing dumb things. If you go down that road, you'll hit an inflection point and things will tumble downhill rapidly. Believe me, Senator. I've seen this play out before."

It's going to go downhill for sure, at least for you, you dumb fuck. His vengeance against Strauss would have to wait for a while longer, but it would come. And then an epiphany struck, as though lightning from a storm cloud. *I'll take care of this myself.* He disconnected without giving anything away.

Just as he felt his strength, his control, building, the

phone call came. He looked at the display and cringed. "Good evening, Reba. What do you want?" He struggled to remain civil.

Her voice sounded as though it were cloaked in ice. The words were intense, but her tone sounded like the very definition of *controlled*. "I'll make this brief. My resources finished looking into the situation over at the network with Sue Hartman and my source in the agency. I'm afraid, Senator Corel, that you are in truly deep shit, excuse my language. Not to worry, though. Your sins can be atoned… for a price."

56

Bonnie Corel's world had been upended. Nothing made sense. She sat in the living room of the condo provided by a Methodist minister. Escaping her abusive husband had started pebbles rolling down the mountainside that grew into an avalanche. Since then, she had focused on trying to make sense of what was left.

What was left, though?

I'm alive. I have means, and I'm pissed. She was angry with the man who had, for the past two decades, passed as her husband. Her parents dismissed her problems when she'd tried to talk to them. Mostly she was angry at herself for being such a dishrag all these years. No more.

"I'm going to fix some dinner. Are you hungry?" Dani Stottman strolled into the room.

Bonnie stared at her for a moment. "He shot you, your boyfriend?"

Dani shrugged. "It's complicated."

"Don't I know."

"He loved me, at least he used to." The young girl

seemed to focus her view on something miles away… or maybe years in the past.

The senator's wife had a hard time believing that this child of wealth knew anything at all about love. Bonnie, herself from money, tried to recall what it felt like in those early years. "It's easy to fake love at first. They can say and do things that make you believe. The real test, though, is time."

Dani's eyes focused on Bonnie. "How long were you married?"

"Twenty-seven years."

The young girl cocked her head, her questioning gaze pressing Bonnie. "You're willing to throw it away? Don't you think it's worth trying to save? I mean, twenty-seven years is a long time."

Amusing. This young thing was barely twenty, if that. "Oh, the marriage ended many years ago. Thom couldn't keep his eyes… or hands… off other women. I thought we could make things work. Even if it wasn't like a true marriage, it could be a partnership. He was a rising star. I believed that the two of us working together could make the world a better place. I was willing to tolerate the other women for the sake of that."

"What happened?"

A bitter laugh escaped. "It wasn't any one thing. The other women began to dominate his attention. By the time we'd been married ten years, it seemed like he could hardly stand to touch me. Then came the words—the horrible names he'd call me and the vicious criticism of everything I did and said. I realized that he didn't want a partnership. He wanted an arrangement. I brought money to the marriage. He wanted that and the appearance of status and respect. He never considered me a partner, though."

"Why didn't you leave sooner?"

Chapter 56

Bonnie turned the question over in her mind. "Like you said, it's complicated. I was always convinced that somehow, we could turn it around." She chuckled. "I honestly have no idea what made me think that."

"But you left?" Dani seemed to be taking a genuine interest.

"The beating started around year twenty-five. Mostly it was throwing me around, kicking me, pulling my hair… that kind of thing. At that point, I think I began to understand that the entire thing was over. I just couldn't figure out what to do about it. I tried running away a couple of times before. They always found me, though. This time, he hit me in the face. My eye swelled shut and my face was bruised. When I looked in the mirror, there was simply nowhere else to hide. That did it for me."

Dani, who had been standing rapt while she listened, collapsed into a chair. She breathed deep and shook her head. "I guess I got lucky. I got out early."

Despite her best intentions, Bonnie burst out laughing. "Lucky? The asshole shot you. If that's lucky, you have an awfully low bar."

"What I mean is that I found out early. I didn't waste twenty-seven years of my life."

Bonnie responded, "As hard as they were, those years had value. We turned my money into more money. He climbed the political and social ladder. While he never saw me as his partner, I met a lot of people whose friendship might eventually help me through. I learned an awful lot."

Dani fell silent.

Bonnie probed, "You're Greg Stottman's niece, correct?"

The young girl shrugged again.

"If you don't mind my asking, how is he connected to

all of this. I mean, how is it that you connected with the good reverend and ended up here in this condo?"

"I don't know. My uncle made the arrangements."

A light went on in Bonnie's head. "He's the money behind all this, isn't he?"

"I'm not sure how all that works."

"Why would a man like your uncle put up the kind of money he has for something that doesn't really affect him? Does he have some kind of relationship with Reverend Polasky?"

The young girl apparently thought Bonnie was talking about a romantic relationship. "I don't know. I mean, he likes her, I think. He doesn't date much, though, and doesn't talk about it."

Bonnie's mind whirled. Greg Stottman was the silent money behind this project. If the rumors she'd heard were true, he was worth billions. Yet somehow, this minister and her project were important enough for him to fork over the bucks plus put his niece in hiding here. He was certainly a man worth knowing.

57

Janet's resolve to keep Greg Stottman out of the day-to-day operations of her project faltered. Given the high profile of her latest client, her funding source had the right to know that, should this all come to light, he might incur some political wrath. The fact that Dani currently shared housing with Bonnie Corel only exacerbated the situation.

After finishing dinner and putting the dishes away, she settled onto her couch. *Eight o'clock—he'd be home by now.* She pulled out her phone and dialed.

"Hi Janet, how's it going?" His voice sounded upbeat, even relaxed.

"I was wondering if you might have some time this evening. There's something I need to speak with you about."

His words came out laced with what sounded like barely concealed excitement. "Of course. Certainly. Do you want me to drop over there?"

"No need. I'll drive over to your place. Is a half-hour okay?"

Forty-five minutes later, she sat on his couch with a cup of steaming tea in front of her. "Thanks for making the time. I really appreciate it."

He smiled broadly. "My pleasure."

She took a sip, set her cup back down, and gathered her words. "There are a couple of things you need to know." She held up her hands, as though urging him to just listen. "I know that you're trying to avoid any direct involvement in what we're doing. I know that your business partners appreciate it as do I. Our latest client... well, you need to know about her."

"Okay, shoot."

"Bonnie Corel."

Greg narrowed his eyes and rubbed his chin. "I assume that she is some relation to our esteemed senator, Thomas Corel."

"Wife."

"Ouch."

A thought flashed through her mind that she quickly banished. *He seems amused.* "Yeah, ouch is right. I'm telling you because I can't know for sure how this turns out. If things don't go well and any of this goes public, you're likely to be on his bad side."

He laughed and slapped the arm of the overstuffed chair in which he sat. "Yeah, that's probably an understatement. I have to tell you, though, it certainly won't be the first time I've been on someone's shitlist."

Janet took a deep breath. "There's more. Right now she's the only client we have. So very likely you can figure out for yourself where we've got her staying."

The humor left his face. "The condo."

She nodded without comment.

"With Dani."

Another nod.

"Why are you keeping her in town? I would have thought by now you'd have her in another state."

"Her choice. I don't necessarily agree with it, but part of what I consider to be our core values is that we honor the wishes of our clients." Janet paused, considering what she'd just said. "We may have to revisit this idea later, but for now, that's what we're trying to do."

"Well, I would say that she's either incredibly stupid or has some kind of agenda."

Janet leaned forward and picked up her teacup. "She doesn't come across as stupid. Something else—she's not taking any financial support from us. She says she has her own money. That tells me that she didn't just up and bolt in the middle of the night. She must have seen this coming." She took a sip.

"Fair enough. I'd be lying if I said that I wasn't concerned for Dani. As I understand it, though, you have an employee working with Miz Corel. I have Kaz keeping in touch with Dani. Between the two of them, they can keep Dani... and your client safe. Do you have any reason to believe the senator is aggressively searching for his wife?"

"Bonnie says that the senator uses some kind of contractor help. I don't recall his name, but she says the man is pretty brutal. Also, and I don't know if this is in any way connected—Sue Hartman over at the DV Network disappeared right after Bonnie left. On top of that, an admin assistant at the network committed suicide at about the same time. Those all may be completely unrelated, but it does cause me some concern."

Greg appeared to process the information. His expression grew intense. "I agree. What do the police say about Hartman? Do they have any leads that you know of?"

Janet shook her head. "I don't know what they have.

My contact with the police, Dee Martin, is with Bellevue. Sue's case as well as the admin assistant's death is being handled by Seattle. From everything I've heard, the suicide is, at least for all practical purposes, a closed case. Sue's case, again, just from what little I've gleaned, is at a standstill."

Greg offered, "I admit that the *hired help* angle is troubling. I could make some phone calls, if you think that might help."

"I don't think it would do any good. If there were anything substantial to be learned, Dee would have figured it out, or at least know that it existed. My bet is that it's one of those cases that nobody really cares that much about."

His eyes took on a distant look as he seemed to lose focus. After a moment, he straightened up. "Tell you what. Here's what I'm going to do. I'll fill Kaz in on the details and have him work this. He's the best in the business and he's not constrained by police policies. If there's anything to be learned, he's the guy to do it. Do you think Miz Corel knows the name of this contractor?"

Worry washed over Janet. "Yes, but there's something else that bothers me. I'm out on a limb telling you all this. We promised Bonnie Corel confidentiality. You're wanting to expand the small circle of people who know. It feels like a betrayal to me."

"I'm sorry you feel that way, and I understand, but Dani's there and I can't stand by and trust this all to chance. Besides, Kaz already knows Miz Corel is there, although I'm not sure he realizes who she is."

Greg paused for a moment and then spoke quietly, "I know this might not make any difference to you, but I trust Kaz as much as I trust myself. The benefit of having him on this might make all the difference in the world as far as Dani's safety… as well as Miz Corel's. If it makes you feel any better, simply put it to her like Kaz is just one of the people working on her case. It's not technically a lie."

"Can I talk to Kaz first?"

"Of course. I'll have him call you this evening. The two of you can talk it over." He stopped abruptly. After a moment, he spoke softly. "After you discuss it with him, I'll honor whatever decision you make. In any event, I may end up having to pull Dani out of the condo."

58

They munched on cheeseburgers and fries in the midday September sun. The city park in north Boise was aflutter with the local denizens out for one last fling in the autumn sunshine. The Sniper considered his cousin, who shoveled the fast food into his mouth. *Disgusting.* Still, Billy had been mostly quiet—not his usual arrogant, ignorant self.

"You have any last questions before we move in?"

Billy swallowed and then took a gulp of soda. "Who is this guy, anyway?"

The Sniper shook his head. "Doesn't matter. He's a job, that's all."

"Yeah, I get that. I'm just curious, that's all. If I'm going to off the guy, I'd at least like to know something about him."

"That's a bad attitude to have, Cuz. You only need enough information to help you plan the hit—nothing more, nothing less. You have everything you need."

His cousin looked particularly unsatisfied by the answer, but didn't respond.

Chapter 58

The Sniper reluctantly continued. "He's a lawyer. Does lawsuits for gays who sue companies, you know, like bakeries and flower shops who won't do gay weddings and such."

Billy's face lit up. "Oh, yeah. I see why you picked the job, then… fucking faggots."

"No, you don't get it. I couldn't possibly care less about them one way or the other. I don't care who's fucking who. As long as it doesn't affect me, it doesn't make a whit of difference. Somebody somewhere apparently cares enough to shell out nine grand. I care about the money. End of story."

Billy's look of joyful enlightenment darkened. His smile faded. He narrowed his eyes as he stared back at the Sniper.

"You don't approve, I take it?" the Sniper asked.

The look on his cousin's face evolved. The darkness gave way to confusion and uncertainty.

"Don't overthink it. We have a job to do. If we do it successfully, somebody will pay us. It's the easiest money you'll ever make."

His cousin shook his head. "Seems like a lot of risk."

The Sniper burst out laughing. "Risk? Cuz, when you shot your girlfriend but didn't finish the job… now that's risky. Killing two cops, stealing a car with Washington plates, and driving into rural Idaho—that's some serious risk. Hell, all you're doing today is lying on the short rise in the trees overlooking the parking lot. You line the guy up in your scope and squeeze the trigger. We'll be home in time for dinner."

He wadded up the burger wrapper and stuffed it into the sack. "You ready?"

Fifteen minutes later, they lay concealed in a small stand of Douglas fir trees overlooking a half-full parking lot. The light midday breeze had dropped off. The flag in front of the building across the way hung limp.

"You're in luck, Cuz. No wind."

Billy stared intently down at the parking lot. "Are you sure he's gonna come out soon?"

"He leaves the office and goes to the courthouse every day at one-thirty."

Just then, their target came out of the office building, a briefcase in his hand. He walked steadily across the parking lot, bound for a silver BMW. "Right on time. Remember what I said, Cuz. Line him up in the scope. You're looking for a center chest shot. Squeeze the trigger; don't pull it. The shot should surprise you."

Billy glued his eye to the scope, his hands fidgeting on the stock of the rifle. He flipped off the safety and eased his finger into the trigger housing.

"Wait until he gets to his car. He'll pause to open the door. That's when you take the shot. Never shoot at a moving target unless you have to." The Sniper paused for a moment and muttered softly, "Wait. Just a little longer."

The man approached the car, clicking with his remote.

Billy grew perfectly still.

"Get ready."

The lawyer stopped at the car and reached for the door.

The Sniper spoke in a voice just over a whisper. "Do it, now."

The muffled shot registered as nothing more than spit. The man at the car dropped.

"Another round, quick."

Billy used the bolt to eject the spent cartridge and chambered another round. He aimed and fired again.

The Sniper took the rifle from him and handed his

cousin a camera. "Get a photo of the body and let's get going. Oh, and grab those spent cartridges."

Thirty seconds later, he stuffed the rifle and camera in his secret camper cache and climbed into the driver's seat of his truck. Billy slid into the passenger side.

"And we're off." The Sniper pulled the gear shift down into drive and eased out onto the side street, turning right at the next stop sign, and then merging into the access road for the northbound highway.

"This is important, Cuz. When leaving, you want to stay with traffic. It's best to pick two or three cars that are traveling close to the speed limit and fall in behind them. Go with the flow. The biggest thing is not to go too fast or too slow. We want to be just another truck."

The Sniper glanced over at his cousin. The boy's hands were shaking. He grasped them together, apparently trying to cover up. "You did good, Cuz. Just breathe. Take in the scenery. We'll be home before you know it."

They rode in silence for about twenty minutes, at which point they found themselves northbound on Highway 55 with very little traffic around. "This is the riskiest part, Cuz. We're alone here on the road. If a cop happens around, either from in front or behind us, we're the only thing they're gonna see. Most times, they won't notice us… won't even care. Thing is, though, keep in mind that we can't hide among other cars."

It all came crashing down about thirty minutes outside of Cascade. A blue flashing light lit up the rearview mirror. "Shit. State cops."

Billy started to reach around for the gun in his back waistband.

"No, Cuz. No gun. Keep your hands in plain view. Don't say anything. When he comes to the window, just look over at him like you're curious. Let me handle everything."

The Sniper eased over to the shoulder, stopped the truck, put it in park, and turned off the ignition. He put both hands on the steering wheel. Watching in the side view mirror, he rolled down the window as the uniformed male officer approached.

"Hey, Officer. What's the problem?" He kept his voice neutral with a tinge of curiosity. He'd been this route before.

The cop who looked to be about forty-five or fifty and stocky, bent down and peered in through aviator sunglasses. "License and registration."

The Sniper smiled. "I'm going to reach into my glove box and get the registration, okay?" He waited for the response.

"You boys got any guns?"

"No sir."

"Go ahead and get it, then."

The Sniper reached over, opened the glove box, and pulled out a piece of paper. "Here you go." He reached around and pulled out his wallet, retrieving his driver's license. "And here's my license, sir."

The cop studied both of them. "Do you know why I pulled you over?"

"Uh, no, sir. I'm pretty sure I wasn't speeding." The Sniper kept his eyes wide as though waiting to be enlightened.

"Your brake lights are out. Did you know that, son?"

The Sniper furrowed his brow. "Uh, I'm sorry, no, I didn't know that. I'll get them fixed as soon as I get home."

"Where is home?"

"I live up on the other side of Cascade." No point in

lying. The cop was looking at his driver's license and registration. "I'll try to get it into Sam's Auto first thing in the morning, sir."

"You see that you do that, son." He bent down further and glanced across at Billy, who nodded to him without speaking.

"You boys be careful now." The cop turned and strode back to his car.

The Sniper sat still, his hands on the steering wheel as the officer pulled out onto the roadway and drove off.

Billy exhaled loudly. "I thought sure as shit you were going to off that guy."

"Why?"

"I figure he'd made us."

"What made you think that?"

Cousin Billy shrugged. "I dunno. I just figured… why would he stop us unless he knew."

"Cuz, if he made us, he'd never try to stop us alone. He'd radio it in, and they'd set up a roadblock. Look, it's nearly three, close to the end of his shift. He's probably headed back to the outpost. This stop was an annoyance more than anything else. He wanted to be done with it as much as we wanted it." The Sniper paused and smiled. "You know what he was looking for?"

"What?"

"Respect. He catches shit every minute of every day. If he's not dealing with a shitty supervisor, he's taking crap from every swinging dick that has a hard-on for cops. Likely he hates the fucking job but can't afford to retire. This time of day, the guy just wanted some respect."

Billy seemed to ponder the idea. "Yeah, I guess. Still, you did grovel a lot."

"I'd rather grovel all day than be forced to kill him."

"Seems like kind of a bleeding-heart thing. You didn't have no problem about offing that lawyer guy."

"The lawyer guy was business. There's no profit in killing cops. You of all people should know that."

59

B ack home at the parsonage, Janet settled onto the couch and phoned Bonnie. She needed to get out in front of this before it got any further.

"Hello."

"Hi Bonnie, this is Janet Polasky. I'm sorry to bother you so late, but there's something I need to touch base with you about. Dani's uncle, Greg Stottman, is concerned about her safety. I know that you said your husband retains a contractor that has, in the past pursued you. We have a person who we use for security purposes in extreme situations. His name is Dimitry Kazarian. I believe you've already met him. With your permission, I'd like to talk to him and then, perhaps tomorrow, bring him over to the condo to speak with you."

"Does he realize who I am?"

Janet replied, "I haven't spoken to him yet."

"I suppose tomorrow will be okay."

Ten minutes later, Janet's ringtone sounded. "Hello."

"Hello, Janet. This is Kaz. Greg said you wanted to speak with me."

She poured out the bare bones framework of the problem without mentioning Bonnie's name or the identity of her husband. "She's willing to meet with you tomorrow, if you're available."

* * *

"Bonnie Corel, this is Dimitry Kazarian." Janet gestured toward Kaz.

The senator's wife stepped forward, her hand outstretched. "We've met. Pleased to see you, Mister Kazarian." She turned into the living room. "We can sit in here and talk."

Just at that moment, Dani strolled into the living from the hallway. "Hi Kaz. What are you doing here?"

Kaz smiled at the young woman. "Just earning a fast buck. How are you holding up,?"

She shrugged. "I guess as well as I can expect. I'm going to make some coffee. Anybody want a cup?"

Janet, Bonnie, and Kaz placed their orders with her.

The senator's wife spoke first. "Okay, then. We're all here. What is it you want?" She tossed the question in Janet's direction.

The minister leaned forward, clasping her hands in her lap. "Here's the situation. Bonnie has indicated she wants to remain local. This is her choice to make. Whatever benefits or drawbacks it has, it also puts her closer to those who are looking for her. By association, this puts Dani closer as well."

Kaz spoke, "If I might ask, who specifically is looking for you?"

Bonnie stared at him for a moment. "Do you know who my husband is?"

"Should I?" His eyes showed what appeared to be genuine curiosity.

"Senator Thomas Corel."

Kaz seemed unimpressed. "Okay, so is he the one looking for you?"

Bonnie appeared to consider the question carefully, finally responding, "Yes and no. He's certainly the one behind it. He has a contractor-type who does his dirty work—Dylan Strauss. He's the one that found me when I left before."

Kaz seemed to ponder the information.

Janet asked, "Do you know him, Kaz?"

"Not personally. I've heard his name. If he's the same guy, he's what I call a problem-solver. Guys like him have few boundaries. They aren't usually hired as hitmen, but they have no problem killing if necessary. Most of them move across international boundaries frequently, working globally. They don't come cheap."

Bonnie nodded. "Sounds right. When he found me, he spoke softly. He almost came across as kind and under-standing… almost. He had an icy look in his eyes as though his heart and soul were frozen. There was no doubt in my mind that he would kill me if I had refused to go with him."

Kaz sipped his coffee as he processed the information. "Do you know, Miz Corel, is your husband's preference to retrieve you or to kill you?"

Janet felt it a blunt and insensitive question. Still, the answer was important.

Bonnie responded thoughtfully, "I'm not at all sure. At first, I was confident that getting me back was what he wanted. But now…." She turned her head and stared out the window for a moment in silence.

"My husband is running for reelection right now. His

position and power are without question the most important things in his life. While I'm at home with him, he thinks he can keep me under control and quiet. I suppose he's right about that. When I'm there with him, I keep thinking that I can make things right." She shook her head.

"That's another story, though. If he had me killed and could make sure that it doesn't lead back to him, it would likely garner him the sympathy vote. That's how cold and calculating he is. If I'm outside his control, I'm his worst nightmare. I could, with a call to a newspaper reporter, bring his entire political career down and he's well aware of that. That's why he's not going to just let me go."

Kaz shrugged. "If that's the case, why not make the call to the newspapers. Once the story is out, he could go after you for revenge, but killing you then would certainly lead back to him, and he knows it. So long as he has a lid on everything, silencing you permanently is his best option."

"In my heart, I know, but that's a huge step, from which there's no coming back. Honestly, I don't want to ruin his career. I don't hate him. I just want to be out of that life."

"I understand. So, look, I'm going to tell you the same thing I told Greg Stottman when I was trying to protect Dani." He glanced over at the young girl, who had taken a seat across the living room and was observing the discussion.

Kaz continued, "All things being equal, defensive strategies are destined to fail. If he continues to search for you with the intent of doing you harm, you have to successfully anticipate and defend against every single attempt. He can strike whenever, wherever, and however he chooses. The worst part is that you have to thwart every single attack. He has to succeed only once. Sooner or later, he'll get lucky unless you stop him first."

"What do you suggest, Mister Kazarian?"

Kaz thought for a few seconds before responding. "Because we aren't going to be assassinating a sitting U. S. Senator, we have to convince him that it's in his own best interest to leave you alone. That has two elements to it. First, he would need to believe that you're not going to blow the whistle on him at some future date. There's no way for you to guarantee that so it would mostly come down to trust."

Taking a drink of coffee, he set the cup down. "Second, and this one's the kicker. We have to show him beyond any doubt that should anything happen to you, the trail back to him would become immediately visible to the entire world. He has to understand that facilitating harm to you, he would be destroying his own life."

Bonnie nodded slowly, a frown on her face. "That all sounds good, but I'm not certain that Thom is in his right mind. Lately, it seems as though he's gone down this deep, black hole. I'm afraid that he may reach a point where he would be willing to give everything up simply to get even with me."

"That's a possibility, for sure. There's nothing we can do about that at the moment short of killing him, which I'm not willing to do. If we can convey the proposed solution back to him, then we might be able to gauge his reaction better. But first things first. Would you be willing to talk to him on the phone to convey these thoughts?"

"I'd rather not." Bonnie leaned back on the couch, her arms folded on her chest. "It could work if we communicate through Dylan Strauss."

Kaz stood. "Possibly. Let me see if I can dredge up

some information on Mister Strauss, including perhaps, a way to contact him."

After a moment, Bonnie turned to Janet. "One other thing. Before this goes any further, I'd like to speak with Greg Stottman in person."

The request hit Janet like a freight train. "Why?"

Bonnie laughed. "This has all gotten very complicated and dangerous. If I'm going to stick my neck out, I'd at least like to meet the guy who's behind all this."

60

With just over a month to go before the election, Senator Corel felt everything closing in on him. His wife remained outside his control—a massive liability —a loose end. He was no closer to getting her back than he'd been when she left. His hired help, Dylan Strauss —useless.

The communication link to Reba Stillings that he'd forced himself to stomach over the years had gone dark. In their last phone conversation, she'd ended any possibility that he could trust her… ever again. She had this farcical notion that somehow, she could exact retribution from him for the situation with the Hartman bitch and that admin assistant. He would, at some point, be forced to deal with Stillings. A smile forced its way onto his lips.

Then there was the minister lady. Strauss had, once again, failed miserably. He muttered under his breath, "I'll fucking do it myself. I can't trust anybody."

Navigating the web, he pulled up St. Luke's piddly excuse for a website. He shook his head as he smirked in disdain. Moving to the tab labeled "Leadership," he stared at the photo of Janet Polasky. He would take care of her in due time. His interest this day was the board president, Rob Young.

"So, what about you, Mister Young? Who are you?" The photo showed a puffy white face. *Probably fat.* The coat, shirt, and tie all looked as though they came off the sale rack at Walmart. But the look on the guy's face—full of self-importance. *This will work.* He grabbed a pen and scribbled the contact phone number for Young, making sure it wasn't the church's business number.

Corel strode into the outer office area and handed the scrap of paper to a staffer, whose name he completely blanked on. "I need to talk to this guy, Rob Young. Could you get him on the phone for me." He started to add *please* but frankly, saw no need. It was the woman's job to do what he commanded.

Back in his office, he waited. Less than five minutes later, his office phone rang. The intercom light lit up. "Yes?"

"Senator, I have Mister Young on line one."

He forced a thank you and clicked on the blinking button. "Good morning, Mister Young. This is Senator Thom Corel. I hope I'm not getting you at a bad time."

After a moment of awkward silence, a voice answered, "Yes, sir, uh, Senator. I mean, no, this isn't a bad time at all."

"I'll get to the point, Rob. As you know, I'm running for re-election. Once the election is over, I want to organize a broad-based community coalition that will help me understand the issues that concern our residents. A key element of this is the faith community. I'd like you to be part of that effort."

Another moment of silence and another hesitant response. "I'm not sure how I could help."

Corel hit his stride. He was in his element. "My focus will be on leadership of community churches and faith organizations. As the president of Saint Luke's board, you're uniquely positioned to interact with me and my staff. The mere fact that you occupy that position of leadership speaks to the respect and trust the congregation has in you. On the other side of the coin, being in a serious leadership position, you understand the realities of organizational culture and how the faith community blends perfectly with our society." He almost gagged at the syrupy cup of horse piss that he was feeding this schmuck.

"Uh, well, yes sir, I understand." He paused.

Corel could almost hear the man sweating. Something wasn't right.

"Thing is, Senator, I've stepped away from my board position for a while. I wanted to spend more time with my family and focusing on my career."

The senator almost burst out laughing. *Career? You're a fucking car salesman.* He forced himself to remain serious. This certainly put a different spin on things. Then it hit him. Something had gone wrong between Rob Young and the church. The *time with my family* thing was the oldest dodge in the book. This could work to the senator's advantage.

"I have to tell you, Rob. I've seen this a lot. The challenges and pressure of leadership rob us of valuable time with those we care about. You know, I think it makes you an even better choice. If you're willing to devote just a little bit of your time, I think this could be incredibly rewarding for you. Tell you what, why don't we meet for drinks. We can go over some of my ideas and, frankly, I'm anxious to hear some of yours. We can grab some dinner first, if you like."

* * *

Corel watched Rob Young ease through the door of the El Gaucho restaurant just before seven o'clock. He wore the same cheap coat and tie as his church photo, albeit with a different cheap shirt. His face reflected delusional self-importance. Approaching the table, he offered his hand.

"Senator Corel, it's an honor, sir. I'm Rob Young."

Corel smiled broadly and gestured to the chair across from him. "Sit, please. Let's not stand on formalities tonight." He held his hand up and snapped is fingers and raising his voice. "Could I get a drink for my friend?"

As a waiter approached, Young said. "Bourbon, over ice."

Corel added, "Scotch rocks for me."

Their drinks arrived and the waiter retreated. Taking a sip, Corel set his glass aside and probed. "I got to thinking about it after we spoke on the phone. I should have made it clear that your wife was welcome to join us. Family is important."

A troubled look washed across Young's face. He furrowed his brow and seemed to clench his jaw. After a moment, he responded softly, "Lucy has been going through some stuff lately. She's back East visiting relatives right now. Her brother hasn't been well."

"That's too bad. I'm sorry to hear that. Please convey my thoughts and prayers for her."

Rob nodded but his gaze wandered down to the table. Corel could see it. The relatives, the brother—lies. There was something else.

"Is there anything that my office can help with?"

The dark look turned to one of near panic. "Uh, no. Nothing. It's nothing, really. Just family stuff."

Yeah, right. "So, you've taken some time off from the

church. It takes a great deal of wisdom to recognize when it's necessary to step away from the responsibilities for a time. That must have been a tough decision."

Young appeared to force a smile. "Yeah, but now I have some time to help you."

Corel moved in for the big push. "What I was thinking, Rob, was that you might help to recruit Reverend Polasky to the effort as well. Between the two of you, we would enjoy a wide range of experience and insight—she from the ministerial perspective and you from the leadership side. It would seem to be a good match." The senator watched closely for a reaction.

What a reaction it was. It seemed as though acid had been thrown in the man's face—a combination of rage, hatred, and fear. The man recovered quickly, though. "That seems like a good approach, but I'm not certain that Reverend Polasky is the right person. She's just not a good fit."

Corel queried, "How so?"

Rob squinted as though trying to form the right sequence of words. "She's… I mean, sometimes she gets caught up in problems that really aren't hers to solve." He smiled and added quickly, "I know, of course, that she means well. It's just that sometimes things are best handled by families themselves without other people meddling."

Epiphany! Rob and his wife had troubles and Reverend Polasky had butted in. *Perfect.* This was going to work even better than expected. Corel summoned his most practiced worried look. He drew his mouth into a tight line and lowered his head.

"These are sensitive and troubling issues, to be sure. During dark times, we need to gather our families around in privacy and solve the problems that haunt us. As well intentioned as some people can be, often they can't see that they are causing more harm than good." Corel turned his attention to the bar. He raised his hand, gesturing that two more drinks were needed.

Rob seemed to be choosing his words carefully, although the truth was slipping out much faster than expected. "Yeah. I'm afraid that she just doesn't understand that."

The drinks arrived. Young polished off his first one and raised the second to his lips.

Corel dug deeper. "You know, Rob, I can appreciate your insight into this. Too often, people like Reverend Polasky get caught up in the details of other people's lives. She doesn't realize that you're balancing family pressures, employment responsibilities, and leadership challenges. In my experience, this is what often separates superior leaders like you from the mediocre workers—that total lack of understanding."

He watched as Rob Young digested the words. The senator forced himself not to smile. The look on the man's face made it clear that he was just about ready.

"Tell you what, Rob. Here's a thought. I'd like to be able to bring you on to my staff once the election is over. You would make an excellent liaison for faith-based initiatives. You bring sound business and leadership experience as well as insight into the spiritual aspect. If I'm reading you right, though, you have some loose ends with your family. Maybe some repair work to do."

"Oh, I'm okay. I'll figure that part out."

Corel pushed ahead. "I've no doubt of that, but I'm sensing that the meddling of the pastor is still an issue. That, I believe, is something I can help with."

Young's eyes darted from side to side. The senator could see that the man was trying to process the underlying message.

Chapter 60

"I'm not sure how you could help. It's kind of a personal thing."

Senator Corel smiled warmly. "Yes, of course it is. What I can do, with your help of course, is to negotiate a truce between you and the minister. With my position and resources, I'm sure that I can convince her that, with her talents, she might be better suited to a larger congregation, perhaps in another state. It's the kind of thing that I can advocate for without being too overt. If I'm not mistaken, that would resolve some of your problems. At the very least, it would facilitate you returning to your leadership position on the board. After that, we can talk about you transitioning to my staff. We could look at a D. C. job or even have you work out of my Seattle office. I'm sure the compensation would compare quite favorably to your current pay." He wondered if this might be too condescending, but Young didn't appear to notice the slight.

Young seemed on the verge... almost ready. "I don't know, maybe...."

Corel clapped his hands together. "This is going to work out fantastic. I'm excited at the prospect of working with you. So, how about we order some dinner?"

Back in his office, Senator Corel pondered his next task, which would be far more difficult than enlisting Rob Young. He pulled out his burner phone and connected.

Dylan Strauss answered after one ring, his voice sounding stressed and irritated. "Yes?"

"Good evening. How are you doing this evening?"

Strauss' voice, while not openly hostile, was certainly not brimming with joy. "What do you need?"

Corel stuffed his anger at the disrespectful tone. "I've come up against a bit of a sensitive problem."

"And?"

The senator fumed, but managed to hold his words. "There are some pointed questions being asked about Hartman and the other one. I'm okay fielding them, but I'd like to talk directly to your employee, Unger, I believe his name is."

"Why?"

Corel gathered his wits and laid it out exactly as he'd envisioned. "I want to hear from him exactly what happened. I'm comfortable that your people did the best they could under the circumstances. Given the potential consequences, though, I want to hear the account from him personally."

He could hear the sound of breathing on the other end of the connection. It sounded angry, confrontational. "What is it you want from him? If I don't know, I can ask him and get back to you."

The senator decided to end the conversation here. "Have him contact me. It won't take a minute."

Ten minutes later his cellphone rang. "This is Senator Corel."

The voice sounded coarse and annoyed. "You wanted to talk to me?"

"Ah, yes, Mister Unger. How are you this evening?"

Corel could hear the uncertainty in the brief silence and the change of tone. "I'm okay, I guess."

"The job you did for Mister Strauss, the one with the Hartman woman and the other assistant. I wanted you to know how grateful I am. I know it didn't go exactly as planned, but I think you recovered nicely, and it all worked out okay." The senator almost gagged at having to utter these words.

"Uh, well, thanks."

"The reason I wanted to talk to you is that I have a job that I'd like *you* to do for me. It's separate from what Mister Strauss is doing, so of course I'll pay you extra, say, an additional ten thousand dollars."

Corel thought he heard a slight gasp. "Must be some job."

"Nothing big. Just a little personal errand."

61

For the most part, Greg felt excited to see Dani without looking like he was checking up on her. He didn't see the point in meeting Bonnie Corel. He avoided politics. Janet's explanation that Bonnie wanted to see him because he was the money behind the project seemed off. Still, on the whole, he was glad for the opportunity to visit the condo.

Dani looked good. The puffiness in her eyes had gone down and she had good color in her face. Mostly, though, it was the soft smile. "Hey, Dani, you look wonderful." He embraced her and hugged tight. And for the first time in recent memory, she returned the hug.

"It's great to see you, Uncle Greg. Thanks for coming over." She stepped back and turned toward the kitchen. "I'm going to grab a cup of coffee. Would you like one?"

"Sure, thank you." He took a quick look around the living room. The condo had a comfortable lived-in look without being messy. A few magazines lay stacked on the end table with a newspaper spread on the coffee table. He stole a glance at the center of the room where, one night months earlier, three men had died. The carpet showed no signs of the blood that had confronted him that night.

"Here you go." Dani set his cup down and took hers over to the wing-backed chair that sat kitty-cornered to the sofa. "How are you doing?"

He took a sip and set the cup back down. "Things are good, although I have to say they'd be better if you were back home."

The smile turned sad and wistful. "Yeah, I wish I knew when this was all going to be over."

"Me too." Greg leaned forward, brushing imaginary lint from his jeans. "I have to believe, honestly, that Billy won't try anything. He's got every cop in Washington looking for him and he's completely disappeared. Coming back here would be stupid."

At that moment, a striking woman who appeared to be about fifty emerged from the hallway into the living room. Her blonde hair, which rested on her shoulders, had streaks of silver emanating from her temples. Her eyes flashed as she strode confidently up to him. "You must be Greg Stottman. A pleasure to meet you."

He stood and offered his hand. "Miz Corel—my pleasure. Have a seat. I was just catching up on things with my niece. By the way, thank you for agreeing to let her stay here with you. It means a lot to me that she's safe."

Her smile exuded confidence. "It's no problem at all. In fact, it's nice to have some company. And please, call me Bonnie."

He nodded and filled the empty space in the conversation by picking up his coffee cup.

Bonnie slid onto the opposite end of the sofa from Greg and turned toward him. "I asked Reverend Polasky to set up this meeting for several reasons. First, and most important, I want to thank you for all of this. I don't think it's an exaggeration to say that this help has saved my life."

It felt odd. He contributed to a lot of causes and programs. Having someone who benefitted set up a meeting simply to thank him was unusual. "You're welcome, but the one you should be thanking is Janet Polasky. It was her brainchild."

"I understand and I did thank her, along with her employee. Given what this all must be costing, I felt it important to recognize your contribution." She smiled broadly.

She was playing him. He resisted the urge to roll his eyes. "You said there were several reasons for the meeting." He arched his eyebrows expectantly.

Bonnie cleared her throat and placed her hands on her knees, as though she needed to keep them still. "Yes, well, mostly it was just to thank you. You and your company are a big part of the Seattle magic. You touch the community in so many ways. You employ thousands. You purchase from local vendors and contractors. Your contributions to charity make the city a better place...."

He lost track of what she was saying. He'd endured this speech so many times he could recite it in his sleep. The delivery always came with a catch or a tagline. She wanted something. "Thanks for the kind words." He got the words out as quickly as he could. Now, if he could just end the meeting that quickly.

"I'll be frank, Greg. I don't recall my husband ever mentioning your financial support for his campaigns." She shot him a questioning look.

"That would be because I don't contribute to political campaigns. I limit my political activity to voting. I'll leave the lobbying and influence peddling to others who are more skilled in that area." He tried to deliver the line with a touch of humor while, at the same time, shutting down any further discussion of politics.

"I respect that, and it's not my intention to affect that one way or the other. I was just curious about someone who had so much at stake in the economy but who steadfastly remained outside the arena."

Weariness got the better of him. "What is it that you want from me, Miz Corel?"

Her smile faded. They locked gazes for a moment. "I will not run from my husband. I refuse to cower in the corner just because he's unable to control his temper. I made the decision to leave him. The reasons are exactly as I told Reverend Polasky and Miz Gomez. He has a violent temper, and treated me like a punching bag. He won't not drive me from Seattle, though. This is my home." Her eyes blazed with anger.

"I appreciate that, but what does it have to do with me?" He was glad that the conversation had at last become real.

"There is something that you need to be aware of. Should it come to light that Reverend Polasky is the one who helped me, she could be in a great deal of danger. On top of that, it could easily be traced back to you. My husband is not a particularly forgiving man and, whatever else I think of him, he does make a formidable enemy. I understand that Sue Hartman from the DV Network is missing. My money is on my husband being at the center of that."

"You think your husband engineered her disappearance?"

Bonnie grimaced and shook her head. "First, and this is just my own personal opinion, I believe that Sue Hartman is dead. Thom didn't kill her personally, but his thugs likely did. Maybe it was revenge. Perhaps it was a crude attempt at prying information out of her. Either way, Thom is involved. I'm telling you this because, while I know you're good at defending yourself in the business and legal arena, he doesn't play that way. He goes for the jugular."

With a feeling of uneasiness, Greg glanced over at Dani. "I believe you're safe here, at least for now. I trust Janet and her employees to stay up on the situation and make the decisions they need to."

"Yes, I agree. That's why I'm here. I'm telling you because, as far as I know, you're not factoring in what his goons might do to you if they find out."

"Do you have any information on these *goons*, as you call them?"

Bonnie paused for a moment, as though gathering her thoughts. "The only one you need to worry about is their leader. His name is Dylan Strauss. I don't know anything about him other than what I observed when he brought me back last time. There was no doubt in my mind that, if I had refused to go with him, he would have killed me on the spot and never given it a second thought. And to make matters worse, I honestly believe that would have been fine with my husband."

"Thank you for that. I'll take appropriate caution. Is there anything else?" Greg tapped the name Dylan Strauss into his notetaking app.

"I will re-establish myself. I'm starting a new life. As you probably know already, I'm not after money. I have my own. I don't intend to try and bring my husband down. Honestly, Greg, I'm looking for friends—people I can count on."

Greg rubbed his chin. "I guess I'm not sure what you mean by *friends*. By definition, at this point, we're acquaintances. I have many people with whom I associate. When I hear the word *friend*, though, it conjures up visions of something very different."

"I understand, and perhaps I misspoke. I know friendship is a thing unto itself." She sighed and regrouped. "Perhaps the term—people with whom you associate—would better describe what I'm talking about, at least for now."

His cynicism grew. He was used to having smoke blown up his ass. It happened all the time. This seemed particularly offensive, though. Most people at least tried to build on some common interest. This woman was offering nothing more than herself. Not that he had anything against her, but he saw no reason for this conversation. "As I said, Miz Corel, I'm pleased to make your acquaintance. I hope that your plans work out. I assure you that you have the best help available in Janet and her people. If there's anything I can specifically do for you, please ask." It was a throwaway line. He would prefer that she get her help from Janet and the others.

She stood and brushed the wrinkles from her slacks. Her smile returned. "I will do that, Greg. Thank you for taking the time to visit." She excused herself and left the room.

62

Val sat at the breakfast room table while Dee poured two cups of coffee. "I could get used to this. Being here with you all night. Going to work like regular people." She laughed. "At least I assume this is what regular people do. Never been one myself."

Dee sat the cup in front of Val and eased into the chair across from her. When she spoke, her voice was soft. "I know. I keep dreading the day when Janet sends you back on the road."

"It won't be today."

Dee continued as though she hadn't heard, "This case seems different. Her project wasn't supposed to work this way." She hurriedly added, "Mind you, I'm not complaining. It's just that it seems so strange."

Val shrugged and sipped her coffee.

"This client of yours must be someone very important. Janet told me about her first client. I'm not sure what's different about this one."

Val tried to put her off. "I assume Reverend Polasky

296

has her reasons. Anyway, I'm just glad for another day in town."

"You can't tell me either, huh?"

"Sorry."

Dee picked at a small wood splinter on the edge of the tabletop. "You don't trust me?"

"Janet said to keep it close. She didn't explain herself, and she didn't ask my opinion. It's just the way it is. It'll be over soon enough." Val felt an uneasiness creeping in. This was beginning to feel like an interrogation.

There was a part of her, though, that wanted to confide in Dee. This… what they had… was the closest thing to a true relationship she'd ever known. There had to be an element of trust somewhere in the mix. She closed her eyes briefly before trying to smooth things over.

"Look, Dee, it's not that I don't trust you. I do. If it was up to me, I'd tell you. You have to understand, I gave my word."

Dee's tone turned hard. She took a sharp breath and turned her head abruptly and stared at the window. "No problem. Don't worry about it."

Val understood completely. The *no problem* meant that this would simmer between them for a while. The *don't worry about it* was intended to underscore that the discussion wasn't finished. She also knew that this wasn't about the identity of a client or even about trust. It was something else—something far worse.

She pivoted and tried to lighten things up. "Anything in particular you want for dinner? I can stop on the way from work and pick up something, if you like."

"What time will you be getting off?"

Val thought about it for a moment. "I'm not sure how things will go. It's unstructured right now. I don't know from one day to the next what's going on."

Dee's words came out matter-of-factly. "Maybe now that we're going to be moving in together, you could look for a different job. Money shouldn't be a big crunch anymore."

It hit Val like a punch in the gut. "What do you mean? You're the one who hooked me up with this job. What happened to the women that need help... the high purpose?"

Dee glared at Val and then her eyes softened. "Hon, this has gotten more dangerous than I thought. It's like... with this new client of yours... I don't know, it's not what I thought it would be"

"Why? Is it because I won't tell you who she is? Or is there something else?"

Dee stood and began pacing the kitchen, her head hung. "No, well, maybe a little. Mostly it's because whoever it is and whatever's going on seems darker, more sinister than what I expected."

"No. I don't buy it. You've seen women and children murdered by violent men. You know what Janet witnessed. You've seen the darkest this world has to offer. Now all of a sudden, because I've got a client that I can't tell you about, it's too dangerous and I should get out."

"It's different now."

Val eased over and touched her shoulder. "Why? What's different? These women still need help. What changed?"

Tears streamed down Dee's face. "I watched you carted off to prison just over ten years ago. I never told you, but it broke my heart. I was in love with you back then. I didn't tell you because, well, you know, you'd been married to a man, and I didn't think you'd...." She turned her head away, her voice falling off.

A few seconds later, she turned back and embraced

Val. "Now that there's a chance, a life that we could have, I don't want to lose you again."

Val returned the hug. The two stood in the kitchen, locked in an embrace. When Val stepped back, she put her hands on Dee's shoulders. "You're not going to lose me, but you need to understand, I have to do what my heart tells me. You were right. There are women who need help. If I can save only one life, it's worth it."

But that wasn't at the heart of what Val thought. Being told what she could and couldn't do brought back trauma that seemed unbearable. It conjured up the memory of her husband ordering her around and then punishing her when she didn't comply perfectly. In that moment, she wondered if she could ever truly be in a relationship. She banished the notion and cleared her throat.

"I have to go. My client will wonder where I am." Val took her half-full coffee cup to the sink, poured out what was left, washed the cup, and put it in the drain rack. Turning, she leaned back on the counter and composed her words carefully.

"It's going to be a long day. I think I'll stay at my place tonight. I need to do some laundry and catch up on my bills. I'll give you a call tomorrow."

Dee looked at her with pleading eyes. "Val, please, don't…." She fell silent and turned her head away. "I understand, I really do. Do what's right for you. Take as much time as you need." She stood, walked over, and gently kissed Val on the lips. "I love you. Don't push me away."

63

Kaz's call came about mid-morning. Greg agreed to a lunch meeting at a bistro about five miles from his office. He arrived just after noon to find Kaz sipping a glass of iced tea. He sat and the waiter immediately swooped in to take their orders. Once he retreated, Greg asked, "Do you have something for me?"

"Yes. Let's do Stillings first. It's easier. As you know, she's an attorney. Does a mix of corporate work and criminal defense, mostly wealthy men accused of violent offenses against partners. The well-heeled men pay the bills, which allows her to do pro bono work. My guess is that the Rob Young case was that way. Her real money, though, comes from the corporate world."

Nothing he said was news to Greg. "Any idea why she had Paulette's office phone tapped?"

"I think the key to understanding is to look at her individual clients. As I said they're all men accused of domestic violence. It's her signature issue, apparently." Kaz folded his hands on the table and leaned forward, as though confiding a dark secret.

"Several of the men she represented ended up murdering their partners. In at least three of those cases, the women were staying in relatively secret surroundings, maintaining a low profile. Somehow, the men found them. One possibility, and I'd say it's the most likely, is that Reba Stillings provided the intelligence that allowed them to locate the women. There's no evidence that I could find that she was complicit in the murders. She's never been charged with anything."

"Do you think she was trying to find Rob Young information on his wife's whereabouts?"

Kaz tapped his fingers on the tabletop as he seemed to think it through. "I'm not so sure about that. I suspect that providing him with intelligence was strictly secondary. I bet that she was attempting to add to her reservoir of information. On the off-chance that Janet was ramping up an effort to help women escape, information on that could be worth a fortune to her. Beyond money, though, it would be a key element in her crusade."

"Is she part of some larger organization or effort? Maybe some deep pockets that fund her efforts?"

Kaz shook his head. "No connection that I could find. As far as funding goes, she makes more than enough off her practice to live comfortably and pursue her philosophical fight. She doesn't need backing."

Greg had trouble getting his mind around her overall motivation, though. "Why? She's a woman. Why would she work so directly in what seems a direct attack on women in general?"

"One possibility is that her work puts her in a position of power with men. In fact, she's known to be quite the bully. It may well be the case that she couldn't care less about domestic violence. Her work is simply a means of exerting power and influence over men."

"That strikes me as shortsighted." Greg had seen a lot of people who ended up painting themselves into a corner in the pursuit of pure power.

"Maybe. Whatever the case, she's good at it. Like most effective attorneys, she uses the pro bono cases as a marketing tool. For every five or ten freebies, she hooks onto a whale. Word is, she milks them for all she can."

Greg sighed. "Okay. Any ideas on how to counter her?"

Kaz laughed softly. "It's a dance. Keep an eye on her. Maintain high security. Sweep offices for bugs regularly." He grew serious. "A couple of other things. First, the women that are helping to move the clients around—they should be armed and have training on how to spot surveillance and defend themselves and their clients. I know that you may get some pushback from Reverend Polasky. I can talk to her if you like."

"I'd appreciate that. Thanks. Now, anything on this Dylan Strauss character?"

Kaz drew his mouth into a tight line and clenched his jaw. He stared into Greg's eyes for a moment before responding. "I know of him… never met him, but he's got a reputation. He's not a lightweight. His work spans the globe. Dylan's what we call a *problem solver*. He fixes things. He has few, if any, boundaries. He's not what you'd call a hired killer, but he has no problem pulling the trigger if he needs to. He doesn't come cheap, which means that his only clients are at the top of the food chain or nearly so."

Greg let his gaze wander for a moment as he digested the information. "You met the woman who's in the condo with Dani—Bonnie Corel?"

Kaz nodded.

"Her husband is Senator Thomas Corel. Not only is he politically powerful, but he's also wealthy, courtesy of his wife's inheritance for the most part. She says that Strauss came after her before... took her back to the senator. She felt, and I have no reason to disbelieve her, that if she'd refused to go with him, he'd have killed her with no remorse."

"That sounds about right. I don't know what specific arrangements Strauss has with this senator, but it makes sense. If she had refused to accompany him, he could have abducted her, you know, drugged her, or just used brute force. The problem with that would be what to do with her once she was back home. Given that the senator apparently has a temper problem, it's likely that he'd just as soon have her dead."

Greg asked, "Do you think Strauss can find her at the condo?"

"Hard to say. It largely depends on what she does. If she stays put, doesn't have any contact with the outside world, there's no easy trace back to her. The only way he could get at her would be to follow back through either you, since you arranged the condo, or Janet, since she arranged the help."

The thought of Janet attracting Strauss' attention brought on a wave of nausea. "How do we handle it?"

"There are several things we can do to reduce the threat. First, as I said, firearms and training. The woman that I met there at the condo when I took Dani over, Val's her name, I believe. We need to get her armed and trained right away. I'll deal with that when I talk to Reverend Polasky."

"Good. What else?"

Kaz continued, "Security at the condo. We need to make sure we have some surveillance video feeds, electronic door locks and security alarms, and some panic buttons that link directly to the police or whoever we want to respond. While we're at it, we need to set up the same kind of security here at your place."

"I appreciate that, Kaz, but you're on a time-limited contract. I'd be happy to extend that, but I'm not sure what other commitments you have coming up."

"Don't worry about it. This situation with the senator and his wife will resolve, probably sooner rather than later. These kinds of stand-offs don't drag on. Once this is over, we can talk about my future."

That one took Greg by surprise. It was the first time that Kaz had implied a longer commitment than what they'd agreed on. "Anything else?"

"One final thing." Kaz took out his phone. Unlocking the display, he showed Greg. "You see that icon there. That calls up a phone encryption app. There are lots of them out there. Some are cheap... and are worth about that much. The better ones are military grade. You pay a little more, but they can keep the conversations unintelligible. Anyone trying to listen in will know there's a conversation going on but won't be able to hear it. That goes for the police as well. The top-of-the-line apps won't even allow law enforcement in."

Greg asked, "How do we get this set up?"

"Eisen is probably a better bet to plan and implement. My general advice is to get a stock of burner phones, purchase an enterprise version of the app we want, and install it on every single phone. Make sure the employees are all using them and give them to the women as well. That goes, of course, for you and Reverend Polasky as well."

"Is using an encryption app legal?"

Kaz shrugged. "It depends. In general, yes, it's legal. Some jurisdictions have tighter constraints than others, and it depends on the specific encryption technology. Here's my advice. Don't worry about it. If Reverend Polasky gets nabbed for it, they may lecture her and try to force her to remove the app. It's unlikely given the issues involved, that it would go any further than that."

"And if it does?"

Kaz shook his head. "We'll cross that bridge when we come to it."

64

Things had turned around. Janet began to feel God's hand guiding her. Bonnie had settled into a somewhat uneventful stay at the condo. She seemed to be getting along well with Dani. Val had been keeping steady company with the two and reported that everything seemed normal, almost boring.

For the first time in recent memory, Janet was in the process of putting the finishing touches on next Sunday's sermon... and it was only Wednesday. She smiled as she savored the return to sanity.

And then the intercom buzzed. "Yes, Margaret?"

A hesitant voice came over the speaker. "I have Rob Young on line one for you."

Frustration and anger swept over her. "Thank you." She punched the button. "This is Reverend Polasky."

Brief silence preceded his words. "Hello, Janet. This is Rob Young. I hope I'm not catching you at a bad time."

She resisted the urge to hurl a challenge at him, deciding instead to allow him to deliver whatever message he had called to convey. "No, of course not. What's on your mind, Rob?" In the back of her mind, though, was the image of that silver SUV following her as she went to pick up Bonnie Corel.

"Things went wrong. I was wrong. What I did, the things I said… Janet, you have to know that those things are not me."

She almost told him that the one who deserved an apology was Lucy. But the reality was, he couldn't tell her anything since he had no idea where she was. "Yes, Rob. That's correct."

She could hear what sounded like labored breathing on the other end. Whatever else might be going on with him, he seemed in genuine distress.

"I know I don't deserve it, but I would like the opportunity to apologize in person to you. There's a lot for me to atone for. Being able to make things right with you would be a good start."

"I understand, Rob, but there's no need. You have the opportunity for a fresh start. I suggest that's where your efforts need to be." His apologies meant nothing to her.

Christ would disagree. Forgiveness.

"I'd like to come to the church. I would appreciate it. After that, I promise I won't bother you again."

Something in his voice was off. He seemed genuinely distressed, but his words didn't ring true. It sounded as though they were someone else's, perhaps scripted for him. On the other hand, maybe he had seen a therapist and they helped him with the spiel. "I'm leaving for the day within a few minutes."

"If it's convenient, I could drop by the parsonage tonight."

A pang of fear struck at her. "I've got visitation with

some congregation members tonight." It was a lie. "Tell you what, how about tomorrow morning at the church at ten?"

After they disconnected, she grabbed her cellphone and called Greg.

"Hey Janet." His voice sounded excited to hear from her.

"I may have a problem, Greg. I know that you're trying not to immerse yourself in my project during the day, but this is kind of urgent."

"No problem at all. What is it." The excitement seemed to have evolved into deep concern.

She related the account of Rob's call and the prospect of him visiting the church the next day. "I don't know, Greg. Something was off. I don't feel good about this. I thought that if I told him no, he would just show up anyway. Better to know exactly when he's coming."

"Kaz and I will be there with you. I'll have him call you in a few minutes. I'll show up at the church around nine-thirty. With the three of us there, he wouldn't dare try anything."

Janet wanted to tell him that he needn't take the day off. Surely having Kaz there would be enough. The truth was, though, she wanted Greg there. The thought of him standing with her made Janet feel safe. "Thank you. I...." she grappled with the words and emotions. "Thank you."

Kaz phoned her ten minutes later. "Greg told me the story. I'll be there early as well. So, in the meantime, here's what I need you to do. If you have other employees there, phone them and tell them to stay home tomorrow morning. You'll have to make up some excuse, but it'll be important that they not be exposed to danger."

His words alarmed her. "You don't really think he'll try anything dangerous, do you?"

Kaz's responded, "I think it's better to play this safe. I only met the guy that one time, but he seemed a little on the unstable side to me. I can't imagine that's improved, what with everything that's happened."

* * *

Margaret questioned why she was being asked to remain home until lunch. Janet came up with the best line she could manage on short notice. "I asked the pest control people to come in the morning. They're going to start with the inner offices. It should be cleared out by noon."

She promised herself that she'd come clean with Margaret at some point. For the time being, though, she just needed the church secretary to remain away from any possible danger.

Janet arrived at the office just after eight. She had at least an hour and a half before Kaz and Greg showed up and hopefully a couple of hours before Rob. Sitting in her office, the silence struck her. She'd been here alone before, but there seemed to be something special today. It felt ominous.

Greg showed up at nine-fifteen. "I worried a little that he might show up early and I didn't want you here alone if that happened."

Janet breathed a sigh of relief. His being there immediately became a source of comfort. "Thanks, Greg. I can't tell you how much this means to me. Hopefully, he'll say whatever he's coming to say and get out."

About that time, Kaz strolled through the door. "Great day out there today, especially for the middle of October. The colors on your trees around the grounds are beautiful." He made his way over and peeked out the window toward the parking lot. "I assume he'll come in that way?"

Janet thought about the layout of the church. "I would imagine so. The only other entrance is through the front of the church into the sanctuary and then down the hall. To do that, though, he'd have to park on the street around front."

Kaz sat on the credenza on the side of the room with a clear view out the window. "Do you have video surveillance out front?"

Janet looked at him aghast. "No. We don't use video cameras here. This is a church."

Kaz smiled and shrugged. "Maybe, but for the next hour, it could turn into a battleground. No matter. Can you see down the hall toward the sanctuary from the outer office?"

"Yes. Stand on the right side of the door and you have a clear view down the corridor."

Kaz turned to Greg. "How about you stand there. Crack the door just enough to see movement. If they come that way rather than from the parking lot through the side door, at least we'll have a little notice."

Janet looked at him in alarm. "You said *they*. He didn't say anything about bringing anyone along."

Kaz shook his head. "He wouldn't. Maybe he will come by himself, but if what you said about his tone on the phone is any indication, he's not up to this alone. Remember, his brother is a cop, too. We'll know in a few minutes."

Greg slipped into the outer office, leaving the door open behind him.

Kaz leaned back, his legs draped over the edge of the credenza and his back up against the wall. "Now we wait."

"Ten minutes later, the waiting ended. Kaz sat up. "Silver SUV."

Janet craned her neck and looked out the window.

"That's Rob's car, but who's that guy with him?" Rob and a tall, husky man with short-cut hair, wearing jeans and a navy blazer made their way toward the side entrance.

Kaz called out, "Greg, we got 'em. Come on in." He reached around and took a handgun from beneath his left armpit.

As Greg entered the room, Kaz handed the weapon to him. "Take this—thirty-eight. The safety's off and there's a round in the chamber. It's ready to fire. Hold it behind your back and pull it around only if you need it."

Greg had a stricken look on his face—deer in the head-lights. "What? Uh, why...?"

"Just do it."

A wave of guilt consumed Janet. She'd dragged Greg into something dangerous. He was risking his life for her. It wasn't for the project. It wasn't for other women. It was solely for her.

Within a minute, Janet could hear them open the outer door. Seconds later, the inner door opened, and the two men stepped in.

Surreal—that's the only way Janet could describe it. Rob stood in utter disbelief. The other man, one that Janet had never seen before, stood rigid, staring at Kaz.

Kaz, for his part smiled. "Hi, Karl. Long time. What brings you to this neck of the woods?" He held his right arm behind him. Although Janet hadn't seen him take it from a holster, she was certain that he held a handgun.

Apparently, the thug made the same assessment. He stared for a moment at Kaz and then glanced first at Greg and then at Janet. He licked his lips as his eyes darted back and forth. This was clearly not in his game plan.

Hapless Rob blurted out, "What's going on here, Janet. I just came by to apologize, like I said."

Kaz spoke before Janet could respond. "We were just here for a Bible study group. What are the odds?"

Karl backed out of the room. "Uh, I need to phone the office. Come on Mister Young, we should leave."

As the two left, Janet would have laughed at the look on Rob's face had she herself not been so terrified. When the three of them were alone, she turned to Kaz. "I'm guessing that you know him?"

"Karl Unger—a common street thug. How do you figure he hooked up with this Rob Young guy?"

Greg gingerly handed the weapon back to Kaz. "You need to take this before I shoot myself in the foot. Do you think they came here to kill Janet?" A horrified look painted his face.

"No. He came to abduct her. If he wanted to kill her, he could have waited outside until she left and fired from cover. As it is, he risked coming inside. Anyone could have seen him. No, he needs something from you, Janet."

"What could he possibly want from me? Do you think maybe Rob hired him to try and force me to reveal Lucy Young's location?"

Kaz responded, "It's possible. but from what I understand, Rob Young lives payday to payday. Unger's not a top-tier contractor, but he doesn't come cheap. My bet is that he was here working for someone else. Rob Young's just a front. In all likelihood, he wanted to get you someplace where they could talk to you. After that, I don't know. What it mostly means, Janet, is that your instincts were good. I hate to break it to you, but whatever it is they wanted, it's not over."

Greg glanced out the window, watching the silver SUV drive away. "Why did we let 'em go? They were here to get Janet." He turned toward Kaz with a look of confused anger on his face.

Kaz laughed. "What should we have done—shot them? We could call the police, but what would we have told them? Two guys came to visit Janet." He grew serious. "We did the only thing we could have under the circumstances. One thing's for sure though—this all just got a lot more serious."

65

Janet felt shaken, but why? She'd watched a woman die in a parking lot. She'd watched Dee kill a violent abuser outside a house after he'd murdered the adult and children inside. Three men had died in a condo right in front of her, their blood flowing out stain the ivory-colored carpet. She'd heard the grisly stories of other assaults and murders. None of this was new to her.

Today it was personal. Rob Young and Karl Unger came for her. The more she thought about it, the more she realized that no matter what information they wanted, she would have died once they got it. Even worse, she had every reason to believe that they would not give up. The two would be back.

Another realization hit her hard. This was probably what happened to Sue Hartman. She pictured in her mind exactly how it might have gone down. One minute Sue was probably going about her business like any other day. The next minute, she was overpowered by thugs, fated at that moment to die.

Janet had been back at the parsonage only a few

minutes when her phone rang. She didn't even bother to look at the number. She simply hit the connect icon and struggled to utter some kind of minimal greeting. "Hello."

"Janet, this is Greg. I'd like to come over and talk to you, please." His tone exuded caution bordering on fear.

"Uh, sure, that would be fine." It would be more than fine, though. She didn't want to be alone. At the moment, she wanted Greg Stottman by her side. When the incident had occurred earlier in the day, he had taken a gun from Kaz and stood ready. He didn't complain and he didn't flinch. He was there when she needed him.

Thirty minutes later, her doorbell rang. Janet peeked out the side window, just to make sure. Opening the door, she stepped aside. "Come in, please." The living room was dark except for the light filtering in from the kitchen. "Sorry for the darkness. I don't want people outside being able to see in."

He took a hesitating step toward her and then wrapped his arms around her, holding her tight. The initial surprise gave way to a sense of safety and warmth. A wave if relief swept over her. She leaned into him and rested her head on his shoulders. "Thank you," she whispered in his ear.

After a moment, she stepped back. "You warned me. I should have taken it more seriously."

He responded, his voice filled with confidence. "You did take it seriously. You've asked for help every time you felt the need. I might add, your instincts so far have been spot on." He shuffled in place, as though there was something else on his mind. "There are some things that I'd like to discuss, if you have the time."

"I'll put water on for tea."

Greg countered, "I haven't eaten yet. Would you like to grab some dinner. I know a quiet bistro where we can talk."

Janet's stomach roiled. The thought of going out in public, after all that had happened, seemed dangerous. She reminded herself, though, that she wouldn't be able to hold up in the parsonage and hide forever.

Ten minutes later, they were seated at a corner table in the Rosemary and Basil eatery. Janet said, "I've been in Bellevue for years and I've never been to this place." She surveyed the customers, who were spread across the dining area. The seating was dense enough to be social. With the din of noise, though, it felt as though private conversations could be had.

"I haven't been in a while. When we were first getting started with the company, Mel and I used to take one evening off a week to eat in a different place. We made it over here several times. I haven't been in years, though. They make a fantastic Rueben or, if you prefer, their Greek gyros are delicious."

The waiter took their order and sped off, leaving them to their privacy. Greg sipped his water and then set the glass aside. "Kaz talked to me the other day about ideas to increase security, and I wanted to suggest something. I know that you select your employees carefully. I anticipate they'll all be women, but how would you feel about employing Kaz full time?"

The suggestion took Janet by surprise. "I don't think having him escort women out of town would be a good idea."

"Escorting women—no. I got to thinking, though, after he made some suggestions about security that we could implement. Maybe the best thing would be for him to implement them himself. He won't come cheap, but there is no one better at these kinds of things. Plus, he's dependable and honorable."

Chapter 65

Janet struggled to process the idea. "I don't know. We haven't factored that kind of expense into the budget."

Greg laughed. "You have plenty of money and, believe me, the extra security will be worth every penny."

The initial shock faded and Janet tried to imagine how the pieces would fit. "Have you spoken to him about it?"

Greg seemed think about the question for a moment before responding. "No. I wanted to run it by you first. This is your project and it's your decision. It's just an idea." He tapped his fingers on the tabletop and glanced over toward the window. His eyes were full of worry. "Janet. I'm frightened for you. You asked for help today and we were there. What might have happened if Kaz hadn't been there?"

Janet considered his words for a moment before responding quietly. "Kaz wasn't the only one there. You stood up to them. I agree Kaz is qualified, but I couldn't do this without you."

"Thank you." He offered a shallow smile. "I was terrified." He seemed to search for some other words. He cleared his throat and continued. "Okay, well, here are some things he suggested." He related the conversation with Kaz including the recommendations—arming and training the women along with encrypted phone apps to start with.

"That sounds good, but we're going to run into a problem straight away. My only employee, Val, is a convicted felon. She's not allowed to carry a weapon. The suggestion that they carry guns would require that we hire only non-felons."

Greg rubbed his chin. "Maybe we could get some kind of special waiver or something."

"I doubt it. For one thing, even if we could, making

any kind of application would reveal the fact that they work for us. I'm not sure how we get around that."

He countered, "Let me talk to Kaz about that. He knows more about these kinds of arrangements than I do."

Janet said, "I'll ask Dee about it, too. She would have some ideas."

The waiter arrived with their orders—a grilled portabella mushroom sandwich for him and for her a Greek salad. After he slipped away, the two of them eased into a more casual conversation as they picked at their food. A gnawing sense of change ate at Janet. Greg had taken on a more active role in her project than she'd envisioned. The prospect both alarmed her and comforted her.

She popped a kalamata olive in her mouth. Chewing and swallowing, she took a sip of water. "Let me ask you a question. You promised your partners that you'd pay more attention to business and less to my project. You said you were going to *step back*. It seems to me that you've actually taken on a more active role. Don't get me wrong, I'm happy that you've been with me on this, but this is going to affect your business."

He thought about it a moment before responding. "It's not so different for you. You try to keep your day-to-day work at the church separate from this. Yes, it's a struggle, but you do it. When the need arises, you do what you have to. It seems to me that you manage handsomely. I have to do that as well. When I'm at work, I need to have my head there. When I'm not at work, I need to be able to switch gears and deal with other parts of my life."

Janet forced a laugh. "For me, it seems like lately everything involves scheduling conflicts and tradeoffs. It's like, recently I had to leave some congregation members in the lurch when I had to move a client. It felt horrible, but I had no choice... or at least it seemed that way at the time. My board president reminded me of my duties." She shook her head as she remembered the stilted conversation with Gayle. "A couple needed me to be with them and I couldn't."

Greg considered her for a moment, his face betraying nothing. Finally, he sighed and locked gazes with her. "I don't have to tell you, Janet. I'm sure you've dealt with this before, but there are choices we make and unintended consequences. You can beat yourself up all day long, but it won't help. At least you're aware of the problem. You'd be surprised at the number of people running around out there that make a train wreck out their days by not paying attention. For me, I try to mind my business while I'm there. Otherwise, I focus on other important parts of my life."

"Like my project?"

He paused, locking gazes with her. "Like your project... and you."

66

They'd reached a turning point. Until now, the Sniper had assigned only transactional jobs to Cousin Billy. He did the job; he got paid—a simple exchange of service for money. The time had come for them to venture into something deeper and more complex.

They both took seats at the kitchen table. As he had two times before, the Sniper slid a stack of bills across. "Here's the payment—five thousand, as agreed."

Billy took the money, thumbed through it, nodding as though he were actually counting it. "What's next?"

The Sniper took a deep breath. "To date, you've earned fifteen thousand. You've also proven that you can follow direction and act when needed. You're almost ready for the big leagues."

Billy narrowed his eyes. "Almost?"

The Sniper leaned back in the rickety wooden chair, his hands laced behind his head. "Look around you, Cuz. Who do you think pays for this cabin, the food, the gas in the truck, and all the other stuff?"

"I guess I assume that you do the kind of stuff we've been doing."

The Sniper offered a tired smile. "Yes… and no. The jobs like the one we just did and running packages to Spokane, those are a part of it. I do other things that aren't directly fee-for-service. I'm paid a set amount over the course of the year. That money allows me to do things that are far more important. They aren't just jobs."

Billy stared blankly as though he had been asked to define quantum theory. "What do you mean?"

"What I mean, Cuz, is that there are things that are important to me. I do them because they need to be done to make a better world. It just so happens that there are like-minded people who provide the funds that allow me to do that. The reason I'm telling you is that I have such a mission coming up. This will be your chance to do some work that helps to pay the bills around here."

"Are you trying to say that I won't get paid?" The words were laced with anger. "It's fucking gonna take forever to get the money I need even when I do get paid for everything. Now you're telling me that I gotta do a freebie?"

"Free?" The Sniper burst out laughing. "How many breakfasts, lunches, and dinners have you eaten here? How many nights have you slept safe here in the cabin? Cuz, you've been working earning money for yourself. You haven't contributed shit to the house expenses. Every once in a while you have to pony up some of the money. Got it?"

Billy clenched his jaw as he glared at his cousin. Finally, he asked, "What's so important?"

The Sniper leaned in, folding his hands on the table-top. "There's a war going on in this country, Cuz. It's a fight for the soul of our culture, our way of life. The traditional roles of men and women have been turned upside down. Men are emasculated. Women are working to enslave men and turn them into eunuchs. We fight the war for men everywhere, to preserve the heritage that made this country great."

Billy looked as though he were about to yawn. His vacant eyes wandered. "So, If I do this job so, men can be men. Sounds stupid to me."

"You and your girlfriend had it out, yes? From what you tell me, the root of the problem was that she wanted to control you. She wanted to make all the decisions. She wanted you to support her. She needed sex from time-to-time, but she wanted it to be her show. That's what I'm fighting, Cuz."

Billy's eyes brightened. "Yeah, I see it, and her uncle has been completely turned against real men like you and me. So, what do we have to do?"

"There's a woman over in Seattle. The people who pay the bills have let it be known that her time has come. You and I are going to be God's messengers of death."

"When are we going to do it?" Billy's face lit up with excitement.

"We're going to make a trip over day after tomorrow. We'll take some sleeping bags, food, and stuff with us. We'll sleep in the camper on the back of the truck. We'll watch her for a couple of days, document her moves, see what she does. We'll come back here, do some final checking and prep work, and then go back over again next week. We'll spend the first day confirming her routine. The second morning, we do the hit and come back home."

Cousin Billy drummed his fingers on the table as he digested the information. "If I'm getting this right, you don't give a shit about that guy we offed yesterday, but somehow this bitch in Seattle needs to die to protect men."

Chapter 66

"I'd say you were paying attention. The contracts that we take are not personal. Someone tells us who the mark is and how much it's worth. We do the job, they pay us. Whether they deserve to die or not is none of my business. The women I hit have earned it. They arc slowly destroying everything our forefathers fought and died for. Like I said, Cuz, this is war, and we're the holy warriors."

67

Senator Corel decided not to explain the Unger situation to Dylan Strauss. One thing was for certain, Strauss would not be pleased. On the other hand, when Unger had extracted the information from Polasky and then disposed of both the minister and Rob Young, the conversation would go much easier. Even better, Unger would make it appear as though Young was the killer. Lord knows he had an axe to grind with Polasky. This would allow Strauss to finish up his mission.

Noon came and went with no word from Unger. Corel knew it would take time for Unger to get what he needed and finish up. The phone call came just after three o'clock.

"What do you have for me."

Unger's coarse voice sounded meeker than the last time they had spoken. "We ran into trouble. She had some help there—looked like she was expecting us. That guy you saddled me with, Rob Young... he must have tipped her off when he called."

The senator resisted the urge to crawl through the cell-phone circuit and strangle the living shit out of this incompetent asshole. He'd fucked up the Hartman job. Now he botched this one as well. *No wonder Strauss can't get anything done… with help like this.*

He forced himself back to the moment. "Who was there?"

"There were two. One I don't know. White guy, medium height, forty-ish. The other—Dimitry Kazarian. He's like a merc. Very expensive. He works mostly international. I ran across him on a job in Algiers a few years back."

"I assume that he recognized you as well."

"We had to get out of there. I'll try again later."

Corel wanted to scream. What a complete fucking idiot. "This changes things." He forced himself to calm down. For the moment, he needed this incompetent shit.

"So, first, things don't go perfectly. You tried and that's important. Making a strategic retreat without playing your hand was probably a smart move. It does, however, alter the playing field. The next time, you're going to have to go alone. Don't take Young with you. You'll have to grab her at some opportune time, like when she's leaving for work or coming home."

"Can do."

The senator composed his next words very carefully. "Here's how this goes. While you won't have Rob Young with you, you'll need to have ready access to him. Once you've gotten what you need out of the minister, you need to finish her." He paused to let that sink in.

"Now, this is the tricky part. You then need to contact Young and lure him in. Finish him off and the set it up so that it looks like a murder-suicide. From what I know, it'll fly pretty easily, since there was a lot of bad blood between them. If my suspicions are right, Polasky helped Young's wife get away. I can find a way to have that information come to light. It'll be a slam dunk."

After he disconnected, Corel sat staring out the window into the late October afternoon. Days were getting shorter. Rain had set in the day before. With the election only a week and a half away, he needed something to raise his spirits. The last days running up to election day would stress everyone's patience. He knew just the thing. Wandering out into the staff work area, he found the person he was looking for. "Alicia, could I see you for a moment, please?"

She leapt to her feet. "Certainly, Senator."

In the inner office with the door closed, he slouched back in his chair. "I was hoping that we might go over some polling numbers this evening." He was confident that she understood what he was asking.

But she looked troubled. "I'm sorry, Senator. I have a prior commitment tonight. Maybe we can go over them first thing in the morning."

Anger flashed through him. He would not be put off so easily. After all, she worked for him. He called the shots. "I need to get on it today. I have a full schedule tomorrow morning."

"I could stay a little late here and we could power through them, if that works for you." She looked hopeful.

Corel could feel the color rising in his face. "If you can't handle it, I'll just find someone else."

Alicia looked horrified. "Let me make a phone call. I'll reschedule my…." She turned and left the office.

68

Corel slouched down in his chair, his head leaned back on the headrest and his eyes closed. He needed to focus. The campaign was on track. The election was his if he could just hold things together. What he needed at this very moment would have to wait until the evening. The thought of Alicia lying on the bed inviting him washed over him. He could see, even feel, her slowly parting her legs to allow him in. He imagined the sheer delight. Her legs would slowly wrap around him as she moved rhythmically, coaxing him on. He felt himself getting hard at the thought. He relished the feeling.

The cellphone pulled him out of it. The display identified Dylan Strauss. *Shit.* He knew exactly what this was about, and he didn't need it right at the moment. Still, he connected.

"Yeah, what do you have for me."

The words exploded through his speaker. "What the fuck do you think you're doing?"

This had to end. Corel was simply not willing to

tolerate this asshole another minute. But his better sense talked him out of what he really wanted to say. "Calm down, Dylan. I'm just trying to help you... and God knows you need some right now."

The voice turned icy. "I don't need that kind of help. You're fucking things up. I'm going to tell you this only one time. I give direction to my people. You tell me what you want, and I'll see it done. Otherwise, you keep your nose out of it."

The senator felt the heat rise to his face. He was felt certain that he must be beet-red. He gritted his teeth for a moment before forcing himself to relax. "What's done is done. What's next?" What wasn't clear from the conversation was whether Strauss knew about his latest instructions to Unger.

"Unger told me about Kazarian. I have some additional information that can help us. The fact that he's associated with the minister tells us that she's chest deep in this. She could not afford his services otherwise. Someone's funding her, though."

Corel responded, "Who?"

"What I have is this. Kazarian has been seen around with a guy named Greg Stottman. He's a tech company CEO with lots of money. My guess is that he's your money man in all this. He donates to causes like this. This tells you who's doing the work and who's paying for it. The thing that throws me is that we've seen no sign of your wife leaving town. If she's hanging out locally, she's not made any legal moves, such as contacting the police or even interacting with the press. I'm not sure what she's up to."

"The stupid cunt is not up to anything. She's likely cowering like a frightened dog in some corner somewhere. We just have to find her."

Chapter 68

"Okay," Strauss agreed. "Now that we know who's helping her and we assume she's in town, we can put tails on the minister, Stottman, and anyone else who comes into contact with them. All we have to do is sit back, watch, and wait."

It came down to this. The senator had given Unger instructions that ran counter to what Strauss had just suggested. There was only one way to go. "Okay, then. I'll stay out of it, and you take it from here."

The response was curt. "Of course." The connection was cut.

Senator Corel immediately dialed Unger's number— no answer. He got voice mail. "We need to put everything on hold. Contact me the minute you get this message." He assumed that Unger would recognize the voice. He considered sending a text, but the idea of committing to words that could be retrieved later made him rethink it. He'd simply have to trust that Unger would listen to the voicemail.

If he could just smooth out this small wrinkle, everything could wrap up within a day or so. He began to feel more relaxed by the moment. A knock on the door brought him out of his thoughts. Alicia stuck her head in and said, "Senator, I'm heading back to my room now. Do you want me to order dinner?"

A shudder of anticipated ecstasy coursed through his body. He stuffed it down. As much as he wanted her this evening, he needed to be available when Unger called back. He shook his head. "I'm sorry. I can't make it. Something's come up." He waved her off.

Her face fell, momentarily, and then took on an unusually angry look. "I cancelled all my plans for this evening. I…." Her face went white as though she just realized what she was saying. She spoke again, this time with a more respectful tone. "Yes, sir. Have a good evening." She closed the door just a little too firmly for his taste. She was beginning to develop an impertinence. that he would not abide. He'd handle that later. For now, though, his mind kept wandering back to the hunt for his wife.

69

Greg leaned forward in his wingback chair. Kaz sat on the sofa. Each nursed a bottle of beer. Greg took a deep swill, savoring the robust flavor. "That was a little unnerving, to say the least."

Kaz leaned forward and set his bottle on the coffee table. "You did great."

"It could have gone differently." Greg imagined all the ways the situation could have ended in disaster. The worst part was that the entire event occurred because someone wanted to get at Janet.

Kaz chortled. "Oh come on, Greg. You of all people know that things can always go differently. We handled it well. Janet did her part, and you did yours. It's all we can do, but we do have to think about where we go from here. It's clear that Janet's in their crosshairs. The problem is that we're not quite sure who it is that's behind it."

Greg took another drink. "Let's work the problem. You said that you knew the one guy, Karl something or another."

"Unger."

"Yeah. From what you said, he hires out as muscle, I think you call it. That means that whoever's calling the shots has access to some amount of money. This Rob Young character certainly has motive, but it seems unlikely that he could afford Unger. As far as I know, Janet's not involved in anything else that could lead to this. That means that it's related to her project to help abused women."

Kaz stared at the coffee table, his eyes seemingly unfocused. Finally, he responded, "Makes sense. Let's go with that. There are two possibilities that I can think of. First is the Stillings woman. She's already shown that she has both the funds and the interest in Janet. The second is obviously the husband of the woman Janet's helping now. I think you said that he's a U. S. senator. As I understand it, he has money and he's used to being in a powerful position."

Greg considered the two options. "Senator Corel, for my money. I may disagree with a lot of what Reba Stillings does, but she's sharp. Going after Janet in broad daylight with a guy like Unger and Rob Young tagging along seems foolish and shortsighted to me."

Kaz countered, "Do you think the senator would be foolish or shortsighted?"

Greg shot back quickly, "He's desperate. He's used to being in control and, if he's like most politicians, he believes the rules don't apply to him. Yeah, I think he'd do whatever he wanted with confidence that he could fix it afterwards."

Kaz shook his head. "One glitch in your theory—we know that Dylan Strauss is working on this for the senator. Strauss is smarter than that. Like Stillings, he'd never try to pull off something that stupid."

"I do have one question, Kaz. This whole thing with Janet... do you think it has anything to do with the disappearance of Sue Hartman. I think I told you about her. She was the director over at the DV network—disappeared without a trace."

"That sounds like a Strauss operation. Sometimes he's heavy-handed. Assuming it was him, they'd grabbed and interrogate her, probably using drugs. Once they got what they wanted, they'd finish her off. If it was Strauss, then her body will never turn up."

Greg took another drink. "Back to the thing with Janet. If we assume that it wasn't Strauss, then would it be possible for the senator to have contracted with Unger directly? I mean, we do think that somehow Unger works for Strauss."

"Those are good assumptions. If it did go down that way and Strauss finds out about it, I wouldn't be that surprised to see him take care of the senator himself. Dylan Strauss runs a tight operation. He doesn't flinch, and he doesn't put up with shit from anyone. This senator fellow may think he's powerful, but Dylan Strauss' client list makes the senator look like the village idiot."

Greg burst out laughing. "Maybe things will take care of themselves, huh?"

Kaz smiled. "It would be poetic justice, but let's not count on it. We need to lay out a plan for keeping Janet safe. It starts by following through with what Miz Corel and I talked about—coming to an understanding with her husband. We can start by telling her that someone came after Janet. That should get her attention."

A moment of silence descended on the room. Each man sipped on their beer. After a moment, Greg switched gears. "What do you think of Seattle, Kaz?"

"It's okay. Why do you ask?"

"I don't know. You live in Brooklyn. I was just

wondering how this compares. You've been here for months."

"It's work. It's what I do. I've spent as much as nine months on jobs around the world. I just get used to it."

Greg probed, "Do you ever think of relocating to another place?"

"You mean like Seattle?"

"It's a nice place."

Kaz paused and then continued in quiet voice. "It's complicated right now."

Something about his tone Greg that it was the end of this particular conversation. "In the meantime, though, I'd like to extend your contract here to help with Janet's project."

70

The previous day had been one fuck-up after another. Everyone had failed him. Strauss hadn't produced any results. Unger was supposed to return his call the prior evening and yet he'd heard nothing from the bungling idiot. For all he knew, the thug was out stalking Polasky.

Meanwhile, Strauss had set up surveillance on the woman, the Stottman character, whoever else interacted with them. This was the first sign of a solid plan. It would be a fucking nightmare if Unger tried an abduction while the plan was in process. *What a dick.*

With just over a week to go before the election, he shouldn't have a care in the world. The polls showed him with what seemed an insurmountable lead. All he had to do was shut everything down for a while and lay low. There was, though, the small problem of his wife. At this point, she was the ultimate loose end. She had to be returned... or otherwise dealt with.

Corel came into the office early and left word that he was not to be disturbed. He needed time to think. By late morning, he'd started to come out of his funk. Presumably, routine work had been going on in the outer office, although the phone lines had been quiet. Leaning back in his chair, he pondered the previous day's misstep with Alicia. Perhaps he had been too hard on her.

He stepped into the outer office but didn't see her anywhere. "Where's Alicia?" he asked, to no one in particular.

One of the new girls whose name eluded him stood and stepped forward, handing him an envelope. "She was in earlier and left this for you, sir."

He took it, responding, "Thank you." Without adding anything, he returned to his office, opening the envelope as he went. As he dropped into his chair, he read:

Dear Senator Corel,

It is with regret that I submit my resignation. It has been one of the great honors of my life to have served with you, both in Washington, D.C. and on the campaign trail. I will be spending some time with my parents in Spokane and I'm thinking of returning to school in the spring to work on my graduate degree. I wish you the best of luck.

Regards,
Alicia Wilkins

Balling the note up, he hurled it at the wall. "Fuck! Is there no one in this entire goddammed world that I can depend on?" He would make her pay for this. She was not allowed to just walk away. No one walked away from Senator Thomas Corel.

He pulled his overcoat from the rack and bolted from the office. "I'll be back later." Fuming, he stormed down the hallway and into the elevator, where he pounded the button for the ground floor. Out in the lobby, he strode toward the front door.

Corel began to calm down, forcing himself to rein in his rage. He started to rehearse the words he would use, with each iteration being kinder and gentler. He hailed a cab and huddled in the backseat for the ten-minute ride.

As he made his way through the hotel lobby, he hoped that she had not checked out. Surely, she would remain, at least for the day. Maybe, if she was willing to hear his points, they might even *make up* and end the whole incident on a passionate note.

He stood in front of her door and composed himself. He'd done this kind of thing hundreds of times. It was no big deal. After all, regardless of any complaints or plans, working for a United States Senator was simply too irresistible. She would relent. He knocked gently.

When she opened the door, her eyes were red and puffy. She wore jeans and a sweatshirt. On the bed, a large suitcase was partially filled.

"Alicia, I'm glad I caught you. We need to talk."

She shook her head. "I'm sorry, Senator. I'm just not cut out for this. I tried, honestly."

He took a deep breath, forcing the frustration to remain in the background. "I know it's hard right now. Believe me, I know the tension and challenges of the campaign, but we can make it right. Of course you know, you're in line for that deputy position once we're back in D.C."

"I know, and believe me, I appreciate that, along with everything else you've done for me. I just can't do it anymore."

The anger bubbled up. This was extortion, plain and simple. The bitch wasn't satisfied with all that she had been given. She wanted more and this was her childish way of getting it. "This isn't all about you. There are millions of voters who are depending on me and this campaign. You're letting them all down. You're letting me down."

She looked shocked. Her eyes widened and she drew back. "I'm sorry if it seems that way. The election is just about over, though. Truthfully, and I think you know it, there's no real contest. You have this in the bag, Senator, but I need to bow out."

"I've invested a lot in you, Alicia. The taxpayers have invested a lot in you. You can't just walk away and tell them all to go get screwed. You have an obligation here."

Her lips drew into a tight line. Her arms wrapped around her stomach as she hugged herself. "Senator, I am an at-will employee. You can fire me any time you want. I serve at your pleasure. The flip side is that I can quit any time I want. I'll always appreciate the opportunity that you've given me, but I need to leave. My decision is final." She drew back from him even more, as if his very presence offended her.

"No! That's not the way it works." He stood over her, his anger boiling over.

Her look of resolve turned first to uncertainty, then alarm, and finally into outright terror. She shrank farther back from him, her eyes widening.

His rage won out. He lunged at her, grabbing for her throat with his hands. She rolled off the bed, onto the floor and stood, backing away from him.

He followed her, his eyes fixed on hers. Every muscle in his body tensed for action.

She bolted for the door, but he hurled himself between the girl and her escape. He swung his balled fist at her connecting with the side of her head. The contact felt good to him, solid. She fell backwards, off balance, her head bouncing off the corner of a table.

Alicia came to rest on the floor, her eyes wide and vacant with blood from the head wound staining the carpet.

Corel wanted to leap on top of her and continue bashing her face with his fists. He fought the urge and won. Gradually, his rage subsided and he regained his composure. He tore his gaze from the dead girl's face and assessed the situation.

Pulling his burner phone from his coat pocket, he selected the number and connected.

"Yes?"

"We have a new problem."

71

Senator Corel sat on the bed, mostly avoiding the sight of Alicia on the floor. Occasionally he stole a glance, but quickly looked away. At first, he'd been horrified at what he'd done, but the more he thought about it, the angrier he grew. This was all her fault. He was the victim. It was beyond irresponsible for her to desert him right in the middle of a campaign. She knew the stress he was under and still chose to slink away like a thief in the night. That didn't even take into account all that he was trying to manage with his wife's desertion. He had expected better of Alicia. He had a right to expect better. As unfortunate as it may have been, he found it hard to feel any sympathy for her.

The expected return phone call came within ten minutes. He checked the display and connected. "Yeah, what do you have?"

"Here's the drill. Within the next thirty minutes, there will be a knock on the door. When you answer it, the person will announce *House Cleaning*. Not *Housekeeping.* That's all they'll say. Let them in. Say nothing to them.

Leave. Exit the building through the main lobby. Take your time, remain calm, but don't stop for anything. Go back to your office and return to work as though nothing has happened. When you get home tonight, burn the letter from the girl. Got all that?"

Corel briefly organized the tasks in his head. "Yeah, got it. Anything else?"

"As soon as you leave, you need to come up with a cover story about your absence from the office. When police begin asking questions about the girl's disappearance, the staffer who gave it to you will certainly remember that. The cops are going to want to know why you left the office immediately after that and where you went. You need to make your story bullet-proof."

Corel thought about it for a moment and then responded. "I can do that. Anything else?"

Strauss' tone turned cold and hostile. "As a matter of fact, yes. Within the next ten minutes, transfer ten million dollars into my account. Once I verify the deposit, I'll green light the house cleaning service."

The senator felt as though someone had punched him in the stomach. "Are you fucking crazy? Ten million? You're out of your fucking mind." Clearly Strauss failed to realize exactly who he was dealing with.

The connection went dead. Corel stared at his cellphone, enraged. He called Strauss again. When the man answered, the senator spat his anger and hatred, "What the fuck? Did you just hang up on me? Let's get on with this. Ten million, is that what you said?"

The icy voice responded slowly and quietly, "The price is now twenty million. Before you launch into another of your tirades, you should know that every time you do, I'm going to hang up and the price will double. Now, do you want this service or not?"

Corel forced himself to calm. He could extract vengeance later. For now, he needed Strauss. "Okay, twenty million. That's a lot of money."

"Yes, twenty million dollars is a lot of money. Senator, I do this kind of thing for a living, and I understand the stakes. This is simple. You want the problem to disappear. I want twenty million dollars. Hopefully, by the end of the day we'll both have what we want. Any other questions? Before you continue the argument, realize that I am not sending the cleaner until the money is in my account. So, the longer you delay, the greater the chance that someone else will discover this. Are we clear?"

After he disconnected, Corel sat stunned for a few seconds. His rage built until he couldn't decide who he hated most, his pig of a wife, the second-rate problem solver who was shaking him down, or the dead girl on the floor whose selfish decision had precipitated this crisis. He hated them all. Alicia was taken care of. His wife, she would follow soon enough. He and Dylan Strauss went back a long way. The man had solved a lot of problems for the senator. On the other hand, he had been well compensated. But twenty million dollars? Holy hell!

He activated the financial management app on his phone. Less than five minutes later his account was twenty million dollars lighter. Given that his wife had tied up much of their fortune, this hit him hard, although he still had a healthy balance. And if... no, *when* he was re-elected, he had some deals working that would easily replenish the account.

A knock on the door brought him out of his thoughts. He opened it. "Yes?"

"House Cleaning."

He stepped aside, allowing the two men and a woman to enter. Each of them took a moment to survey the entire room and then each set about a different task. Corel's impatience got the better of him. "Don't forget to wipe the fingerprints."

The two men ignored his words. The woman, however, turned and glared at him for a moment. Without speaking, she nodded toward the door and then returned to her work. He resisted the urge to strangle the bitch—he could do it. He'd just killed that twit of an assistant. He could certainly end the life of this pitiful excuse for a woman. He turned and left, allowing the door to close behind him.

As he made his way out of the hotel, his cover story began to coalesce. He stopped by a magazine stand and picked up a newspaper and magazine. After that, he dropped into a nearby branch of his bank and withdrew two hundred dollars in cash. Finally, less than a block from his office, he stopped into a coffee shop and purchased a latte.

Twenty minutes later, he was seated at his desk going over the latest poll numbers. He often wondered why he did that. He knew what the projections were. The election wasn't even close. The numbers gave him comfort, though. They told him what he enjoyed hearing. They didn't argue with him, and they never deserted him.

About fifteen minutes later, his door opened after a quiet knock. A young woman, whose name escaped him, stood at the threshold. "Senator, excuse the interruption, but how do you want to handle Alicia's workload? Are you going to hire a new assistant?"

He wanted the problem to go away... at least initially. He motioned the woman in. She was not wearing a wedding band. Thinking quickly, he checked her name tag. "Zoey, have a seat, please." He gestured to a chair beside his desk. "Things are crazy right now, and Alicia's departure comes as a surprise. Still, there's only a few days left until the election. Do you think that you could handle her workload?" He quickly added, "With a pay raise and the official title, of course. After the election is over and we head back to D.C., we might want to have a conversation about how you could fit into our structure there. What do you say?"

She looked a little plain, but her figure was inviting. He could imagine undressing her for the first time. He could almost feel what her trembling body would be like as he gently guided her to the bed.

Zoey blushed. "I suppose so, Senator, if you think I could do it."

He clapped his hands together once and then rubbed them. "Then it's settled. Call HR and let them know that Alicia has resigned and that you'll be taking her place. Have them call me for verification, if necessary."

"Yes, sir. Once the admin details are done, what do you need me to do first?"

He licked his lips. "I think the most pressing thing right now is for the two of us to go over the polling numbers. I'm tied up right now, but do you have time after dinner this evening?"

"Yes, of course."

"Tell you what, then. Why don't we have some dinner ordered in and we can work here in the office... that is, unless you think we might be more comfortable in your hotel room."

"The office would probably be best, since I'm staying with my parents while we're here."

Why was it that no one could be depended on? He'd given her the opportunity of a lifetime and she wasn't bright enough to see it. Why was everyone aligned against him? "That'll be fine. We can work here."

His brooding gave way to planning. After one more

Chapter 71

week he would be able to rid himself of everyone who had betrayed him, starting with that asshole Strauss. *Twenty million dollars just to clean a fucking room.* Corel promised himself that the twenty million he'd given Strauss would end up being the worst deal that man had ever made.

72

Janet sat in her office on the late October afternoon trying to get enthused about St. Luke's annual report, which would go out to congregation members after the first of the year. It was a chance to highlight all they had done this year, where she and the board thought the church should go during the next year, and their financial health.

She had mostly recovered from the near miss with Rob Young and the other man. It had taken several days before she realized just how lucky she was. Greg Stottman had been by her side and arranged for Kaz to be there as well. A sickening sense of dread overtook her whenever she considered how it might have gone if they had not been there.

The buzzing intercom interrupted her brooding. "There's a young lady out here to see you—Abby Miller."

Janet eye's shifted to the clock—just after two in the afternoon. Did school let out this early. "I'll be right out."

She found Abby sitting in one of the chairs, her hands

clasped in her lap. The look on the young girl's face shouted *indifference.*

Janet sat down beside her. "Hey there, Abby. It's good to see you." She hugged the young girl, who barely acknowledged the act. "Did school let out early today?"

Abby shrugged and turned another page. "I quit school."

Janet stared in disbelief. When the shock wore off, she queried, "What do you mean you quit school?"

"I don't like it there. They don't like me either."

The minister stood. "Let's go into my office so we can talk."

Once inside, Abby slouched in one of the chairs. Her face looked blank as if she cared about nothing. Janet pulled her chair around to sit in front of the young girl.

"Why don't you tell me about it?"

"I don't know."

Janet's mind whirled. The first question she asked herself was whether or not to take Abby literally—*quit school.* "Did you just walk out of class today?"

Abby nodded and turned her head to stare out the window.

Janet took Abby's hands in hers. "What happened? Tell me all about it."

"The other kids don't like me. My dad killed my mom and it was my fault. My teacher doesn't like me either." Her eyes moistened.

"What makes you say that, Abby? I can't imagine anyone not liking you."

Abby twiddled her fingers in her lap as she furrowed her brow. The question apparently stumped her. "I don't know."

Janet slowed down. This was not going to resolve itself quickly. "What were you doing in class today?"

"Nothing. They were talking about the Thanksgiving play. The teacher asked how many parents would be coming. All the kids raised their hands, but I didn't. Then one of the girls said my parents wouldn't come because my dad killed my mom. And then nobody said nothing." The tears flowed down both cheeks.

Janet understood some of the girl's pain. Abby had lost her parents in perhaps the most horrible way possible. Having other children ridicule her for it seemed beyond anything that even an adult could endure, despite the reality that kids did that sort of thing. She wanted to fold her arms around Abby and pull her close, driving out all pain. "I'm glad you came to see me. We'll figure this out, I promise—you and me together."

Abby wiped her face on her sleeve. "I wanted to go over and see that other woman, you know, the one I talked to that day when you went to see that man."

Janet searched her memory. "Oh, do you mean Dani?"

"I think that's her name. She was nice. Her boyfriend shot her. She would understand, but I didn't know how to get there."

An idea popped into Janet's head. "Tell you what, how about I phone over and ask Dani if she'd like to come over here and have dinner with you and me. We can even ask your grandmother. What do you think about that?"

Abby's eyes brightened. "Would Dani come?"

"All we can do is ask. First, we need to call your grand-mother and let her know where you are. I'm sure she's worried sick about you."

The young girl's face fell. "Okay."

"Let's go out in the reception area. You can wait there while I phone them."

Once Abby was settled outside, Janet thought it through. Roberta Klein would be the first call. She would also need to get Greg's okay if she wanted to invite. "Okay, then, let's do this," she muttered.

Roberta Klein answered on the third ring. "Hello."

"Good afternoon, Miz Klein. This is Reverend Polasky. I called to let you know that Abby is here with me. She came to the church from school. I thought you might be worried." There was a lot more that she needed to say to this woman, but this was as good a starting point as any."

"The school called. They said she ran away. The principal wants me to come in tomorrow."

Janet asked, "Did they tell you about the circumstances?"

"They just said that they can't have students leaving the school any time they want. They want to talk about whether to suspend her or not." Roberta's voice was flat and unemotional.

"She left the school because the other children were teasing her about her parents. I'd say that the principal has a lot to answer for." Janet could feel her anger building.

Roberta Klein sighed. After a moment, she spoke softly. "I know she's hurt, but she might as well get used to it. It won't get better."

For the love of God, does no one care about this girl? "If you'd like, I can go with you to the school tomorrow, although I have to say, I'm not likely to be as forgiving as you sound. It's unconscionable that the administration didn't intervene."

"What are they gonna say, Reverend? You call it teasing, but it ain't nothing but kids telling the truth. Abby's papa killed her mother. Nothing dresses that up."

In that moment, Janet knew that Roberta Klein needed help every bit as much as Abby did. The difference was that Abby was willing to ask for it and accept it. Her grandmother built walls to keep help out and pain in.

Solving that, though, would have to wait until another day.

Janet offered, "If you don't mind, I'll swing by and see the principal in the morning. If he needs to talk to you after that, he can call you. I think I can manage it alone, though."

"If you want."

Janet moved on to the next topic. "Anyway, Abby's here right now. We're going to have some dinner at the parsonage. There's another young woman that will be here. Abby's met her and likes her so I'm hoping it'll cheer her up. You're welcome to join us. I'd love to have you."

"Please have her home by nine."

Janet's next call was to Greg. "I'm sorry to bother you in the middle of the day, but I wanted to check with you on something."

His voice sounded upbeat and cheerful. "It's no bother at all, although you don't need to check with me on things."

Janet laughed. "This isn't about my project. I wanted to know if it would be okay with you if I invited Dani over here for dinner tonight. I have Abby Miller, the young girl I had with me at the condo that day. She's had a hard day and I think she's made a connection with Dani."

"Sure, that would be fine. I'm sure Dani would jump at the opportunity to get out of the house. I have her new cellphone number if you'd like it."

Janet copied down the number and was about to disconnect when another thought struck her. "Oh, and I almost forgot, you're invited as well, if you can make it. We'd love to have you."

His voice sounded giddy. "Yes, I'd love to come over, I mean, if you're sure it's okay with the little girl. Oh, and when you call Dani, please tell her about me coming. If she's not enthusiastic about it, no problem, I understand."

"Six o'clock. Nothing fancy. See you then."

Janet turned the lights out in her office and opened the door into the outer office. "Okay, let's see if we can get some things together for dinner."

73

J anet took off early. With Abby in tow, she went by the supermarket and picked up a few things. She and Abby had decided on homemade hamburgers, potato salad, and baked beans. It wouldn't be the healthiest of meals, but it was comfort food, and this little girl needed some comfort. She picked up a frozen apple pie and some vanilla ice cream as well.

Once back at the parsonage, Janet set about making it all happen. Everyone had agreed on six o'clock and it was only four, so they had plenty of time. "First things first. If I get you a stool to stand on, can you wash the potatoes for me?"

Abby nodded. As the little girl scrubbed four russet potatoes, Janet put some white beans on to cook.

"Once we get the potatoes on to boil, we'll get some hamburger patties ready to go, what do you think?"

Abby stared with a curious look on her face.

Janet paused with the pan of beans in her hands. "Have you ever made hamburger patties before?"

"Mom always used the hamburgers that were frozen."

The minister smiled warmly. "Those are good too, and they're really fast to make." She didn't want to say anything that would in any way diminish Hanna in Abby's eyes. "You can help me pat out the ground beef and we'll make these patties by hand. It'll be fun."

Two hours later, the meal was close to ready. The first doorbell rang at about 5:55. Janet answered the door to find Greg with a bouquet of colorful autumn flowers—reds, golds, and oranges. He spoke as he offered them to Janet. "I grabbed these on the way. I thought that anything that would bring a little cheer to the evening would be good."

Dani arrived about ten minutes later, dropped off by Kaz. She nodded to Janet as she entered. Once inside, she went straight to Abby and gave the young girl a tight hug. "I'm so glad to see you again. Thanks for inviting me."

Abby's smile lit up the room. The young girl took Dani's hand and led her over to the couch, where the two sat and became immediately engaged in some quiet conversation.

Janet turned to Greg. "I can't tell you how much I appreciate this. It's not something I expected, but Abby is really taken with your niece."

"I'm glad it worked out that way with them. How are you holding up? I'm still a little rattled by what happened."

"Come on. We can talk while I finish preparing dinner." She led him through the doorway into the kitchen where the only two chores remaining before putting the burgers on to cook were to mix up the potato salad and the baked beans.

He offered, "Can I help with anything?"

"Do you know how to make potato salad?"

He began pulling out ingredients. Janet could tell by what he had on the counter that he'd done it before. He put two eggs on to boil and began chopping dill pickles and onions. "Do you have any black olives?"

Janet shook her head. "Sorry, no."

"No problem." He pulled mayonnaise and mustard from the refrigerator and took down a bottle of apple cider vinegar from the shelf over the stove. "I'll have this done in about fifteen minutes."

The minister smiled. "That's just about how long it'll take me to finish up the beans."

Twenty minutes later, the four of them sat down to dinner. Janet offered grace. Since she was unsure of Greg and Dani's spiritual inclinations, she kept it short. "For what we are about to receive may God help us to be truly thankful. Amen."

In that moment, Janet realized what a mine field any conversation would be. If Greg or Dani asked Abby about school, it was certain to create an awkward moment. The upcoming Thanksgiving holiday might also be an unpleasant topic for the young girl.

Dani saved the day. "This is delicious." She turned to Abby. "Reverend Polasky said that you helped with the potatoes and the hamburger patties."

Abby, caught with a full mouth, chewed and swallowed as the nodded. "I never made patties before. It was fun."

"They're perfect. You know, when you get a hamburger out at one of those fast food places, the patties are always too thin. You can't even taste the meat." The young woman scrunched up her face. "This is what a real hamburger is supposed to taste like." Dani took another bite of her burger.

As they settled into the rhythm of the meal, Janet felt increasingly grateful to Dani. This young woman had gone through hell and was still being bounced around, unable to get her life back on track. Yet her entire focus this evening had been on Abby. After dinner, Janet pulled Greg aside. "Did you see that? Dani changed that little girl's entire day. Greg, I can't even begin to tell you how grateful I am."

He seemed flustered, as though there was something he wanted to say but couldn't figure out the words. Finally, he managed, "I'd be willing to bet that it's helping Dani just as much. I wish that I could give her the kind of joy she's giving Abby."

Janet took his hand in hers. "What you give her is different, but every bit as important, Greg. You've stuck with her through all of this. Right now, you're the one person in the world who she knows she can depend on."

He nodded. She could see that his eyes were getting a little moist. She lightened up the conversation. "I'm going to put some coffee on and hot water for tea. We have apple pie and ice cream for dessert."

Dani put on her coat to leave around eight o'clock. "Kaz is supposed to pick me up." She laughed. "It's strange having a babysitter."

Greg hugged her and they spoke quietly for a few minutes before she left. Abby walked her to the door, holding on to her hand. Greg watched the scene with what appeared to be wonder. Seeing those two together—Dani and Abby—was like watching a miracle in process.

After Dani was gone, Janet put the dishes in the sink. "We're going to have to get you home soon, Abby. Why don't you gather your things while I say goodnight to Mister Stottman."

Greg, as though taking the cue, grabbed his coat from the closet. "Thanks for inviting me, Janet. This has been the most enjoyable evening I've had in years."

Janet followed him to the door and walked out onto the porch with him. The darkness of the late October evening was broken only by the pale porchlight. Her doorway was obscured from the street by several shrubs.

He turned to her and took her hands in his. "Thank you, Janet. What you did tonight, it was incredible."

"It was my pleasure. I'm glad it worked out."

Her legs began to tremble. She'd felt this before. The look in his eyes told her that he was making the same journey. *No, not now.*

Greg moved closer. She knew that she needed to stop it, but the word would not come. With his face only inches from hers, she closed her eyes and felt his lips on hers. Her heart raced and the trembling spread to her entire body. She momentarily wrapped her arms around his neck as he embraced her. She parted her lips and felt her entire body melting.

Then she eased away. "I'm sorry, Greg. I shouldn't have."

He touched her cheek with his hand. "Yes. You should have."

74

E ating homecooked meals with a partner turned out to be a mixed experience for Val. She, of course, had eaten dinner with her husband more than a decade ago. That experience, though, had always been an exercise in damage control—a constant balancing act of trying to be a family while not doing something to set him off. More often than not, something at the dinner table turned into a catalyst for violence.

It was different with Dee. This woman was sharing, kind, and respectful. She was everything that Val had wanted in a marriage all those years ago. She listened to Val, avoided criticizing, and knew how to disagree without attacking.

She was also an excellent cook. "Good salmon," Val offered between bites. The lemon-honey glaze worked perfectly with the broiled fish. "I guess it's be harder to get the fresh stuff in winter."

"We'll find substitutes. The cod is excellent as is rock-fish, and we can get both of those at the market all winter."

Dee spoke, though, as if something else occupied her mind.

Val set her fork down. "You seem bothered tonight."

Dee took a deep breath as she seemed to turn the question over in her mind. Finally, she asked, "Did Janet tell you about what happened the other day... with those two guys?"

"No. I haven't spoken to her since early in the week. What was it?"

Dee responded, "Two guys came to see her. One was Rob Young, Lucy's husband. Janet was expecting him, so she made sure she had help. Greg Stottman and another guy... a security type... were there with her. Turns out, the man who came with Young is a thug who works for some powerful people. Her best guess is that they came to abduct her, hoping to get information about what she's doing with this project."

Val put the pieces together. Senator Corel, Bonnie's husband, must have been the one behind it. "I guess that as we go on, this kind of thing will happen again. That's the point of the project, after all—to move women away from abusive and powerful husbands."

"It's also dangerous. You know that Sue Hartman over at the DV Network disappeared. She's most likely dead, and that admin assistant there that committed suicide—I'd bet a month's pay that it's more than that. I'm telling you, Val, I'm more than a little scared."

Val reached over and put her hand on Dee's. "Yeah. I hear you, but this is what we do, huh? How long have you been a cop? You go to work every day not knowing whether or not you'll come home. You do it because, at least for you, it's the right thing to do."

Dee lashed out, "But I'm a cop. It's what I do for a living. I've been trained. I made that decision years ago. I know how to handle myself. You stumbled into this gig. I'm afraid for you."

Val could feel the resentment building. "Dee, it's what I do for a living too. I made the decision. I didn't stumble into it. I was offered a job, and I took it knowing full well what kind of dangers were involved. Don't forget, I lived with a man who beat me just because he wanted to."

The detective grew insistent. "It's different. I've got years of experience, and I know how to avoid danger. In your job, you put yourself right smack in the middle of trouble."

"Who should do the job then? Is there someone else whose life isn't worth much who should take my place? Dee, you said it yourself—this is important work. Women's lives depend on what I do. What kind of person would I be if I ran away from this because there's danger involved. These women live with the danger every day."

Dee bit her lower lip and stared at the half-eaten salmon on her plate. "I don't have any answers, Val. I used to think I knew how everything works. But now…" she shook her head and furrowed her brow, "I don't know."

She raised her head and stared into Val's eyes. "I just know that, for the first time in my life, I'm with someone who matters. Life is different when you're in it. Better than anything I've ever known. I don't want to lose that."

"I understand all that, I really do. Think about it, though. Do you really want to be with someone who spends their time hiding at home, afraid of everything that might harm her? Dee, life is dangerous and then we die. It comes for all of us. I could get hit by a car. The furnace could go haywire and I could be asphyxiated by carbon monoxide. I could get a chicken bone stuck in my throat. There are thousands of ways to go and I can't run away from them all."

Dee shot back angrily, "You don't have to run toward them."

Val could see where this was going. It wasn't just about danger or the threat of losing someone. She'd seen all this before. This was about control. "Dee. I know how you feel, but I don't try to tell you how to make a living. I get to make my own decisions."

"That's not how partnerships work. These kinds of decisions should be made together."

Val was just about at the end of her rope. She could see the end coming into view. "I suppose that you're willing to put your job as a cop up for a joint discussion, or is that off the table, you know, grandfathered in?"

Dee hurled her retort. "That's not fair and you know it. I was a cop long before we ever met. It's the only job I know. You just started doing this and you've done other jobs."

Val smirked. "Like making license plates in prison?" She pushed her plate back and stood. "I'm sorry, Dee. I can't do this. I love you, but I'm not willing to give up control of my own life." She started toward the hall closet, where she'd hung up her coat. "Let's give it a little space."

She hastily threw her coat on, and left, closing the door quietly behind her.

75

Mixed feelings haunted Greg all night. The kiss with Janet took him to an emotional place he'd never known before. He'd kissed women before. He'd had sex. He remembered college relationships. They were fun. They had seemed like more at the time, but when all was said and done, it had been about two people having their physical needs met. This was different. For the first time in his life, he could imagine building a life with someone he cared about. It was about sharing himself with another person.

On the other end of the emotional spectrum, though, was the memory of Janet's reaction to the kiss—regret. He'd seen it on her face, especially in her eyes. Guilt crept in. Had he forced it on her, if not physically, then emotionally? She depended on him for funding of her project. Did she feel obligated to return the kiss?

He tossed and turned until daylight. He needed to fix this. By the time he arrived at work, Greg had come up with a plan. Sitting in his car idly scanning the parking lot, he decided to act before going into the building. He pulled out his phone and connected.

"Hello?" Her voice sounded tired.

He closed his eyes and carefully proceeded. "Hi Janet, this is Greg. Do you have a minute?"

A short pause preceded her muted response. "What is it?"

"About last night. I wanted to—"

She cut him off. "It's okay. Don't worry about it."

"No." He shot back quickly. "It's not okay. If you'll let me, I'd like to talk to you about it."

"Okay."

He shook his head as though somehow she could see him. "Not now. I mean, could I come over this evening and talk to you?"

"I don't think that's a good idea."

He knew, or thought he knew, what her concern was. "Just talk, I promise. Nothing else."

"Seven o'clock." The tone embodied a mix of resistance and anger.

After he disconnected, Greg felt a wave of helplessness. Was he pushing her too hard? Did she agree to let him come over only because of his funding? He and Janet had always been able to talk. No matter what the topic, there had always been openness and honesty. At this moment, though, he felt as though she wanted as little to do with him as possible. What made it worse is that he had no idea what he would say that evening to change things, short of just being honest. He muttered under his breath, "Yeah, like that'll work." A tortured laugh escaped.

Once in his office, work drove the demons away as best it could. He picked up a bound report entitled *Public Policy Issues and Artificial Intelligence: The Road Ahead*. With the rapid deployment of AI imminent, questions abounded regarding the role government would play, especially concerning privacy. He scribbled notes in the margins— questions, observations, and challenges. It felt nice falling into his old familiar rhythm.

By ten, he needed a break. As he ambled down the corridor, he tuned out the faint din of noise emanating from the side offices. At the small snack kiosk in the main atrium area, he purchased a chocolate chip cookie and black coffee. Grabbing a table by the window, he lost himself in the colors of the late October morning. The bright blue sky promised relatively warm temperatures for the afternoon. Everything outside looked peaceful.

Suddenly, a shot of panic invaded. He and Kaz had not really spoken much about the event with the two men at Janet's office. The incident had ended as a stand-off. It was sheer stupidity to think it was over.

Moments later, he had Kaz on the phone. "What do you have going on today?"

"Not much, just finishing up some final pieces on the Reba Stillings thing. I should be able to have a report to you within the next day or so."

Greg said, "I need you to do something for me. We can talk about a longer strategy later, but for today, I'd like you to keep an eye on Janet. I assume she's at her church. I'm kind of afraid that the thing with the two guys the other day is going to pop up again."

"Is it okay if she knows I'm watching."

"I'll call and let her know. I'm just a little nervous about her being there alone with no protection."

"Okay, no problem. I agree, though, that we need to talk about a longer-term strategy."

After they disconnected, Greg tried Janet, but his call went straight to voice mail.

76

Janet rose early. She skipped her daily run. A full day lay ahead of her. The minister decided to get a jump on things. Before she could even begin to organize her thoughts, though, Greg's call had come. At the moment, he was the last person she wanted to talk to. Her feelings were complicated. She found it harder and harder to ignore the attraction she felt for him. Every time she got close, though, the memories of her late husband swept over her. She had never even considered the idea of someone else. Here it was in front of her, though. She tried to put him off, but he insisted. *I'll talk to him tonight.*

With that resolved, the next item up was Abby's school situation.

The bell that signaled the beginning of the school day could be heard from the sidewalk. Janet entered the school and signed in at the reception desk. "I'm here to see the principal," she told the young lady.

"Can I ask what this is about?" The woman shuffled papers as she asked the question. She was no doubt just getting set up for her day.

"I'm here about one of your students, Abby Miller."
Janet kept her voice even and soft. Whatever the school
was doing wrong with regard to young Abby, it wasn't this
woman's fault.

"Are you her mother or guardian?" The receptionist
looked up, seeming to notice Janet's clerical collar for the
first time.

"I'm the minister at her church. Her grandmother,
who's her legal guardian, was unable to come this
morning."

The receptionist responded, "Uh, I'll have to call her
grandmother to get permission." She clicked on the
computer keyboard, staring at the screen until she apparently found what she was looking for. She dialed the phone
and, after a brief conversation with Roberta Klein, she
turned to Janet. "I'll let the vice principal know you're
here."

Janet stepped back. *Vice Principal.* This meant that the
school most likely considered this to be a routine discipli-
nary issue. If it were more sensitive, such as something that
might draw adverse publicity, the principal would handle it
personally.

"He'll be with you in about five minutes." The receptionist offered a shallow smile and went back to her paper
shuffling.

Janet took a seat and waited. It occurred to her that, if
she were to resolve this, it would require the presence of
Abby's teacher and also any counselors who might be
available. This was not something that a vice principal or
even principal could fix by themselves.

Within a few minutes, the receptionist peeked up over
the counter. "The vice principal will see you now. Second
door on the right." She gestured down the hallway.

The minister knocked and then opened the door. "I'm

Reverend Janet Polasky. I'm here to discuss the situation regarding Abby Miller." She closed the door behind her and pulled a chair up close to the desk.

The vice principal was a stout man who appeared to be in his late forties. His thinning brown hair was combed over and trimmed short on the sides. He wore a pale blue shirt with a navy tie. A blazer hung on the coat rack behind him beside a raincoat. "Good morning. I'm Vice Principal Stewart. I was expecting Abby's grandmother. I believe she's the legal guardian." He forced a slight smile which morphed quickly into a look of concern.

"Miz Klein was unable come today. She asked me to speak with you. I'll be meeting with her later today and will convey the details of our discussion. Before we start, I think it would be preferable that we include Abby's teacher and your school counselor in this conversation. This isn't some kid with discipline problems. There's a lot going on here. If you want to resolve it with the best results for both the school and Abby, then all the players need to be here."

He shook his head. "Abby's teacher is with her class right now. Pulling her out would be disruptive. I can get the counselor, if that would work."

Janet pressed her case. "I appreciate that, but the teacher is at the heart of the problem. Without her, nothing we say is going to make a difference. I would hope that we can finish this up within fifteen or twenty minutes. Maybe you can have an admin person stay with the class for that short period." She locked gazes with him and waited.

After a moment, the silence worked. He picked up the phone and made the arrangements. When he was done, he said, "It will be just a moment." His voice sounded both tired and bothered.

"Thank you."

About five minutes later, the door opened, and two women entered. They introduced themselves and sat. As silence set in, Janet realized that the floor was hers.

"As I told Vice Principal Stewart, I'm Reverend Janet Polasky from Saint Luke's Methodist Church, here on behalf of Abby Miller. She's a member of my congregation. Abby left school yesterday after an incident in class and showed up at my church shortly afterwards. What she told me was disturbing. Layered on top of this was the fact that you phoned her grandmother and asked her to come in to discuss a possible suspension. This seems a little harsh based on the circumstances."

Stewart sighed. "Reverend Polasky, students bring all kinds of troubles with them to school. We do the best we can to help them with what we have. We do require that they follow a few simple rules, the first of which is that they are not allowed to simply get up and leave any time things become uncomfortable."

Janet forced a tight smile. "I understand that, and I'd be willing to bet that Abby does as well. You have to consider context, though. I would ask her teacher," Janet nodded toward one of the women, "What occurred in class that set Abby off. I think having that information might be a good place to start."

The teacher, a small chubby woman of about thirty, cleared her throat. "It was all pretty simple. We were talking about our Thanksgiving play. Students were talking about having their parents attend and then Abby just got up and left."

Janet sat in utter bewilderment. "Correct me if I'm wrong, but my understanding is that you asked the students whether their parents would be attending or not."

"I suppose, yes, that's a standard question I would ask

about something like this. It engages the students and connects them to the event."

The minister continued, "I understand that several students ridiculed Abby. Maybe you're not aware of the situation, but last spring, her father killed her mother and then himself. In that short span of time, Abby went from having two parents, at least one of them functional and loving, to being an orphan. She's now in the care of her grandmother, who herself is struggling with this tragedy. That's an awful lot for a twelve-year old to bear, wouldn't you agree?"

Of the three school officials in the room, the counselor was the only one who reacted. The young woman who appeared to be no older than her mid-twenties, said, "No. I wasn't aware of that." Her face reflected what appeared to be genuine distress.

The other two—the teacher and the vice principal— seemed outwardly unmoved. The Vice Principal Stewart said, "Yes, that's tragic. I agree that the young girl probably has a lot of healing to do, but I fail to see how that applies here. I mean, surely you can't be suggesting that the rules don't apply to her just because of this event. I feel for her, but we have a school to run. If she needs mental health services, there are agencies in town that can provide those. Our teachers are charged with maintaining discipline in class so that learning can occur."

It was at this moment that Janet realized that Abby's relationship with this school was over. They were simply not inclined to recognize what the young girl needed. The fact that the teacher remained completely uninvolved during the discussion said volumes. No matter what decisions were made with regard to Abby, this woman would have no part of it beyond what was absolutely forced on her.

Chapter 76

Janet sighed. "It seems to me that your school is not equipped to deal with this. I'm a little surprised, since you are funded for counseling services. Until now, I always thought that middle school teachers took an interest in students. That's clearly not the case here. I'll discuss this with Miz Klein, Abby's grandmother. My recommendation will be for her to get Abby enrolled in a private or charter school that can meet her needs."

Vice Principal Stewart held his hands up as though to forestall her argument. "I think maybe you're overreacting. I didn't say that we don't care, and I never said we wouldn't try to find solutions. I'm merely expressing a view that we have many students to consider. Our teachers are overworked and asking them to put everything on hold to deal with one student's problems is a lot to ask. Also, I'm not certain what kind of accommodation you're looking for. We have school events, such as the Thanksgiving play. Parental involvement is crucial. What you seem to be suggesting is that we shouldn't mention parents to the children because of Abby's situation."

Janet shot back. "No. You have that wrong entirely. I'm suggesting no such thing. What I am saying is that, if children ridicule her, the teacher should intervene. If that intervention doesn't work, the parents of the children doing the harassment should be called regarding their behavior. You're trying to lay the blame on Abby. That's not going to work. Period."

The teacher appeared as though she wanted to say something, but the vice principal put his hand up in her direction. The meaning was clear. He didn't want her saying anything. "We're willing to discuss this, but we need Abby's legal guardian to come in and talk to us. Before we look at any accommodations, though, we still need to

369

determine what, if any sanctions should be applied as a result of her leaving school without permission."

Janet stood. "You've made your position clear. I'll discuss this with Miz Klein, and we will search for another educational option for Abby. In the meantime, Abby is ill, which should come as no surprise to you. I'll make sure that she has a doctor's note, so you won't mark her as being truant. We'll be in touch."

With that, Janet turned and left, shutting the door behind her.

77

K az pulled into a parking spot on the street about a half a block from St. Luke's Methodist Church. He sat in his car, taking note of everything around him. Nothing seemed amiss.

Reverend Polasky's car was not in the parking lot. Kaz pulled out his phone and connected with Greg. "Hey, just wanted to let you know that I'm here at the church, and Janet's not here. Did you have a chance to talk with her?"

"My call went to voice mail. I left a message for her to get back to me."

Well, crap. Kaz asked, "Any idea where she might have gone?"

After a moment, Greg responded, "She did say something last night about having to talk to the principal at Abby's school this morning. If she's not at the church, I assume that's where she is."

"Do you happen to know the school?"

"Sorry, no."

Kaz sighed. "Okay, then. I'll hang tight here and wait."

Twenty minutes later, Janet's Subaru pulled into the parking lot. She eased out of the car, moving in what seemed slow motion. From where he sat in his own parked car, he couldn't make out any clues on her face. She moved as though she was weary. She started for the church door and then suddenly stopped, as though something caught her attention.

Internal warnings kicked in—nothing explicit. He could see no visible signs of trouble, but Kaz's gut told him something was wrong. He jumped out of his car and started down the road at a fast clip. He needed to get her into the church. Hopefully Greg had told her about the protection detail. If not, well, the two of them could sort it out.

He told himself he was being too cautious. There was nothing to suggest that anything out of the ordinary was afoot. His instinct refused to relent. It was just something he felt but couldn't explain.

Kaz picked up the pace. He drew closer but Polasky didn't seem to notice him. *Odd.* He was almost running across the parking lot in plain view, and it wasn't like they didn't know each other.

Movement caught his attention. From the right, another figure closed on her—Karl Unger. Fortunately, the man had not noticed Kaz either. Unger moved in, keeping his right hand in his coat pocket.

Shit, shit, shit! It was clear that Kaz wouldn't reach them in time to prevent a confrontation. He broke into a run.

Unger, his back to Kaz, pulled his hand from his pocket. As expected, he held handgun. Bringing it to bear on the minister, Kaz could hear him speak.

"You need to come with me, Reverend Polasky."

The look on Janet's face was sheer terror.

Chapter 77

Kaz pulled his own gun, aimed at Unger, and stopped in his tracks. "Hold it right there," he shouted.

Unger whirled around, his gun pointed generally in Kaz's direction. The two men locked gazes.

"Don't try it, Karl. You're not that fast." Kaz clicked the safety off and took a deep breath. The front sight of his 9 mm came into sharp focus. He could see Unger's stocky body as a fuzzy outline. Kaz shifted his focus to his adversary's eyes. "Don't do it."

But Kaz could see it in his eyes. Unger brought his weapon up as he crouched.

Time ran out. Kaz squeezed off the first round, then a second, and a third. Karl Unger crumbled to the ground.

Janet stood staring for a long moment and then stumbled backward against her car, slumping to the ground. Kaz ran by Unger, kicking the man's weapon away, continuing on to the minister. Going down on both knees beside her, he asked, "Janet, are you okay? Are you hurt?"

She stared at him with glazed eyes, apparently unable to speak.

"I'm going to check you for injury, okay. I'm making sure you're not hurt." He pulled her coat away. The black blouse she had on didn't appear to have any blood on it. He saw no apparent injuries.

"I don't see anything. Can you hear me, Janet?"

Eyes wide, she nodded slowly.

"Are you injured, are you hurt?"

Not moving her eyes or speaking, she shook her head slowly. Her entire body trembled.

"Good." He glanced back toward Unger's body, which lay completely still. "I need to check on something. I'll be right back." He rose and eased over to check on the man. He quickly confirmed what he already knew. Karl Unger was dead.

Back by Janet's side. He forced a smile. "I need to call the police. This is likely to get messy. Sorry."

She stared at him as though not comprehending. Finally, she spoke. "How did you know?"

78

Greg had spent his lunch hour trying to structure in his mind the conversation he wanted to have with Janet. This wasn't just about a kiss. It was about two people who cared about each other. The only problem—he wasn't certain that she cared about him, at least in *that way*. Surely, though, she wouldn't have kissed if there wasn't something there.

The call came at one in the afternoon. He checked the display—Kaz. "Hi. Did you manage to catch up with Janet?"

The somber voice came out as little more than a whisper. "You need to get over here, Greg. We're at her home."

Terror struck at his heart. "No, God no, Kaz. Tell me she's not…."

"Janet's safe. We'll talk when you get here."

He called over his shoulder as he passed his assistant in the outer office. "I'll be in tomorrow." He half walked and half ran down the hall, breaking into a complete run as he exited the building.

A half-hour later, he pulled up at the parsonage. Bolting from his car, he ran to the front door and entered without knocking. Kaz intercepted him as he entered the living room.

"She's okay, Greg. Rattled but okay."

Greg sidestepped him and moved toward the couch, going down on both knees as he approached her. Janet trembled, her eyes red and swollen. She wrung her hands in her lap and hunched her shoulders.

He took her hands in his. "I got here as quick as I could." He desperately wanted to make everything okay.

She looked through him to a place far away. He could see that his words and actions weren't registering. He felt a touch on his shoulder. When he turned, Kaz motioned him to the other side of the room.

"That same guy, Karl Unger, came for her. He intercepted her at the church. I got there just as it was going down."

"Did the police arrest him? Do they have him in custody?"

Kaz lowered his head. "I killed him."

Greg searched for the right words. Of course, he was glad that Kaz had been there. The fact that Unger was dead didn't upset him, but Greg could see that his friend was not particularly happy about it. "How are you doing?"

"I'll be fine. I gave a statement to the police. They wanted to question Janet, but she wasn't up to it there at the church. I suspect they'll be by later today."

Greg nodded his understanding. "Do you need anything? I mean, is there anything I can do?"

"You need to be with her. If you hadn't called me this morning, this would have gone much differently. She knows it and it terrifies her. It's going to take some time."

"Thanks, Kaz. I can't even begin to tell you how grateful I am." In spite of himself, he hugged the man.

Greg sat beside Janet on the couch, held her hands, and spoke softly. "I'm here, Janet."

She turned, seemingly aware of him for the first time since he'd arrived. "I should have known."

He squeezed her hands harder. "You're safe. That's what matters."

A single tear rolled down her cheek. "If Kaz hadn't been there…."

"But he was."

She shook her head. "How did he know?"

Greg paused a moment, not knowing how she would take his answer. "I told him to keep an eye on you. I was afraid that guy would show up again."

Janet squeezed his hand back. "As much as I've talked about men who have the resources to pursue their wives, I never imagined…."

"We can talk about that later."

Her eyes searched his. "If you'd been here, he would have killed both of us."

Greg let the comment go unchallenged. There was nothing to say. He took one of his hands away from hers and wrapped an arm around her, pulling her to him. In that moment, he remembered the night in the hospital when he had been close to breaking. She had been there holding him and listening as he poured his heart out. Now it was his turn to be there for her.

Two hours later, a female police detective showed up at the door. Sitting down beside Janet, she spoke so quietly that Greg couldn't hear the conversation. Realizing that it was that way by design, he asked, "I'm going to make some coffee. Would either of you like a cup?"

The detective responded, "Thank you. That would be nice. Black."

Janet nodded.

Greg felt a pull on his heart as he left the two and went into the kitchen. He needed to remain by her side. As he filled the coffee maker with water, he found himself wanting to be with her as she endured the questioning. Placing the coffee grounds in the filter, his thoughts turned to Kaz, who had left the parsonage a few minutes earlier. Greg assumed that there would be no legal repercussions. After all, Kaz was defending Janet.

As he sat the cups down in front of the detective and Janet, he asked, "Can I get you anything else?"

"No thanks," the detective answered. Janet just sat there, her hands squeezed between her knees.

Greg wandered into the kitchen and parked at the table with his steaming cup in front of him. It occurred to him that this was the very thing that Mel had warned him about. This was dangerous business and Janet had almost been killed. On the other hand, if he had followed his partner's advice, Janet would be dead at this very moment. The thought chilled his heart. He sat for a while and then moved back into the living room, sitting in a chair across the room from where the two women were speaking.

An hour later, the detective rose and turned off her notepad. She touched Janet on the shoulder and handed her a business card. On the way out, she stopped to speak to Greg. "I have what I need for now, but I'd like to ask you a few questions tomorrow."

He nodded. "Of course. Do you need me to come down to your station?" He felt uncomfortable having the police show up at his office.

"I know where your office complex is. I'll drive out,

probably around ten." She handed him a card and then was gone.

He returned to Janet's side and put his arms around her. He wanted to keep her forever safe. Her eyes had dried, although they remained red and swollen. "I don't know if I can do this. It's never going to end. You know that, don't you?" Her voice was flat.

"There's a lot to talk about. Truthfully, I don't have answers right now. I do know that what you're doing is important. It makes a difference. If it didn't, that guy wouldn't have shown up. We just have to figure some things out."

"What if Abby had been with me?"

Greg once again put his arm around her and pulled her to him. "She wasn't. Kaz was there, and you're safe. Those are the things that matter."

Out of the blue, she said, "Does the kiss last night matter?"

The question floored him. Of all the things he expected she might say, this was not on the list. "It matters a great deal to me, more than I thought a kiss could."

He felt her lean into him. She laid her head on his shoulder. Together they sat until the daylight outside faded and the room was washed in shadow.

Finally, Greg asked, "How about we get something to eat?"

"I'm not really hungry."

"You need to eat, Janet, even if it's something light. I figure that you skipped lunch."

She reached up and touched his hand, the one on her shoulder. "Okay."

"I'll order for delivery, just a couple of sandwiches and some salad."

A half hour later, the food arrived. Greg turned on a

few lights and set the bag on the dining room table where just the prior night, he, Dani, Janet, and Abby had enjoyed a remarkable evening. Janet rose from the couch and shuffled into the kitchen. She spoke as though in a trance. "I'll get some silverware and napkins. Is water okay?"

It would probably be a long night for Janet Polasky.

79

Janet trembled. Despite the safety of Maddie's cozy home, she could not control the fear. The previous day's attack had slammed home the inherent danger on the path she traveled. The brush with death underscored the speed with which events could spin out of control. The sleepless night following the incident had destroyed her reserves.

"It must be something bad. You brought these delicious tea biscuits and haven't touched a one of them." Maddie always cut straight to the point.

Janet reached to pick up her teacup, but her shaking wouldn't allow it. Instead, she tucked her hands between her knees. "It was horrible."

She poured out the story. Her voice cracked as she cobbled it together. She remembered the man. The huge black barrel of his gun dominated her attention. She heard shots. The world spun and grew dark. After a moment Kaz was there and spoke to her. She remembered being on the ground with lots of people around. Then, somehow, she was inside the parsonage. How did she get there? Didn't the shooting happen at the church? The police came and talked to her at home. Were they at the church parking lot? And then Greg was there beside her.

After the rush of words trickled to nothing, silence reigned for a few minutes. Finally, Maddie spoke. "God was certainly with you."

Janet thought it an odd thing to say. If God had been there, wouldn't he have prevented the entire thing? Why did he let that man pull a gun on her. Why did God leave it to Kaz to save her? God had not saved Hanna Miller.

She swept the thoughts from her mind. *My faith will not be shaken.* Still… so many questions; so many doubts. She shrugged. "I guess." It seemed the safest answer. She refused to give voice to those doubts, especially to Maddie, who at one time had been her board president.

"You should consider taking some time off. Have you spoken to the board president?"

"I told her about the shooting. We have services this Sunday. I need to be there." Janet felt strange, as though she was hovering above herself and listening to this discussion. The words she uttered didn't feel like they came from her.

"What you need, Dearie, is to spend time with people who care about you. It's good that you showed up here today, and not just because I wanted some Russian tea biscuits." She offered a warm laugh.

"Hold your friends close, and understand, they need to be with you as much as you need them." Maddie took another bite of a tea biscuit and sipped her tea. After a moment, she spoke with a seriousness unlike her usual playful banter. "You've chose a dangerous road, Janet. You see that now and you have to know that it won't become less so. The safe bet would be to leave this work to others—

those who are trained for it and have chosen it as a career. You might say it would be the prudent action."

Janet started to object, but Maddie quickly continued, "If you're right though. If God did indeed call you for this…." Her voice faded into silence for a moment. When she spoke again, it was with a curious tone of objectivity, almost as though she were citing some authoritative text.

"When my family fled the old Soviet Union, my father told me that the families that helped us risked losing everything, including their lives. This was not an occupation for them. They weren't paid professionals. I choose to believe that they felt called by God. They understood the stakes. Certainly, they were careful and didn't take any unnecessary risks. Still, they refused to sit by and do nothing."

She smiled warmly. "Janet, you've chosen to do the same. You made the decision to put your own life in jeopardy so that abused women and children might have a chance at a new life. Only you can decide whether to stay the course or pull back. You must know, though, that while I fear for your safety, I am proud to call you my friend. Even more, I'm sure that God is proud of you as well. Now, you need to gather those friends to you and heal from this experience."

Janet thought about Dee and Val, neither of whom she had called. "I suppose. Greg Stottman was with me all afternoon and evening."

"It sounds to me like he cares about you."

Janet remembered the kiss. "It's not like that, Maddie. He's wealthy and could have any woman he wanted. He was being nice to me. That's all." She was less sure, though, what she wanted.

Maddie continued to probe. "Did he tell you that or is that just you making things up?"

Janet laughed in spite of herself. Her dear friend was

just not going to let this go. "We've talked about this before. Even if he did feel more, it wouldn't be fair to him. I'm still carrying the memory of Mark. I don't know that I'll ever be able to completely give my heart to anyone else."

"I'm going to give you some completely free and unsolicited advice, Dearie. You'll always carry Mark with you. He is and will always be a part of you. That doesn't mean, though, that you can never love again. Your time with your husband helped shape you into who you are today. Any man worth having would understand that, and I'm guessing that Greg would fall into that category. I'm just an old woman, though. Don't take my word for it. Talk to him about it."

Janet suddenly remembered that, before the incident the day before, Greg had wanted to talk to her. She was certain that it had to do with their kiss. Maybe he would tell her that it was just a passing thing that happened and didn't mean anything. Perhaps he would say that he didn't have time for a woman in his life. Most likely he would say that he hoped she didn't misunderstand his attention. He just wants to be friends. *That's what I want, isn't it?*

She cleared her head of the Greg thoughts. "Do you remember the young girl I told you about, Abby Miller?"

Maddie asked, "Do you mean the one whose father killed her mother?"

"She's having problems at school. It seems an impossible situation. She's incredibly fragile right now and, well, you know kids that age. They can be insensitive, to say the least. She left class the other day and came to the church. I went down and spoke with the principal and her teacher. They claim they're not equipped to deal with all of her grief. I think that's a lot of BS, but I don't really have any standing with them. I'm going to recommend to her grandmother that Abby be enrolled in a private school."

"What makes you think the children at a private school would be any less insensitive?"

Janet responded, "I don't know. At least with a private school, we could put more pressure on the administration to try and deal with it."

Maddie chuckled. "Who is this *we* you're talking about? From what you've told me, her grandmother is not in any condition to be putting pressure on anyone, and she's the young child's legal guardian."

"I'm sure that I'd have to help, at least for the foreseeable future, but I can't just stand by and let Abby face this alone."

The old woman rubbed her chin and furrowed her brow. "Let me ask you a question. This project thing you're working on—is there some way that it could play a role?"

Janet hadn't considered that angle. "I'm not sure. What I'm doing is about helping women and their children get to safety. That's not really the situation that Abby's in."

"No… and yes. She's not running from a violent father, but she is suffering from the effects of what a violent father did. It doesn't seem like much of stretch to me to try and use some of your resources to help. It would be worth talking to Greg—he is the man that put up the funding, isn't he?"

80

Time healed. Janet knew this. She'd been through pain and suffering before. Books on dealing with pain and trauma filled shelves at the bookstores. TV celebrities offered every manner of solutions. Experience, though, had taught the minister that time was essential—the passing of days, months, and years.

The shooting in the parking lot remained fresh in her mind. Every time she flashed back, Janet felt a horrible wave of nausea wash over her. Maddie had suggested spending time with friends, people who cared about her. Her mentor had offered that this would be the best medicine. For her part, Janet felt more inclined to crawl into bed and stay there until the memories of the event vanished.

She stared alternately at the framed art on the wall, the book shelves full of wisdom, and her desk, stacked with enough work to keep her busy for weeks. She tried to will her attention to the membership list. It simply looked like a list of names. Her sermon for Sunday was as done as it was going to get, and it would certainly not be her best work.

She had a schedule of special church events coming up—Thanksgiving festival, Christmas with all its activities and special services, and a New Year party. All sat stalled at various stages of planning. Her heart told her they would not advance this day.

Her cellphone chirped around mid-morning. Janet forced some small amount of cheer into her voice. "Hi, Dee."

Detective Martin sounded strained. "Have you got a little time this morning? I was hoping to drop by and talk to you."

Janet sighed. She didn't feel much like talking, but the visit would give her some justification for getting absolutely no work done. "Sure, swing by any time."

Twenty minutes later came a knock at the door. It opened and Dee entered. "Hi." Her tone seemed bathed in the same pain that Janet felt.

"Have a seat." Suddenly, it seemed as though Janet had lost her casual conversation skills. She had no idea what to say.

"I heard about what went down at the church. You should have called me." There was no enthusiasm in Dee's admonition.

"Sorry. I haven't been up to talking about it."

Dee said, "I got the rundown from some of the uniforms that were there. Jesus, Janet, do you have any idea how close you came to…?" Her voice trailed off and the sentence went unfinished.

Janet just stared at her.

"Did you arrange to have that guy there, Kazarian?"

"No. I had no idea. Greg asked him to keep an eye on me."

A look of desperation came over Dee. "You're going to have to make some kind of security arrangements. You can't... I mean, there may not be anybody there to help next time."

Janet took a deep breath. "I'm rattled right now. I knew the danger when I agreed to go down this road, though. We'll learn from this. I'll figure it out." She had no confidence in those words.

If Dee sensed Janet's fear, she didn't let on. She pivoted and switched topics. "Say, Janet, do you remember Luellen Pickering?"

"Sure. She's the woman that we were going to try and help in the beginning. Her husband got to her kids and killed them before we could get there. Why do you ask?"

Dee furrowed her brow as though she trying to solve a complex problem. "Funny thing. Her brother called me this morning. He lives over in Eastern Washington, near Spokane, I think. Anyway, he called to tell me that Luellen had gotten out of the mental health facility. Apparently the staff there was satisfied that her condition had improved enough to let her go. He seemed to think, though, that she wasn't ready—that she might try to harm herself."

Janet sighed. "I can't even begin to imagine what it must be like for her, having lost her kids like that... just as she was trying to get away from the violence. What did the brother want from you? I mean, you're not in a position to do anything about that."

"He didn't say. I got the sense that he was searching for any kind of solution he could find. I'm afraid I didn't have any good answers for him." Dee fell silent, sadness in her eyes. Something seemed off about her. Janet had known her for years. She'd seen the detective worried. She'd been with her during some dark times. This seemed different.

"What is it, Dee?"

"So much death. It's like it's everywhere just waiting to jump."

Chapter 80

Something told Janet that this wasn't about her, or at least not completely about her. "Yes." Janet decided to let the silence work for her.

After a few minutes, the truth came—a trickle at first. "I'm scared, Janet. I've worked around crime and death for years. It's different now."

"Why?"

Tears filled Dee's eyes. "Do you know about me and Val?"

Janet nodded.

"I'm afraid for her. All this stuff that's happening and she's out there alone. No one's going to ride up and save her if that kind of thing happens to her."

"We're working on it, Dee. So far, we've assumed that if we kept a low profile and moved quickly, we could avoid these kinds of confrontations. No such luck, though."

The detective stared blankly through the tears. "She left."

Janet did a double-take. "What?"

"We had an argument about this. I wanted her to quit and find something safer."

Janet didn't know how to respond. Val was her only employee and up until this point, had done an incredible job. In the short time she'd been working, the woman had earned her trust.

Before Janet could respond, though, Dee continued, "I know that wasn't fair of me. I was trying to control her life. I've never felt this way about anyone before and I'm terrified that I could lose her. Because of that, I did the same thing that abusive husbands do."

Janet shot back, "No, you didn't, at least I'm pretty sure you didn't beat her. There's a world of difference between wanting your partner to be safe and trying to beat them into submission. I know what it feels like to lose someone you love. You're right, it's crushing."

She slid her chair around beside Dee and held her hands. "Which is better—living without her and knowing she's in danger or finding a way to accept that danger and learn to live in the moment? My guess is that Val is not going to change her mind about this. Even if she did, you have to know in your heart that it would breed resentment."

Dee remained silent.

Janet paused and spoke softly. "I'm going to share something with you, something I usually don't like talking about. Years ago, when Mark was diagnosed, we knew pretty quickly that it was terminal. The doctors were remarkably frank with us. There were simply no words to describe the horror, the pain, and the desire I had to crawl into a dark, black hole and never come out. Instead, I held him. I spent every minute I could with him. We talked. We laughed. We cried a lot. It seemed beyond hard at the time. Today, I'd give anything to have just one of those days back."

Dee squeezed her hands.

Janet continued, "If you love Val, don't throw this time away. Yes, she may be in danger. Neither of us can know the future, but it will undoubtedly bring both good and bad. Each day with her is a gift. You can choose to squander that if you like, but I promise you'll regret it."

"I don't know if she'll even talk to me now."

Janet laughed and it felt almost good. "Unless you're telepathically inclined, then the only way you'll know is to call her."

Dee shifted her attention back to Janet. "What are you going to do about your own safety?"

"I'm working on it."

81

The golden leaves swayed in the light autumn breeze. The Sniper surveyed the scene across the parking lot. "Wind is left to right between ten and fifteen miles an hour. We're at fifty yards. Do you need to adjust the windage?" He tossed the final test at Cousin Billy.

Billy stared across the lot as though confused for a moment. "It ain't that far. Don't seem like a big deal to me."

"Cuz, I asked you a simple question. With a ten to fifteen mile an hour breeze left to right do you need to adjust the windage. It's a yes or no question." The kid had totally missed the point.

"No." Anger bathed the response.

"Good. What about a thirty mile per hour wind— would that make a difference?"

The Sniper could see Billy's face turning red with rage. *Good.* He needed to push the kid into his anger zone. It was the one thing that was sure to bring him down if he didn't conquer it.

"Yes. I need to adjust the… the wind thing."

The Sniper rolled his eyes and shook his head. *The wind thing.* "Windage." He paused and continued, "Okay, anything else?"

"All set."

"Good. Same drill as before. Wait until she stops. Center chest. Confirmation shot. Photo. Then we're out of here."

Billy settled into his seated position, the rifle extruding out through a narrow opening in the rear camper window. Looking through the scope, he appeared tentative, unsure.

The Sniper watched him for a moment and then took up position behind. Nine-fifteen came and went. The woman was running late. Her apartment door opened at nine-twenty as she trudged across the lot. "There she is. Wait until she's stopped at her car."

Cousin Billy didn't respond but rather continued peering through the scope.

Everything moved according to plan until the woman was halfway across the parking lot. She stopped and turned to her right. It appeared as though someone had called out to her. The Sniper took his binoculars and scanned the area. Sure enough, another woman, standing by her own car, was waving and saying something.

Their target resumed her walk to her car and then stopped suddenly, turning back toward the speaker.

That's when the unthinkable happened. Billy pulled the trigger.

Their target lurched back to her left and fell to the pavement. The Sniper heard the scream, apparently from the other woman. Two men appeared in the parking lot looking bewildered and began scanning the area. Another woman came running from the right side of the lot.

The Sniper took one last look at the victim. It wasn't a killing shot. She had apparently turned, presenting a side profile. "Goddammit, I said wait until she got the car. For fuck's sake, man. Let's get out of here."

"You want me to take another shot?"

The Sniper couldn't believe what he'd just heard the man say. It was the height of stupidity. "Let's go. You pack the rifle, I'll drive." The conversation he needed to have with this total imbecile would have to wait.

He eased away from the curb and drove slowly down the street, turning right onto a main cross street. The interstate access road was less than a mile away. He frantically watched the rearview mirror and scanned the road ahead and on both sides. *What a complete fuck-up.*

A police car with blue and red lights flashing shot by them coming from the opposite direction. The Sniper heard sirens from ahead. In the distance, an ambulance with red lights flashing moved in and out of traffic. He turned on his blinker and made a turn onto another side street, maneuvering to access the interstate farther to the north.

The scene faded into the background behind them. Billy remained in the camper, out of sight. *Just as well. If he were up here, I'd be tempted to stop and strangle the fucking life out that dumb shit.*

Once on the interstate, he picked up speed. Billy crawled through the access window that led from the camper into the truck. "Are we clear?"

The Sniper clenched his jaw and forced his gaze to remain on the road.

When Billy spoke again, it was with a maddening casualness. "I guess we'll have to try again on that one, huh?"

The Sniper began to re-orient himself to reality. Whatever could have been was past. He had to work out a plan to go from the here-and-now. "We're done with her."

"Why?"

"We'll talk about it later. For now, our concern is getting back to Idaho. First, we have to get out of the city. So do me a favor. Keep your fucking mouth shut."

Well, Aylin Freyberg, today was your lucky day, thanks to my dimwit cousin.

82

Greg listened without speaking as Eisen rattled off the information he'd uncovered about the now-defunct extremist website. The techno god spoke without any discernible emotion, as though everything was exactly as it should be. Greg Stottman, on the other hand, sat horrified. Then, with a final few points, his world began to spin and come unglued.

Eisen paused and checked his notepad again. "This hit list, assuming that I'm right about it, is buried deep within the new site. The page is aptly called *The Well of the Damned*. It contains the names of individuals who have been deemed to be a threat to society. Two names at the top of the list stand out. One is Aylin Freyberg. She's important because she's in this area. Unless I'm off the mark, and I'm sure I'm not, she'll be the next victim. The name below hers, though, is… well," he paused as though composing himself. "Janet Polasky."

* * *

The call came just after lunch. It was a call Janet had not expected to get. "Hi, Tam." Tam Wiggins at the Church Association had not been happy with Janet after the now infamous *Thursday Night Ambush*. Janet and her allies had successfully fended off an attempt by the more extreme faction to alter the Association's position on domestic violence services. In the process, Janet had humiliated the board president with regard to their firing of Aylin Frey-berg. Tam felt that everything had come back on her shoulders. This would not be a pleasant conversation.

Tam's words, though, caught Janet by surprise. "I don't know whether you heard or not, but Aylin Freyberg was shot this morning. She's in ICU over at UW Medical Center Northwest." Her voice sounded subdued with a tinge of guilt woven in.

Janet felt the panic set in. "Is she... I mean, what's her condition, do you know?"

"I don't know the details. I'm headed over there now."

Janet stood and grabbed her coat from the rack with one hand while holding the phone with her other. "I'll meet you there."

On the way out, she paused and spoke to Margaret, her secretary. "I need to go to the hospital. Aylin Freyberg from the Association was shot this morning. Call if you need me." And with that, she was out the door.

Once she hit Highway 520 across Lake Washington, she heard her cellphone chirp. In the heavy traffic, though, she chose not to answer. Odds were, it was bad news and she didn't need any more of that at the moment. A long half-hour later, she pulled into the parking lot and bolted for the emergency room door.

Once inside, she remembered that Tam had said that Aylin was in intensive care. Checking the signs, she made her way to ICU. She found Tam Wiggins seated in the visitor area, her face reflecting pain. Janet slid into a seat next to her. "How's she doing?"

"Stable. That's about all they would say."

Janet took Tam's hands. "She'll be fine. She's too ornery for anything else. You know that." She forced a shallow laugh.

Tam nodded and turned to stare out the window. "How does this kind of thing happen?"

"What actually happened? Do you know?"

The woman answered without turning to face Janet. "She was shot. What else is there to know?"

Janet replied, "There's a lot to know. How did she get shot? Who was it? Do they know why? Was it random? Was it someone she knew? Believe me, Tam, it matters."

"I don't know any of that. All I know is that the Association screwed her and now this."

It seemed a curious statement. "I'm not sure about that. Yes, we can agree about the Association's actions." Janet was careful not to pile on by acknowledging that Tam had played a major part in that. "I'm not convinced, though, that her being terminated had anything to do with her being shot. I don't see how that figures in. It could have been totally random."

Tam sighed and continued to stare out the large picture window.

Janet noticed several police officers in the waiting area along with one seated at the entrance to Aylin's room. Their presence gave some sense of safety. She stood. "I'm going to grab a coffee. Can I get you anything?"

"No thanks."

As she made her way down the corridor, Janet turned this latest event over in her mind. Had the world suddenly grown more violent or had she just lived a terribly sheltered life? Had this level of death always been there, simply hidden from view?

It felt strange though. Rather than frightening or intimidating her, she felt rage building within her. *I will stand against this.* As a warmth washed over her, she felt the presence of God soothing her soul and telling her in no uncertain terms that this was why she had been called.

As she approached the small coffee bistro, she remembered the call on the drive over. Checking, she saw a voice mail from Greg Stottman.

The voice came out frantic, filled with fear. "Janet, please, call me as soon as you get this. And for God's sake don't go out anywhere until you talk to me."

83

Janet huddled in a corner of the small hospital bistro, the cellphone to her ear. The din of noise gave her some comfort that no one would be listening in, although it also made the conversation more difficult.

"Slow down, Greg. I'm having a hard time hearing you. What's going on?"

Greg's voice sounded frantic. "Where are you? I've been trying to get you for the past hour."

"I'm at the hospital—"

He interrupted her. "Are you okay? What happened?"

"I was going to say, I'm at the hospital with a friend." She was about to add that Aylin, her friend, had been shot when Greg dropped a bomb.

"Would that friend happen to be Aylin Freyberg? Was she shot?"

The words stunned Janet. "Uh, yes. How did you know?"

"I'll fill you in later. Don't go anywhere, Janet. Stay at the hospital until I get there. I'll explain everything then. Just don't leave, promise me."

"I'll stay. Promise." She bit back the questions that tore at her. "We're at UW Northwest—ICU."

"We're on our way. We'll be there in a few."

After they disconnected, another question surfaced. Who was the "we"—*we'll* be there in a few? Who was Greg bringing with him? How did he know about Aylin? Maybe it was on the news. *Yeah, that's it. He heard it on the news.* To her knowledge, though, Janet had never mentioned Aylin to Greg. How did he make the connection? Janet realized that she was recycling all the questions she wanted to ask Greg on the phone—the ones he said he would answer when he… *they* arrived.

Twenty minutes later, Greg and Kaz arrived in the ICU waiting area and Greg rushed over and hugged her tightly. He frantically looked around the waiting area all the while wringing his hands. In what almost seemed an afterthought, he asked, "How is she?"

"Holding her own. She was lucky."

He grabbed her hand. "Janet, we're going to have to build in some protection for you and it can't wait until later. It has to start today."

As much as Aylin being shot frightened her, Greg's demeanor seemed worse. It was as though he was suggesting that the shooting had been aimed at Janet. "Why? I mean, yes, I agree that we need to look at security and safety, but what does this have to do with Aylin."

For the second time in less than an hour, Greg's words dumbfounded her. She sat in stunned silence as he rambled through a narrative that, while it seemed disjointed, held one very clear fact. Janet was on someone's hit list. She slumped down in her chair, a sense of helplessness overwhelming her. "You're sure about this?"

"You're going to have to change your routine. Avoid the places you normally go. Change things up."

Chapter 83

Janet pushed back. "Greg, I have a job to do. I can't hide in a closet for the rest of my life. I agree that we need to do something, but in the long term, the police will have to solve this case. That's the only real solution."

"I get that, yeah, but in the meantime, today, you can't go home. You can't go to work. We can get you into a hotel room and arrange for security there. That'll give us some time to work the problem." His words flooded out as though he were barking orders to some cowed subordinates.

"That's not going to work, and you know it. I have responsibilities and they don't go away simply because of the possibility of danger. I knew this going in and so did you."

"This is different. Whoever did this is a professional assassin. This isn't some bumbling, angry husband. This guy is a cold, precise killer. He's patient and relentless. Your name is next on the list."

Janet shot back, "If he's that good, how did he manage to leave Aylin alive. We're not even sure this is the same guy that killed the other domestic violence workers."

"Trust me, he's the one."

Kaz, who had remained silent up until this point, intervened. "Let's take a few steps back. Janet, Greg's right in that you can't just pretend as though nothing's going to happen. We do have to take some major precautions."

He paused and turned to Greg. "You need to put your strategic hat back on. We need to act, but we don't have to do it this instant. You need to think this through with a wider scope. Whoever shot this young woman won't likely be in a position to try again this quickly, especially if they're a pro. He'll wait until things settle down. Very likely he knows that he missed and will be watching to see how law enforcement reacts before he moves again. When he does move, in all likelihood, he'll be motivated more by self-preservation than any sense of mission."

The combination of the two men suddenly gave Janet a warm sense of safety. Greg Stottman was passionate about protecting her and seemed willing to do anything required. Dimitry Kazarian—Kaz—remained calm and focused. Between the two of them, she felt confident that they could solve this problem.

As though reading her mind, Greg seemed to slip into a more pensive mood for a moment before speaking. "Right, yes. Let's agree that, while we don't need to make crucial operating decisions right this instant, we need to get the ball rolling."

Janet nodded, noting that Kaz seemed content to let Greg do the talking.

"First, Janet, as much as I respect your right to make decisions for yourself, I'm going to push back on the notion that this is a police issue. I got this information from Eisen, and I'm pretty sure that he didn't pay any particular attention to the law, constitutionality, or anyone's privacy. He was able to do within a couple of days what the police have been unable to do over months. To get to where we are using police methods would likely have taken years."

Kaz responded simply, "Fair enough."

Greg continued, "Involving the police in our efforts might bring some slight advantage, such as the ability to easily access government databases. Their constraints would slow us down, possibly even stop us. By contrast, I think we could get the same type of information using Eisen with virtually no boundaries."

Janet offered meekly, "And possibly get us all thrown in jail."

Kaz burst out laughing. "Somehow, I don't think law

enforcement is competent enough to catch on to what that guy can do. I have to agree with Greg on this one."

Janet found herself surprisingly in agreement as well. "Okay. Where do we go from here? Eisen can get the information, but once we have it, what do we do with it?"

Greg nodded, "Good question. That would suggest that we need to widen our effort to include some other people—people who would be able to weigh in on our response."

Janet immediately thought about Dee. "While I generally agree about the police, I have a detective friend that I believe is crucial to the discussion."

Greg asked, "Is that the same one who was involved with the condo thing? I think her name was Martin? That didn't turn out so well."

Janet felt compelled to defend her friend. "Yes. That's right, but she didn't cause the problems. She did the best she could with what she had to work with."

"All that considered, it would still present some difficulties. There is no doubt in my mind that at some point along the line, we're going to drift into illegal territory—most certainly in the information gathering phase and probably in the action stage. That would put her in a tenuous position."

"I have a good relationship with her. I'll simply ask her the question—whether or not she could live with that possibility. If she's willing to go along with it, she could bring valuable insight."

Kaz weighed in again. "I've seen plenty of circumstances in which individual cops were willing to suspend their devotion to the rule of law in order to accomplish some goal. Sometimes it's noble; sometimes not. It's worth asking. Additionally, she might also have some ideas on who else to involve in this discussion."

Greg's face suddenly changed. It was as though something struck a nerve. "There may be someone else—the detective who's investigating my niece's shooting. I can't say exactly why I feel this way, but I just have the sense that she might have something to offer as well. If you trust me, I'll approach her and try to get a sense about the possibility."

Kaz nodded.

Janet said, "I'm fine with it, if you think it'll help."

Greg leaned back in the chair and exhaled. "Okay, here's where we are. The people we want involved, to the extent possible, are the three of us, Eisen, Detective Martin, and Detective Wharton. This is not an exhaustive list. It's just where we start."

Janet closed her eyes and nodded. "Let's get to it."

84

The Sniper had intentionally avoided the conversation for the past two days. His dipshit cousin had failed the mission. A forced reality check, though, reminded him that it was also his own fault. He had trusted Billy—a misplaced trust to be sure. Still, he owned some of it. The question that begged his attention was—where do I go from here?

"So, really? We ain't getting paid nothing for that? All that work and no pay?" Billy, despite what should have been a humiliating experience, remained fixated on entitlement.

The Sniper closed his eyes and willed away the rage. In that moment, he almost knew what it was like to be completely ruled by emotion—*almost*. "What is it that you think you should be paid for? We had a job. We didn't do it." He paused and watched Billy's face closely for any sign of recognition. Did the kid even have a clue?

"We get paid for results, not work. No results—no money. It's that simple. In this case, you messed up." The Sniper fought back the urge to unload on his cousin.

Instead, he tried to focus on the future. "It happens. Don't let it get you down. The important thing is what you do with that screw-up. You can ignore it and keep doing the same shit. That usually brings the same results. Or you can learn from it and not make the same mistakes again." He calmly placed his hands on the tabletop. "What's it gonna be?"

Billy shook his head. "Look, I'm sorry about how it went down. How was I supposed to know that bitch would turn around again? She stopped, just like you said. I shot when she stopped. If you wanna be pissed at somebody, you should look at the cunt that waved to her. If it hadn't been for her, I'd have nailed it."

The Sniper tamped down the building rage. "Do you see what you're doing wrong?"

Cousin Billy stared, eyes wide. "What?"

"You spend all your time and effort trying to shift blame. You took a bad shot. Leave it at that. You can do better next time, but don't pretend it was anyone else's fault. Nobody out there is obligated to help you kill someone."

"Fuck you. You just don't get it, do you? You've never had to deal with the shit I have. I get dumped on from all sides and you sit here like some high and mighty expert or something. The least you could do is take my side once in a while. We're family. We're supposed to stand together."

It had become a pointless discussion. "You need to take care of a few issues. We'll give the contract work a rest while things settle down. In the meantime, you need to get rid of that car out there. Sooner or later, some cop's going to run the plates and notice that they don't match the vehicle. When that happens, you're toast."

Billy looked at him with incredulity. "What, you want me stranded here with no way to get around?"

Chapter 84

The Sniper answered calmly. "For now, I'll help you get where you need to go. In the long run, we can get you another vehicle. For now, though, that one has to go."

"So, do we just drive out into the woods and leave it?"

"If the vehicle is found here, the cops will quickly learn that it's stolen. They'll put two and two together and figure you're in the area. This place will be crawling with 'em. No, Cuz, we have basically two options. We can try to take back across the state line into Washington or we can make sure it never gets found. Both have the pros and cons."

Billy shot back, "Yeah?"

The Sniper sighed. This was getting tedious. "Getting it back into Washington is risky since it involves a long drive. You could get stopped anywhere along the way. Once you get there, though, you could abandon it by the side of the road in a rural area. They're going find trace evidence tying it you, but there won't be any other real information that would help them find you."

"What about the other way?"

"There are several deep lakes north of here. We could take the car up during the night and run it off into one of them. If we do it right, it'll be in water so deep it'll never be found. The problem with that is that, if we screw it up and it ends up in shallow water, you don't get a do-over. You have to nail it the first time."

"You want me to choose, then?"

"Not a chance, Cuz. I'll make the decision. You'll help me with the work."

"Which is it going to be, then?" The look on Billy's face was full of bluster and confrontation. He was clearly not happy with the direction things had taken.

"Before we nail it down, let's consider the other thing you have to fix. You left that girlfriend of yours alive.

That's not going to work. You need to go back and finish the job. While you're at it, you should take out the uncle, too."

Cousin Billy shook his head. "That's stupid. That puts me right over there where they're trying to find me anyway. Why would I do that?"

"Because she's a fucking witness. You shot her and she can testify in court to that. Even if that doesn't come to pass, her uncle is rich. He's likely to hire some mercenary to track you down. Believe me, a good one can find you long before the cops ever will. Once they're both dead, there's nobody left to care."

Billy stared without speaking.

"Here's what we do. We're going to kill two birds with one stone. You'll drive your car and I'll follow you in my truck. Once we're in Washington, you can dump the ride and we'll continue on in mine."

"You make it sound easy."

"It won't be." The Sniper stood and started down the hallway toward his bedroom. "On the other hand, if you can pull this one off, then maybe you'll be ready for some more contract work."

85

G reg wasn't looking forward to the coming conversation. He and Detective Wharton had definitely not hit it off when they first met, and things hadn't improved much since then. Now he was there to engage her in an effort that would, at some point, almost certainly put her on the wrong side of the legal line. Still, she might have something to offer and, if things went right, it could help her with the Billy Robinson case.

"Thanks for agreeing to speak with me." Greg stood awkwardly at the threshold of her cubicle at the King County Sheriff's office.

Wharton nodded toward a chair. "What can I do for you, Mister Stottman."

Greg scooted the chair up next to her desk. "I've thought of a way that we might be able to help each other, if you're willing."

"Go on." She arched an eyebrow as though interested but doubting.

He took his time, trying to think through the words before he uttered them. "I seem to recall that you had floated the idea of Billy Robinson perhaps contacting some relative in Idaho." He paused, waiting for a reaction. None came. The detective sat still, a neutral look on her face that betrayed neither irritation nor enthusiasm.

Greg continued, "Some people that I work with developed information that might be of use to you."

Anger flashed in her eyes. "Am I to understand that, despite my warnings, you're still out there playing detective?" She leaned back, her arms crossed on her chest.

"No, at least nothing to do with your case." He hated groveling, but he wanted her help. "I'm working on something else entirely. It struck me that some of what we're learning might also apply to your case, that's all."

The angry look eased to more of a stern but not hostile appearance. "Okay, so what's the information?"

This was where it got tricky. Greg had no intention of just blurting out what he knew. He needed her help. He figured that the only way he'd get it would be to make sure she had something to gain. Giving her information at this point would eliminate any motivation for her to work with him.

"Not so fast, Detective. I'm willing to include you in the effort, but in return, I expect you to contribute to the effort."

She immediately shot back, "What effort?"

"It's complicated." He held his hands up to forestall what he was certain would be a very hard pushback. "I'm happy to fill you in completely, but before I go through the hassle of trying to explain, I need to know if you're willing to at least consider it."

She scrutinized him for a moment before quietly responding. "Mister Stottman, you can't be so clueless as to think I'd agree to help you with something without having any idea what I was agreeing to. I have an active case on

Billy Robinson. That's my priority. If you have information that can help, fine. If I have information that you want, you should ask. If I'm legally able to tell you, I will. Don't play games with me, though."

That was just about what Greg had expected. This was the moment. "Fair enough. Are you familiar with the series of murders involving domestic violence workers over the past year?"

She nodded without speaking.

"I'm working with some people who are putting together an innovative DV program and there's an indication that at least one of them is being targeted by this assassin. I'm not going to reveal exactly what I know or how I know it right now. The reason that I thought of you is that the best information we have puts the killer in Idaho. We also know that he's part of a larger effort aimed at the DV community."

She stared at her desktop for a moment, subtly shaking her head. "What has all this to do with my case?"

It was a good question. Greg wasn't certain they were connected at all. Admittedly, it was a long shot. "I can't say for certain. I know that you were looking for a connection in Idaho. What you told me about Billy Robinson's family sounded like something that could be associated with what we're looking at."

"Except that Billy Robinson's cousin was killed in Afghanistan. I'm sure that I told you that."

Greg responded with confidence. "No. You didn't say that. You said that he went missing while awaiting a courts martial. They assumed he was dead. As I understand it, his body was never recovered and, unless you omitted something from the account, they never got any additional information on him."

"Same difference. Even if he's not dead, he was in Afghanistan. That puts him a long way from Idaho."

He shrugged. "Maybe, and I agree it's tenuous at best. I admit there's no real evidence that connects the case to Robinson. It is, though, more than you have right now and I can promise you that the people we have working on this can run circles around anything the county or state can do, especially in the area of data mining."

Wharton took a deep breath. "This takes us back to the original question. What do you want from me and what are you offering me in return?"

"What I want, is simply to have you as a part of the team—on your own time, obviously. I'm not asking you to reveal police secrets. You have insight into criminal behavior that could explain things. You know of data sources that we might be able to request help from. Finally, and don't let this go to your head, you seem pretty smart. It's nice to have smart people with you."

The detective smirked. "You're a real smooth talker, huh? You won't say exactly what you want from me and you're not offering anything substantial in return. With all of that, I'm supposed to enthusiastically jump in… on my own time, no less."

Greg considered her for a moment before responding. "Yeah, that sounds about right."

Silence descended for a few minutes. Finally, she asked, "Who else is on this?"

He went with his strength first. "We have a detective out of Bellevue PD helping. I've got a couple of private investigators, one of whom is a tech expert. There's a Methodist minister who's running the new program and she'll be there."

"I'll be honest with you, Mister Stottman. You haven't been the most honest or forthcoming guy I've ever met.

Quite frankly, there's little reason that I should throw my lot in with you. In the interest of second chances, though, I'll meet with your group and see what's up. If it's convincing, we can go from there."

"Thanks. That sounds fair. I'll be in touch." Greg stood to leave, moving the chair back to its original location.

"Oh, by the way, how's your niece doing?"

Greg studied her and, in that moment, she seemed genuinely concerned.

86

Kaz settled onto the sofa holding his coffee cup with both hands. Bonnie Corel sat in a wingback chair across from him while Janet staked out the other end of the sofa. "I recall that we talked about communicating with your husband, possibly through Dylan Strauss. I guess it's time, huh?"

The look on Bonnie's face was one of confusion. "I thought that Mister Stottman would be here for this as well."

Janet responded, "That was not my understanding. We all agreed on the need for action, but neither of us was under the impression that Greg Stottman needed to be part of this." She bristled at the notion of having to justify herself.

Bonnie looked uneasily at Janet and then back to Kaz. She hesitated as though unsure of whether to proceed or not. Finally, wringing her hands together, she spoke. "Well, I see." Disappointment bathed her words. "That being the case, yes, I'm ready to do this if you have the contact information."

Kaz exhaled and set his cup on the coffee table. "I have it. So, here's how this is going to work. For a one-time communication, it's not that hard. First, use a clean burner phone. We'll get rid of it when we're done. Second, you travel to a distant location in the city—some place that's relatively populated but not heavy with surveillance cameras. Finally, you make the call, get to the point, and terminate within a few minutes. I'll destroy the phone and we'll get you back here."

"How long will I have to talk to him, you know, before he can track me?"

"That shouldn't be a worry. If you obscure the number you're calling from, he won't be able to track you in real time. He can find your location after the fact, but it will take hours, maybe days. That's not a concern since the location from which you call won't be connected with you or Reverend Polasky in any way. The real question is whether he'll deliver your message and how your husband will react."

"Okay, anything else I need to do?"

"You need to convey to him that, should any misfor-tune come to you, arrangements have been made to widely distribute evidence that would ruin your husband. Also, that can't be an idle threat. We do need to come up with something. A detailed personal statement, perhaps accom-panied by documents or photos that you can come up with. You can think about it later, but for now you have to deliver that message."

* * *

Kaz drove. Janet sat in front and Bonnie in back. They rode in silence, each lost in their own thoughts. The dreary early November weather seemed to have darkened everyone's mood. After an hour of navigating heavy, late morning traffic, they arrived at their destination. They pulled into a public recreation area about twenty miles south of SeaTac airport.

There were no visible surveillance cameras and foot traffic was light, probably due to the poor weather. Turning off the ignition, Kaz twisted around to speak to Bonnie. "Take that path over there, the one leading into that stand of trees. Walk in maybe fifteen or twenty feet—far enough that you're not readily visible from the road but where you can still see out into the parking lot through the trees."

"Got it."

"Make the call. No chitchat. Say what you need to say then disconnect. Bring the phone back here. I'll smash it and dispose of it later. We'll drive around for a short while, just make sure we haven't by some chance picked up a tail. After that, I'll deliver you back to the condo."

Bonnie nodded and opened the door. "Okay."

Before she closed the door, Kaz added, "Just remember, don't engage him in conversation. Say what you intend to say and disconnect. He'll try to keep you on the phone. Don't do it."

"Okay, okay, I've got it. I'm not an idiot." With that, she was gone.

* * *

Bonnie made her way along the path as instructed. Once into the trees, she turned to assess her location. She could easily make out the car in the parking lot but felt confident that, unless someone was specifically looking for her, she was nearly invisible. She wore a forest green jacket and heather brown slacks—not camo but at least it would more or less blend. She felt nauseous. She was about to call a man who wouldn't lose a moments sleep over killing her. *What am I thinking? This is madness.*

Removing the phone from her purse, she took a deep breath, and punched in the number on the piece of paper Kazarian had given her.

Strauss answered on the second ring. "Yes?"

Bonnie struggled to keep her tone steady. "Hello Dylan. This is Bonnie Corel. I have something I'd like you to convey to my husband. I'm away from the area now, safe from him and you. I won't be returning, but I'm willing to agree to a truce. If he terminates the chase, I'm willing to let things go. He'll win re-election and can continue his life. I would like a divorce—we can keep it no-fault, if that works for him. If he's not amenable to this, then we can take this fight public—his choice."

"Miz Corel, let me see if I understand—"

Bonnie cut him off. "Also, should anything happen to me, the media and police will receive packages detailing events of late. I've already put these arrangements in place. Deliver the message. I'll contact you again in a few days for the answer." She hit the disconnect button. Relief swept over her. She stuffed the phone in her purse and left the stand of trees, focused on keeping her pace quick but even.

Back at the car, she slid into the back seat and, with shaking hands, gave the phone to Kaz. "Here you go."

"Any problems?"

"None. You were right, he did try to engage me and keep me on the line."

Kaz got out of the car, and using a hammer that he'd brought along, smashed the phone, and returned to the driver's seat. "I'll get rid of it on the way back."

Bonnie said, "I'm going to need another fresh burner. I'm going to call him back in a few days for an answer."

87

J anet fought back the sense of intimidation. Navigating the topic at hand with this eclectic group would not be easy. Greg Stottman, Kaz, Dee Martin, and Charlotte Wharton all sat waiting in the church conference room. Once they were ready to go, Janet would make a phone call and put Eisen on speaker. The tech wizard was not willing to meet in person with a group of strangers.

"Thanks for coming tonight. I appreciate it. We can do any necessary introductions in a few minutes, but first I'd like to make sure we're all on the same page. This relates to a series of shootings over the past year—assassinations and attempts on women associated with domestic violence services. We've come into information that might give us some insight into who and why. I want to say upfront that I have a vested interest. My name is the next one on the hit list. A friend of mine has just come out of ICU today, having been shot a few days ago."

She paused, waiting for comments or complaints. Hearing none, she plowed on. "We asked you here because each one of you has some interest in this and potentially something to offer. For Dee and Charlotte," Janet nodded at the two, "I want to be clear that we didn't invite you here as representatives of your respective organizations. You're here as interested individuals. To the extent that what we discuss can help you in your jobs, so be it. We're not, at the moment, in collaboration with any law enforcement agencies."

Wharton shot back, "Why not? There've been murders. You have relevant information. Why is this like some private party rather than trying to help law enforcement solve the crimes?"

Janet treaded carefully, "Good question. Although I know this is going to sound trite, the situation is complicated. I ask that you hold your reservations until you hear what we've learned. I will assure you that we are not attempting to mount some vigilante effort to solve it on our own. Whatever we learn, in the end, will end up with law enforcement to do with as they will. My goal—I hope *our goal*—is to keep people safe until we have the information that will allow the case to go forward in the legal system."

Detective Wharton stared for a moment and then nodded. "Okay, for now. Go on."

Janet continued, "I became involved when Dee Martin brought some information to me about a now defunct website that advocated violence against women and DV workers. By the time law enforcement learned about it, the site had been taken down. Since it was hosted on an offshore server and there was nothing to directly tie this site to the murders, the investigation went nowhere within the legal system, at least so far."

Wharton again interjected, "Which agencies are working the case?"

Dee inserted herself into the conversation. "This is where it gets complicated. It obviously started out as a single murder, then two, then three, and so on. That means that a number of different jurisdictions are involved. The state has taken the lead and I believe they are consulting with the FBI. Since Bellevue PD isn't a part of it, I've only been able to get bits and pieces of information."

With a irritated look on her face, Wharton asked, "Why not turn over what you have to the state, then? Sounds pretty simple. They have lots of resources and can take it from here."

Janet retorted, "As I said, it's more complicated than that. I agreed to address this concern at the end, but for now, please let us get through what we have. We'll spend substantial time and effort on deciding about our next moves."

Silence.

Janet continued, "With what Dee told me, I took this to Greg Stottman. I should say at this point that we've just started up a new DV project with some unique features. Greg is the sole funder of this project, which is why I consulted him and why he's here. Anyway, he and some of his people were able to gain considerably more information about this website. Rather than me trying to explain all this, I have a gentleman on the phone who can walk us through it. Eisen, are you there?"

After a brief pause, a voice came over the speaker. "Here's what I found. The old website, righteousfire dot com, was hosted on a server in eastern Europe—Budapest, to be more precise. The administrator of record was someone who went by the username of Refiner's Fire. I was able to run some traces on that name and found a lot of IP activity in the central and southern Idaho area. As the minister said, the old site has been taken down, although the servers weren't scrubbed so I was able to get content from them."

Wharton jumped in again. "Can I ask how you managed to do all that?"

Eisen laughed. "You can ask anything you want, but I'm not going to be revealing my methods or sources. Let me continue. The site shut down just about the time that the dark web started to get more mainstream traction. I ran some searches and found the site "Strength is Truth." It's more of a networking platform than a typical website. The name is different from the original site, but the content is similar, including some that's identical, to the original website. Plus, one of the main posters in that platform is none other than Refiner's Fire. He neglected to change his username."

Greg asked, "Is he the administrator of the new platform?"

"Doesn't look like it. He's active in the forums but keeps it very general—no bragging or confessions. I'll get to administration and funding in a minute, but let's continue on with content for now. The site does mimic the antagonism toward women's services in particular and feminism in general that the old site had. Additionally, there's lots of railing against gays, immigrants, Jews, Muslims, and a lot of other minority groups. They take political stands off and on, but their main bread and butter seems to be anti-feminism."

Dee asked. "What leads you to believe that it's tied to the killings?"

Eisen's tempo picked up. "This is where it gets interesting. There is a sub-level to the platform. It's called the 'Well of the Damned.' In it we find a list of people and brief descriptions. There is an icon associated with some of the names—a skull, to be exact. When I cross-checked, those names that have the skull have been killed."

He grew quiet for a moment and then continued.

"Along with that, for each person killed, there is an uploaded jpeg that shows the body. These were clearly posted by the killer as a means of verification. As the minister said, she is the next person on the list after the lady who was shot the other day."

Greg nodded. "Maybe now is a good time to talk about administration and resources."

Eisen added, "Yeah, right. So, the thing about an operation like this—it takes money and expertise to maintain. Given what they're doing, it also requires substantial security effort. The question is, where does this money come from? Typically, these operations have three potential funding sources. The first is state sponsorship. You see this a lot in Eastern Europe and Asia. I doubt seriously that this is the case here. The second way is through a wealthy donor who's doing it for ideological reasons. That's possible here. Someone who has substantial resources and doesn't mind putting up few million here and there could certainly drive the site. The final method is the use of diverse business enterprises. For example, this site and its missions could be financed through the arms trade, drug trafficking, or prostitution, human trafficking things like that."

Wharton asked, "Any idea which one they're using or any details about it?"

"Nope. There's no financial connection on the site, at least none that I've been able to penetrate at this point. As for which one they're using, this is conjecture, but I'd bet it's a combination of a large donor and business enterprise. I don't have any specifics yet."

Wharton said, "I know we agreed to wait until the end to talk about involving law enforcement, but if we have the hit list, wouldn't it be prudent to alert the authorities so that these individuals can be protected?"

Kaz stood and cleared his throat. "For those that don't know me, my name is Dimitry Kazarian. I work for Mister Stottman in a security capacity. I'd like to address this, if I may."

Everyone around the table nodded.

"All things being equal, the detective raises a good point. We could bring this hit list to the attention of the authorities and, if nothing else, throw a wrench into the works. At the end of this, we may decide to do just that. There are, however, a couple of other considerations. First, there's only one name on the list after Reverend Polasky's. We might be able to help directly and more effectively than the police could."

He held up his hands toward Wharton as though fending off her objections. "I don't mean that to sound critical of the police. You have to admit, though, law enforcement is primarily about investigating crimes and prosecuting cases. They generally have a poor track record when it comes to protecting people. In fairness, they don't have the resources to protect everyone in their jurisdictions who happens to be at risk."

Wharton seemed to be visibly struggling to hold back the anger.

Kaz continued, "Second issue. What I'm going to say now is likely going to piss you off, Detective Wharton. Sorry about that. Nothing personal. I'm sure that if you do the research, you'd find that law enforcement agencies are not monolithic homogenous organizations. They're composed of diverse individuals who happen to share a vocation. Many share similar values. As with any large group, though, there is enough variance in people that you can expect to get what some euphemistically call 'bad apples.' In the case of domestic violence incidents, that could mean something as simple as a bias in favor of abusers or, at the most extreme, people who themselves are perpetrators of violence against women."

The room was momentarily cloaked in silence before Kaz continued. "We also know that, among our law enforcement resources, there are people who are associated with violent alt-right movements across the country— everything ranging from white supremacy to anti-feminist and everything in between. If we go to the authorities with what we have now, there's the distinct possibility that someone associated with the organization would be tipped off to what we have."

Eisen jumped back in. "You have to remember that these people are engaged in some high stakes activities. They survive by operating in the dark. If they have any level of competence at all, there are layers of security. They'll have flags and traps set up to catch the nosy visitor. They maintain sophisticated levels of verification and credentialing. You don't get there by accident."

Wharton challenged him. "If they're that good, how did you manage to get in?"

Eisen answered, his response remarkably restrained. "As I mentioned earlier, I'm not inclined to reveal my methods. My fees reflect my level of competence. Let's leave it at that. Back to the matter at hand, if these people get the least bit suspicious, they'll shut down immediately. Again, given what they're into, they probably have contingency plans that would allow for an immediate locking and shutdown and simultaneous restart. Without some inside information, it would be nearly impossible to find them again."

Wharton leaned back in her chair, her arms folded on her chest. "Assuming you're right, what is it that you intend to do."

"The Holy Grail of our effort is to identify one individual and find out where they're located. With that, it doesn't matter how many times they switch the site. That's what we'll work on, given that we've already started down that road with our first subject, Refiner's Fire. He's our target. As soon as Mister Stottman gives me the green light, I'll get on it."

After a moment's silence, Greg said, "You got it."

The meeting broke up around ten o'clock. As they made their way to the door, Greg took Janet by the arm. "I need talk to you."

88

They eased toward a couple of chairs in the corner of the conference room and waited for everyone to clear out. Janet was weary but the worried look on Greg's face told her that she needed to hear him out.

Once the noise had faded, Greg said, "We need to talk about some security for you. We may be on to something with that website, but right now we have no idea who the shooter is or how soon they may try to strike again."

Janet had tried to ignore the personal danger for the past few days, losing herself in the details of the project and her duties at church. "I know." She sighed and shook her head. "I know."

Greg pushed gently, "I don't mean to pile on here, but you need to switch gears. We've got this website thing going and there's no need for you to put any more thought into that for now."

"Okay, well, do you have any particular ideas, because I don't?"

He motioned toward the chairs. "Let's sit." Once they settled in, he leaned forward and continued, "I'd say the first order of business is to get you relocated to new residence. If I understand things correctly, the assassin has been striking as victims leave for work in the morning. Getting you away from here would at least give us some breathing room."

Janet had a foreboding that the conversation was about to slip into an area that she didn't want to visit. "Greg, I know you're worried and so am I, but I can't just drop everything and move. My being at the parsonage isn't only about a place to sleep. It's where the members of the congregation know they can reach me after hours. Even if I did relocate to another place, it wouldn't take long before he found me. After all, he likely knows where I work."

Even as she spoke, Janet could see the worry in his eyes. His mouth drew into a tight line, and he clenched his jaw and seemed to hold his breath as though preparing for battle.

Finally, he exhaled and lowered his gaze. "I'll have Kaz work with you. If anybody can figure this out, it's him."

"I appreciate that, Greg, but I'm sure you have other things you need him to be doing."

Greg shot back, a note of fear in his voice. "There is nothing more important than your safety at the moment."

There it was. Janet wasn't ready for this conversation. "I tell you what, I'll mull it over tonight and give you a call tomorrow." Her problem was that she herself had no answers. The danger was real. A man had come for her and would have killed her had Greg not had the foresight to alert Kaz. No matter how she turned the issue over in her mind, it came up the same. There was simply no foolproof safety to be had.

Greg switched gears. "Oh, by the way, I meant to ask the other day. This other woman who was shot, Aylin, she's a friend of yours?"

"Sort of. More of a colleague, I'd say. Why?"

He said, "It seems strange to me that you're both on that list, one after the other, and that you know each other. Maybe it's coincidence, but I'd bet that if we look at where the two of you intersect, we'd find a trail back into that website."

She stared for a moment, not really surprised but not wanting to accept the assumption. "Until recently, Aylin worked at the King County Church Association. My church is a member and I've been active there over the years. That's our only connection. You think there's someone there who could be connected with the shootings?"

He shrugged. "Otherwise, it just seems strange that both of you show up on the list together. What are the odds?" After a pause, he continued, "Can you think of anyone there that might fit the bill?"

Sadness suddenly washed over her. It felt like betrayal. "Six months ago I would have said no. Now, though, I'm not so sure. Things have been… different."

"Maybe we need to get together with Eisen. If you can give him a few names, he may be able to work some magic. This could get us to some answers much quicker than might otherwise be the case."

She sighed. "We can talk more tomorrow."

He nodded but didn't move. "Janet, one other thing."

A sense of dread came over her. This was what she had been emotionally avoiding.

"About the other night—I wanted to—"

"Let's not go there, Greg. It happened. I'm not sure what else to make of it." She struggled for the right words.

"I want you to know it was something important to me. I'm not inclined to go around kissing women. I certainly didn't plan that, but I have to admit that I've thought about it. It was not some one-off random thing. I'm not asking you for any kind of commitment. I need for you to understand that I care about you." He reached over and took her hand, holding it for a moment before releasing. "That's all."

Janet felt as though she were perched precariously on the edge… but the edge of what? The idea of a relationship terrified her. A spark of warmth inside, though, reminded her of how wonderful it was to be in love. "I have to go. We'll talk tomorrow."

Before turning to leave, she scoured through her purse and pulled out a small notepad and pencil. She took a deep breath and scribbled two names on the sheet of paper —Carl Broward and Millard Conyers. She handed the page to Greg and left.

89

Janet had been certain that she would fall into bed and be out like a light. Instead, she lay awake in bed staring at the ceiling. The wind had picked up and she could hear the rain slapping against her bedroom window. Her myriad of problems competed with each other for attention.

The protection and security issue seemed unsolvable. She couldn't in good conscience move out of the parsonage. Leaving for a day or so might be okay, but to relocate for any extended period would seem too much like abandoning her church and congregation. Still, Greg was right. Remaining in the house would make the assassin's job much easier.

She muttered out loud, "Maybe Greg and Kaz will have some ideas." She could think of no other options. On top of that, even if they protected her in this one instance, the path she had set upon would bring the problem back again and again.

The issue of the website and the terrorist group, or whatever they were, seemed less urgent. There was nothing she could do directly, other than protect herself. She'd help bring people together to work on it, but that seemed the limit of what she could contribute. In the end, the police needed to catch the guy or guys doing the killing.

Greg Stottman. The kiss. That night. Although the question seemed straightforward, it was anything but. *What does he want from me?* She laughed out loud. "Sex, for starters." He wanted her to believe it was more than that, though. He said he cared about her. *Not likely.* Why would someone with his money and power be drawn to her? She didn't fit into his universe, and he didn't fit into hers, except that he had become a fixture in her world.

Do I care about him? Certainly. He was a nice guy, and he funded her project to the tune of a billion dollars. *No, that's not what this is about.* The kiss—what did that feel like? *Not going there.* She argued with herself. *Why not?*

At some level, deep inside, Janet knew that she could no longer make this about Mark. Her husband had passed ten years ago. Using his memory as a means of fending off a potential lover seemed unfair to him and his memory. If she wanted a relationship with Greg, she needed to own it. If she didn't, then she needed to shoulder the responsibility of telling him *no* point blank.

With that realization, she felt better, although she still didn't know what the answer would be. *I'll come up with that later. What's next on the problem list?*

Abby! "Oh my God." She had completely forgotten about the young girl and her school situation. Janet recalled Maddie's advice—using project resources to pay for a private school for the young girl. In order for that to happen, she needed to speak with Greg.

Why? He had, after all, told her that he didn't want to micromanage. This was simply a decision about how to allocate funds, of which she had plenty at this point.

No. This is different. Her conscience told her emphatically that, while he might likely agree, this problem was special enough that he at least needed to know about it.

Okay, then, first thing in the morning.

* * *

"Hi, Greg. I hope I didn't catch you at a bad time." Janet sat in her office with the door closed.

"Not at all." He paused, as though uncomfortable. "Look, I'm sorry about last night. I was pushing and it was wrong."

"It's fine, and after some thought, I agree that we should talk about it. I'm calling about something else, though." She gave him the story, not as clearly and concisely as she'd intended, but she conveyed the idea.

"Okay, so what's the problem?"

"It's an unusual allocation of funds. I wanted to make sure that you were aware of it before I committed."

Greg responded, "I've already told you—I'm not getting into the weeds on this, at least not with regard to how you spend the money."

After the conversation ended, Janet grabbed her coat and bolted through the door and past Margaret. "I'm going to see Roberta Klein. I'll be back mid-afternoon."

On the drive over, she struggled with how to approach the issue with the woman. Janet had worried about dealing with the school administration, letting Greg know about the use of funds, and having to locate another school. She hadn't given any thought to how the grandmother would react to everything. Roberta had alternatively pushed back on offers of help, claiming she didn't need charity and passively accepting anything that came along.

Janet was struck by the darkness inside the house. The

curtains were drawn and there were no lights turned on. Roberta met her at the door and unenthusiastically invited her in. She gestured toward a chair while she sat on the couch. "Abby's asleep."

"That's fine. I came to talk to you anyway. You know how it went with the school—I think we talked about it a few days ago. Miz Klein, I'm afraid that keeping Abby in that school isn't going to work. I was thinking about a private school. If nothing else, that would give us more leverage in demanding that they address Abby's problems."

Roberta sat stiffly on the couch, her face empty. "I can't afford a private school."

Janet continued, "That's what I wanted to talk to you about. I have some funding that we could use. It will be enough to get her into whatever school we choose as well as covering any other costs associated with it."

"Why would you do that?" Roberta cocked her head slightly, her eyes intense. She appeared genuinely curious.

"It's very simple. I believe that's what would be best for Abby. I can work on finding a school and providing funds, the decision is really yours."

The woman leaned back in her chair, her eyes seeming to lose focus. "What do you want me to decide?"

It was at that moment that Janet knew. Roberta Klein wasn't up to making decisions of any importance. The woman needed help as badly as her granddaughter.

I'll have to deal with that later. Part of that sentiment stemmed from the fact that Janet wasn't sure how to even approach helping her. "I'll do some research on private schools in the area. I'll be in touch with you early next week." As she left the house, Janet tried to envision how she was going to navigate all the problems that were biting at her ankles.

90

Senator Corel turned things over in his mind. The election was days away. He needed to keep a clear mind. This was not the time to engage in knee-jerk reactions. If he could just lay low and keep things running, he was a shoo-in. Still, Bonnie had been gone nearly three weeks.

Three weeks and he'd heard nothing from her or even about her. If she intended to sabotage his campaign, she was certainly waiting until the last minute. *No, that's not likely.* He tried to put all the pieces in logical order. If she'd wanted revenge, she'd have gone to the police or the press right away. There had to be something else.

On one hand, his life was considerably less complicated without her around. On the other hand, having her there provided some useful benefits, not the least of which was access to her inheritance money. The funds had been kept in her name, but she drew on them frequently to support their joint needs.

His mind wandered to their marriage. He didn't hate her, and he certainly didn't enjoy hurting her. It was as though she took great pleasure in provoking him. *Why can't she just do what she's told to do and leave it at that? Why does she always have to create a scene… and always at the worst possible time?*

In the long run, though, it was worth it. He would accomplish great things. There were so many wrongs that screamed to be righted. He was the perfect instrument for that. Also, if history was to be believed, all great men had to make hard decisions. They all were forced to do things that, under normal circumstances, they would not want to do. Sometimes people such as Bonnie have to suffer for the greater good. There could be no progress in the world without sacrifice.

His cellphone ring brought him out of his reverie— Dylan Strauss. "Yeah, what do you have for me?"

"I spoke with your wife this morning."

Finally, some good news. "So, you have her. When will you have her back at the house?"

"I said that I spoke with her, not that I have her. She contacted me using a burner phone, which she evidently destroyed as soon as she hung up. She asked me to deliver a message to you."

"What the fuck? I don't pay you to be a messenger boy. Your instructions were to bring her back. Now, when can I expect that to happen?" Corel could feel the pressure building up inside him. His heart pounded. He could almost feel the color rising in his face.

"Take a step back, Senator. We've had this discussion before. If you want to hear what I have to say, fine, listen. If not, I'll be going."

Corel gritted his teeth before spitting out the word, "What?"

"She says that she has no desire to hurt you or your campaign. She wants to be left alone. She'd like a divorce

—simple settlement, all kept quiet. You go on with your life, she gets hers. She's going to call back within a few days for your response."

Despite his fuming, his reason began to kick in. He had been right. She was apparently not out to cause trouble. Still, this was not okay. She didn't get to decide whether it was over or not. He would make that decision if and when the time came.

Strauss continued, "One other thing. She made clear that she'd made some kind of arrangements to have documents, statements, and the like delivered to police and news outlets should anything happen to her."

Focus on the problem. The election... days away. Everything aligned. The voting itself was little more than a formality. It would be a coronation. His victory speech, though, would be far more impressive with a wife behind him on the stage.

Then there was the issue of all the people who had wronged him—Dylan Strauss, Reba Stillings, and even that preacher lady who had apparently helped Bonnie desert him. *I'll tend to them after the election.*

He shifted his attention back to the phone conversation. "Where was she calling from?"

"South of the city. That's as close as we can get for now. I'll pinpoint the location later, but honestly, it doesn't matter. The fact that she used a throwaway burner and kept it very short, tells me that she had help. While we're on that subject, I learned the identity of the guy who killed Unger. He's the hired gun I told you about—Kazarian. He's expensive and competent. My guess is that he's the one advising your wife. If that's the case, there's not going to be a lot to go on."

Kazarian. It made sense. Unger had said that the man was there with Polasky at the church along with some other guy. Strauss had later told him that Kazarian had been seen around town with.... *Stottman?* That's how she was doing it. Greg Stottman, Mr. Billionaire was financing the operation while this Kazarian character was on running the security. The Polasky bitch was the brains.

Strauss' voice interrupted his thoughts. "What do you want me to tell your wife?"

"You tell her that if she wants to have a discussion, she knows my number. I'm not going to engage in this little game she's playing. In the meantime, you figure out how to get this under control."

After they disconnected, Corel swiveled around to stare out into the autumn rain that steadily drenched downtown Seattle. He reached a decision. He was done with playing around. Strauss would be the first. The Stillings bitch would follow him to hell. The preacher would be easy enough. After that, he'd reassess.

91

Janet girded herself for the difficult conversation that she knew lay ahead of her. During the short walk from her car to Roberta Klein's front door, she tried to put the words together. She knew, though, that it wasn't really a matter of the words or even the school arrangements that she'd made for Abby. The challenge would be that Roberta Klein was so mired in depression that any reaction at all seemed unlikely. Still, there was no other option. Abby had to go to school and her grandmother was unable to facilitate that.

The idea briefly swept through Janet's mind that this was a more appropriate task for state Children's Services. After all, Roberta Klein was hardly providing the support that Abby needed. *No. Abby's already lost her mother and father. Losing her grandmother as well would be too much.* Janet would just have to work with what she had.

When the door opened, Janet found herself looking into sunken, haunted eyes set deep in a gaunt, blank face. She forced, "Good morning, Miz Klein." She almost asked whether or not it was a good time to talk. She had, though, already phoned Roberta and set up the meeting. Good time or not, this conversation needed to take place.

The old woman stared blankly. She stood in the doorway looking so frail that the slightest breeze might blow her away. Roberta Klein was in desperate need of help.

Janet gently prodded, "May I come in?"

Roberta stepped aside without speaking.

Once inside, Janet decided to get straight to the point. "I made the arrangements for Abby's school. I was able to get her enrolled at Northlake Academy. It's just east of Bellevue, about ten miles from here." She leaned forward, clasping her hands together.

"It's an excellent school. They specialize in what they call STEM—science, technology, engineering, and math. Since it's private, they have considerable leverage over student behavior. I went through the situation with them, and they assured me that they can manage things."

Roberta sat with her hands folded in her lap. She nodded, although her eyes didn't reflect any meaningful understanding.

Janet continued, "The school day starts at eight-thirty and goes until four. We can work on arranging transportation to and from school."

"Okay."

It was clear. There was no *we*. Either Janet would arrange it or there would be no transportation. "I'll work on that later today." She glanced down the darkened hallway. "Is Abby here?" *Of course she's here. Where else would she be?*

"I think she's still in bed."

Janet pushed. "I need to speak with her, please."

With what appeared to be her last shred of energy, Roberta stood. "I'll get her."

A few minutes later, Abby straggled down the hallway, dressed in flannel pajamas, with a look of confusion on her face.

Janet moved to meet her, embracing and squeezing her tight. "I'm so happy to see you again, Abby. I was hoping to talk to you this morning about school."

Abby mumbled, "I don't go to school." Her voice sounded devoid of all hope.

"I know, I know." Janet took her by the hand and guided her to the sofa. "I've got some good news for you."

Abby allowed herself to be led. She slouched onto the couch and stared blankly at Janet.

Janet pulled a chair up directly in front of the girl and took both hands in hers. "Abby, I was able to get you enrolled in a very special school. They have a lot of classes in math and science." She poured every ounce of enthusiasm she could find into the description.

The young girl's eyes brightened for a moment and returned to the blankness. "Okay."

"This afternoon, I'm going to be arranging for someone to take you to school in the mornings and bring you home in the afternoon."

Abby cocked her head, her eyes widening. "What about Dani? Could she take me?"

The question stunned Janet. Why would Abby even think to ask this? "I don't know. I hadn't thought about that. I mean, I'm not sure what she's doing right now." Janet was at a loss. Dani Stottman had her own problems, not to mention the security issues involved. What would Greg say about an idea like this?

The young girl seemed to consider the answer and then shrugged without speaking.

"This school doesn't require uniforms, so tomorrow, you and I will go shopping for some school clothes. Maybe while we're out, we can have lunch together. Would you like that?"

"I guess. Maybe. Could Dani go with us?"

What was this all about? Why was Abby so fixated on Dani Stottman?

"I don't know, Abby. I'll ask." Deep inside, though, Janet wondered about the wisdom of bringing this up to Greg and Dani.

After leaving the Klein household, Janet swung by the Dancing Russian Bakery, picked up some tea biscuits, and made a beeline for Maddie Kavanaugh's small home.

* * *

"Funny. I was just thinking how nice it would be to have some of these biscuits with my tea this morning." Maddie burst out laughing. "Oh, and of course it's nice to see you too." She took the white paper bag from Janet and shuffled into the kitchen, speaking over her shoulder. "You get yourself settled. I'll put the kettle on."

Five minutes later, the two women sat—Janet on the sofa and Maddie in her well-worn wing-back chair. "Now, Dearie, what brings you here this morning, and don't tell me this is just a casual visit? Something's up. I can see it in your eyes." Maddie's voice rang clear. She smiled and took a sip of tea before nibbling on a tea biscuit.

Janet laughed. "I should've known you'd see through me." She grew more serious.

"I told you about Abby and her problems at school. Well, I got her enrolled in a private school. Hopefully that will resolve some of her issues. I still have some things to take care of, you know, like transportation. There is, though, something really curious I wanted to ask you about."

Maddie took a sip of tea. "Ask away."

"Abby seemed fixated on Dani Stottman. I may have mentioned her. She's Greg Stottman's niece. She had some problems with a violent boyfriend and she's staying at the same house as Bonnie Corel at the moment. Anyway, Abby and Dani met when I went over to meet with Bonnie and my employee who's managing the case. I'm not sure what they talked about, but Abby asked if Dani could take her back and forth to school and also go school shopping with us."

Maddie rubbed her chin as she listened. "Maybe you're making too much of it. Dani is a young woman. I think you said she's either eighteen or nineteen. It could be nothing more complicated than Abby seeing her in sort of an older sister role. The young girl has no siblings."

"The other issue is that Dani's boyfriend, the one who beat and shot her, is still out there. The police haven't caught him yet. What if he manages to locate her? That could put Abby in danger too."

"Yes, it could." Maddie's eyes seemed to lose focus for a moment. When she spoke, her voice came out soft and cloaked in kindness. "If you had to guess, what would you say is the biggest threat to Dani?"

Janet almost blurted out the probable violence if Billy Robinson found the young woman. Something didn't seem right, though. "Aside from the obvious danger, I think that loneliness and a sense of betrayal combined with a feeling of helplessness. The man she thought she was going to build a life with turned out to be her worst enemy. Her world turned upside down. She hasn't found her way back into the light yet."

Maddie's eyes sparkled as she clapped her hands together once. "Excellent, Dearie! Yes. You're right that there is some danger from the young man. What's eating at her, though, is not that imminent threat. You hit it right on the head. Knowing that, what effect would being with young Abby have?"

"I guess it might help, but it's a lot of responsibility to put on Dani—taking Abby back and forth to school every day."

"What else does she have to do? If I remember correctly, she doesn't have a job and she's not currently in school. It might give her days some structure. From what you tell me, it would bring some joy to Abby as well."

Janet sighed. "I guess I could mention it to Greg, although I'm not sure how he's going to react to the idea."

"All the more reason to talk to him." Maddie paused for a moment and then grinned. "I suspect that you and he have a lot of other things to talk about as well." She winked.

Janet laughed. "You're bad, Maddie."

"I try."

92

Dani wasn't prepared. The request had seemed so simple and straightforward. Reverend Polasky had asked her to go clothes shopping with her and Abby Miller and have lunch afterwards. It was just a few hours out of what would have been an otherwise boring and uneventful day.

She stood in front of a house, the light rain adding darkness to the late autumn morning. No light shone from within the home. It was as though all life had deserted the dwelling, leaving it to suffer the coming winter alone.

Dani's heart wrenched. She began to understand an inkling of what this young girl must be going through. "Are you sure she's expecting us? It doesn't look like anyone's home."

Janet pulled her raincoat hood over her head. "They're home." She mounted the front steps and rang the doorbell.

The woman who answered the door seemed little more than a wraith, her frail body lost in her tattered-looking housecoat. Her sunken eyes appeared flooded with pain. She looked from Janet to Dani as though unsure what the two were doing there. After a moment, she stepped back and to the side. "You should come in out of the rain."

Everything happened at once. Once inside, Dani saw young Abby sitting silently on the couch. They locked gazes. Abby stood with what seemed a great deal of uncertainty. Dani rushed to her, sitting down beside her and embracing the girl. "Oh Abby, I am so glad to see you again."

Abby hesitated for a moment and then threw her arms around Dani's neck and squeezed. A single tiny sob escaped the young girl as the two locked in the embrace.

Dani heard Janet talking to the older woman. "Are you sure you don't want to go with us?"

"I'm fine." The response came with no enthusiasm.

"We should have her back by three or four. Can we bring you anything?"

"No." The woman added in what seemed an afterthought, "Thank you."

As they left the house, Dani took Abby's hand. "Why don't you ride up front with Reverend Polasky. I'll sit in back. That way, you can talk to both of us."

Abby squeezed Dani's hand. "Okay."

"This is going to be fun, huh?" Dani glanced down at the young girl. The dour, hopeless look had faded into one of muted curiosity and anticipation.

After a few attempts at light conversation, Dani withdrew, and they rode in silence. She watched Abby staring out the passenger window into the dreary early November day.

A half-hour later, they navigated the aisles in the department store. "The hoodies are over in that aisle." Dani pointed to their right. Grasping Abby's hand, she guided the young girl over to racks of clothing. "What's your favorite color?"

Abby stretched her head back and forth looking at the different tops. "Mostly blue, I guess." She reached over and touched one of the plush pullover hoodies.

Janet offered her perspective. "I was thinking two or three of these, some long-sleeve pullover shirts, a few button-up blouses, some jeans, and maybe a dress or two. How does that sound?"

Abby stared up at her as though in disbelief. The first smiles appeared as she began to try on the tops. She stared into the mirror as she rubbed her hands on the fabric. One after another, the blue, green, and pink hoodies made their way into the shopping cart.

After an hour of shopping, Janet announced, "That should do it for now, what do you say, Miss Abby?"

The pronounced nod and accompanying smile said it all.

They decided on Red Robin burgers for lunch. As they waited on the food, Janet said, "I need to make a phone call. Can I trust you two to occupy yourselves for a few minutes?" The minister offered a warm smile as she touched Abby's arm. With that, she slid out of the booth and over toward the entrance to the restaurant.

Dani seized the opportunity. "Between you and me, how are you doing, Abby?"

The young girl looked confused. "Okay, I guess."

"Yeah, I know. It's hard. I've been hoping we could talk some more."

Abby cocked her head, eyes wide, and asked, "Does it still hurt, I mean, where you got shot?"

The directness of the question was like a punch to the gut for Dani. "I guess, well, yeah, it still hurts some, but mostly I hurt inside, you know. The person I thought loved me did it. I don't really understand that."

Abby nodded, understanding in her eyes.

Dani continued, "There's so much to try and understand. At first, I blamed my uncle for everything. Then I blamed myself—I must have done something to deserve it. It took a while, but I finally got it. The only one to blame was the man who did it."

"Why did he do it?"

It was the question that had haunted Dani for weeks. "I don't know, Abby. I suspect that the only person who can answer that is he himself. Maybe even he couldn't answer it. What I do know is that what's helping me is having people around that care about me. My uncle never gave up on me. He helped me even when I tried to refuse him. Reverend Polasky over there," Dani pointed in the direction of the entrance, "she was there for me, too. There were others—people who cared and would help."

Dani reached across the table and took Abby's hands. "Then there's you. When I talk to you, it makes me feel better. When I see you smile, it lights up my whole world. Abby, you're important. It's not just me. Reverend Polasky would do anything to help you."

Abby responded quietly, "I like her."

Dani laughed. "I know. Me too." She whispered conspiratorially, "I'll let you in on a little secret if you promise not to tell. I think my Uncle Greg likes her too."

Abby giggled. "Do you mean like boyfriend and girlfriend?"

Dani felt the warmth wash over her. "You have to promise you won't say anything, but, yeah, I think he kind of likes her in that way."

93

J anet sat inside the foyer entrance to the restaurant as she waited with the phone to her ear. She wanted to have one more check-in with Greg before asking Dani about transporting Abby back and forth to school.

Greg's voice sounded full of cheer. "How are things going?"

"Incredible. I am so thankful for Dani, I just can't tell you. The two of them are really hitting it off. Honestly, I was beginning to wonder whether Abby would ever smile again."

"Great to hear, really. I have to say I was kind of wondering the same thing about Dani. Trying to recover both from the physical injuries, which were bad enough, and also the trauma of having her boyfriend… well, you know. It's a lot for one person to go through."

Janet took a deep breath. She couldn't put it off anymore. "There's something else I wanted to ask. I was able to get Abby enrolled at Northlake Academy. It's east of Bellevue, about ten miles from her home. I'm working on transportation issues now."

Chapter 93

Greg interjected, "Shouldn't be a problem. You should have plenty of funds to contract with someone to do that."

"Yes, I can do that. Abby made a strange request, though, and I wanted to at least run it by you before I decided. She asked if Dani could take her to school and bring her home." Janet closed her eyes and waited for the objections.

"Hmmm. I didn't see that one coming. Let's see, well, first I'd want to talk to Kaz and hear what he thinks of it. He'll know more about the security risks than I do. What does Dani say about it?"

"I haven't asked her yet, and I won't mention it unless I have your blessing. I understand the issues with her safety and that has to take priority."

"I'm in the process of leasing a new car for her, one that can't be linked to her personally. That should be finalized within a few days. As far as I know, there's no real connection between Abby and Dani, other than the personal relationship that's recently developed. That means that unless someone just stumbled onto it, it's not something that I'd expect Billy Robinson to know."

"That's what I thought, but I didn't want to presume."

Greg responded, "Why don't you run it by Dani and get her reaction?"

Janet had conflicted feelings. On one hand, if Dani agreed, it would do wonders for Abby's mental health, and would probably benefit Dani as well. On the other hand, if anything went wrong and either of them were hurt…. She refused to let herself go there. "I'll do that. Thanks. I'll give you a call tonight and let you know how the conversation went. If you could talk to Kaz before then, we can at least have everything on the table."

They dropped Abby and her bags of clothing off just before three. On the way to the condo, Janet broached the subject. "I wanted to ask you this alone, so you'd feel free to respond however you choose. Abby asked me if you could be the one to take her to school and bring her home every day. I asked your uncle about it, you know, from a safety standpoint, and he said to run it by you. We'd be happy to compensate you and pay your driving expenses."

Dani asked, "Me? She wants me to take her and bring her home?"

"It was her idea. I had no idea she was even thinking about it."

After a moment of silence, the young woman replied, "What if I say the wrong thing to her? She's going through a lot and I'm not exactly the poster girl for emotional stability right now."

Janet forced a shallow laugh. "I'm not sure any of us are the picture of emotional health at the moment. She reacts to you in a way that no one else seems able to reach her. If you feel uncomfortable with it, I understand, but I trust you to help her."

Dani's laugh seemed more genuine. "I'm not sure who will be helping who, but I'd love to."

94

Corel increasingly struggled to contain his fury. Stillings, Strauss, his wife, the Polasky woman—he wanted them all dead. Even Alicia, dead though she was, served as a constant irritation. What, was he supposed to feel sorry that she was dead? Why? It was her fault. She'd brought it on herself. The bitch thought of no one else. Everything was always about her. It was the same with Bonnie. *Fuck! It's the same with all women. They only care about themselves. They don't understand that they're part of something bigger than themselves.*

Sadly, though, there was simply no substitution for them. He'd gone without sex for a week or so before, but the current dry spell was particularly onerous. Alicia, his preferred lover, had betrayed him. Bonnie, his option of last resort, had abandoned him as well. He could, he supposed, find one of the other staffers to fill in, but that would take time and effort. He had neither to spare at the moment.

It was barely ten in the morning, and he had already worked himself into near rage. The intercom buzzing brought him out of it. He closed his eyes and took a deep breath. Punching the speaker button, he answered, "Yes?"

"Senator, I have two police officers out here. They'd like to talk to you."

A wave of panic washed over him. This had to be about Bonnie. The bitch was trying to sabotage his life at this crucial moment. He knew this was going to happen. He should have had Strauss just end her.

Back in the moment, he composed himself. "Certainly, show them in, please."

A moment later the door opened, and two plain-clothes officers entered—a man and a woman. Both wore badges affixed to straps around their necks. The looks on their faces betrayed nothing.

"Come in, please, have a seat." He motioned toward two chairs.

As the two sat, they introduced themselves, although he promptly forgot their names. He studied their faces for any sign of what was coming. He saw nothing.

The woman spoke. "Senator, we're investigating the disappearance of a young woman that I believe worked for you until just recently—Alicia Wilkins."

Not about Bonnie. Corel quickly shifted mental gears and put on the most concerned face he could muster. "Disappearance, you say? I wasn't aware that she'd gone missing." He summoned the cover story he'd concocted.

"She did work for you, correct?"

"Uh, yes, she was my aide up until, I don't know, what, two weeks ago, maybe." He tried to sound as though the entire thing meant nothing to him.

The female detective continued to speak. "When was the last time that you saw her?"

The senator's mind raced. He furrowed his brow as he tried to focus on dates. "Let's see, I think it was probably the day before she resigned. I'm not sure of the exact date, but I can get it for you if you like."

"That would be good, thank you."

He punched the intercom button and said, "Could you bring me a copy of Alicia's resignation letter, please?" He smiled at the detectives. "It'll be just a few minutes."

He knew that his staff would not find the resignation letter. He'd burnt it as Strauss had suggested.

Corel's internal frustration built. Suddenly, he found himself hoping that the *house cleaners* had done their work well. The staffer rang back within a few minutes. "Uh, Senator, we don't have a copy out here. Could it be in your office?"

He snapped. "No. I don't keep administrative correspondence in here. Look again." He punched the button on the handset, ending the discussion. "I'm sorry. It's been hectic around here. I'm sure they'll find that letter somewhere. Like I said, though, I think it was about two weeks ago."

Both officers nodded but remained silent.

He continued, unable to keep from talking, "If I remember correctly, the letter said something about her going to see her family and then going back to school, you know, to get her graduate degree." He could feel the sweat forming on his brow.

The male detective asked, "Did you happen to discuss the resignation with her?"

The first feelings of panic set in. What did they know? "No. I mean, she'd mentioned going back to school on a number of occasions. I think she wanted to get a master's degree in political science. As you probably noticed, though, I have a number of staffers out there and it's difficult, especially during election season, to keep track of what all of them are doing."

That sounded stupid. He wanted to kick himself. His statement made it seem as though he couldn't manage his staff. "I mean, right now, everyone has assignments. We all focus on what we're doing. I have to trust that the staff are working on their tasks." He forced himself to shut up. He knew he was just digging himself in deeper.

The male detective probed deeper. "What was your relationship with Miz Wilkins?"

The senator's stomach roiled. He felt as though he was about to vomit. They knew something. They had to. "Relationship? Well, she was my primary aide, if that's what you're asking. She supervised the other staffers and did research for me. I had a great deal of trust in her."

"Was there anything more to the relationship than that?" The detective stared straight into Corel's eyes. There was a steely determination in his face.

"I don't know, I guess we were friendly."

The female resumed the questioning. "Anything more?"

"Like what?" The senator's panic built.

The woman arched an eyebrow. "You tell me."

Corel gritted his teeth. "Detectives, I've told you what I know. I've been open and forthcoming. If there's something else you want from me, ask directly. I don't want to seem rude, but I've got too much going on right now to play games with you." He tried to sound forceful and confident. He was, after all, a United States Senator. These two were just grunts, flunkies.

The female detective asked, "Senator, we understand that you left the office shortly after receiving her resignation letter. Could you explain that?"

The senator cleared his throat. "Well, yes… let's see." He paused a moment as though trying to remember a distant, insignificant bit of information. "As I recall, her resignation took me by surprise. If she'd been here, I would have spoken to her about it. Unfortunately, she'd already left. I went out to get some air and clear my head. That kind of thing tends to upend plans, you know. I remember stopping at a newsstand—I purchased, I think, a paper and a magazine. After that, I went to my bank and withdrew some cash. Oh yes, and on the back to the office, I stopped for a latte." He smiled and put on his most sincere face.

"Which vendors did you stop at?"

"I don't know, that's been a few weeks ago. The coffee shop is the one right down the street, I think. I don't remember specifically which newsstand. If it's important, though, I used my credit card. It would be on there." As he finished speaking, Corel scribbled down the name of his bank on piece of paper and handed it to the detective. "You should be able to get what you need from them."

The two stood and the male spoke. "When you find that letter, give us a call." He handed Corel a business card. "We may have some other questions for you later. Thank you for your time."

After they left, he grabbed his cellphone and punched in Dylan's number. As much as he despised this man, Corel needed some reassurance.

"Yeah?"

The rude greeting was not lost on the Senator. This, however, was not the time to make an issue of it. "The work that your house cleaners did for me... did that all work out right?" He didn't know how else to ask the question.

"Why?"

"The police were just here asking about Alicia."

"And? What, did you expect that she would disappear, and no one would notice? The authorities are going to ask questions. They're going to investigate. It's what they do. Your job is to play dumb and appear to cooperate. I'm sure you're smart enough to know what that means. Anything else?"

Corel felt on the verge of crawling through the connection and strangling the living shit out this asshole. "What if they pull the video surveillance from the hotel?"

"Not a problem. They won't see anything."

"That sounds all good and well, but I spent twenty million on house cleaning. For that amount, I expect certainty of success."

"They did their job. Do yours and everything will be okay. Now, if there's nothing else, I'm busy." Strauss disconnected.

95

Bonnie Corel stepped out of the car and wandered casually over to a picnic table. The damp, cold weather ensured that there was no company in the vicinity. She took out the phone and punched in the digits seared into her memory. Her stomach churned as her mind raced, trying to consider all the different possibilities.

"Yes."

"Dylan, this is Bonnie Corel."

Silence.

"Did you deliver my message?"

His tone was matter-of-fact. "I did."

"And?"

"And what?"

She grew exasperated. "What was his response?"

"About what you would expect. If you want to have a conversation with him, you know his number." The tone of his voice suggested something between boredom and mild annoyance.

"That's it?"

"Miz Corel, I'm not being paid to be your messenger

boy. If you want your husband to know anything else, call and tell him. I delivered your message, and I just conveyed the response. If there's anything else you need, do it yourself."

She turned it over in her mind. This didn't sound like the Dylan Strauss that she'd dealt with in the past. This man sounded like he couldn't care less. Maybe Thom had given up. The campaign was in the bag, to be sure. He didn't need her around anymore. "Can I assume that you no longer have any interest in finding me?"

He laughed. "I can assure you, Miz Corel, I have never had any interest in finding you. I did what I did because your husband is a client and it's what he wanted. Beyond that, you're just about the furthest thing from my mind."

Not for an instant did she believe that. "Very well, then. Our business is concluded. Good-bye." She waited for a few seconds before disconnecting to see if he would try and keep her on the line. He disconnected without saying anything.

Hmmm. Maybe he is done with me. She didn't buy it, though. Thom wouldn't let her go that easily and Strauss worked at his beck and call. It was a ploy, but why? What did Strauss or, for that matter, her husband, gain by feigning disinterest?

Returning to the car, she handed the phone to Kaz. "I guess that's it. He didn't even try to keep me on the line."

Kaz turned his head and stared out into the afternoon rain. "No, he wouldn't have. You disconnected quickly last time and destroyed the phone. He probably assumes that you're being coached and would be ready for it. My guess is that he knows that trying to track you through the call would be impossible. If he's still looking for you, he's probably looking at Reverend Polasky's relationships and connections. I'm pretty sure he knows that she's involved in this."

"Because of the guy you killed?"

"Karl Unger, yes. He was Strauss' thug, and he came after Janet directly. That was no coincidence."

Bonnie asked, "Does that mean that she's in danger?"

"She was in danger the minute she decided to go down this road. More to the point, though, yes. It's likely, given that the Hartman lady disappeared, they view Janet as the most likely source of information."

Bonnie felt guilty. People were in danger because of her. People had been killed. She tried, with little success, to banish that idea. "What are you going to do?"

"Did you put that package together, you know, the contingency for any injury that might befall you?"

"I made five copies—one for the Seattle Police, one for Bellevue PD, another for the Post-Intelligencer, one for my attorney, and a copy for me."

Kaz answered, "That should do it. I'm confident nothing will come of it, but it's better to be on the safe side. So, for now, we'll try to keep an eye on Janet. In the long run, I may need to come to an understanding with Dylan Strauss."

Bonnie forced a humorless laugh. "Good luck with that."

96

Election Day dawned with a brilliant cobalt sky lightening to soft magenta on the eastern horizon. A beautiful start to a remarkable day. *As it should be.* Senator Corel stood in his office, taking in the view from his window. Nothing would spoil this. He had stopped by his election precinct to cast his vote and provide a photo op for several news outlets. If the polling was to be believed, he would cruise to an easy victory.

Shortly after 9:00 a.m., his assistant knocked and opened the door. Stepping inside, she consulted her pad before offering him a smile. "We have the preliminary results for the first exit polls, if you're interested, Senator."

He nodded his approval. "And?"

Her smile grew broader. "It's shaping up to be an incredible day. So far, it looks like you're carrying just under seventy percent."

He waved it off with a good-natured laugh. "That's great. Keep in mind, though, that you're talking about Seattle sites, for the most part. It's going to be tougher going in the eastern part of the state."

Corel's mood continued to soar as the morning went on. Several news outlets called to get his reaction to the exit polls. Without pouring cold water on their speculation, he tried to come across as humble and realistic. "Things could change. We won't know until the polls close, and the votes are tallied. The voters have the final say."

Noon came and went. The sun journeyed to the western sky. The election news just got better and better. Exit polls from across the state—even in conservative eastern Washington—showed him cruising to an easy victory. At two-thirty, he pulled up his draft victory speech on the computer and began tweaking it. In several spots, he made a point to declare that he would be the senator for all Washingtonians, not just those who voted for him.

As afternoon deepened, he watched the clock. The polls close at eight in the evening. Corel had to remind himself, though, that most votes in the state were cast by mail. The state Elections Division would already be counting mail ballots. As the day ended, there would be a huge block of results published. He would leave the office around five and head over to the State Convention Center, where his campaign had leased one of the ballrooms. Everything was primed for his victory speech. He had all but forgotten about his issues with Bonnie. *Just as well. I don't need her slinking around on the stage to detract.*

Four-thirty rolled around, and another phone call demanded his attention, although this one was less welcome. He sighed and rolled his eyes as he connected. "Good afternoon, Reba."

"I wanted to be the first to offer my congratulations, Senator. I have it on good authority that it's not even a contest."

"Thank you, but I think it wise to wait and see what

the voters say. You and I both know that exit polls are noto-riously inaccurate."

Stillings laughed. "I assure you, Senator, I was not talking about exit polls."

It figures. She always has her sources. "Well, then, thank you for the congratulations."

"While I have you on the phone, I wanted to briefly touch on our relationship and your debt to me."

Corel shot back, "And I will remind you that I have no idea what you're talking about."

"Of course, you do. Don't worry, though. What I want from you isn't that onerous. You win—I win—everybody's happy."

Corel lost his patience. "What is it you want?" He spat the words out.

"Strike the prohibition on firearms ownership contained in Violence Against Women Act. Make it go away."

"Bullshit. You know that I can't do that, even if I wanted to."

The laugh returned. "You have a way of making things happen, Senator. Make this happen."

"Or?"

"Oh come now, let's not toss threats and ultimatums around. We're simply two professionals exchanging favors. I let sleeping dogs lie. You do some of that Thomas Corel magic. Like I said, everybody wins."

"I have to go." He almost added that he would talk to her later but was not able to spit those words out. If all went well, he would never talk to her again.

The first news outlet called the election at nine-thirty —an unbelievable precedent. Others followed suit. At eleven-fifteen, his opponent made a concession speech and offered congratulations. Senator Thomas Corel basked in the glow of what had indeed turned out to be a coronation. *And I did it without that bitch of a wife hanging around.* The thought occurred to him that perhaps he should take her up on the offer—a quiet, low-profile divorce—irreconcilable differences. The pressures of public service and constant scrutiny had created schisms. They both would, of course, remain amicable as they pursued their respective lives.

He arrived home shortly after two in the morning. Too keyed up to sleep, he paced through the rooms, a glass of scotch in his hand. With the pressure of the election over, he could turn his attention to other matters. An instant of regret swept over him and then disappeared. It would have been nice to have the company of Alicia. Despite her betrayal and self-absorption, her skills as a bed partner would have eased his tension. *Fucking cunts. Always screwing things up.*

Unlocking his safe, he pulled out a single sheet of paper, on which were typed three series of alpha-numeric strings. With these codes, he could settle up accounts that had gone sour. He also retrieved a non-descript cellphone that he had religiously kept charged for this one eventuality.

Going first to his computer, he navigated to a website that appeared to sell men's clothing. He selected three specific items, placed them in his shopping cart, and then proceeded to check-out. This is where he was prompted for his account information. He entered the first coded string.

The system began it's typical "thinking" as it processed his input. The next prompt asked him to confirm his account number. He entered the second alpha-numeric code and waited. After a moment, the system presented him with a security question.

What was your first grade teacher's name?

He entered the third alpha-numeric code and waited. The screen turned white and a brief message appeared.

Thank you for your order. Reference A387GF49PP

Less than a minute later, the cellphone rang. He connected. "Yes."

"This is in regard to your recent order. Can you confirm your order number please."

He read the code that the screen had displayed and then waited.

"Just a moment."

He heard a series of clicks followed by a background hum.

"We're secure now. What can we do for you?"

"I need level one services. Time frame—one week. Three copies."

"Very well, I'm ready for the first copy information."

"Janet Polasky, Minister, Saint Luke's Methodist Church, Bellevue, Washington."

"Stand by." After a brief moment, the voice returned. "The price for that item is twenty-five thousand. Next copy?"

"Dylan Strauss, system contractor."

A silent, uncomfortable pause preceded a curt, "Stand by." After a moment, the person on the other end spoke. "The price for that item is three hundred-fifty thousand. Next copy?"

Corel spoke clearly into the phone. The words gave him great pleasure. "Reba Stillings, attorney, Seattle, Washington."

An audible gasp came from the connection, followed by another "Stand by." When the voice returned, the words came slowly and clearly. "The price for that copy is fifteen million."

It was Corel's turn to gasp. "Verify, please."

Chapter 96

"The price for that copy is fifteen million." The voice was firm and cold. "Do you wish to proceed to checkout?"

His first inclination was to argue with the voice. He knew that it would be fruitless. The senator did some quick math in his head. This arrangement would almost deplete his liquid assets. It would take months, maybe years, to recoup these costs. Was this really the best use of his money? His emotions won out. "Yes."

"Your transaction code is one three one seven two nine four eight seven. Status valid for twelve hours. We will confirm when processed."

Corel had used this service before, although not for this specific purpose. Still, the arrangement was the same. He needed to deposit the funds into the account identified by the transaction code. Once that was verified, things would be set in motion.

He disconnected from the call. Turning back to the computer screen, he navigated to his financial account website. A quick assessment showed that he had just over thirty million available to him. He began transferring funds. All things would be made right. *The world will be a better place.*

97

Despite things running smoothly, Janet felt plagued by several issues. Roberta Klein was in desperate need of help. All of Janet's attempts to engage the woman had fallen flat. Abby was once again enrolled in school. That pressure was eased. Maybe it was time to attend to her grandmother.

Bonnie Corel seemed to be managing her own problems. She remained at the condo. Val checked in with her daily. Fortunately, there were no other women asking for help at the moment, so there was some breathing room.

Security and protection were at the top of Janet's list. There had already been one attempt on her life. Then she found out that she was on some other hit list. Her friend Aylin Freyberg had already been shot and Janet was supposed to be next. She and Greg had discussed it, but nothing had come of it.

Then there was Greg Stottman. This was the one problem that Janet could not get her mind around. He had declared an interest in her. To be fair, he hadn't really said what that interest was. *Probably sex.* The problem, though, was that she didn't know how she felt about him. How should she feel? She was married, well, had been married. Mark had been the most incredible person she'd ever known and now he was gone. Intimacy with him had been more than just sex. How could she ever do that again? How could she simply move on with her life?

What's wrong with moving on with my life? Janet understood, or rather thought that she understood, that moving on would mean leaving Mark behind. She was not ready for that. Whatever else came her way, she would not turn her back on his memory. She would simply have to explain this to Greg.

* * *

"Would you like a cup of tea or coffee?" Greg stood, poised at the kitchen door, while Janet took a seat on the couch.

"I'm fine. I don't want to take much of your time."

He laughed. "Take as much as you want. It's not like I have a lot going on tonight." He gestured around the silent living room. "The place feels really empty without Dani."

Janet sat back on the couch drumming her fingers on the arm. "I can imagine. Living alone takes some getting used to." She knew all about that.

He slouched into the overstuffed chair across from the couch. "Okay, then. What is it you wanted to talk about?"

She considered him in silence for a moment. He knew exactly what she wanted to discuss. Janet could see it in his eyes. "We agreed a few nights ago we'd talk about this." They both knew what *this* was.

He nodded, but said nothing.

"First of all, Greg, and I really mean this. You're a great guy and I do like you."

His face betrayed disappointment. His eyes fell, his nod was almost imperceptible. "I sense a *but* coming."

"There are several of them." She smiled and tried to make it sound casual. "First, we live in different worlds. You're wealthy and run with some very powerful people. I'm a minister who lives payday to payday. It's been great working with you, but I worry that the feelings you have are just what close colleagues feel."

He started to say something, but Janet held her hand up as she continued, "Second, I worry that allowing things to become personal between us will hurt what we're trying to do together. So far, we've accomplished amazing things. It needs to stay about the project, though."

She paused, expecting him to object. He didn't.

"Here's the hardest part. I told you I was married before. My husband died ten years ago. I know that sounds like a long time, and believe me, it sometimes seems like a lifetime. He's still a part of me, though. Being in a relationship and feeling the way I do would be unfair. Mark would always be there between us. At this point in my life, I don't have it within me to banish him. I can't do it." Tears gathered in her eyes and rolled down her cheeks. She fell silent.

He looked down at his clasped hands for a moment before speaking. "I could sit here and argue each of those points, well, at least the first two. I'm going to take a bold leap here and say that I don't think either one of those is what's bothering you. Yes, I have money and my work is different than yours. I also realize that there can be complications when relationships develop between people who work together. My sense, though, is that both of those are just filler. It's that last one that gets you."

She nodded and wiped the tears from her cheeks.

"I'm not going to try to win you over tonight. Even if it were possible, which I doubt that it is, I wouldn't want you dragged into a relationship against your better judgment. Instead, I'm going to tell you some things that you can mull over. With regard to your husband, Mark. You will never get over him, nor should you. He is and will always be a part of who you are. Anything that you become or do in the future will include him as a part of that. Anyone with whom you are in a relationship will need to understand that."

The words struck Janet as odd. They were virtually the same ones that Maddie had uttered as the two of them had discussed this issue.

Greg continued, "I care about you—all of you. That includes your marriage, your grief, your journey out of that darkness, and whatever else there is. I'm not interested in picking and choosing the parts I like and leaving the rest behind."

He leaned forward in his chair and gestured. "Janet, the last thing I want you to feel is pressure from me. I'm not asking anything from you. It's not going to affect how we work together. I know that I'm anxious over your safety right now, but, honestly, I'd be anxious no matter how I felt about you personally. So, let's leave it at this. You know how I feel. I know what your reservations are. I promise not to push this on you. All I ask is that, if you do change your mind, let me in on it.

98

A heavy rain pelted the tin roof of the cabin. The Sniper sat across from Billy as they studied the map. The tension between the two had been building steadily since the botched mission. The Sniper had concluded that this upcoming venture was Cousin Billy's last chance. He even entertained the thought of just ending it right away. *Why go through the motions?*

"We need to be out of here around noon."

Billy shot back, "Why so late? Why not get started at first light?"

The Sniper fought back the urge to tell the kid to keep his fucking ideas to himself. "Several reasons. To start with, we want lots of traffic around us. It's harder for cops to focus on any one vehicle if there are lots on the road. That's why you're going to follow all traffic laws and keep your speed about the same as other cars around you. You want to be just like everyone else."

Billy scowled but remained silent.

"We want to get to the drop-off site just after dark. From here, it's going to be about eight hours. If we leave at first light, that puts us there early afternoon. Your car's going to be found pretty quick. If we drop it off after dark, it will most likely not get noticed until the next morning. By then, we'll be long gone."

"Where's this drop-off point?" Billy stared at the map.

"We're going to head south to Boise and pick up Eighty Four West. That will take us into Oregon. Just to the east of The Dalles, we'll turn north on Ninety-Seven and into Washington. There's a small town a short ways up—Gold-endale. We'll go through there and drop the car between the town and the Yakima Indian Reservation. Once we're clear of Goldendale, we'll find a small side road. That's where we dump it."

"Am I going to need to wipe it down for fingerprints and stuff?"

The Sniper laughed. The kid was genuinely funny, in a stupid kind of way. "We won't have that much time. Still, it's not a big deal. They'll find the prints and connect you. By then, though, we'll be long gone."

Billy nodded as though he was in complete command of the facts. *What a fucking idiot.*

"What's the plan when we get up to Seattle?"

The Sniper pointed to the map. "Renton—that's our destination. I did some checking. Greg Stottman has a condominium there. If what you tell me is true, he's got the girl there with him."

He pulled out a black box with wires attached. "I'm betting he's got a digital lock on his front door. This little gadget will hack it in less than twenty seconds."

"How does it work?"

The Sniper held up the end of the cable, which was fitted with a transducer. "This is military grade hardware. You hold this cup-like thing right below the keypad and press this." He indicated a small red button. "It induces a signal into the internal wiring of the box and runs every possible combination of numbers until it senses a match. It'll work on any consumer-grade lock. After that, you should be able to just open the door."

"Won't they hear me doing it? I mean, I'll be standing right there on the front porch."

The Sniper sighed, but it occurred to him that it was a good question. "The key is to look confident as you go up to the door and work quickly. We'll watch and wait until the living room lights go out. Give it an hour and then go. When you get the green light on the box, turn the door handle very slowly and quietly. When you enter, make sure your weapon is drawn. I have a noise suppressor for you. Once inside, you'll have to figure out where the bedrooms are. Hopefully, they'll be asleep and won't hear you."

"Okay, so I hit them both. Anything else I need to do?"

"Get out alive." The Sniper smirked. "Once you're clear, we'll come home by the northern route, though Spokane. I'll try to time it so that we hit the city during rush hour. That'll put us home late, but once we're in Idaho, we should be okay."

Billy grinned. "Easy peasy."

"Yeah, right. Don't get cocky. You saw what happened last time you went down that road."

99

The week had flown by. Congratulatory calls came non-stop. Senator Corel scurried from meeting to luncheon to media interviews. On top of that, he'd received verification that his payment had been received and delivery was scheduled. Soon all debts would be repaid.

Friday morning, he arrived at his office looking forward to the day. He'd been invited out to the Governor's home on Bainbridge Island for the weekend. He had a light schedule for the day. Standing in his favorite spot in the office, he took in the view of Seattle. As he thought through his plans for the weekend and beyond, he became more and more certain that a peaceful dissolution with his wife would work in his best interest. In a perfect world, he would have added her to his debtor list, the one that was about to be cleared. Having her killed, though, would bring attention to him. That simply wouldn't do.

The knock on the door came at nine-thirty. He turned just as it opened and was struck by a beautiful, if unknown woman who strode confidently in. "Good morning, Senator. I have the media reviews ready for you." She set a stack of papers on his desk.

"Wonderful. Thank you. I don't recognize you. You are…?"

"Oh, I'm sorry. I'm new, just this morning. Your campaign manager hired me a few days ago. My name is Claire Montgomery."

He offered his warmest smile. "Welcome, Miz Montgomery. Are you from Seattle?"

"Originally from Portland. I came up here to study PolySci at UW about eight years ago. Liked it so much I decided to stay."

He liked what he saw. "You have family in the area?" She had real possibilities.

"No. My folks still live down in Oregon. I was staying with a roommate until about a week ago. Depending on how this job works out, I'll either get a place here or maybe relocate." Her coy smile definitely got a physical reaction from him.

Oh yes, you could certainly have opportunities. "That's wonderful. I'm going to be restructuring my Washington D.C. office staff. Perhaps you and I could discuss that over lunch."

She nodded and smiled. "I have a room over at the Grand Hyatt. They have good luncheon specials. We could meet there."

His mind raced. "That sounds great. Hopefully, they won't be too crowded. In this business, it's not wise to have such discussions in public places." It was a flimsy line, but it would have to do.

"We could order from room service and talk in my room, if you prefer."

Chapter 99

Holy Shit! A perfect ending to a perfect week. "That might work better, yes. I can be over at, say, about eleven-thirty." No point in wasting time. It had been a few weeks, after all.

* * *

Senator Corel strode confidently through the lobby and entered the elevator at eleven-twenty. He needed to meet the governor at the ferry around five-thirty. That gave him the entire afternoon.

Things only got better when Claire opened the door for him. Dressed in a silk top that came to just below the thighs, her nipples clearly showed how excited she was. She held up a bottle. "I ordered champagne. After your win, I figure there's lots to celebrate."

He embraced her and they kissed. Her mouth tasted sweet, with just a tinge of liquor. Setting the bottle down, she wrapped her arms around his neck and kissed him back, rubbing up against him as though giving him just a taste of what he was in for.

She picked up the champagne and smiled seductively as she poured. He stared, almost mesmerized as the golden liquid filled the goblet. Handing it to him, she whispered in his ear, "Congratulations, Senator. You win the prize." Her other hand slid from his shoulder down to his chest, then his stomach, and then to his crotch.

Corel could barely contain himself. He started to set the full glass aside.

She stepped back and poured a drink for herself, raising the glass in toast. "To you, Senator."

He raised his glass in return. "To us," and took a deep drink. The liquid warmed as it went down. The sweetness lingered, accompanied by some other, unfamiliar taste.

Claire set her glass aside without drinking any. "Now, where were we?"

He felt his head spinning as he allowed her to unbutton his shirt.

100

The two rolled into the Seattle-Tacoma area as the sun retreated for the night. The Sniper and Cousin Billy had dropped off the car the previous evening north of Goldendale, in southern Washington, without incident. They'd slept the night, tucked into sleeping bags in the back of the truck at one of the many pull-off areas that allowed overnight camping. They drove with Oregon plates until changing to Washington plates at the state line. Sniper had an extensive collection of stolen license plates from all the western states. It wouldn't even get them through a traffic stop, but it would reduce the likelihood of being noticed.

The Sniper broke the long silence that had dominated since they dumped Billy's car. "We'll shoot for about eleven. It's not so late that someone walking up to the door would be noticed but hopefully they'll be in bed or at least getting ready for bed."

Billy continued to gaze out the passenger side window without acknowledging the plan.

His cousin's silence annoyed the Sniper. The key to

success was planning and execution and Billy couldn't have seemed less interested. The Sniper decided to let it go. He didn't need his cousin's approval of the timing. "Are you up for this?" He asked the question with a deliberate pointedness. It was not by any stretch a formality. The kid would need to gain entry and move quickly between rooms. There would be no time for taunting or words. Find the targets, do the job, and get out.

"Yeah." Billy's voice reeked of boredom and a touch of insolence.

This lackadaisical attitude gnawed at the Sniper. This was no walk in the park. One wrong move, one hesitation, one misstep—could spell disaster. "Run it back to me? How does it go down?" He pushed Billy harder.

His cousin turned to face him. "What the fuck? Why is it that you can't just trust me? We've been through this a hundred times. I go in, I take 'em out, I leave. What's so fucking complicated about that?"

The Sniper could feel the anger emanating from his cousin. He exerted every ounce of restraint he could muster. He spoke softly. "What's so *fucking complicated* is that you're dealing with two people who could react in any number of ways. You can't control that. Once inside, their responses will drive your actions. They might freeze, like deer in the headlights. If so, no problem. One might freeze while the other takes evasive or even offensive action. Both of them could rush you. You have no idea, at this point, how they're going to handle it. That's the complication. The reason I'm not ready to just *trust you* is that, number one, you've already fucked up once so I know it's possible. Number two, your fuck-ups could come back on me. So, humor me. Run it back to me. How does it go down?"

Billy's exhalation was bathed in frustration. "I use the box to get inside. I look around. If either is in the living room, I take them out. Otherwise, I walk down the hallway and to the first bedroom I come to. I open the door and shoot whoever is there—multiple shots. Go to the next room—same thing. Then I go back and finish each with one final head shot. I leave the condo. Close the door. Come back to the truck. Watch for anybody that notices me."

"And *if* someone notices you?"

"If they're close, like five or ten feet, I take 'em out too. If they're farther away, ignore 'em."

"Good." The Sniper grasped the steering wheel tighter and continued, "We'll spend some time finding the right parking spot. It needs to be in an area where a parked vehicle wouldn't draw attention. We need a good view of the front of his condo, but not too close. I've never been there before so it may take some time. I checked on Google Earth and it looks pretty accessible, but until we're there, we won't know for sure."

Billy nodded and turned his head back toward the passenger window.

This isn't going to work out. The Sniper had tried—given it his best shot—but it seemed increasingly clear that the relationship between the two had soured. His cousin wasn't taking this seriously. Billy apparently wasn't ready to grow up. It did, however, raise a serious question—was the night's mission a waste of time and an unnecessary risk? He could divert to an out-of-the-way spot and end it without a problem. It was tempting.

He decided to let it play out. After all, it was Billy who would bear the brunt of the risk. The only problem would be if he got captured. In most cases such as this, either it succeeds, or the occupants kill the intruder. Rarely are they captured. "How about some supper? Micky Dee's is right up the road."

Another thought occurred to the Sniper. Was Billy the hesitant about killing Dani. Sure, he'd shot her and left her for dead before, but that was in a fit of rage. A cold, calculated kill is something far different. On reflection, he decided it was too late to ask.

A note of enthusiasm crept into Billy's voice. "Sure, that'd be great."

101

Greg and Kaz sat in the gathering shadows of Greg's living room. It was the first time in the last week that they'd really had a chance to sit back in the quiet and have a casual conversation. "We're coming up on the end of your six-month contract. Any idea what you're going to be doing next?"

Kaz tilted his head back as though searching for an answer among the swirling patterns of plaster and paint on the ceiling. "Not really. Funny thing about this business, something else always seems to come along. It's not anything you can really predict, but it just seems to work out."

Greg nodded. He'd heard that sentiment before, especially from independent contractors. They moved from job to job, with no guarantees for the future. Yet somehow, it always seemed to work out for them. "Have you ever given any thought to taking on something more permanent?"

Kaz laughed. "You mean, like a regular job?"

"Sort of, I guess."

The contractor grew serious. "It's complicated. If it

was just me, I might think about it. My mother, though, is in a nursing facility. She's Medicare, but there are a lot of out-of-pocket expenses. My current line of work ensures that the money's there to pay for it."

"So, it's money? That's what keeps you where you are?"

"What else would it be? I think we'd both agree that I charge outrageous fees. That companies, governments, and individuals are willing to pay them keeps me coming back."

Greg considered the words for a moment. This was as good a time as any. "Suppose you were to find a job where the pay was comparable?"

"Jobs like that are hard to come by."

"I'd like you to stay on—help Janet with her project. We can make it worth your while." Greg held his breath.

Kaz eyed him with what seemed keen interest. His words came slowly and carefully measured. "I don't know. I like the work and, believe me, I respect both of you. My mother, though, is in a place in Brooklyn. I would worry about being so far from her."

"I can imagine. My mother and father died years ago, but it would kill me to be apart from them, especially if they needed me. Let me ask you, though, how often do you get to see her? After all, you've been here nearly six months and haven't gone back during that time. If you worked full time here, you could easily fly back and be with her every month or so, if you wanted. You might even see her more often." Greg was trying to walk that fine line between having a persuasive conversation and pushing too hard. After a brief moment, he added, "You might even consider moving her out here. The insurance that goes along with the job would cover the costs for the best care available."

Chapter 101

He was well aware that he was making this all up as he went along.

"I wasn't really expecting anything like this, so I'm not prepared to give you an answer tonight. I promise, though, I'll consider it."

Greg nodded. "Fair enough." He stood. "I think time kind of got away from us. Why don't we put some dinner together?"

The two moved toward the kitchen, leaving the living room in near darkness. Kaz stopped abruptly and pointed up into a corner of the ceiling. "I never noticed that. What is it?"

Greg responded, "It's a warning light. I've got hidden video cameras and a motion sensor mounted out front. Anyone coming up the walkway will trigger it. I get the warning light and the cameras switch on. I can check the feed on my cellphone. Pretty slick, huh?"

"Yeah, I'd say so. I've never even noticed it myself, and I'm paid to notice things."

"What do you feel like? I have pasta, sandwich fixings, salad stuff, or a burger."

Kaz backed into the kitchen, never taking his eyes off the warning light. "Nice."

Greg laughed. "Burgers it is."

102

The Sniper decided on a spot in the main parking area about thirty yards from the condo. He parked facing away from the unit and climbed through the access window into the covered bed of the truck. Opening up the floor panel, he unlocked the storage unit and retrieved a Smith and Wesson nine-millimeter handgun and noise suppressor. Fitting the noise supressor onto the pistol, he slammed a magazine into the handle, released the slide, and set the safety.

"There you go, Cuz. You have fifteen rounds with one in the chamber. The silencer will prevent alerting the neighbors. If you can't finish it with that, we'll send you back to school." He laughed as he handed the weapon to Billy.

Billy took the gun and held it in his hands for a moment, turning it over and around and examining it from different angles, as though hoping to find some hidden secret. Finally, he tucked the weapon in his waistband beneath the small of his back. "No problem."

"Good. Now we wait." The Sniper took out a pair of

binoculars. Cracking open the rear sliding window, he peered at the target condo. "Not a lot of lights on. Entry area not that well-lit. Looks like some muted light behind that, maybe a kitchen or something. I'm not seeing any movement yet."

"What if nobody's home?"

The Sniper considered the question—it was actually a good one. "Based on my research, that's Stottman's car over there." He pointed in the direction of a sedan with the license plate fully visible. "Let's give it some time and see if we spot any kind of movement inside."

They sat for about an hour. Finally, the Sniper noticed it—a movement of shadows that appeared to come from the area behind the entrance. "Got something. Looks like they may be in the back area. My guess is it's a kitchen."

"Maybe I could take them both there. If I come in quietly, they'll be in the light, and I'll be in a dark area. That gives me an advantage."

"Not a bad idea, but let's wait a little longer. Also, keep in mind that one of them could be in the kitchen and the other in the bedroom. You said that they didn't get along that well. That works in our favor too."

Billy laughed. "Yeah, that cunt hated her uncle. I think he was trying to get some of that, and she wasn't going along with it."

Annoyance swept over the Sniper. It wasn't that he thought the idea was impossible. It was just that his idiot of a cousin was always making shit up just because he thought it sounded good. It had a way of distracting him from what he should be thinking. "Another half-hour."

The Sniper reached up into the truck cab and grabbed the white paper sack. "Apple pies. Enjoy." He handed one of the pies to Billy and bit into the other himself. They sat and munched without talking.

A half-hour later, the Sniper picked up the binoculars again and gave the condo one last scan. "Nothing new. It's time. You all set?"

"Ready."

Billy climbed back through the window into the cab and exited the truck from the passenger side. The Sniper watched him glance from side to side as he wandered casually toward the unit.

As his cousin approached the front walk, something struck the Sniper as out of place. He reached into the hidden compartment and grabbed a spotting scope. Looking at the detail around the front of the condo, he saw it—a video camera. It was well disguised, almost invisible, but there was no mistaking it. Uncle Money Bags had a surveillance system. "Shit."

It was too late. Billy made his way up the walk to the front porch. Taking a quick look around, he pulled out the black box and went to work.

Contingency Plan B—the Sniper accessed his hidden compartment and pulled out his sniper rifle. Loading a round in the chamber, he positioned himself as he watched the unfolding events through his scope.

103

T he red light flashed. Greg stared at it for a moment before whipping out his cellphone. With a couple of touches, he accessed the camera feed. "Some guy coming up the walkway."

Kaz stretched his neck as he looked across the table at the display. "Anybody you know?"

"Can't tell. He has a hood up over his head. Keeping his face down."

"That doesn't sound promising." Kaz pulled a weapon from the shoulder holster that he'd hung over a chair. Reaching down, he pulled a smaller weapon from a leg holster just above his ankle. Chambering a round and setting the safety, he handed it Greg. "Just click this switch and fire—pretty simple."

Greg took it without argument. He felt a tightness in his chest and his stomach churned, although it was less intense than his previous experience with a gun.

They watched as the man stopped in front of the door and started working with some kind of box. Kaz nodded. "Yep, not good at all. He's trying to bypass your electronic lock. If he knows what he's doing, it shouldn't take him more than about twenty or thirty seconds."

Greg froze as he watched the intruder operate on the lock. A sense of dread built and he felt on his brow.

Kaz stood and whispered, "Let's go say hello."

They positioned themselves on either side of the living room in the dark, weapons pointed at the door. Greg stood by the light switch. He heard some clicking and then silence. The handle squeaked ever so slightly as the door cracked open—a little wider and then a little wider. The figure stepped inside.

Greg switched on the light.

Kaz yelled, "Freeze. Don't move a goddamned inch."

Greg moved forward, his shaking weapon pointed at the man's chest.

Kaz recognized the intruder first. "Well, now, this is a surprise. I was certain we'd seen the last of you."

Billy Robinson stood, paralyzed in the light. Holding the black box in his hands, he appeared to be carrying on an internal debate.

Kaz lowered his voice, "There's no way you can do it, son. You're just not that fast. Now drop the box and put your hands above your head. I'm not fucking with you here. I can drop you where you stand and no jury in the world is going to convict me. Hands over your head or you die—your choice."

After a moment of silence, Billy dropped the box and raised his arms.

Kaz moved swiftly across the room, shutting the door behind Billy. The kid rotated around slowly, watching Kaz's every move.

"That's it. See, you can make a good decision when you try." Kaz pulled a straight-backed chair from the edge of the living room into the center. "First of all, I want you to reach behind you with your left hand. Take the gun that I'm sure you have in your waistband and drop it to the floor. Then, with your left foot, slide it away from you. I'll remind you. I have a weapon pointed at you as does Mister Stottman over there. One wrong move and it's over."

Billy reached around slowly with his left hand, pulled the gun from his waistband, and dropped it as directed.

"Very good. Now, have a seat and make yourself comfortable while we wait on some company." He turned to Greg. "Call nine-one-one. Tell them we have an armed intruder secured."

As Greg completed the call. The Renton Police Dispatch assured him that help was on the way. After that, he stood for a moment watching the kid, whose eyes kept darting toward the front window into the darkness as though expecting salvation to come from outside.

"I'm going to call Wharton from King County as well. She'll want to know this." Greg picked up his phone again. Scrolling through his contact list, he made the call.

"Hello."

"Detective Wharton, this is Greg Stottman. I hate to bother you at night, but I wanted to let you know that we got Billy Robinson. He tried to break in here."

After a moment of silence, she asked, "Is he alive?"

"Yeah. We called Renton PD and they're on the way."

"I'll be right over." She disconnected.

104

This was the Sniper's worst nightmare. Billy had not killed his targets, nor had he himself been killed. Instead, the idiot had allowed himself to be caught. There he sat, probably waiting to be rescued. The Sniper surveyed the scene through his spotting scope one more time. His cousin was clearly visible through the living room window. With the lacy curtains in place, it was not ideal, but sometimes one had to make the best of what one had.

Setting the spotting scope aside, he returned his right eye to the scope atop his rifle. He briefly looked at nearby trees—no wind. *Good.* He steadied his rifle, and, with no sense of emotion one way or the other, acquired his target. His finger began to squeeze the trigger. The fitted noise suppressor rendered the sound little more than a spit. The Sniper smoothly retracted the bolt, ejected the spent shell, and seated a new round. Quickly re-acquiring his target, he squeezed again.

For a short moment after that, he simply watched. The figure sat slumped in the chair, chin on his chest. "Sorry Cuz."

105

The sound of tinkling glass broke the silence. Billy jerked. A red spot spread rapidly on his chest. Greg stared with incredulity, unable to make sense of what had happened or even to move.

In that instant, he felt himself knocked to the floor with Kaz on top of him. "Get down. Crawl over behind the sofa."

As Greg scrambled over on his stomach, Kaz rolled over toward the end table on which the lamp shone. He reached up and, with a single motion, swept it off the table. The light went out.

Kaz shouted, "Watch the door, but don't shoot unless I tell you to. I'll call nine-one-one. They should be here in a minute… I hope." Kaz's voice sounded far too calm.

"What the hell happened?"

"Right off hand, I'd say that whoever was helping Billy had second thoughts."

Greg's mind raced. "What are we supposed to do?" The hand in which he held the gun shook controllably. His stomach roiled.

"Stay put. Don't stand up. Don't move around. It's dark in here and, unless whoever it decides to come in, they won't be able to see us if we stay down."

Although it seemed to be hours, Greg was certain that it was only a few minutes before the strobing red and blue lights found their way into the living room through the window. "I guess that's the police." Greg breathed a little easier.

Then came a pounding on the door. "Renton Police."

Kaz called out. "Yes. There's two of us alive in here. One down. There's a shooter outside, though."

The reply from outside came quickly. "Any shooters inside?"

"No. All clear in here."

The door opened and two figures slipped in, shutting the door behind them. "You say there's a shooter outside. How many?"

"I can't say for sure, but there were two shots fired. Could have easily been done by one person. Probably rifle with a suppressor."

"The vic, do you know his condition."

"My guess is that he's dead. Took two to the chest. That's him in the chair over there." There was just enough ambient light filtering through the curtains to make out Billy's slumped form.

One of the cops crawled over to the slumped body and reached up, feeling the wrist. "No pulse that I can feel. I can't say for certain, but most likely dead. I'll call for medical and back-up."

Fifteen minutes later, more vehicles pulled up. Barked orders and shouting filtered in from outside. A few minutes later, a voice called from outside. "Initial sweep finished, negative."

Chapter 105

One of the cops stood. "Okay, let's get some lights on and secure the scene."

That started what was sure to be a long night for Greg and Kaz. They were shuffled out of the way and quickly separated by detectives who began to ask questions. EMTs arrived and pronounced Billy dead. They called for the medical examiner.

Ten minutes later, Detective Wharton showed up. She flashed her badge to the uniforms posted at the door. After stopping to look at the victim, still slumped in the chair, she eased over to where one of the detectives was questioning Greg. "Well, I see you got your revenge." Her words were filled with venom.

Greg shot up from his chair and got in her face. "Fuck you! I called you as a courtesy. He was alive. I didn't shoot him and neither did my friend. Whoever killed him did it from outside. If you were such a good cop, you would have caught him yourself. Seems like you don't manage to accomplish anything. So, get the fuck out of my face."

Wharton turned crimson, her jaw clenched. The local responding Renton detective sat silently, staring at the showdown.

Greg, trembling with a combination of rage and trauma, stood his ground, glaring at her.

Finally, she nodded and lowered her gaze. "It's been a long night." She turned to the other detective. "This is the guy who killed two cops in Spokane. He also shot a young woman and nearly killed her. The entire state's been looking for him."

The Renton detective shrugged. "Well, I guess you found him." He turned his attention to Greg. "I think we have everything we need from you tonight. I may need to ask you a few more questions sometime in the next few days."

Greg felt drained and overwhelmed. "Okay, yeah, thanks. I suppose I need to start cleaning up this mess."

"Nope. This is a crime scene. Until we're done, you need to leave it as is. You might want to find yourself a hotel room."

Greg felt a hand on his shoulder. He turned to see Kaz standing beside him. "Come on, let's find a place to crash tonight."

As Greg stuffed a few pieces of clothing into a backpack, another thought occurred to him. *I guess I need to call Dani.*

106

The Sniper set his rifle aside and took up the spotting scope. The lights in the living room had gone out. Whoever had been in there knew what they were doing. He could make out no movement. Unless he was wrong, flashing red and blue lights would show up shortly.

He quickly stowed the rifle, scope, and spent shells in the hidden cache and pulled the covering over the floor. Slipping through the access window into the cab, he buckled up and started the ignition. With one last look around, he eased out of the parking space and navigated down a small side street. He took the first left and went two more blocks before turning on his headlights.

Three more turns and another couple of miles brought him to the I-5 interchange. He turned and headed north to pick up I-90 eastbound, which would take him to Idaho. Once out of the Seattle area, he would find a place to sleep for the night. Making the drive during daylight hours would bring less scrutiny.

A new thought found its way into his mind. For the first time since he'd returned from Afghanistan, he was in danger. This outing had been a mistake and had gone to hell. The whole entanglement with Cousin Billy had been a fuck-up from beginning to end. Everything changed. His organization—Truth is Strength—was not forgiving of screw-ups. There would be no going back. He would have to find a way forward.

107

Janet sat in a chair as Greg sat on the sofa, his arm around Dani. He had phoned just as she arrived at the church and related the events of the previous evening. He'd seemed happy when she offered to come over to the leased condo and sit with him and Dani.

She watched the interaction between the two of them. There was a tender quietness about the moment. Dani had taken the news about Billy Robinson's death with what seemed to Janet as relief tinged with sadness. Greg, for his part, had remained solemn and had avoided saying anything negative about the boy.

Dani broke the silence. "It's hard to believe that the person I wanted to spend the rest of my life with broke in to kill the two of us. Why?"

Greg pulled her closer. "I don't know, Dani. I honestly don't. I wish I had more answers for you."

"Do you really think that whoever brought him there or was helping him was the one who killed him?" She spoke with what seemed resigned sadness.

"We never even heard the shots. Whoever did it was a

pro. I know that Detective Wharton said Billy's cousin was killed in Afghanistan, but I'm not so sure. From what she said, they never found the body. The way that Billy was shot, that seemed an awful lot like a military sniper. It was cold, precise, and mechanical. I don't know of anyone else that he was close to that would have helped him. It would answer a lot of questions."

She sighed. "It's hard to know where to go from here. I'm not sure I could ever trust a man again after this."

Greg laughed softly. "There are tons of good men out there, I promise you."

It felt funny, but it seemed a side of Greg that Janet had not noticed before. Sure, he'd been there for Dani at every step, and he'd been as loyal as a person could be to Janet and the project. At this moment, though, he seemed to be opening up in a way that put his heart on display. As much as she felt the urge to second Greg's assertion, Janet remained silent—in the background.

After a few more minutes, Greg said, "Would you like to go out and grab some lunch?"

"I don't know. I'm not really that hungry." Dani sat limp, allowing Greg to hold her close.

"You could do with some sunshine, though."

She laughed. "It's raining."

"Restaurants are open even when it rains."

She stood. "Give me few minutes to get ready." She started down the hallway and then stopped and turned around. "Say, Janet, maybe you and Abby could come along."

Janet glanced over just in time to see a flash of excitement on Greg's face. "If it's okay with your uncle, I'll phone over and see if Abby can go."

Greg answered immediately. "Of course, it's okay with me. I'd love it."

Chapter 107

Before Janet could call, though, her cellphone rang. She glanced at the display. *What would she want on a Saturday morning?* "Hey, Dee, what's up?"

"Are you watching the news?"

"Uh, no. I'm over at the condo talking with Greg and his niece. What's happening?"

"Special news bulletin. Senator Corel died. They found his body this morning."

A wave of conflicting emotions washed over Janet. There had been so much death over the past month. Would it never end? This also meant that Bonnie Corel's dilemma was solved. "How did he die?"

"Okay, here's where it gets weird. They found his body at a downtown hotel just after eight o'clock this morning. A friend at Seattle PD said that an autopsy was signed just before noon citing a heart attack as the cause of death."

"That's a shocker alright. Did he have a history of heart problems?"

Dee's voice ratcheted up a notch. "No idea, but it's beyond strange that a guy is found just after eight in the morning and the autopsy is done by noon. But listen to this. Word is that his body will be cremated within the next hour."

"That's absurd. His wife is in her bedroom down the hall, and I can promise you she doesn't know about it. How can they do that without her permission?"

"I don't know, but my source is reliable. It sounds to me like someone somewhere wants to make sure that there's no further inquiry into this."

The remark stunned Janet. "That would mean—"

Dee interrupted, "Yes. That's exactly what it would mean. Heart attack my ass."

Janet thought about it for a moment. "Yeah, well, I'll have to let someone else sort that one out. I guess I should go back and tell Bonnie, though. I'd hate for her to have to hear it on the news."

After disconnecting, Janet turned to Greg. "Senator Corel died—heart attack, they say."

Greg shook his head. "Well, I assume that it'll take some of the pressure off his wife."

Janet made her way down the hall and knocked on Bonnie's door.

"Come in."

108

Janet opened the door and slipped in, closing it behind her. "Hi, I have some news for you." She sat in corner chair while Bonnie sat on the bed. For the first time in her memory, Janet had no idea how this would play.

"The media is reporting that your husband died last night. They've ruled it a heart attack. My guess is that they're trying to contact you to provide notification, but your old phone number is obviously not working."

Bonnie stared with what appeared sad curiosity. After a moment, she shook her head. "I don't even know what I feel. We had some good years, followed by some okay years. It turned bad…." Tears gathered in her reddening eyes, but she wiped them before the tears could flow. "I guess it's finally over."

"A police friend of mine says the body will be cremated shortly. I have no idea how that's even possible, but I thought you should know."

"It's just as well. I think everyone will be best served if this goes quickly. We can arrange a memorial service later. He'll be remembered for the good things. I'll figure out how to live with the bad part." Bonnie flashed the briefest of smiles.

Unsure about whether this was the right time or not, Janet decided to plow ahead with what was bothering her. "There's something that I've wondered about for some time, if you don't mind my asking."

Bonnie's reaction was one of reserved caution. "Of course."

Janet picked her words carefully. "You came to us for help, presumably to escape the violence at home. Once you were here, though, it appeared as though you were strong, confident, and more importantly, had some kind of plan in mind."

"What's the question?"

"I guess what I'm asking is whether you had this in mind all along. It seems to me, and I could be wrong, that someone with this kind of strength would have left long ago. Why stay with him that long and why leave now?"

Bonnie stood and eased over to the bedroom window, parting the curtains to survey the clear morning. "I don't mean this to sound rude or judgmental, but it strikes me that you're drawing heavily on stereotypes—helpless women trapped in violent relationships. It's far more complicated than that."

Janet suddenly realized that Bonnie was right and, more importantly, this could be a unique opportunity to learn something. "How so?"

"Thom wasn't always violent. In fact, when we were first married, he was the very essence of consideration and respect. There was a time when, at least from where I stood, we were very much in love. We talked about the things we were going to do together. The change came gradually." She paused, seemingly transfixed by whatever she was seeing in her head.

Janet let the silence work for her.

"At first he seemed to be more stressed. Sometimes he would snap at me, but invariably he'd apologize. It was easy to write it off as him being in a tough spot or having a bad day." Bonnie turned and smiled. "We all have them, you know."

Janet nodded.

"Over time, he became more verbally abusive. He never got physical, at least not back then. He'd fly off the handle, yell for a while, and then leave. I thought at the time that he was just getting away to cool off. It never lasted. He'd always come back either like nothing happened or, in more extreme cases, full of contrition and apologies, promising it would never happen again. He took to buying me flowers as a way of making up. Sometimes he'd take me out for a lovely dinner, or we'd share some wine at home and then make love. I hated the outbursts but loved the making up." She picked at a loose thread on the sleeve of her blouse.

"The violence came later. The first time he beat me, I was too stunned to even know what to think. Before I could react, though, he swept me up in his arms and apologized. Then came the familiar 'making up' part. Something had changed though, and I knew it. The next time he hit me, maybe a month later, I left."

Janet probed, "How did that go?"

"I think I told you before, Dylan Strauss came after me. I have no idea how long the man had worked for Thom, or what he did. Plus, I was very naïve and went about it as clumsily as one could do. Strauss found me at a hotel."

Bonnie paused and clenched her jaw, her eyes narrowing. "When he confronted me, it was one of the worst experiences of my life."

"Did he physically abduct you and take you back?"

"No. It was much worse than that. He simply told me to get my things—that we were going back. His voice was quiet, but his eyes said everything. They were cold and lifeless. I was nothing more than dollar signs to him. There was not a shred of doubt in my mind that, if I didn't do exactly as he said, he would kill me on the spot." She laughed softly but her trembling hands betrayed her trauma.

"Looking back, I suspect that assumption was more hyperbole than real. Still, he had a way of commanding the situation. It never occurred to me that I could challenge it."

Janet asked, "How long ago was that?"

"It was just after Thom was elected the first time, about six years ago. Things got a little better after that, and we never talked about the incident. It was one of those situations where he acted as though nothing had happened."

"So, it got better?"

"For a while. When it started back, it accelerated fast. It went from the occasional outburst to the verbal assaults to the beating within a matter of months. I went through wild mood swings. Some days, I was certain that it was my fault, just as he told me. I would work on finding ways to avoid setting him off. I thought if I could just do what he wanted, everything would be fine. It was never enough. Some days I would have given anything just to die. Then there were the days when I grew angry, furious. On those days, I was determined not to live like that. I started small. I set up new financial accounts that I kept secret. I funded them with a trust that my father left me. Thom didn't have direct access to that."

"He didn't notice?"

"No. I typically moved money from that into our joint accounts. He was never good with details. I moved small amounts at first. Then I began moving small amounts from our joint accounts over to the secret caches. The amounts grew larger. At some point, maybe six or seven months ago, I realized I had enough set aside to start over, especially given that I could access my trust account too. I began to think about the mechanics of leaving. The problem, of course, is that there were still those days when I deluded myself into thinking we could still work things out. Finally, the dam broke. You know the rest."

"You didn't say—did you have some sort of plan for after you left?"

"Yes, and no. I had the money set aside. I had no desire to thrust our problems into the public eye. I knew that, with the election coming up, he would be reluctant to do anything that would draw unnecessary attention. The key was to find a place or arrangement—like what you have here—that would allow me to remain hidden. I figured that, the longer I was out of his reach, the more likely he was to steer his own life in a different direction. I'm not sure why, but I was certain that the last place they'd look for me was in Seattle. I felt confident that his desire for power—getting reelected—would overshadow his obsession with me."

Janet wanted to lash out. Sue Hartman had gone missing and was probably dead because of that assumption. Still, it was past and nothing she could say would change it. "Was it worth it?"

"Honestly, I don't know. A lot of people have helped me and, I know what you're thinking—the Hartman lady. I can't even begin to say how that news devastated me. I never wanted anyone hurt. You and Val have done an incredible job of taking care of me. I want you to know how much I appreciate that. As for my plan, it remains as it was. I just want to restart my life. I don't know what that looks like yet, but I will be out of here shortly."

"One other thing, Bonnie, and if you don't want to answer this, I understand. When I first broached the idea of Dani coming here to stay with you for a while, you pushed back. When you found out that she was Greg Stottman's niece, your attitude seemed to change, almost like day and night. What was that about?"

Bonnie laughed. "You got me. Yes, it did change. Greg Stottman is powerful. Although he doesn't seem to exercise that power, he has the capability of great influence. I had no idea what starting over would look like, but I thought that if I could at least forge an amicable relationship with him, it would be nice to have him in my corner. Before you ask, I don't really even know what that means. It was like this plan that I was developing and executing at the same time. When you mentioned him, it struck me as a possible opportunity. As it turns out, I never really got to know him. His niece is a wonderful girl and I'm glad I made her acquaintance. Who knows, maybe one day I'll connect with him through her."

Janet could see it in Bonnie's eyes. The response had been genuine. Maybe there wasn't really any romantic interest after all. Janet stood and eased over and put her hand on Bonnie's shoulder. "Thank you. I'm sorry about your husband, all of it. Let me know if there's anything I can do."

109

Dani felt her emotions changing as they pulled up to the Klein home. The sadness, defeat, and resignation she'd endured when she heard about Billy Robinson's death melted away. In its place, a surge of optimism and compassion washed over her. She found herself looking forward to the lunch with Abby, Janet, and her uncle. More than that, she felt something she'd lacked for a long time—an emerging sense of purpose. She would be taking Abby to school and returning her home in the afternoon. Dani would be a part of helping someone regain their life.

She leapt from the car and bounded up the stairs, leaving Janet and Uncle Greg behind. She turned and checked on them as she rang the doorbell. Roberta Klein, with her haunted eyes and gaunt face cracked the door and peered out. After a moment, the woman opened the door and gestured her in.

"Hi, Miz Klein." Recalling that she'd met the woman only briefly once before, she reminded her, "I'm Dani, we met a few days ago."

Roberta nodded. "Abby'll be ready in a minute." She

turned away and gestured toward the couch.

By this time, her uncle and Janet had come in. The three of them stood, shuffling their feet and waiting. The old woman retreated into the kitchen and out of sight.

Abby appeared out of the darkened hallway, her demeanor clearly conflicted. She seemed an odd mixture of happy and sad. She said nothing.

Dani approached her and gave her a big hug. "Hey there, Abby, how are you doing today?"

"Okay, I guess." Abby hesitated for a moment before returning the hug.

"We're gonna get some pizza. What do you think of that?"

Abby glanced first at Janet and then at Greg. "That's good."

In the car, Abby sat in back with Dani while Greg drove, and Janet sat up front with him. As they pulled onto the road, Dani was struck by how much her uncle and Janet looked like the perfect couple. Janet seemed to be keeping her feelings close, but Uncle Greg was clearly in love. Her thoughts strayed to her parents. It had been a long time, and many of the memories were faded. The one thing of which she was certain—her father had never hit her mother. Maybe they had bad times and maybe they argued, but it was never violent.

She turned her attention to Abby. "Are you ready for your new school next week. This is exciting."

Abby shrugged. "I don't know. Maybe I'm a little nervous."

Dani sighed. "Yeah, I hear you. I always get nervous with new things. On the other hand, you'll be able to meet lots of new friends, and we'll get to see each other every day. I'm really looking forward to that."

The young girl smiled.

Chapter 109

* * *

The waiter brought a couple of medium pizzas—one pepperoni and cheese, the other vegetarian. After he left, the four of them ate in silence for a few minutes. Finally, Abby asked, to no one in particular, "What's going to happen to my grandmother?"

Janet responded, "What do you mean?"

"She's not good. I can't make her feel good. I try but it doesn't work. Can you help her?"

Janet nodded and set the slice of pizza down on her plate. "I'm going to try, Abby. Here's what you have to remember … and please don't ever forget this. What your grandmother is going through is not your fault. You both have been through a lot. People heal in their own time and in their own way. You love her and you're there with her. That means a lot. It may be hard to see sometimes, but she loves you dearly and will do anything for you."

"I know. She cries a lot, though, and I don't know the things to say."

Janet reached across the table and took Abby's hands in hers. "You don't have to say anything. Sometimes if you just put your arms around, it will make her feel better."

Dani was grateful that Janet had stepped into the conversation. Abby was asking hard questions. Would she ask those kinds of questions on the way to and from school? Janet seemed to have good answers. Dani wondered how she would handle it.

In that moment, she understood how her uncle must have felt over the past months. All of the problems—all the grief and tragedy—all seemed to come back on him. Never for a moment did he give up. His answers weren't perfect, but he was always there for her. That would be her charge with Abby. *I have to be there for her every day.*

110

The weekend had been a blur. In her wildest imagination, Bonnie Corel never thought things would unfold as they had. Since learning of Thom's death, she'd been on an emotional roller coaster. The medical examiner with whom she spoke, confirmed that her husband had died of a massive heart attack. For reasons the coroner either couldn't or wouldn't reveal, the body had been cremated Saturday afternoon. Why they didn't wait on her permission escaped her, although to be honest, she didn't really care that much. Even stranger, no one from the police department had contacted her, despite the fact that she left her name and phone number with the ME.

Monday morning brought no greater sense of clarity. Instead, Bonnie mentally prepared for the task of moving out. Her first thought was to find an apartment or even a condo, but she cast that aside almost immediately. She had an incredibly beautiful and well-appointed home in North Seattle.

Janet Polasky showed up at the condo just after nine that morning. They each grabbed a cup of coffee and moved to the living room. Dani was taking Abby to school.

Janet was the first to broach the subject. "Have you given any thought to what's next?"

Bonnie responded, "All weekend. I guess what you're probably most interested in is when I'll be moving out." She allowed a good-natured laugh to accompany the words, if for no other reason than to take the sting out. She didn't necessarily intend the words as a barb. They just came out that way.

Janet seemed oblivious to the dig. "Not necessarily. I am interested to know, though, if there's anything more you need from us. I don't have any other clients at the moment, but I will need Val's services if something comes up."

"Of course. I can't see a good reason why I'd need her help."

Before Janet could respond, Bonnie's cellphone rang. It seemed odd because this was a new phone with a new number. She'd only given it out to one other person—the medical examiner on Saturday. What really caught Bonnie's attention, though, was the name on the display. "Hello."

"I'm trying to reach Miz Bonnie Corel."

"Speaking."

The confident female voice continued, "Would you please hold for Governor Ethridge?"

"Certainly."

Bonnie sat in a daze as she waited. After a moment, a somber voice came over the speaker. "Hello, Bonnie. This is Charles Ethridge. I wanted to phone and offer my deepest condolences on the loss of your husband."

"Thank you, Governor. That's very kind of you."

"This has been an unexpected tragedy, I know, and I don't want to burden you with a lot of extraneous talk. There are just a couple of things I wanted to convey. First, please let my office know if you schedule a memorial service for Thom. He was a dear friend. I would be honored to attend."

"I'll do that. I'm not sure when it will be. This hit hard and I'm still trying to make sense of it."

The governor continued, "The other thing that I wanted to run by you—and you don't need to decide today —is that I am going to have to appoint someone to fill the senate seat won by your husband. There will likely be a special election called sometime next year, but we can't have that seat vacant until then. I would like to appoint you, if you are willing to serve."

The statement stunned Bonnie. After a moment of stuttering, she managed to respond, "I'd be honored, Governor. I must tell you that I have no experience in governance, though."

He laughed heartily. "That's simply not true, Bonnie. You were at Thom's side throughout the campaigns and while he served. No one knows his priorities and connections as well as you. Additionally, you're known and respected as an honorable person with no hidden agenda. You will, of course, have to run if a special election is called, but we can talk more about that later."

Bonnie's mind raced. "Oh, well, yes, thank you. What do I need to do next."

"Absolutely nothing. We'll arrange a public announcement. My office will contact you. I hope that you might join me on the stage for the event. It will be at least a week from now, so there's no need to bother with anything right now."

After she disconnected, Bonnie became aware that Janet Polasky had been sitting there listening to one side of the surreal conversation. The phone had not been in speaker mode.

"That was Governor Ethridge. He asked me to fill Thom's senate seat."

111

Janet had come to a place where she felt she could actually take a deep breath. Bonnie Corel's situation, at least as far as Janet's involvement was concerned, was resolved. The incident with Billy Robinson's death seemed more and more to be somehow linked to the assassin who had been murdering DV workers, although Janet couldn't pinpoint exactly why she felt that way. The consensus from Detectives Martin and Wharton seemed to be that whoever the killer was, he was likely to be laying low for a while. Abby was enrolled in her new school and, at least so far, things had been going well. Dani's help had turned out to be an incredible bridge in bringing Abby back to the world of the living.

Other uncertainties remained. Roberta Klein needed help. There was still the need to come up with some kind of security arrangement for herself and Val, along with any future employees. Most important, though, Janet felt the strong need to re-commit to her congregation. It wasn't that she'd completely neglected the church. It was just that it had not been the uppermost thing in her mind. That needed to change. Maybe this lull would help.

Her sense of calm was shattered by a phone call that came around ten on Tuesday morning. Her cellphone display showed the call coming from the DV Network. "Good morning. This is Reverend Polasky."

"Hi, this is Sara Menendez. I'm the interim director at King County DV Network. I have some notes here that Sue Hartman had in her drawer. They indicate that you might be a resource for women who need to relocate with a high degree of secrecy."

"What is it that you need?"

"At the moment, maybe nothing, but I have two women who are in precarious situations. We have them here at the shelter right now. Both have expressed some degree of fear that their husbands might try something drastic. There's nothing firm at the moment, but I'm trying to line up potential resources in case we need them."

Janet decided to keep it general. After all, she didn't know this Menendez woman. "Okay, well, if there's something specific that you need at any point, give me a call."

Two women. That meant that Janet was going to have to hire at least one other person. Her first thought was to contact Dee and ask for a recommendation. After all, that's how she'd found Val. Another idea came to her. She grabbed her coat and, on her way out, stopped at Margaret Shemanski's desk. "I need to visit a friend in the hospital. I should be back by early afternoon."

She found Aylin Freyberg in a sullen mood. The woman had pulled through the worst of her injuries and was on the mend.

Janet asked, "When are they going to kick you out of here?"

Aylin grimaced. "Not soon enough. This is going to cost me a fortune."

Janet laughed. "Oh come now. It won't be that bad. After all, the Association had to hire you back, so you've got insurance."

"Uh, I never contacted them to get reinstated."

"Doesn't matter. You weren't technically ever fired."

Aylin stared for a moment, seemingly unsure how to take Janet's cheerful assessment. Finally, she turned and stared out the window. "I guess we'll see."

Janet pulled her chair up closer to the bed. "What are your plans now?"

The woman turned back toward Janet and propped herself up in bed. "I guess that you think I should go back to the Association."

"Is that what you want?"

Aylin's laugh contained no small amount of bitterness. "Just how do you think that would work out? I get that the way they went about it wasn't by their own rules, but it doesn't change the fact that they don't want me there. Have you ever worked someplace where you weren't wanted or valued? It sucks."

"So, if you don't intend to go back to the association, then what are your plans?"

Aylin's body stiffened, her face hardening. "I don't have any at the moment."

Janet ran the idea through her head one more time before speaking. "I may have something you'd be interested in."

Aylin's demeanor changed. Her eyes widened slightly and she cocked her head. "I'm all ears."

Janet poured it all out, watching Aylin's eyes grow wider with each revelation. "I can have you up and running as soon as you're able. The only problem might be your daughter. The job would have you on the road a lot."

Aylin narrowed her eyes and chewed on her bottom lip for a moment. "My daughter's sixteen. She can stay on her own for a few days at a time. I have a cousin who lives up in University Heights. She might be able to help out a little. When do you need someone?"

"There's really two parts to the question. First, I'd like to get someone hired as soon as possible. One thing I can tell you is that once the need arises, trying to get employment set up at the same time you're trying to get the woman out of town is a formidable task. Better to do the admin stuff ahead of time."

Aylin nodded. "I guess I could sign on right away. You say that you have one other person working for you. Does she move clients out of town as well?"

"Yes. Right now, we have no clients, but I understand that there are two women at the shelter who might need help soon. That's all I know at the moment."

Aylin's face grew hard, her eyes filled with determination. "Count me in."

112

For Greg, it seemed that the light at the end of the very long tunnel grew nearer with each day. Dani was safe and, at least for the time being, seemed to have a purpose in life. Janet had hired another employee and the operation was beginning to look more and more like a functioning organization. For his part, Greg was ready to return to managing his own company.

This left one nagging loose end. He sat on the couch next to Janet as Kaz occupied the chair opposite them in the living room. "Have you thought any more about the job offer?"

"I have, although I'm not completely sure what the job entails. I've seen the types of security issues you're dealing with. Some can be handled with tightening up communications and setting up protocols for dealing with unexpected events. What concerns me most, though, is that at some point, these kinds of defensive strategies aren't going to do it for you. There will come a time when you will be forced to wander across a legal line or two; either that or die. How do you intend to deal with that?"

Chapter 112

Greg could sense Janet tensing up next to him. It was a topic they'd broached from time to time but had never truly resolved. "That's a tough one, Kaz. It's not because I think it'll never happen. It's just hard to plan on breaking the law. Janet can speak for herself, but I know that I kicked in Billy Robinson's apartment door when I went after Dani. That was clearly against the law. I'd do it again in a heartbeat. Still, it's one thing to act in the moment or the situation to solve a problem and quite another to base a strategy on illegal operations."

He expected Janet to weigh in. She had been vocal about her opposition to breaking the law in the past. At this moment, though, she remained silent.

Kaz prodded her, "Revered Polasky?"

She sighed and then offered a shallow smile. "When I started all this, I had a naïve notion that we could all ride around on our noble steeds, doing good deeds and saving everyone in danger without crossing the line. That was a stupid notion. I've watched people at every level of society wander effortlessly across the legal line with no apparent consequences. The women we serve depend on us. My guess is that when it comes down to whether they live or die, they likely won't much care about legalities. I agree with Greg. I find it hard to plan on breaking the law. That said, I find it equally hard to accept that I would stand by and let a woman die simply to avoid crossing a legal line."

Kaz laughed and nodded. "Then we are of a mind. People in my line of work don't get up in the morning with this unfulfilled desire to go out and break the law. All things being equal, I'd prefer to remain legal. Unfortunately, I'm not always driving the bus. More times than not, my actions are driven by those on the other side. I won't shrink from what I have to do."

Greg jumped back in. "That's exactly why I want you

for this job. The stakes are as high as they could possibly be. I want to know that we're doing everything we can do to keep employees and clients safe."

Kaz responded, "I need to go back to Brooklyn and see my mother. I am interested. I'll think about it over the next week or so and give you a firm answer when I get back."

Greg understood that it was the most they would get for now. "Fair enough."

Janet cleared her throat. "Before you go back east, I was wondering if you might do me a favor—a very big favor."

"And that would be?"

"You've probably heard us talk about Sue Hartman, the director over at the DV network, the one who disappeared. I'm convinced that what happened to her is somehow linked to Senator Corel. His henchman, Dylan Strauss, I think his name is, I was wondering if you might have a conversation with him. If nothing else, Sue's family would like some closure."

Kaz considered her for a moment. "I suspect that you're right. I wouldn't hold out much hope of getting information from Strauss. I don't know him personally, but guys like him—like all of us in this line of work—don't discuss operations, especially with people on the other side. I'll ask, but don't count on any help from him."

113

Kaz parked in a corner seat in the lounge area of the private airport. From this vantage, he could see the entrance as well as enjoy the view through a large picture window. Winter, such as it was in Seattle, had nearly arrived. That meant rain, wind, and constant raw dampness. Still, the prospect of winding up the contract with Greg Stottman offered a respite—time to go home, visit his mother, and generally relax. The offer of a permanent position with Janet's project felt better and better. Even if he decided against it, though, he had enough funds to see him through for the foreseeable future.

A voice brought him out of his reverie. "Mister Kazarian?"

He turned to see an unremarkable man—five feet ten inches or thereabouts, short brownish hair, and a trim build. What threw Kaz was the clothing. He expected to see someone in a pilot's uniform. Instead, the man wore dark gray twill slacks, a pale blue button up shirt, and slip on black shoes.

"Yes. Are we ready to leave?" Kaz had been told that he'd be flown to a different location to meet with Strauss.

The man laughed. "*We* aren't going anywhere. When I finish this conversation, I'll be taking a flight."

"Dylan Strauss?"

"You wanted to talk to me. So, talk." The man's demeanor was neither friendly nor hostile. To an outside observer, it could have been nothing more than a discussion about stock portfolios. He slid into a seat opposite Kaz.

"Where are you headed after this?"

"I don't enjoy meaningless prattle, Mister Kazarian. What do you want?"

Kaz regrouped. In passing, he realized that Strauss' response was to be expected. "Very well. Sue Hartman."

The look on Strauss' face gave nothing away. He remained silent.

"Her family, they'd at least like to know what happened."

"I see. They're looking for... what do you call it... closure?"

"Something like that."

Strauss leaned back in his seat, his hands laced behind his head. "Funny thing about closure. Once they know what happened, things change. Then they want justice. This meeting, it's about revenge."

Kaz shot back, "I don't do revenge."

"I know. I checked up on you. Some punk beat up your mother. She ended up in an institution where she'll remain for the rest of her life. You refused to seek retribution. The cops never caught the guy and you're okay with that."

"This isn't about me."

"Sure it is. This meeting is at least in partly about you."

"Your boss is dead. I assume your contract no longer

exists. Talking to me about Sue Hartman shouldn't cross any one of the many moral boundaries you have." Kaz struggled to contain the sarcasm.

"If you're referring to Senator Corel, neither he nor his contract are of any concern to me at this point."

Kaz shrugged, "You wouldn't have had anything to do with his death, would you?"

Strauss' laugh seemed out of character. "Do you believe that if I did, I'd just tell you?"

"Well?"

Strauss remained silent for a moment before speaking quietly. "No. I had nothing to do with it nor any knowledge about it ahead of time. What I will tell you is that he wandered across a line. You and I, Kazarian, we're in more or less the same business. One might say that we both swim with sharks. One of the first rules you learn in this business is that you never attack the other sharks. Sadly, Senator Corel either was not aware of the rule or chose to ignore it. There's always a heavy price to pay for violation of that particular law." He locked gazes with Kaz, although there seemed to be no hostility in his eyes.

Kaz smirked, "Hopefully you got your payment up front."

"We both know how to build insurance into our arrangements. The hitch here is that I figure you owe me. You destroyed my asset—one that I poured considerable time and money into."

Kazarian laughed, his humor genuine. "Do you mean Karl Unger? I did you a favor. You and I both know he was a thug—a liability for you. I took him off your balance sheet. No thanks needed."

Strauss nodded thoughtfully and considered Kaz for a moment before speaking. "You're familiar with Boris Bunin, the Russian mob boss in New York, I understand."

"I know him. We've crossed paths culturally and socially. We don't run in the same business circles. What does Bunin have to do with all this?"

My understanding is that he was almost like a big brother to you. I'd call that more than *crossing paths*, as you put it. Anyway, he contacted me recently. Did you know his wife, Larissa?"

Kaz replied, "Never met her."

"Lovely woman, or so I hear. Seems she was murdered by some cop from Alaska. Boris is looking for *closure*, as you call it."

Kaz shook his head. "Boris is old school. Revenge is a vital part of his business model. Tell me, Dylan, you don't strike me as the type to take on a job like that."

Strauss laughed. "Not hardly. My point is this. If Boris came to you with this offer, would you take him up on it?"

"I've already told you, I don't do revenge. This is, by the way, the same thing that I've told Boris on a number of occasions."

Strauss leaned forward, raising his index finger as though to emphasize his words. "My point exactly. Even for your dear friend Boris Bunin, you wouldn't go down the revenge road. Why do it now for someone you don't even know?"

"These people aren't players, Dylan. They're ordinary folk trying to make sense of things. They just want to know what happened to Sue. Can you at least tell me where she is?"

"I don't know where she is."

Kaz searched the man's face. Strauss wasn't lying, at least not in the technical sense. "I assume you're going to tell me that Karl Unger knew where she is."

"Alas, we shall never know. You killed him, remember.

Whatever he knew or didn't know went to the grave with him."

"Do you think the family be justified in assuming that she won't be returning?" It was one last ditch attempt to get something concrete.

The response came matter-of-factly. "The family can assume anything they want. If I were a betting man, I'd say that the fact that there's been no word from her for this long reduces the probability that she'll show up in the future."

In truth, Kaz had expected not much more than this. "Switching gears, would it be fair to assume that Reverend Polasky is no longer in danger, at least from any residual issues related to you?"

"That's a hell of a convoluted question." The smile disappeared and Strauss' voice became serious. "I had nothing to do with events surrounding that woman. Before you toss out the snarky remark, yes, it was Unger working directly for Corel without my knowledge. In fact, I warned the senator off Polasky on several occasions. The reverend is in no danger from me, or anyone associated with me. Clear enough?"

After a moment of silence, Strauss stood and turned to leave. He paused and spoke over his shoulder. "You know as well as I do, Kazarian. Sometimes things go wrong. Take care."

114

The house remained the same. Everything else had changed, though. Bonnie Corel didn't want to admit that the fear that constantly gnawed at her as she desperately tried to prevent her husband's violent outbursts had taken its toll. Now that fear had mostly transformed into sadness. They had once been in love, but that was another time and he had been a different man.

Mixed with the sorrow, though, was a sense of hope. Her appointment to Thom's senate seat was a part of it, but it was more than that. Life opened up ahead of her. She didn't know where the road would take her, but that gave her strange sense of optimism.

She sat on the sofa with a cup of coffee on the rainy, cold mid-November morning when her cellphone sounded. The display showed a blocked number. She considered letting it go to voice mail, but, given that she was beginning to enter a very public period in her life, she decided to answer.

"Good morning."

"Miz Corel, this is Reba Stillings. I'm a local attorney

here in Seattle. I was wondering if you might have a few minutes to meet with me during the next few days?"

* * *

Bonnie settled into the chair, taking full measure of the blonde woman sitting behind the desk. The hurried research she'd conducted suggested that Stillings was a strong, competent woman and fierce advocate for men's rights—especially those men accused of domestic violence. This seemingly put them on opposite sides of the issue.

Reba Stillings appeared completely at ease. "I appreciate you taking the time to see me. I know that what with the announcement from the governor and all the preparations for the coming session, you must be quite busy."

Bonnie responded warily, "It's overwhelming at the moment." She knew that Reba Stillings represented views that were far removed from her own.

Stillings smiled warmly and leaned back in her chair. "I'd like to offer my condolences. I knew Thom for many years. We didn't always see eye-to-eye, but we did manage a productive and civil relationship."

"Thank you." Bonnie wondered for a moment whether that relationship included romps in the bedroom. Taking stock of the woman, though, she decided it likely didn't. Thom preyed on younger, impressionable women. Reba Stillings, as beautiful and feminine as she was, looked as though she would have chewed Thom Corel up and spit him out in short order. There was an icy coldness in her eyes, giving the impression of a battled-hardened warrior. He would have never sought out that kind of relationship with a strong woman like this.

"On that vein, I'm hoping that you and I can cultivate the same kind of relationship. When the subject of replacing Thom arose, I spoke to the governor on your behalf. I believed and continue to believe that you're the best choice to fill his seat. I think that, should you choose to run in the special election, you'll easily win."

Stillings' words seemed oddly out of character. The attorney was the antithesis of what Thom had campaigned on and what Bonnie felt she would endorse. "If you don't mind my asking, Miz Stillings, why me? All else being equal, surely you know that I'm likely to follow in Thom's footsteps with regard to policy."

Stillings sat with her hands folded on the desk, her posture erect, and made direct eye contact with Bonnie. "Please, call me Reba. Yes, I know that, and your implication is accurate. I'm not cut from the same ideological cloth as your husband. You and I will, on many issues, be adversaries. That shouldn't, however, mean that we have to be enemies. I'll gladly share my priorities with you and am anxious to hear yours. What I can offer you is a safe sounding board. I can give you insight into what reactions will be to your policy proposals. If we do it right, I can offer my limited support, along with the support of other like minds, for some of your ideas. What I would ask in return is that you at least consider some of my points. Trust me, I'm not asking you to betray your beliefs and ideals."

Bonnie could hear the calculation behind the carefully chosen words. "Thom had a habit of quoting overused cliches, one of which was 'the devil's in the details.' What you say sounds practical, if overly general. What I can promise you is that I'll listen. I haven't decided about running in the special election. My focus, at the moment, is on representing the people of Washington until then. I intend to do my best to represent all Washingtonians, both those who voted for my husband and those who didn't."

Stillings laughed. "Noble words, and I believe you." She paused and cleared her throat. "The federal Violence Against Women Act is coming up for renewal. The basic elements are in place, and I wouldn't expect them to change much. Whether the reauthorization makes it through will depend heavily on how willing both sides are to sit down and talk. I'm going to make the first move here. My priority with this act is having the prohibition on firearms ownership be time limited. I think we could both agree that, after a period of time with no problems, men should be able to regain that right. What you might be able to take away from such a deal would be closing the boyfriend loophole."

Bonnie recalled the question that Janet Polasky had posed many months ago at the church association meeting —the boyfriend loophole. "The governor hasn't even announced my appointment yet, so any kind of deal is premature. That said, I will take what you've said in good faith. If I have questions, I'll get back to you."

The attorney smiled. "That sounds like a fair arrangement."

Bonnie stood to leave, but something bothered her. "My husband's death was quite sudden, and he had no history of heart problems. Also, it was odd that the autopsy and cremation were both done so quickly, don't you think?"

Stillings' smile faded. "The loss of a spouse is always a tragedy." She paused for a moment before speaking again in a low voice. "I know what the last few months have been like. I know that you left. I know he was trying desperately to find you. I know all about that. I mean no disrespect to you or the memory of your husband, but it's entirely possible that, in his obsession, he crossed some lines that he perhaps shouldn't have."

Bonnie felt as though she should be shocked. She wasn't. Stillings' words seemed to confirm the only thing that really made sense. Toward the end, Thom had become unhinged. He had lost control of his temper, and his judgment disappeared. If the attorney was to be believed, he had likely not treated others any better than he'd treated her. "I have a lot to do this afternoon. It was a pleasure meeting you, Miz Stillings."

115

F riday drew to a close. Janet had just put the finishing touches on her sermon for Sunday. Margaret had taken off early, wanting to get an early jump on the weekend. Thanksgiving was the following Thursday and the church secretary intended to bake all weekend. Janet found herself wondering what that would be like—baking and preparing for a Thanksgiving feast with a large family.

Just as she was putting her coat on, Dee Martin knocked and entered. "I'm glad I caught you. I was afraid you'd be long gone by now."

"I was just headed out."

Dee responded, "You want to grab some dinner out?"

Fifteen minutes later they sat across from each other in a booth at the Chinook Ale House, a local brewpub. The aroma of robust beer, baking bread, and fish dominated the dining area. Janet looked over the menu. "It all looks great. I think I'm going to get the blackened salmon salad with cilantro lime dressing."

"Halibut and chips for me. The beer batter is fantastic here."

Janet closed her menu and took a sip of the deep amber ale. "Okay, so tell me. You seem awfully cheerful tonight. It's not like you. You're always the queen of serious."

Dee set her beer aside and picked at a piece of bread. "I'm going to talk to Val tomorrow. I've thought a lot about what you said. After everything that's happened, I'm terrified for her, honestly, but you nailed it. I would rather have her with me in a way that she wants than force her to be something she doesn't."

"Good luck."

"I don't know. The last time we talked, she was pissed at me. I've given her space, so hopefully, she's willing to talk."

Janet responded, "Just be honest. You're scared for her. There's nothing wrong with that, in fact, I'd argue that's a good thing."

Dee nodded and took a drink of beer. "Oh, did you hear the news today? Some guy was gunned down early this morning, right outside his house."

Somehow, the announcement invoked a sense of weariness in Janet. "Why should today be any different than any other day? So much death."

"Yeah, but it's like the last one I told you about, you know, Peter Cook, the guy accused of murdering his estranged wife and kids up in Bellingham. The guy who was killed this morning had been charged with assault on his wife, but the case fell apart in court. I don't know the details, but that's gotta suck for the wife."

"Did she do it?"

"The news report didn't say."

Janet shook her head. "If it was her, then I guess it wasn't the same as the Peter Cook case. I mean, in Cook's situation, it couldn't have been the wife since she was dead. His murder had to be committed by someone else."

Dee stared at Janet for a moment before responding in quiet voice. "I don't know. I'm not sure of anything anymore."

* * *

As Janet walked into the parsonage about eight-thirty, her cellphone rang. She checked the display and connected. "Hi Dani."

"Hey Janet. Look, I wanted to let you know something. I wasn't sure what to do about it. This morning when I went to pick up Abby, the house was dark. I knocked on the door. After a few minutes, Abby answered. She was still in her pajamas. We got her dressed and barely made it to school on time. I asked her where her grandmother was. She said that she was in bed sick. When I brought her home in the afternoon, the grandmother still wasn't up."

Dread washed over Janet. She had been hoping that Roberta could hold it together. Apparently, that hadn't worked out. "I'll check on her right away. Thanks for letting me know. You handled it perfectly."

After she disconnected, Janet decided against waiting until morning. Twenty minutes later, she pulled up in the driveway. A dim light shone through the living room window. It appeared as though someone was up. When she rang the bell, a haggard looking Roberta Klein answered. The woman looked confused, almost as though she didn't recognize Janet. She stood and stared for a moment.

"I'm sorry to come over so late, Miz Klein. May I come in?"

Roberta stepped aside without speaking.

Inside the living room, Abby was nowhere to be seen.

As if reading Janet's mind the old woman said, "Abby's in bed." There was no offer to get her up or provide any other information.

"That's okay, I actually came to talk to you." She stood awkwardly in the center of the room. Roberta made no move to sit.

Janet eased toward the sofa. "Why don't we sit down."

Once seated, Janet asked, "How are you doing?" She wasn't sure how else to begin this difficult conversation.

The woman looked around the room as though trying to find an answer in her surroundings.

Janet started to offer help but decided for the moment to give the woman some space and time.

"I don't know what to do."

Janet listened intently.

"I know Abby is hurting. I can't say anything to make it better."

Janet asked, "Does she talk to you?"

"Sometimes. She thinks she can save me, but it doesn't work that way. I try to tell her, but she's too young to understand. Why did her father kill her mother? Why is Abby an orphan? What kind of God would let this happen?"

Janet wasn't certain whether Roberta was relating Abby's question or whether these questions ate at her. "I wish I could give you some answers. There are no good reasons why people kill each other. I promise you—those questions haunt me too."

"I'm an old woman. My life is spent. It doesn't matter much what I think or feel. Abby has her life ahead of her, though, and she's already been overloaded with death and sadness that even adults can't handle. What's going to happen to her?" Tears rolled down the woman's face.

Janet leaned over toward Roberta, who sat in a chair

across from her, and took both hands. "Abby has people who care about her—you, Dani, and me, just for starters. The school is good for her. She's an incredible young girl. I want to help you, though. Your life is not over. There are people who care if you will let them in."

The woman bowed her head, tears dripping on her robe. She nodded but kept quiet.

Janet stayed with her for another hour. They spoke little. Janet made some hot tea, sweetening it with honey from Roberta's cabinet. Janet invited Roberta to church on Sunday, offering to pick her and Abby up and deliver them back home. The old woman wouldn't commit. Her eyes, though, didn't give Janet much hope. Janet invited them to Thanksgiving dinner at the parsonage—again, no commitment but her face conceded a possibility.

Janet arrived back home at ten-thirty, ready to fall into bed. As she hung up coat, her phone rang. Weary to the bone, she briefly toyed with idea of just letting it go to voice mail. The display showed that the number was blocked. *This cannot be good.*

She connected. "Hello."

"Is this Janet Polasky?" The voice was heavily accented —perhaps India, Afghanistan, or Pakistan.

Janet asked, "Who is this?"

"I need your help."

Coming 2025

Garden of Lilies (Book 3, *Lilies of the Underground)*